Praise for
The Sinclair Sisters of Cripple Creek Series

"A beautiful tale. Intriguing. Inviting. Inspiring."
— CINDY WOODSMALL, author of *The Hope of Refuge*
and *When the Soul Mends*

"It's always a joy to read a historical novel that isn't afraid to let its women escape the farm. Cripple Creek's cast of colorful characters play host to a new romance, as well as pulling back the curtain on a local family tragedy. This sequel does more than simply tell the "next" story; it revisits the characters we've already come to love and creates a complementary depth to an entertaining new tale."
— ALLISON PITTMAN, author of *Stealing Home*
and *The Bridegrooms*

"Ida believes her future is secure in a man's world. After all, she has drive and determination. But what happens when she meets a man who makes a withdrawal from her heart? Author Mona Hodgson makes discovering the answer to this question a rich, rewarding adventure."
— DIANN MILLS, author of *A Woman Called Sage*
and the Texas Legacy Series

"All the ups and downs of a romance with a delightful dose of history, with characters that will sneak into your heart and take up residence. More, more, we want more."
— LAURAINE SNELLING, author of *No Distance Too Far*
and the Daughters of Blessing Series

TWICE A BRIDE

TWICE A BRIDE

A Novel

MONA HODGSON

Book Four

The Sinclair Sisters of Cripple Creek

WATERBROOK
PRESS

Twice a Bride
Published by WaterBrook Press
12265 Oracle Boulevard, Suite 200
Colorado Springs, Colorado 80921

All Scripture quotations or paraphrases are taken from the King James Version.

This is a work of fiction. Apart from well-known people, events, and locales that figure into the narrative, all names, characters, places, and incidents are the products of the author's imagination or are used fictitiously.

ISBN 978-0-307-73032-9
ISBN 978-0-307-73033-6 (electronic)

Copyright © 2012 by Mona Hodgson
Cover design by Kelly Howard

Published in association with the literary agency of Janet Kobobel Grant, Books & Such, 52 Mission Circle, Suite 122, PMB 170, Santa Rosa, CA 95409-5370.

Published in the United States by WaterBrook Multnomah, an imprint of the Crown Publishing Group, a division of Random House Inc., New York.

WaterBrook and its deer colophon are registered trademarks of Random House Inc.

Library of Congress Cataloging-in-Publication Data
Hodgson, Mona Gansberg, 1954–
     Twice a bride / Mona Hodgson.—1st ed.
         p. cm.—(The Sinclair sisters of Cripple Creek ; bk. 4)
     ISBN 978-0-307-73032-9 (alk. paper)—ISBN 978-0-307-73033-6 (electronic)
  1. Widows—Fiction. 2. Sisters—Fiction. 3. Cripple Creek (Colo.)—Fiction. I. Title.
   PS3608.O474T84 2012
   813'.6—dc23

                                                    2012017189

Printed in the United States of America
2012—First Edition

10 9 8 7 6 5 4 3 2 1

Written for the Lover of my soul—Jesus!

Hear my cry, O God;
Attend unto my prayer.
From the end of the earth will I cry unto thee,
when my heart is overwhelmed:
Lead me to the rock that is higher than I.

PSALM 61:1–2

ONE

1898

Jagged edges marked the sculpted granite at Willow's feet. Love was like that. Smooth in places. Sharp and dangerous in others.

'Tis better to have loved and lost than never to have loved at all.

Willow stared at the white rose in her hand. She agreed with Alfred Lord Tennyson's statement. But on this last day of August, churned clods of Colorado dirt formed a blanket over her father's grave. Was it the loss of her father so soon after their reunion, or was it fear threatening to rob her of air? Both were cunning adversaries.

She glanced at the shiny black carriage where her loved ones awaited her. Aunt Rosemary hadn't looked at her today, but Willow had seen the apprehension clouding Mother's eyes. Her brother, Tucker, had stared at her during the graveside service, worry rutting his brow. Even her sister-in-law watched her the way one would watch a pot on the brink of a boil.

If Willow dared to look in a mirror, she'd see the same question lurking in her own features. Could this insatiable sorrow pull her back into a tide she couldn't withstand any more than Sam could survive the undercurrent in the San Joaquin River?

She bent to the ground. "Father, I'm sorry for the anguish I've caused you. I wanted to be strong." She laid the rose on the grave. "I won't be a Weeping Willow this time." Squaring her shoulders, she brushed away the tears spilling onto her cheeks. At what point after Sam's death had her mourning become abnormal? Would she recognize warning signs if it were to happen again?

"Willow?" Tucker's voice wafted on the breeze, just above a whisper.

Drawing in a fortifying breath, she looked at her brother and stood. His eyes narrowed as though he expected her to crumple. Tucker had been the only one to visit her at the asylum after Father had her committed, and he'd visited her once a week despite never receiving notable response from her.

Tucker met her gaze. "Are you all right?"

"Yes." She brushed a blade of grass from her mourning gown. "I needed some time."

"I can't help but worry about you."

She offered him a slight grin. "I know."

He slid his hands into his trouser pockets. "You shouldn't be alone."

Willow agreed. She'd expected by this time in her life to be a pastor's wife and herding at least two or three little Peterson tykes.

"I'm not alone." Was she trying to convince him or herself? "Mother and Aunt Rosemary are at the boardinghouse with me."

He looked at the rose she'd placed on their father's grave. "Saturday they'll return to Colorado Springs."

"But Miss Hattie is under the same roof, and she's not going anywhere." Willow added a lilt to her voice to see if she could cause his brow to soften. "And I have you."

Perhaps it was a mistake to live this close to her brother. He had a wife, a church to shepherd, and the Raines Ice Company to oversee. Worrying about her was not a pleasant way for Tucker to live. But if she didn't settle in Cripple Creek, where would she go? Nothing, and no one, awaited her in Stockton, California, where she'd grown up and married Sam.

Tucker's shoulders sagged. "It's not the same as having a spouse to... I'd feel better if you'd agree to move into the parsonage."

Willow pressed the squared toe of her dull black shoe into the grass. "We've already talked about this, and my answer is the same."

"You can't blame a brother for trying."

"I don't." She patted his bristled cheek. "I love you for it."

Tucker offered his arm. "We best get to the house. A supper awaits us."

A bereavement supper, to be exact, replete with long faces and self-conscious commiseration. She matched Tucker's pace, determined to remain above the shared sadness.

At the wagon, Willow stepped onto the wrought-iron foot brace and seated herself beside her sister-in-law, Ida.

Concern laced Mother's green eyes—the source of Willow's own eye color. "Are you all right, dear?"

Willow nodded, her lips pressed against another swirl of grief. She wasn't the only one burying a father or a husband today. "What about you, Mother? Are you all right?"

"As well as can be expected, I suppose."

Tucker raised the reins. As the wagon jerked forward, Ida's tender hand rested on Willow's palm, and she squeezed her sister-in-law's hand. Tears stung Willow's eyes. She needed to find her own path, but she didn't let go.

Uncharacteristically quiet, Tucker guided the horses down Second Street toward the rustic home their parents bought when they left Stockton. How ironic that when Father's consumption got the best of him, nearly two years ago, he ended up in a sanitorium. An institution, of sorts. Mother had moved in with her sister in Colorado Springs to be close to him. Tucker lived in the cabin until he and Ida married and moved into the parsonage. Now Otis and Naomi Bernard and their four sons called the cabin home.

As they approached the creek-side property, Tucker slowed the horses. Mother let out a fragile moan, and Tucker reached over and patted her arm.

Willow had seen the place once when she first came to Cripple Creek for her brother's wedding, but she'd never viewed it as her parents' home. Home was the clapboard two-story house in Stockton where she and Tucker had grown up. The house where she'd planned her wedding.

She wanted to believe everything happened for a reason—that God had a divine plan. Last year she'd found it easy to believe He'd left her here on earth and healed her so she could help her parents through her father's illness. But now? Father was gone. Mother planned to return to Colorado Springs with Aunt Rosemary. And her brother had a new life with a pregnant wife.

"Here we are," Tucker said. A few horses and wagons formed a line between the cabin and the barn. Otis, the biggest man Willow had ever seen, stepped off the porch. His oldest son stood at his side. Even at ten years old, Abraham was already a miniature of his father—dark skinned and broad shouldered.

His wife, Naomi, awaited them at the open door. A paisley-print apron added a bright spot to her black broadcloth dress. "Please accept our condolences, Missus Raines." The petite woman reached for Mother's hands. "Mr. Raines was good to us. You both were, and I'll never forget that." Sincerity shone in her dark eyes.

"Thank you." Mother glanced at Abraham. "We appreciate all you and your father did to keep the ice deliveries going when Mr. Will took sick."

Nodding, Abraham twisted a floppy hat in his hands. "Ma'am, Mr. Will did have a big bark, but he never bit me."

Tucker was the first to laugh, but Willow and Mother soon joined him.

Naomi didn't laugh. She glared first at Otis, then at her son. "Abraham, you will apologize for your disrespect."

Abraham's brow crinkled. The boy obviously didn't realize that what he'd said was, by some standards, inappropriate. He straightened nonetheless, his arms tucked into his sides in a contrite manner. "I apologize, Missus Raines. I didn't mean any disrespect. I liked Mr. Will. He always gave me a penny for candy or gave me a Tootsie Roll—my favorite."

Mother smiled. "He liked you too, Abraham." She patted the child's head, then looked at his mother. "Naomi, your son is right. My husband did sound off with quite a bark now and then."

Willow remembered her father's bark, and she already missed it.

Naomi opened her mouth to speak, but Mother beat her to it. "No harm done."

"Thank you." Naomi stepped away from the open door. "Lots of folks have come to pay their respects."

They entered the cabin one after the other, Willow stepping into the front room last. Before she reached the food tables, a stout woman stepped in front of her.

"I'm Mrs. Henry."

"Your husband drives one of the ice wagons."

"Yes." Mrs. Henry narrowed her hazel eyes, looking at Willow but not meeting her gaze. "According to everything I've read in Scripture, if your father is in heaven, he's in a far better place."

If? Willow coughed as if she'd just swallowed something sour. She covered her mouth, more in an attempt to stifle her retort than as an act of propriety. Mrs. Henry had good intentions, didn't she? Offering the woman the benefit of her doubt, Willow nodded, then glanced across the crowded room. Hattie Adams stood with Ida at the dessert table, and Willow suddenly had a hankering for something sweet—their company.

Her sister-in-law brushed a tear from her cheek. Tucker had found a good wife. Ida had a big heart and was mourning the loss of a man she barely knew. Hattie pulled a handkerchief from her apron pocket.

Willow regarded the stout woman still planted in front of her. "If you'll excuse me."

"Of course." Mrs. Henry tugged the white collar on her black shirtwaist. "Just remember, it's always darkest before the morning."

And just before one woke up. Biting her lip, Willow started across the room. *Don't make eye contact. Don't smile.* She didn't want to be stopped by any more misguided well-wishers. She was a woman on a mission.

Flight. Straight into the sanctuary of Ida's and Miss Hattie's company.

Ida looked Willow's way and extended an arm to her. Willow took Ida's hand and glanced at the dessert table. She'd recognize her landlady's three-layer carrot cake anywhere.

"I remembered." Miss Hattie's smile highlighted the laugh lines that framed her blue-gray eyes.

Hummingbirds and eagles were more closely related than Mrs. Henry and Miss Hattie.

Willow squeezed her sister-in-law's hand. "Are you all right?"

"Yes." Ida sniffled. "I was thinking about the baby."

And the grandfather he or she would never meet. Willow nodded. The grandmother too. Ida's mother had died more than a dozen years ago. The Sinclair sisters had expected their father to arrive in Cripple Creek this past spring, but so far they'd seen no sign of him.

Ida dabbed her face with a handkerchief. "I was about to grab a piece of carrot cake and take it out to the bench. Join me?"

Willow caught sight of a pinched-face woman in a black shirtwaist with a white collar. "I suppose that depends on whether or not we're faster than Mrs. Henry and her trite expressions."

≈≈≈

That evening, Willow pressed a butterfly seal to the envelope on her dressing table. She'd written a letter to her friend at the Stockton State Asylum. Maria Lopez had taken good care of her even when she was in a stupor and wasn't aware of the older woman's tender care. When Willow had awoken and become aware, Maria brought her homemade tamales every Sunday.

Willow had buried her father today and still missed Sam something awful.

But she was a blessed woman. God had put people like Maria and others at the asylum in her path. She still had a brother, her mother, and an aunt who loved her. And now she had Ida.

Miss Hattie's laughter winged its way to the second story. Mother and Aunt Rosemary were downstairs with her landlady.

Tucker was right about her being alone soon. Mother and Aunt Rosemary would board the train for Colorado Springs in three days. Tucker and Ida were busy with each other and their pursuits.

Willow had wasted two years of her life in the asylum. Two years she could've spent apprenticing with an established painter.

She returned her writing box to the bedside table. There had to be something she could do to support herself and her artistic ambitions. It'd be even better if she found purpose in it. Her landlady thrived on coming alongside others—especially young women experiencing a big change, as each of the Sinclair sisters had. Following Miss Hattie's example, Willow decided to search until she found purpose.

But right now, her quilt-covered bed looked more inviting than the blank canvas propped in the corner. Yawning, she left her bedchamber and strolled down the staircase to the parlor to say good night.

Aunt Rosemary sat on the sofa beside Miss Hattie, chattering between sips of tea. Her mother looked up from where she sat on a Queen Anne chair and motioned for Willow to join them.

"Come in, dear. I was hoping you'd come down before you retired." Mother nibbled a lemon bar and then glanced at the plate of nuts and red grapes. "I couldn't eat at the house. Not right after...with all those people."

Willow seated herself in a rocker on the other side of the table that held her mother's teacup. "I couldn't either." But sitting by the creek between the two willow trees Tucker had planted, she'd managed a generous slice of carrot cake just fine.

"I was beginning to think you'd gone to bed." Mother pulled the napkin from her lap and wiped her mouth. "What were you doing up there for so long?"

"I wrote a letter to Maria, my favorite attendant at the asylum."

Mother popped two grapes into her mouth. Willow gnawed her bottom lip. Her stay there—the very fact that she needed to be tucked away—was still a hush-hush topic.

"Would you like something to eat, dear?" Miss Hattie pointed to the tray of sliced ham and cheese, and lemon bars.

"No, thank you." She'd be ready for a big breakfast, but right now she wanted her pillow. "I came down to say good night."

"You do look tired, dear." Aunt Rosemary added a slice of ham to her plate, along with a dinner roll.

Mother picked up her cup and saucer. "Before you go back upstairs, I have something to tell you."

Willow squirmed in the rocker. Mother's statement usually preceded a serious announcement or declaration.

"I had a chance to speak to Ida when she came back from the creek."

"About your grandchild?"

"About you."

"Me?"

"Yes. Ida said she couldn't offer you full-time work, but she'd welcome your help in the icebox showroom."

"You didn't." It came out louder than Willow would've preferred.

Mother's teacup rattled in its cradle. "Indeed, I did. And you should be grateful. Rosemary and I will be leaving soon, and as lovely as this boarding-house is, you can't just sit around. It wouldn't be good for you. You need some-thing productive to do."

She did need something productive to do. But selling iceboxes?

Two

*T*renton Van Der Veer stood at the worktable just outside his dark-room and leveraged a pry bar at one corner of a crate. A delivery wagon had hauled the two crates from the morning train—his first big order since he'd opened the studio two months ago. He applied pressure to the iron bar until the nails gave way with a shriek, then carefully lifted a paper-wrapped flask from the wooden box. He set it on the table and smoothed out the sheet of parchment paper. Repeating the process with bottles of fixer and flasks of developer, he stacked the paper he could use to protect his finished prints. After he'd emptied the first crate, he set the bottles in neat rows on one of the new shelves he'd built in the darkroom. He lined up the chemicals according to their role in the developing process—developers on the left, washes and fixers on the right.

Trenton pulled two new glass plates from the crate and examined them. Obviously, the train offered a smoother track than the rural road he'd maneuvered in Timothy O'Sullivan's photographic van, a glorified and enclosed buckwagon. No matter how well he'd wrapped the plates, at least one would crack on most trips. He tucked the new plates into one of the shallow wooden boxes on the shelf below the counter. The metal slides went into the next box over, and he placed five cans of negative emulsion into the third box.

This new shipment alone was twice the bulk of supplies that would have fit in the wagon. But working as an apprentice traveling photographer was his past. He was thirty-seven years old, and he'd grown tired of living out of a van. It was time he settled down; time that his clients came to him. That was why he'd opened the Photography Studio, although Colorado hadn't been where he'd expected to hang his shingle. He'd spent some time in New York during his traveling years and had been set to return there with an ambitious wife to photograph the cream of society—magazine editors, newspaper moguls, and the latest songbirds of the opera.

Trenton's eyelid twitched, and he reached up to still it. He'd expected to return to New York with a wife, but then—

The bell on the outer door jangled. He had company.

Opening his mouth to speak, Trenton contested the persistent cramp in his tongue. "B-be…r-right there." After adding the last sheet of parchment paper to the stack, he stepped into the office and closed the door to the darkroom behind him. Mollie Kathleen Gortner stood at the counter in a navy blue suit. An angled hat eclipsed the mine owner's narrow face.

"G-good day, m-ma'am."

"And to you, Mr. Van Der Veer." She stared at the leather apron he'd donned to unpack the boxes. "You telephoned. My print is ready?"

He'd telephoned Monday and had expected her to come by yesterday. As he opened his mouth to speak, he felt the muscles on the right side of his face contract. "Y-yes. Right here." He lifted the portrait from a stack of prints beneath the counter and laid it in front of the businesswoman. She'd brought in a mine-claim certificate and a feathered fountain pen for her sitting.

She examined the sepia image. "Nicely done, Mr. Van Der Veer."

"I'm g-glad you approve." He'd like the image better if Mrs. Gortner hadn't looked so serious. Perhaps women in Kansas weren't alone in taking themselves too seriously. He shrugged. If only shrugging were enough to rid him of the memories.

Mrs. Gortner pulled a fan from her reticule and flipped it open. "Has Mrs. Hattie Adams spoken with you yet?"

No more than a handful of women had visited his shop. Mostly businessmen. Miss Mollie O'Bryan and Mrs. Gortner being the exceptions. "No. Sh-should I ex...pect her?"

"Mrs. Adams is a widow and the owner of Miss Hattie's Boardinghouse over on Golden Avenue. She's been in town for at least a dozen years and is a good woman to know." Mrs. Gortner fanned herself. A strand of red-brown hair streaked across her forehead. "As the co-chairwoman of the Women for the Betterment of Cripple Creek, I mentioned you and your photographic services at our meeting last Friday. Several of the women seemed taken with the idea of scheduling a sitting, Hattie Adams in particular."

"Thank you." The two words jerked out as one.

"You're welcome." Not seeming at all put off by his stammering, she returned her fan to her reticule and pulled out the balance she owed.

After writing out a receipt, he slid the print into a crisp manila envelope, hoping the mine owner had the kind of influence that would bring him business.

She held the photograph as if it were a fragile baby. "Do you know what else would help to make your business boom, Mr. Van Der Veer?"

An articulate spokesman wouldn't hurt.

"Painted portraits are all the talk now, you know. You need to hire someone who can paint portraits from your photographs. The time saved from a portrait sitting would be a wonderful selling point."

He rubbed his jaw. He'd read all about photographic portraiture in *Peterson's National Magazine* but hadn't given it any thought.

"Mark my words, Mr. Van Der Veer. You hire someone who can paint mantel portraits from your prints, and your quiet little business will boom."

"I'll g-give it some thought, Mrs. Gortner, and let you know wh-what I decide."

Trenton opened the door for her, then looked at the clock above the door. He had a sitting in thirty minutes. Inside the studio, he set up his tripod six feet from the Greek column he used as a stationary elbow rest.

The more he thought about Mrs. Gortner's suggestion—almost a demand, really—the more he liked the idea of partnering with someone who could paint portraits from his photographs. It'd be all the better if the artist could also colorize existing prints. That, too, was a popular service in the bigger cities. Two months in business may be too short a time to be considering expansion, but if he could find the right man for the job, they'd both benefit.

While waiting for his two o'clock appointment, he made a mental list of the artists he'd met. Jorgensen and McGregor in New York, and several in Chicago and Kansas City. It was doubtful he could lure any of them to Cripple Creek. From his darkroom, he pulled out the plates for this sitting, then returned to the studio and inserted the first plate into the back of the wooden box on the tripod.

It'd be better to solicit help from someone local, anyway. Someone with connections in the district could help stir interest in the Photography Studio. His friend Jesse had been in Cripple Creek for several years and was certainly doing his part to help spread the word, but as much as Trenton appreciated his friend's enthusiasm, a blacksmith and livery owner's sphere of influence in the arts was admittedly limited.

He'd write out an advertisement for the *Cripple Creek Times* and deliver it to the newspaper this afternoon. He might even pen a letter to Susanna while he was at it.

When the studio met his satisfaction for the next client, Trenton pulled a sheet of scrap paper and a fountain pen from the top drawer of his desk. He needed just a short advertisement, direct enough that he wouldn't waste his time with anyone who wasn't qualified for the job.

Painter Wanted: A skilled portrait painter to work with photographer.
Send letter of application and a sample of your painting to The
Photography Studio at North First Street.

He returned the pen to its cradle in the desk and greeted Mr. and Mrs. Updike as they arrived for their sitting.

∽◦◡◦∽

The rope of bells on the door jangled, and Susanna looked up from the tray of chocolate-dipped strawberries.

Helen bounced into the confectionary with a newspaper tucked under her arm. Her pointy nose sniffed the air. "Oh, I do love the smell of warm choco-late." She glanced at the strawberries, only a slightly brighter red than her braid, then jabbed a boney finger toward the door behind the counter.

"My father went to the bank," Susanna said in answer to Helen's silent question. "But you still can't have one."

"We'll see about that." Helen studied her the way one would a butterfly specimen. "Have you been sour all day, or did you save it all for me?"

Sighing, Susanna returned the last strawberry to the tray and wiped her hands on her apron. "You do this every day, week after week. *Then* tell me how you feel about sticky, gooey candy and the people who rot their teeth eating it."

Helen's tongue darted out. "You didn't seem to mind it so much when Trenton fed you the chocolate-coated strawberries."

Susanna's stomach knotted. "You have a lot of nerve mentioning him."

Helen planted a hand on her hip. "It wasn't my fault that downhearted man left you."

"You were there!"

"And so were you." Helen waved the newspaper. "I thought this might help you feel better. But thanks to your foul temper, I can see I'd be wasting my time."

Susanna slid the candy tray into the oak icebox against the back wall. "How is a Podunkville rag going to help?" If it couldn't take her out of this place, it wouldn't make her feel even one iota better.

Helen raised the rolled paper, holding it like a summer fan just below her sparkling green eyes. "It's not the *Scandia Journal*, dearie."

"So you dropped coin for the *Topeka Capitol-Journal*." Susanna rearranged the tray so the icebox door would close. "A clear waste of your money. My father brings the *Topeka Journal* home from the smoking club."

"Once again you've underestimated me." Helen pressed the newspaper to her chest. "Do you consider Denver Podunk?"

"Well, it's not New York. Or even San Francisco. But it is out West, away from Kansas." Susanna tossed her apron into a basket under the counter. "How did you get hold of a Denver newspaper?"

"The *Denver Post,* no less." Helen held the newspaper out to her as if it were a meaty bone. When Susanna reached for it, Helen took a giant step backward.

Susanna crossed her arms.

Helen cackled. "Can't blame a girl for trying to have a little fun around here."

"Why should I care about the *Denver Post*?"

"My brother Harold lives in Denver, and he's been trying to talk my father into moving us all out there. He sent the paper, thinking all the talk about mines and mills would entice him."

Susanna took the newspaper from her and spread it out on the counter. "Page five, right side."

She flipped pages. "I'm in no mood for chasing rabbits, Helen." Page five. "Can't you just tell me what you found so fascin—"

The headline in the upper right-hand corner of the page froze the word in her throat. "Photographer of the rich and famous drawn to wealthy Colorado."

"Trenton?"

"Keep reading." A smug smile dimpled Helen's freckled cheeks.

Sure enough, the article was about Trenton Van Der Veer. *Her* Trenton Van Der Veer. "He moved to Colorado...set up a studio in Cripple Creek."

Her finger trailed the margin as she read. "Says here Cripple Creek is on the southwest slope of Pikes Peak. 'The bulk of Colorado's millionaires call it home.'" Her pulse quickened. "He is still photographing the wealthy."

And where there was wealth, there were opera houses and theater companies that needed singers. Given a chance, she could revive Trenton's plans to marry her, take her to live in New York, and introduce her to the top tier there.

Helen tapped her perky chin. "Feeling better, are we?"

"Much better." Susanna took quick steps to the icebox and pulled out the tray of strawberries. "That information, my dear friend, has earned you not one but two chocolate treats."

Helen picked out the biggest strawberries on the tray.

"I've heard good things about Denver," Susanna said. "It's called the land of opportunity, you know." That was especially true if it moved her closer to Cripple Creek.

Nodding, Helen licked a smudge of chocolate off her bottom lip. "You're starting to sound like my brother."

The information about Trenton was worth the whole shop's worth of chocolates. Susanna held the tray of dipped strawberries out to Helen. "Any chance your father is considering the move?"

THREE

Willow drove Miss Hattie's surrey down the hill on Fourth Street. She would have suggested she and her mother and Aunt Rosemary walk to the Midland Terminal depot this morning if not for the five bags between the two women. Tucker and Ida had planned to come along, with Tucker in the driver's seat, but he'd telephoned the boardinghouse just moments ago. Ida wasn't feeling well, and he thought it best they stay home until Ida felt better.

She'd rolled out of bed with dawn's first peek through her upstairs window. This was the day her mother and her aunt would return to the house they shared in Colorado Springs, which meant this was also the day she'd begin her new, independent life in Cripple Creek. She'd visited the city for her brother's wedding and for Vivian's wedding, and she'd returned with her folks for Christmas at the parsonage last December, but now it was her home. A bittersweet beginning.

Her mind had awoken in a sprint, and she had yet to catch up to it, let alone rein it in. Her father had passed. Her mother was moving on with her life. She couldn't help but think God had brought her here at this time for a purpose.

"It's not too late, dear." Aunt Rosemary sat behind Mother, shouting over the cacophony of braying donkeys and screeching wagon brakes on the steep road. "Are you sure you don't want to come with us? I still have that third bedroom. We could take the later train to give you time to pack."

Going home with them would certainly be easier than starting over here. Especially if staying meant working at the icehouse. Willow made the mistake of glancing at her mother.

"You know you're welcome." The tears glistening in her mother's green eyes pleaded with her.

Willow drew the horses to a stop in front of the depot and looked at her aunt. "Thank you, but it really is time I start a life of my own." Even if she was the only one who believed she could start over and survive it.

A porter met them at the hitching rail with a baggage wagon.

No more than thirty minutes later, the three of them stood on the platform, the locomotive rumbling and belching steam behind them. They'd said their good-byes. Her face damp with tears, Mother stepped up into the train with Aunt Rosemary.

On the top step, Mother twisted and shouted over her shoulder. "You'll think about the job Ida offered you, won't you?"

"Yes." Willow waved. She'd thought of little else since her mother's announcement Wednesday night.

After the train pulled away from the platform in a series of jerks, Willow offered a final wave and walked back to the surrey.

What now?

As she loosened the reins from the rail, Miss Hattie's horses nickered. Willow patted the old mare on the withers before she climbed into the seat. Mother was right—she did need something to do. Ida would birth a baby in the spring, and if working in the icebox showroom would help Ida, that would be productive work.

But not very creative. She wasn't quite ready to give up on finding work better suited to her abilities, or at least to her interests.

She didn't even know if Ida needed help. Chances were good Mother had gently reminded Ida that the Raines Ice Company was a *family business,* then broached the subject of Willow's desperate need for occupation.

Willow loosened the reins and clicked to start the horses up Bennett

Avenue. She wanted to go by the parsonage to check on Ida, but first, a trip to the library. She could pick up a book or two to sink her mind into, and while she was at it, she'd peruse the area newspapers for job advertisements.

Unlike the big library in Stockton or the memorial library at the seminary in San Francisco, the Franklin Ferguson Memorial Library in Cripple Creek was housed in a simple clapboard house on B Street.

Stepping into the entryway, Willow drew in a deep breath. To her senses, the leather bindings and ink-dappled pages of books cast an aroma nearly as sweet as that of Miss Hattie's carrot cakes.

The square-jawed woman behind the desk didn't look much older than Willow. "May I help you?"

"I'd like to pick up copies of *Little Women* and *The Friendship of Women* while I'm here, but first, do you have any copies of Cripple Creek–area newspapers?"

"We do. You may not know this, but our fair city now boasts several newspapers, some of them dailies."

"I'm looking for employment."

"Then you'd need something local." She glanced toward a side door. "That's easy enough. You'll want to start with the *Cripple Creek Times*. It's a daily, popular with local businesses, and most likely to earn their employment advertisements. We keep several issues of some of the most popular local, state, and countrywide newspapers in the resource room."

Following the woman through the doorway and toward another, Willow passed row after row of stocked bookcases and drew in another deep breath. She'd much rather work in a library than in a store full of wooden iceboxes.

In a room that Willow supposed had once been a formal dining room, they stopped in front of a wooden dowel rack where the librarian selected the most current edition of the *Cripple Creek Times*.

"Here you are, Miss."

"Mrs. Peterson. Thank you."

"I'm Alice. Let me know if you need anything else, Mrs. Peterson." She smiled, then left the room.

Willow carried the newspaper to the oak library table located at the back of the resource room and flipped the pages until she found the classified advertisements for employment on the next to the last page. She drew in a deep breath and began reading.

Wanted: Muckers: Irish or Chinese, all shifts.
Wanted: Powder monkeys, young and quick.

Turning the page, she moved on through domestics and chambermaids for the wealthier residents to advertisements for cooks, for a laundress, for woodcutters, and even for girls for the purpose of entertainment.

Willow kept reading.

Painter Wanted: A skilled portrait painter to work with photographer.
Send letter of application and a sample of your painting to The
Photography Studio at North First Street.

She blinked and read the listing again. *"A skilled portrait painter."* She would more readily choose the word *experienced* to describe her portrait painting, but if experience produced skill, then she was qualified. And if the job involved painting a portrait from a photograph, it would be much easier than trying to capture the facial features of a squirming neighbor child or a sleepy grandmother. Admittedly, she didn't know much about photography, but if she could trust the ad, that didn't seem to be a requirement. She pulled a notepad and a pencil from her reticule.

When she'd copied the information from the advertisement, she closed the newspaper and returned it to the rack on the wall. Showing her work in a photography studio could be the first step to having her paintings hung in an art gallery. That would be much better than selling boxy appliances. And if she already had a lead for a more suitable job, Ida wouldn't feel obligated to hire her. She'd return to the boardinghouse, compose a letter of application, and select a sample of her painting. Then she'd go tell Ida of the exciting possibility.

Ida pulled the bed sheet to her chin. The Lover's Knot quilt Aunt Alma made for her wedding lay draped over the rocker.

Her legs felt like anchors, and she hurt everywhere. If she could, she'd roll onto her side. But she couldn't, not with Doc Susie bent over her bottom half. If only she could move onto a dry spot, away from the wetness. She'd feel better if she could go back to last evening when her family was gathered around the dinner table at the boardinghouse. Miss Hattie was hostess to her mother-in-law, Tucker's Aunt Rosemary, and Willow. All three of her sisters and their husbands had joined them for dessert. If only she could turn the clock back to before the first spear of pain.

This morning she'd awakened first. Tucker lay on his back, his left hand tucked behind his head. She'd watched his chest rise and fall and then rolled to her right side and laid her sleepy head in the cradle of his shoulder. He'd wrapped his arm around her, pulling her close. They'd both drifted back to sleep, her dreaming of sitting on the bench at the creek. In her dream, her daughter sat beside her, dangling little legs and twirling the golden curls above her ears.

That was when everything was right...before the aching began. An ache that felt like the jaws of death gnawing at her womb. Chomping at her baby's developing heels.

Doc Susie stood and pulled the bed sheet over Ida's legs. No words were necessary to tell her what she already knew—death was feasting on her emptiness.

"Mrs. Raines." The voice drifted in a fog above her. "I am afraid you have miscarried."

Ida pressed her hand to her aching abdomen. *Miscarried.* What kind of a word was that? Failed to carry? Mistake? Or had she just failed?

What had she done wrong? She'd made cherry pie for dessert last night and eaten a piece rather late. Ida cringed. She didn't remember feeling sick. She'd worked at the icehouse showroom yesterday. Did this happen because—

"I'll go find your husband." The door clicked shut.

Ida's chest cramped and her lips quivered. She'd just lost her baby. The child for whom her sister Nell was knitting a blanket. The one Willow had said was the living answer to her father's death.

And Tucker. She'd lost her gift to him. What would she say to him? He and Otis had already started work on the cradle.

Muffled voices permeated the fog that enveloped her. Was someone crying? Or was it her own sobs trapped just below the surface that she heard? Death had paid her another visit. First her mother. Then her father-in-law. Now—had she lost a son or a daughter?

Footsteps pounded the wood flooring outside the bedchamber. Why were they so loud? Any life left behind should be silent, still in death's wake.

The door creaked open, and Tucker entered the room, his face solemn and his steps suddenly tentative. Ida didn't want to move, didn't care to open her eyes, but she sat up anyway. Tucker arranged their bed pillows to support her.

He stroked her mussed hair. "Are you all right?" His brown eyes were dulled but dry.

Biting her bottom lip, she nodded, lying. She wasn't all right. Children were a heritage, and God had just taken back His gift.

Willow walked into the room. Tears shimmered in her green eyes as she knelt beside the bed and captured Ida's hand. "I'm so sorry."

Ida sniffled. Her sister-in-law had buried a husband. Willow hadn't failed to carry a baby, but she understood. Ida could see it in the lines framing Willow's mouth.

"You're not all right, are you," Willow said.

Ida shook her head. The dam broke, and the tears stinging her eyes ran down her face.

Tucker squeezed her arm through the bedcovers.

Ida met his clouded gaze. "I'm sorry."

"Me too." He looked past her, at the wall. "All that matters is that you're well."

That wasn't all that mattered. The baby she carried had mattered.

He brushed her forehead with dry lips. "I'll be in the parlor."

Ida held her breath to stifle her cries and nodded.

When he closed the door, Doc Susie stepped up to the bed, and Willow stood.

"What you're feeling is normal," the doctor said. "When a woman conceives, her body reacts with feelings of euphoria. An opposite reaction occurs when her body aborts the—"

"Baby."

"Yes." Doc Susie moistened her lips. "Your body expelled the baby naturally. It may take a few days, but your body will soon return to normal."

Normal would have been her body clinging to a life and her midsection expanding to accommodate a growing baby. Like Kat's. Like Vivian's.

Doc Susie leaned forward. "Are you experiencing any more bleeding?"

"No."

"You should be fine then." The doctor looked at Willow. "Telephone me if she has any problems." She laid a hand on Ida's shoulder. "You can come by my office in a few days, or, if you'd like, I can stop by the icehouse to check on you."

"Thank you." Gratitude was the last thing Ida felt right now, but none of this was Dr. Susan Anderson's fault. Her own body had betrayed her, and no one else was to blame.

FOUR

*T*renton positioned his camera and framed the family of three seated on a deacon's bench. He'd seen bait worms less squirmy than this toddler. How was he to capture a good shot with her looking everywhere but at him? No wonder he preferred capturing landscapes. Too bad the Indian paintbrush, Dome Rock, and the Rocky Mountains didn't pay to have their images recorded.

The mother sighed, the lines at her mouth deepening. "I apologize, Mr. Van Der Veer." She glanced at the man beside her. "Perhaps we should reschedule for another time when she's tired."

Midnight? Trenton stepped out from under the cape of his Kodak. "I have an i-idea." He'd seen Timothy O'Sullivan use distraction, and it had even worked for him a time or two. He pulled a metal tub full of toys from a cupboard and dug out a bright yellow cloth bird. He met the mother's gaze. "Her n-name?"

"Ruby."

As in ruby-throated hummingbird with very busy wings. Trenton held the felt-billed duck at the child's eye level. "Ruby, this is Bo the bird. Can you help me?" When the words finally came out, they ran together as one.

The child nodded and reached for the stuffed animal.

He pulled it back. "Not yet. B-Bo wants a picture, b-but he likes to wiggle. Can you keep him still?"

This time the little girl's nod was so big it sent her chin to her chest. Trenton couldn't help but smile.

"I do it." She snatched the bird from him. Her fingers tight around the toy's middle and her knuckles white, the child could have been a statue.

Trenton returned to his camera and retreated under the cape to focus the grouping on the etched glass pane. He pulled the photo plate off the small table beside the tripod and pushed it into the camera. The slide came out in one smooth motion.

"Ready." He squeezed the bulb and held up a tray of flashpowder. *Poof!* "P-please hold s-still while I change the p-plate." He flipped the plate and refilled the flashtray. Another *poof.* "Th-that should d-do it."

Mr. Flinn blew out a long breath. "Are we finished?"

"We are." And none too soon.

The man loosened his tie. "My family lives in Cleveland. Never seen Ruby. I know folks who had their photographs colorized back East. You do that? Can you show them Ruby's blue eyes?"

"I'm hiring someone who can do that." Trenton pushed the bellows back into the body of the camera and latched the wooden door shut. He'd received a handful of applications for the job of portrait painter. If he had the right person, they could add appropriate color to his sepia prints. "I'll have your p-prints ready by Thursday. I'll let you know about the c-colorizing then."

The man led his family out of the shop.

Exposed plates in hand, he headed to the darkroom. As he was about to enter, the bell jingled on the outside door. "One moment," he called.

"I have a delivery."

A courier. Another application? Trenton set the plates on the worktable and stepped into the front office.

The postmaster's son stood at the counter holding a thin, two-foot-square, string-wrapped package.

Trenton reached into his pocket and pulled out a dime. "Thanks, son."

"Anytime, sir."

When had he become a "sir"? Probably the day he'd pulled that first gray hair from his temple.

A thick string double-wrapped the white butcher paper that was addressed to the studio. The sender had printed, "Do not bend or fold" across the front and back of it. Definitely another application for the job of portrait painter. Hopefully this applicant would hold more promise than the first four.

The package held an envelope and more paper folded over a wooden frame. He slipped a piece of stationery out of the envelope first and unfolded the letter.

To whom it concerns:

Please accept my application for the job of portrait painter. I am a sketch artist and a painter. My formal training includes several art courses with Mrs. Agnes Gibson of Stockton, California, whose work is sold in galleries in Sacramento and San Francisco.

The sample I've chosen to include is the portrait I painted of my husband, Samuel Peterson. Please note that whether or not I gain your employment, I require the painting be returned to me.

I look forward to hearing from you in respect to the details of the position available at your photography studio.

With best regards,

Mrs. Peterson

Miss Hattie's Boardinghouse

Golden Avenue, Cripple Creek

Trenton dropped the letter on the countertop. A female applicant. He unwrapped her sample painting. Dark cherry wood framed a stunning portrait of a young man. Mrs. Peterson's work displayed a keen understanding of composition and shading. Her abilities with depth of field were unmatched by the previous applicants. Leaning against the counter, Trenton pinched the bridge of his nose.

Jesse stepped onto the boardwalk outside the door, and Trenton waved him inside. His childhood friend looked around the studio. "You ready for some lunch?"

Trenton grinned. "You buyin' today?"

"Yep." Jesse hooked a thumb in his overalls. "Sold that black stallion."

"Then, yes, I'm ready." Trenton tucked the latest application into the drawer and pulled his hat from the hook. Mollie Gortner might be in a hurry to have a portrait painted from her photograph and Mr. Flinn might be anxious to have his daughter's eyes colorized, but he couldn't be in such a hurry that he hire the wrong person for the job.

After he locked the door, Trenton fell into step beside his friend. "Since you're buying, I might even indulge in a generous slice of pie."

Jesse chuckled. "You looked awful intent back there. You hear from another artist about the job?"

Trenton waved at the elderly woman sitting in front of the cobbler's shop across the street. "A Mrs. Peterson submitted an application."

"A married woman."

"Yes." Trenton turned left on Bennett Avenue and headed for the Third Street Café.

"S'pose neither of us should be surprised. More and more married women are working now." Jesse raked his yellow hair with one hand. "Reverend Tucker Raines's wife is a businesswoman. She manages the ice company and sells iceboxes."

A pastor's wife, no less. Trenton patted the pocket watch in his vest pocket. "Times are changing, all right." He didn't have anything against women who took jobs away from their home. That was a woman's business to work out with her husband. But he'd assumed he would hire a man.

"Did your female applicant send a sample painting?"

"Yes."

"Any good?

"Didn't expect to hire a woman."

"That good, huh?

Trenton nodded.

"Not all women are like that one in Kansas, you know."

It would be far easier to believe that if he didn't still have the sour taste of duplicity stuck in his throat.

FIVE

attie covered her mouth, but the giggle escaped anyway. Boney Hughes lay under her kitchen sink, his upper body concealed by the cupboard. His legs sprawled over her linoleum flooring.

Boney scooted out from under the sink and peered up at her. "You think me rappin' my old knuckles on these leaky pipes is funny?"

Unable to stifle her amusement, Hattie nodded. "You look like a…" She fanned herself, trying to regain her composure while he stood. "Like a fish out of water."

Boney's winter-white eyebrows arched. "A big old river catfish?"

Giggling, she studied him from his wiry beard to his worn boots. "A smaller fish perhaps, but surely one with a big heart."

"You're still a charmer, Hattie." He hooked his thumbs in his bib overalls. "Wore my best duds for coffee this morning. If I knew you planned to put me to work—"

"You would've shown up anyway." She smiled and pulled two mugs from the buffet.

"You know me all too well, Adeline Prudence Pemberton…Adams." He said her married name with an air of reverence.

George had died within months of finishing the boardinghouse. He would have relished the ever-changing company the house afforded. Hattie sighed, picturing her late husband leaning against the sink.

Boney cleared his throat and looked out the window. "I still miss him too."

She poured the coffee and set their cups on the kitchen table beside the lemon-meringue pie she'd baked that morning.

Boney washed his hands under the running water, then bent to look at the pipes beneath the sink. "Fishy or not, ma'am, I fixed it. Not a single wayward drop." His eyes shining like polished silver, he joined her at the table and gulped his coffee.

Hattie stirred a pinch of cinnamon into her cup. "You're a good man, Mister Hughes."

Bracing her cup with both hands, she sipped and savored the bold warmth as she did the same with the memories. "It's nice to have someone to share coffee and a chat with. The house has been too quiet lately."

"You got spoiled having the Sinclair sisters in the house."

"I surely did." Melancholy softened her tone. She missed witnessing the first hints of affection between the ladies and their gentlemen, the questions, the discoveries, the surrendering of two hearts to become one. Their journeys to the altar. She missed the excitement of the weddings.

She couldn't love those four girls—young women—any more if they were her own daughters. George would have too. Each of them had found a good man and married him. Vivian, the last born and the last to arrive in Cripple Creek, had wed nearly a year ago.

The house had definitely been too quiet these past few months. Willow Raines Peterson was back in town, and she was as close to being a Sinclair sister as one could get without the blood, but—

Boney cleared his throat again, derailing her thoughts and drawing her gaze. Her friend had cut the pie and dished up two pieces. "Where'd you go?"

"I was on Tenderfoot Hill, May 30, 1896, watching Kat and Nell wed Morgan and Judson. The next minute, at the church, listening to Ida and Tucker's vows. Then in the parlor remembering Vivian and Carter's ceremony. And just now, I was wondering about Willow. Praying she is...content."

"You think she'll marry again?"

"I don't know." Hattie spread a napkin on her lap. "Widows aren't easily convinced."

"Don't I know it." Boney slid her pie plate across the table to her. "You ever miss Missouri?"

She tucked errant gray hairs behind her ear. "I miss the river. Especially during the summer."

He nodded, his mouth full of pie.

"And at times, I miss that girl."

"The one with hair the color of molasses?"

"That's the one." Although she wouldn't have used a pantry item to describe her hair.

"Well, as time would have it, I was fond of that girl and happen to be quite fond of the woman she is today." He scooped up another forkful of lemon meringue. "Her cookin' ain't half-bad either."

"You always were one to flatter the females, Mister Hughes."

"Friends call me Boney." He winked.

The telephone jangled. Hattie lifted herself out of her chair with a *hmph*. Just as well. She'd been dawdling too long on memory lane. Some anniversaries of George's death did that to her. Today was a tougher one. She reached for the telephone, lifted the earpiece, and spoke into the cone. "Hello."

"Miss Hattie, there's a Mr. Harlan Sinclair on the line for you."

"Sinclair?" Oh, the girls' father.

"From New York."

"Yes, thank you."

"Hello, Mrs. Adams!" The line was more scratchy than usual, and he sounded as if he were shouting. "My four daughters have all stayed at your boardinghouse."

"Yes. Delightful girls, each and every one."

"Thank you."

"I've been wishing you'd had more daughters." Her cheeks warmed. *What a thing to say.* "I only meant that I enjoyed having Kat and Nell, Ida, and Vivian here in the house."

"That's what I'm calling about, ma'am."

"About your girls living in my house?" She glanced over at Boney, who was sliding another piece of pie onto his plate. "That's interesting. It's been nearly a year since the last one moved out."

She couldn't be sure but she thought she heard him sigh. "Mrs. Adams—"

"Begging your pardon, Mr. Sinclair, but your girls call me Hattie."

"Very well, Hattie Adams, I need to secure two rooms for the third week of September."

This was September 9, the second Friday. Hattie opened her mouth.

"Week after next." Mr. Sinclair's words were clipped. "I expect I'll need at least one of the rooms, perhaps both, for a month or more."

She thought about asking why he didn't plan to stay in one of his daughters' homes, but the man clearly wasn't given to chatter. But then costly long-distance rates from New York wouldn't invite windy conversations. Still, she wondered if his daughters knew he was no longer in Paris.

"Do you have two rooms available for that time?" he asked.

"I do, and they're now reserved for you."

"Very well. Until then."

After a click, the static on the line fell silent. Hattie shivered, staring at the telephone for a moment. The girls had obviously inherited their warmth from their mother.

She returned to the table and regarded Boney, a man with a very warm heart. "That was Mr. Sinclair."

"Father to our Sinclair sisters?"

"The very one." She scooped up a generous bite of pie. "Mr. Sinclair will arrive in Cripple Creek in about ten days, week after next. And he's bringing a guest."

"He's bringing a friend with him?"

"He let two rooms. He didn't say who would fill them."

"Perhaps it's the girls' aunt coming with him."

"Yes, of course. That's probably who it is. Aunt Alma." The prospect made her smile. Alma Shindlebower could brighten a room any day. Perfect!

Hattie raised her cup as if she were toasting her grand inspiration. The lively Alma Shindlebower was just what her friend Boney needed in his life. Willow might not be ready for a match, but those two were long overdue. And soon the Sinclair family would fill her home again.

Six

*F*riday morning Trenton carried his second cup of coffee and the artist applicant packages out to the front porch. He set his mug and the stack of applications on the table and settled into one of the rockers, then looked at the empty chair on the other side of his coffee cup.

A familiar ache stirred in his chest. The chair would remain empty unless Jesse or a neighbor stopped by for a visit. Some men were meant to remain single. That was what his mother had told him when he hit courting age and couldn't gain the interest of the girls in his small Maryland town.

This spring he'd learned that gaining a female's interest wasn't the prize his colleagues had built it up to be. He needed to find contentment as a single man. And he couldn't think of a better way to start than to focus all his attention on the task at hand. Two weeks had passed since he'd placed the advertisement in the newspaper.

He pulled the stack of applications onto his lap. Before he left for the shop this morning, he'd choose who was going to help him expand his business. It needed to be someone skilled and personable. Someone who wasn't bothered by his *disability*. Another of his mother's terms, straight from one of the many speech therapists she'd dragged him to see.

His first applicant was also new to Cripple Creek. As the town had boomed in size in just two years, most folks here were relative newcomers. Mr. Zwall was not a nomad, however. He'd lived in Chicago for twelve years straight before moving to Colorado, and he'd studied art in Boston. But his sample painting qualified for still life, not a portrait. While the bowl of fruit he'd painted was colorful and boasted human characteristics, such as a mouth on a pear, it hardly qualified him for the job.

One artist from the Dakotas submitted a caricature. Trenton chuckled. It was doubtful that an impressionist image was what Mollie Kathleen Gortner had in mind for her mining-office wall. A third applicant talked about his portraits as sculptures. Another form not conducive to wall displays. The last two packages contained true portrait paintings. Mr. Davis of Denver planned to relocate to Cripple Creek to be closer to his mother, a mine widow. The man's credentials were impressive and his work above average.

But Mrs. Peterson's painting was exquisite. She'd captured emotion in her subject's face. Trenton pulled her application from the bottom of the stack and removed the sample she'd provided. She'd read love on her husband's face and captured it in the glint of his eyes, the shaded curve of his mouth, and the slight tilt of his head toward the portrait painter.

Trenton blew out a long breath, then slid Mr. Peterson's image back into the butcher-paper packaging and added it to the stack on the table. He sat back in the chair and lifted his cup to his mouth.

He'd made his decision.

⤬

Willow finished writing the paperwork for the sale of an icebox, then glanced at the mismatched couple. The woman was at least four inches taller than the man. "All I need now is payment." She pointed to the total.

Two weeks ago she'd sent her application to the Photography Studio. The photographer had no doubt chosen someone else for the job by now. Just as well. Ida needed her.

The woman pulled money from her coin purse and counted it out to Willow.

"Thank you, again, for your patronage, Mrs. Johnstone. Otis will see that your icebox is delivered on Monday afternoon to the address you've provided."

On their way out the door, the couple dodged Miss Hattie and a large, flat package. Perhaps the phantom photographer had finally returned her portrait. Willow locked the cash in the desk drawer.

Miss Hattie set the paper-wrapped package on the desk and glanced at the door. "Business is good?"

"It is. I just sold them a top-of-the-line icebox."

"I'm sure Ida will be quite pleased with the job you've done."

If she ever returned to work. Sinking into the chair, Willow ran her finger over the wrapping of the package.

"It came this morning," Miss Hattie said. "I was headed into town for my women's Bible study and decided to bring it by."

Willow pulled scissors from the drawer and cut the string. "It's the portrait I sent with my job application."

"I thought it might be important."

"When I hadn't heard anything, I thought I'd have to hunt it down." Willow pressed the paper open and stared at the face on the canvas, remembering.

Her landlady sighed and sank into the chair across from her. "Sam?"

Willow nodded while swallowing a bitter bite of grief, then lifted the portrait to give Hattie a better look. "He had the best smile."

Hattie leaned forward. "Warm." She met Willow's gaze. "With a spark of mischief, I see."

Willow giggled. Perhaps she'd done a better job of capturing his personality than she'd given herself credit for. "Yes. He could be quite mischievous. My mother lost her voice many a time, scolding him and Tucker for teasing me with all manner of bugs and critters."

"Before he noticed you were more than his best friend's sister, I presume."

"Mostly." Willow's cheeks warmed in the memories. She pulled the wrapping paper over the top of the portrait and leaned it against the wall. In the process, an envelope slid onto the wood floor. Probably a letter of polite decline. She retrieved the sealed envelope and reached for the letter opener, then unfolded the stationery and skimmed the brief message.

"Your work is the best I've seen." Her lips began to quiver.

Miss Hattie straightened in her chair. "He offered you the job, didn't he?"

"Mr. Van Der Veer wants to meet with me first, but it does sound like he intends to hire me." Willow handed the letter to her friend.

Hattie leaned back in the chair. "When?"

"Late this afternoon."

This job could give her a new path in life. But Ida still needed her. Willow looked around the icebox store.

"I had tea with Nell and Vivian this morning," Hattie said softly. "Neither one of them has seen Ida out yet."

Willow was about to ask Miss Hattie what she should do when a dapper gentleman sauntered into the showroom. She looked at the wall clock. Precisely eleven. Her considerations and her response to Mr. Van Der Veer would have to wait. She still had a full day of work ahead of her.

"Mr. Davenport?"

"Yes. Mrs. Peterson, I presume?"

When Willow walked out from behind the desk, Miss Hattie touched her arm. "I'll leave you to your business, dear."

It wasn't her business, but Willow nodded anyway. "Thank you."

While Miss Hattie walked to the door, Willow joined the hotel owner at a row of iceboxes on the left side of the showroom.

"This is one of the three iceboxes I spoke of on the telephone yesterday."

Nearly an hour later, Mr. Davenport had looked at every one of the twenty iceboxes on display—small and large, plain and fancy, least expensive to the most costly. She pointed out each feature, from the construction to the ice block size that would fit in each one and approximately how long it would last, depending upon the quality of insulation in the icebox. Her voice was spent and so was her patience. Right now, all she wanted was a tall, cold glass of lemonade and a shady tree to sit under with a canvas and a palette of paint. But she'd settle for sending the man on his way to think on his decision.

"I'll take ten of the large Emenees and five of the smaller oak White Clads."

Willow gulped. Sweat beaded on her palms. She'd only sold one icebox at a time until now. Ida didn't keep that many iceboxes in stock. She probably had a special form for such a large order tucked away somewhere. "I'll need to order them. You said ten of the larger ones and five of the smaller ones."

He traced his thin mustache. "That's correct."

"Very well then, Mr. Davenport. If you'll join me at the desk, I'll prepare the paperwork necessary for your order." If she could find the paperwork.

Seated behind the desk, Willow opened the top drawer and flipped through the various folders. Completed order forms. Catalogs of iceboxes. A listing of ice customers. No blank order forms. She pulled open the second drawer.

The businessman sat in the chair on the other side of the desk, cracking his knuckles. "Mrs. Peterson?"

Willow moistened her lips and looked up.

The knuckle cracking ceased. He leaned forward. "Is there a problem?"

Her smile was no doubt thin but the best she had to offer at the moment. She wiped her damp hands on her linsey-woolsey skirt. "I'm filling in for the woman who normally works here. I've never processed this big an order before."

He arched his thick eyebrows.

"I wouldn't call it a problem, but I do need to find the proper form. Then I'm sure I can figure it out."

Mr. Davenport glanced at the wall clock.

If she didn't act fast, she was going to lose the sale. "Let me telephone Mrs. Raines." Willow lifted the earpiece and gave the crank a spin.

The operator answered.

"Yes, please connect me with Ida Raines." Willow listened to several buzzes. Her pulse raced. She'd been able to pretend to be a businesswoman for two weeks, but the shoe didn't fit, and right now she felt the squeeze clear up into her throat.

The operator sighed. "I'm sorry, Mrs. Peterson, but I'm unable to reach Mrs. Raines. You'll have to try again later."

Later would be too late. "Thank you."

She should be glad Ida finally felt good enough to get out, but why now?

She was hanging up the earpiece when she heard the bell on the door and glanced up to see her sister-in-law enter the showroom. "Ida!" She stood, and so did Mr. Davenport.

Ida apparently recognized her desperation and took long strides toward them.

Her customer tugged on the hem of his suit coat. "Are you the woman who normally works here?"

"I am." Ida shifted her attention to Willow. "Is there a problem?"

Willow stepped out from behind the desk. "This is Mr. Davenport. He'd like to order ten Emenees and five White Clads."

Ida smiled. "And you've not handled any large orders."

"Exactly."

"Well then, I'd say my timing is spot on." Ida extended her hand to the customer. "I'm Mrs. Raines, and I'd be happy to help you with your order." She seated herself behind the desk and slid her reticule into the bottom drawer. She pulled a file folder out of another drawer.

Thank You, Lord, for Ida's improvement. And for the timing.

Ida belonged behind a desk. Willow didn't. But did Ida know that? Was she back to work for good, or had her visit been a fluke?

Willow pulled a chair beside Ida and watched a true businesswoman at work. Facts, details, and numbers seemed to roll off Ida's tongue so easily.

When her sister-in-law had completed the order form and taken the deposit, she stood and shook the man's hand. "Thank you for your business, Mr. Davenport. Willow will telephone you when she has a delivery date for you."

Willow cringed. There was her answer. Ida wasn't back to work. And, even worse, she expected Willow to carry on here for her. At least long enough to secure a delivery date.

When the man stepped outside, Ida pulled the cashbox out of the second drawer and looked at Willow. "You've been working here for two weeks, and without any payment. That's no way to treat such good help." She counted out thirty dollars and handed it to Willow. "Is that enough for ten days' work?"

"It's very generous. Thank you." Willow had heard miners made three dollars a day for many more hours' work on a very dangerous job. This may not be a good time to mention the photographer's advertisement or the letter she'd received today, but…

Ida pulled her reticule out of the desk drawer and stood as if she intended to leave.

Willow stood too and stuffed the bills into her seam pocket.

"I appreciate your help, Willow."

"You're welcome." Willow smoothed the ruffle at her neckline and met her sister-in-law's gaze. "When you came in today, I thought perhaps you were ready to return to work."

"Hattie came by the house."

"She went to see you after she'd been here?"

"Yes."

That was why Ida showed up when she did. "We're concerned about you."

Ida's lips quivered, and she pressed her hand to her chin. "I'm not ready."

Willow watched Ida go until the tears blurred her vision. Just when she was finally ready to leave the birdcage and fly again, Ida slammed the door shut.

SEVEN

*V*ivian walked up Bennett Avenue toward the Cripple Creek Police Department and the man she loved. She'd thought it would be fun to rest the tin plate she carried on the shelf of her swollen belly but decided against it. As active as her son was in the womb, the dish was sure to end up on the ground. Instead, she held Carter's dinner out in front of her, away from her overactive kicker. A cloth sack of goodies for Ida, her second stop, hung from her arm.

Approaching the corner, she slowed her steps and tugged her shawl tight. Not that long ago, she fairly hopped from the boardwalk to the dirt-packed road. But the baby she carried had sorely altered her balance. She was about to step down when she heard her name.

"Vivian? Mrs. Alwyn?"

Oh, but she loved the sound of her new surname. Vivian looked toward the familiar voice. Her friend waved, her smile warm. She stood nearly as tall as the street sign.

"Opal! Good to see you."

Opal stared at Vivian's expanded middle. "Has it been that long since I came to the house for tea?"

Vivian gave in to her whim and rested the plate on top of her belly. "A month."

Opal raised a thick brow. "You've grown that much in a month?" Her whistle drew scowls from a shopkeeper with a broom and a beak-nosed woman with a baby on her hip. Supposedly, ladies weren't given to whistling. Or had Opal's previous profession earned their disdain?

Vivian shifted her weight to the other leg. "If the baby keeps growing at this rate, I'll be as big as Miss Hattie's Boardinghouse. I already feel as wide as a freight wagon."

Opal's riotous laughter drew more attention. "I stopped at the shop to see you."

Vivian glanced across the street and down a block. From that distance, the slate sign she'd hung on the door of Etta's Fashion Designs looked like a postage stamp.

Opal regarded the plate in Vivian's hands. "Dinner for our legendary chief of police?"

"Yes." Vivian felt her face warm with memories of her and Carter. They'd been married nearly eleven months now. Before their first Christmas as man and wife, he'd traded his job as a county-roaming deputy sheriff for his new role in law enforcement. A job that afforded him the opportunity to remain close to home and her the chance to surprise him with an occasional visit at the office.

"You know I'm happy for you." A cloud shadowed the smile on Opal's face.

"I know. Thank you." Vivian glanced toward the police department on the next block. "You were looking for me?"

"Yes. To tell you I'm no longer working at the confectionary. I wasn't making enough money to pay the rent."

Vivian swallowed the trepidation threatening to overwhelm her.

"Don't worry. I didn't go back to the Homestead." Opal straightened her shoulders. "I'm done working in the red-light district."

Vivian's deep sigh surprised even her, and they both giggled. "Good," she said, "but what will you do?"

"It seems Mr. Updike feels guilty about leading a double life."

"Oh?"

Opal's green eyes sparkled in a wide grin. "He holds a lot of stock in the telephone company here."

Vivian nodded. "He was the reason I was fired." At least that's what that sourpuss Mara Wilkening had said.

Opal nodded. "Yes, well, apparently our nocturnal banker was feeling guilty and suggested I apply for a job at the telephone company. I start work tomorrow."

"Good for you."

"I know you had trouble there, but—"

"You'll do fine." Vivian moistened her lips. "We'll have to swap stories over tea."

"Soon." Opal looked at the plate in Vivian's hand. "Right now you'd best take that to your man."

Vivian nodded. "God bless you."

When Opal turned onto Third Street, Vivian continued up Bennett Avenue and breathed a prayer for her friend to find a godly man who loved her.

A new two-story brick building in the middle of the block between Third Street and Second housed the Cripple Creek Police Department. At the glass door, Vivian shifted the plate to one hand.

Before she could grab the handle, the door swung open. Officer Gleason pulled his cap from his balding head. "Good day, Mrs. Alwyn." He stared at her face as if looking at her pregnant belly was a sin.

"I brought him some dinner."

"That's good, ma'am. I was headed out to find him something to eat." He glanced toward the short hallway on his left. "Chief's in his office."

"Thank you." She dipped her chin and walked past a desk and a file cabinet and stopped outside the closed doorway.

"If that's you, Gleason, you'd better have a big biscuit or a steak…something for me to eat. Otherwise, I may take to chewin' on this paperwork. Probably the only way to rid myself of it."

Barely able to hold back the laughter bubbling inside her, Vivian opened the office door and peeked in at her man. "Chewing paperwork? Wouldn't want to miss that, Chief Alwyn."

Carter jumped out of his chair, sending it crashing into a file cabinet. "Mrs. Alwyn, am I ever glad to see you." Taking long strides toward her, he pointed to the dish in her hand. "And that."

She held the plate away from him. "What's it worth to you?"

He gave the door behind her a shove. It hadn't even clicked shut before his lips found hers. "Mm-mm."

Vivian agreed. Carter's affections still made her heart sing. "Another one of those, and the veal cutlet is yours."

"My pleasure." Love and hunger smoldered in his dark eyes. Bending to kiss her again, he rested his hand on her belly. Just as their lips met, their baby kicked at his hand. He laughed and met her gaze. "Not too surprising she's a feisty little miss." He tapped Vivian on the nose.

She pretended to snap at his finger. "Or an ornery lad like you."

He gave her a lazy smile. "Either way, we'll have our hands full." He took the plate from her. "I thought you were designing a winter ball gown for Mrs. Johnstone."

"I was." She removed her shawl. "Then I remembered that my poor police chief left the house early, before I could make his dinner plate. I knew you wouldn't take the time away from your city council reports to go to the café."

"Pretty *and* smart." After kissing her on the cheek, Carter placed his other hand in the small of her back and guided her to an armed chair near his desk. Seated, he uncovered the plate and pulled a fork from a desk drawer. Midbite, he regarded the sack on her lap. "More surprises for me in the sack? Dessert?"

"You started with your dessert, remember?" She winked. "Going to the parsonage from here. I have apple scones for Ida."

"Still not back to work?"

"No. She's not leaving the house much. Miss Hattie's concerned about her. We all are."

"I'm sorry."

Vivian nodded, automatically pressing her hand to her middle, inviting a kick. She and Carter didn't talk about Ida's miscarriage. For obvious reasons.

Fifteen minutes later, Vivian left Carter to his paperwork and walked up the street. When the white steeple of the First Congregational Church came into view, her mind strolled down memory lane. She remembered the first time she visited the parsonage, saw the church and the steeple. She'd arrived in Cripple Creek earlier in the day feeling like a lost sheep. An outcast in disguise. She'd felt unlovable. But in a matter of months, God and Carter Alwyn had extended amazing grace to her and proven her wrong.

So much had changed for her.

And for Ida.

As Vivian walked the graveled path to the parsonage, she asked God to give her the words to encourage Ida. Should she even be here? Her big belly was probably the last thing Ida wanted to see. She'd never understand God's ways. And today she was having trouble accepting His way with Ida.

Vivian knocked three times. Ida may have gone out. But what if she was all alone, melancholy and refusing to see anyone?

Vivian leaned forward. "Ida, it's me. Are you in there?"

She heard sniffling, and then the door crept open. Her big sister stood before her, stoop-shouldered, her face blotchy and damp. A stream of sunlight striped the drab frock Ida wore.

Vivian breathed another prayer. "I'm coming in."

Ida nodded.

Inside, Vivian closed the door behind her and glanced into the parlor. "Your curtains are drawn."

"I was in the bedroom."

"Are you feeling ill?"

Ida sniffed. Red rimmed her dull blue eyes. "I'm a terrible person, Vivian. The worst sister-in-law ever."

Vivian had never seen her sister like this. "Willow adores you."

"How can she?"

"Let's go to the kitchen." Vivian held up the sack. "I brought scones. We'll have some tea."

"I'm not good company."

"I can see that." Her turn to be the big sister. "Let's go to the kitchen anyway." She drew in a deep breath and held her hand out to Ida.

Ida gripped Vivian's hand and followed her to the table.

Vivian pulled out a chair. "How about you sit, and I'll serve you for a change."

The tea made and the scones set out on dessert plates, Vivian carried the serving tray to the table. She sat across from Ida and slid a teacup to her silent sister. "Did something happen with Willow? Was she here?"

"I went to her."

"To the showroom? You were out?"

"Hattie came by." Ida tucked a strand of light brown hair behind her ear. "Said she'd had tea with you and Nell this morning."

Vivian nodded. "You were invited."

"I didn't feel like going out. Hattie said Willow might appreciate seeing me, said a stroll to the icehouse would do me good." Ida stared at her teacup. "Hattie was wrong."

That was hard to believe. "Do you need a lump of sugar?"

"I don't know what I need." Ida reached for the sugar bowl. "Willow needed me. She had a big sale and didn't know how to fill out the order forms." Her spoon clanged against the sides of the cup.

"It's good you went to the showroom." Vivian sipped tea, savoring the tingle of mint on her tongue.

"Willow was happy to see me, and so was the impatient customer." A frown dimpled Ida's chin. "I couldn't stay. As soon as the papers were signed, I remembered my baby. Two weeks ago tomorrow." She let the spoon fall against the cup and met Vivian's gaze. "I get sad."

"There's nothing wrong with feeling sad."

Ida quirked a thin eyebrow.

"It's what you do with the sadness. It'll push on you every chance it gets, but you can't let it hold you down."

"How did you get so smart?"

"By making mistakes."

"Maybe you should've been the big sister."

"No, thank you." Vivian tilted her head. "It's far too much work for me."

Ida blurted a giggle. "But you're so good at it."

"I am?"

"I'm out of bed and sipping tea, aren't I?" Ida raised the cup to her mouth.

Vivian slid a dessert plate toward Ida. "It's apple. If you like the scone, I'll give you the recipe. It's a specialty of Carter's mother."

"How is he?"

"Happy and full of veal. I took him dinner before coming here."

"You're a good wife."

"So are you."

"I don't know. Lately…"

"You'll feel better."

"You're easy to believe, little big sister."

They both laughed and Vivian dropped a bite of cinnamon-laced apple pastry into her mouth. "Mm-mm. Delicious. Even I have to say so myself."

Ida pulled the dessert plate closer, then scooped a forkful of the scone into her mouth.

Her eyes widened and she licked her lips. "I need to get the recipe."

They finished the scones and drained their teacups, and Ida stood and started filling the tray with the dirty dishes. Vivian leaned forward to slide her empty cup to Ida and felt as if she'd run into a brick wall stomach first. She looked down and stared at the space between her and the table.

"What's wrong?" Ida returned the tray to the table.

"I don't know. Something doesn't feel right." But just as suddenly as the sensation appeared, it left. She blew out a breath, relieved.

Ida sank into a chair, her brow creased. "Are you having the baby?"

Vivian's pulse quickened. "Now?"

"I don't know."

"The baby needs to wait. I wanted Father to be here first."

Ida dipped her chin and raised an eyebrow. "You may not have much say in the timing."

"Everything felt tight, but not for long."

Ida stood. "We should call Kat. She's had a baby, and her husband's a doctor."

"Did you call her when—"

"This is different."

Vivian pressed her lips together, wanting to believe her big sister. But what if it wasn't different? She'd heard of too many women who'd lost their babies well into pregnancy.

In an instant, Ida stood beside the telephone on the wall talking to an operator. Then she said, "Hello, Kat. You need to talk to Vivian." She waved Vivian over.

Vivian joined her sister and took the cone from her.

"Viv?" Kat's calm voice seemed to mock the storm brewing in Vivian's thoughts.

"Yes."

"You're at Ida's? Is she all right?"

"Better. But—"

"Something's wrong with you?"

"I don't know. I had a… It wasn't actually a pain, but it was my belly."

"Feel like someone was squeezing you around the middle?"

"Yes, that's what it felt like."

Ida pushed a chair toward her, and Vivian sat.

"How long did it last?" Kat asked.

"It takes me longer to blow my nose."

"How many times has it happened?"

"Just that once."

Ida wrung her hands. No, it wasn't easy being a big sister.

"How long ago, Viv?" Kat asked.

"Just before we called you. Four or five minutes."

"And you're not feeling anything else?"

"Like I drank two cups of tea." Vivian giggled.

"But you haven't felt any leaking or seen any blood today?" Kat could've been interviewing her for a magazine article.

"No, nothing else."

"It could be a false start then. I had some of that before Hope was born."

"How long?"

"About a month."

"A month? What do I do? How will I know?"

"If my niece or nephew is ready to come, you'll have more of the tightening *and* pain, closer together."

"I feel fine now. I was about to leave."

"I wouldn't just yet. Wait a few minutes to be sure nothing more is going on." Hope fussed in the background. "I can have Morgan stop by on his way home to check on you."

"That's not necessary." At least she hoped it wasn't. "I'll telephone if anything else happens."

Vivian hung up, and she and Ida visited for another forty minutes without incident before Ida walked with her to the road.

"Thank you for coming to see me. And for the scone and the distraction." Ida gave her a gentle hug. "Amazing how thinking of others can so affect one's disposition."

"It certainly works for me." And right now the baby had her full attention.

EIGHT

renton set his camera in its leather carrier and latched the bag. He switched the light off in the darkroom and locked the door behind him. He checked the studio to make sure he'd left everything in its proper place—the tub of toys, the deacon's bench, the Brady stand, the tripod, the lights.

He shut that door behind him and stepped into the office area. A lone file lay on the desk in front of his chair. He'd returned Mrs. Peterson's portrait sample this morning by courier and included a letter asking her to visit the studio by four o'clock this afternoon if she was still interested in the job. He pulled his watch from his trouser pocket. Twenty past five, and he hadn't heard a word from the woman.

His own fault. He'd received her application two weeks ago and sat on it. Mrs. Peterson had no doubt found other work by this time.

He slid the file folder into the top drawer. Monday, he'd take another look at the package from the man in Denver. Not as solid a painter yet as Mrs. Peterson, but probably good enough for a starter.

He'd just pulled his hat off the coat rack when the door opened. A young woman rushed in and stopped in front of him. A pleasantly photographic woman. Her lashes were thick and a deep brown like her hair. Prominent cheekbones. A graceful jaw. Eye-pleasing lines from her statuesque shoulders to her...curves. Trenton cleared his throat as if by doing so he could clear his mind as well.

"I'm c-closing, ma'am."

"I came as soon as I could," she said, slightly breathless.

"No sittings until M-Monday."

"A sitting?"

"To have your photograph taken."

"You have to take my photograph for the job?"

Trenton blinked. "Mrs. P-Peterson?"

"You sent me a letter and told me to—"

"Come by before f-four o'clock." What, the woman didn't own a timepiece?

"I wanted to comply, but I was working."

So she *had* found other employment. "It was…k-kind of you to let me know you're no longer av-vailable."

"I haven't found another job."

"B-but you did say—"

She whirled around and marched out the glass door. She pressed her hands to her cheeks, then held her head high and reentered the shop with a smile on her face. "Good day, sir. Are you the proprietor here?"

Trenton cocked his head in disbelief. "You know I am."

"Well then, I'm pleased to make your acquaintance. I'm Mrs. Peterson. I applied for the job of portrait painter, and you expressed interest in hiring me."

"Yes, I know." He hadn't meant to sigh.

She dipped her perfectly rounded chin and raised an eyebrow.

Intrigued by her resolve, he straightened a notch and gave in to the regeneration. "Yes, I'm Trenton Van Der Veer."

She extended her hand to him, and he shook it.

"I've been filling in for my sister-in-law in the icebox showroom at the Raines Ice Company," she said.

Trenton remembered his conversation with Jesse about married women in business. Mrs. Peterson was related to the pastor, or at least to his wife.

She pulled the shawl off her shoulders. "It's a temporary position. I'm still interested in learning more about the job as a portrait painter." She paused. "That's why I'm here."

Suppressing his amusement, Trenton returned his hat to the rack. Mrs. Peterson had spunk. They'd gotten off on the wrong foot, or at least he had. Her going out the door midway through his sentence seemed rude, but with the fresh start, their communications skills had improved.

He turned to face her. "Of course." It jerked out as one word. He motioned toward the chair in front of the desk.

She seated herself, her hands folded over the reticule on her lap. "In your letter today, you mentioned a need for an artist who can paint a client's portrait from a photograph and colorize photographs." She met his gaze. "I can do both."

"You're hired."

Blinking, she raised her hand. "I have a few questions for you before accepting any such agreement."

Spunky *and* direct. Trenton leaned back in his chair and motioned for her to proceed.

Mrs. Peterson squared her shoulders. Was she this bold with her husband or only with potential employers? "Would you require that I work here in the office?" She glanced at the doors to the darkroom and the studio. "Or would I be able to do the painting elsewhere?"

"Elsewhere is f-fine."

A slight smile pressed into a dimple on the left side of her face. "What would be the terms of my employment?"

"I would advertise your p-painting services." He paused to alleviate the spasms in his jaw. "Take…any requests." Another pause. "And send the w-work orders to you, along with any photographs."

"And payment?"

"Per job." He reached into the top drawer and pulled out the folder he'd made for her. "I listed the various painting services and assigned fees. You'd receive seventy percent." He'd managed to make it through the whole sentence without any stammering.

"Seventy-five percent seems more equitable." She glanced at the closed door again.

"Seventy-five percent." He shifted toward the studio door. "Those are my w-work rooms—a d-darkroom and a studio where I do the sittings and take the photographs. Would you like to see them?"

Her eyes widened, and she shook her head. "I'll wait until your office hours."

Trenton gulped. "Of course." Had he lost his mind, asking a woman into private rooms after working hours? Hopefully she wouldn't include his question when relaying their conversation to her husband. He leaned forward. "Are you still interested in w-working with me?"

"I am."

"You're hired, then?"

"Yes." She stood, and he did likewise. "Thank you. How soon did you want me to begin?"

"Is yesterday too soon?"

She laughed. Mr. Peterson no doubt enjoyed her laugh—if not her directness—immensely.

❧

Rounding the corner onto Golden Avenue, Willow pulled her shawl tight and glanced up at the coral and crimson stripes across the clouds. The sun had disappeared behind the Sangre De Cristos, leaving a nearly full moon visible. Thankfully, this long day would soon come to a close. She took slow steps to the boardinghouse.

She should be excited Mr. Van Der Veer had hired her and that her new job would allow her to work as an artist. She would paint from a photograph or add color to printed portraits. It wasn't selling her landscapes in a gallery, but she *would* receive payment for painting. A much better prospect than spouting the features of myriad iceboxes and adding numbers on a sales sheet.

But what about Ida?

Mr. Boney's mule, Sal, stood tethered to the hitching rail in front of Miss Hattie's. As Willow approached, Sal bobbed her head and brayed.

"I'll tell Mr. Boney you're getting impatient with him. But I wouldn't expect him anytime soon."

Talking to a mule? It wasn't necessarily a symptom of melancholia, but conversing with animals probably didn't bode well for good mental health. Willow shook her head and stepped onto the porch.

She needed more friends. Like Ida. And right now it was important she be a good friend herself. She couldn't abandon Ida when her sister-in-law needed her, even if Ida's siblings would have been better candidates in the showroom. But Kat was a writer with a daughter to care for and a baby on the way. Nell had a toddling son and her benevolent work with the Sisters of Mercy. Vivian was plenty busy designing clothes for Etta's Fashions and would soon deliver her first child. They all had families to care for.

Willow stepped into the entryway and was welcomed by a robust march coming from the Edison phonograph, which meant her landlady was in the parlor with Mr. Boney. Again.

Perhaps it was time she turned the tables on Miss Hattie and did a little matchmaking herself. Hattie and the old miner had been spending more and more time together. Still sparring like good friends, but wasn't friendship the best foundation for a lasting relationship?

Thanks to Tucker, Willow and his friend Sam Peterson had started out as sparring partners at the age of twelve. Then quite suddenly, friendship grew and blossomed into a love she still craved. Granted, Miss Hattie and Boney were older, but Willow believed the same could happen for them.

"Willow, is that you?" Miss Hattie's voice rang out above the staccato beat of the march.

"It is." Willow shed her shawl.

The phonograph went silent, and Miss Hattie stepped into the entryway. "Dear, you look like you're all in but your shoestrings. A busy day?"

Nodding, Willow laid her shawl and the wrapped portrait of Sam on the entry table beside a vase of daisies. "The man who came to the showroom while you were there ordered fifteen iceboxes. Two different kinds."

"Oh my."

"Thankfully, Ida stopped by in time to complete his order form."

"She didn't stay?"

"Only long enough to send Mr. Davenport on his merry way." Willow raised her finger to emphasize an important detail. "After she told him I would telephone him with the delivery date for his iceboxes."

Hattie sighed, deepening the lines framing her mouth. "That doesn't sound promising." Her blue-gray eyes narrowed. "You didn't tell her about—"

"How could I?" Willow carefully removed her hat. "What kind of a sister-in-law...friend would I be if I were to walk out when she needed me?"

"Dear, what kind of a friend would you be if you didn't tell her the truth?" Miss Hattie brushed Willow's arm. "You and Ida are like sisters. She would want to know about your opportunity."

Willow laid the pins in the bowl of her hat and set it on top of her shawl. She glanced out the window at the mule that stood outside, then toward the parlor. "I see that Boney is here again. He can't find good coffee elsewhere?" She pressed a fingertip to her chin and grinned. "Must be the company."

"A woman can have a good friend who happens to be a man." Hattie clucked her tongue, her face turning pink. "I'll go see about our meal and pour you a cup of tea. Could you let Boney know I'll return momentarily?"

"Certainly."

"And no teasing allowed." Her landlady wagged her finger, then sashayed toward the kitchen.

Willow couldn't help but smile. Hattie Adams was a woman with a servant's heart. She deserved to be happy, to have a man who would love her and help her around the house. Boney seemed to fit the bill to the letter. Well, a little crusty around the edges for some, but her landlady didn't seem bothered by that in the least. Neither did Mr. Boney seem put off by Miss Hattie's refinement. Perhaps the charming miner just needed a little push.

Willow, her steps lighter, fairly waltzed into the parlor. At the sight of her, Mr. Boney set his coffee mug on the hearth and stood.

"Willow. I thought I recognized your voice."

Had he heard their conversation?

"Hello, Mr. Boney." Willow shook his hand and met his gaze. "Did Miss Hattie have another problem with the sink?"

"No ma'am. I think I fixed it to last a good while."

But he was here in the evening, and no less close-lipped about his visits than Hattie was.

"Miss Hattie went to pour me a cup of tea. She said she'd return to you soon."

He didn't so much as blink.

"She's a good woman, our Miss Hattie," Willow said.

"Indeed she is, and a mighty fine cook."

He only visited Hattie because of her cooking and baked goods? Willow seated herself in the Queen Anne chair. She doubted Hattie's cooking was the only draw for this man. Her stuffed pork chops and carrot cake were delicious, but...

"Hattie tells me you're selling iceboxes while Ida, uh, recuperates," Boney said.

"Yes. But I'm afraid I'm not as good at bookwork as she is. I hope she's not sorry she left me in charge." And that she returned to work soon, preferably before Mr. Van Der Veer began sending her painting jobs.

Boney sat back down on the hearth. "I'm sure you're doing fine." He picked up his mug and swirled the coffee. "Hattie's glad to have you back here at the house. The company is good for her."

Well, at least they agreed on one thing—Miss Hattie needed company. Now if she could only make him understand Miss Hattie needed more than boarders, or even female friends, to keep her company.

Miss Hattie strolled in carrying a tea tray. Boney took it from her and set it on the table in front of Willow.

Hattie smiled. "Thank you, kind sir."

"You're most welcome, lovely lady." Boney held his snowy beard to his chest and bowed.

About to choke on their sap, Willow pressed her hand to her mouth. The display had been for her benefit. These two were having far too much fun teasing her.

Hattie laughed, then met Willow's gaze. "Boney and I are good friends. We have been for a very long while." She glanced at the miner. "Perhaps we'll tell the story sometime."

Willow stirred a spoonful of honey into her teacup. "A story I'd enjoy hearing."

"Me too." Boney chuckled. "Right now, however, I best be on my way." He kissed Hattie's hand with royal flair. "I doubt it's proper for a man to call on such a pretty girl this time of night."

Hattie giggled and fanned herself like a giddy schoolgirl.

Willow shook her head. Perhaps there was no matchmaking to be done here. Those two were already a pair.

NINE

*S*inging the last bars of "The Sidewalks of New York," Susanna set the stack of extra dressing gowns and petticoats into the trunk at the foot of her bed. She lowered the front of the writing desk and stared at the wooden box at the back. Her grandmother had carved the image of a phoenix on the lid. She was that bird, and she would rise from her ashes in Scandia, Kansas, and make her perch in Colorado. In Cripple Creek, to be precise. Until Trenton was ready to marry her and take her to New York.

She carried the box to the bed and sifted through the stack of photographs inside it, all of them images of her. Just days after Trenton had arrived in town with his photographic van, he'd followed her around with his camera. Pictures of her at the confectionary shop wearing her father's crisp white candy-maker's hat. Standing in front of a flowering crab-apple tree. Dressed for dinner, seated on the settee in her parents' parlor.

If she hadn't been so shortsighted, she'd already be singing for the upper tens in New York's high society. Feeling the sting of his rejection again, she returned the photographs to their nest and latched the lid.

She was adding the box to the trunk when her mother stormed into the room and stood over her, boiling like a swollen rain cloud.

"I've just spoken to your father." Lightning flashed in Mother's brown eyes. "Of all the foolish things you've ever done, daughter, this move would top them all."

Susanna added her silk beret to the trunk.

Mother slammed the lid shut and pinned her with a stormy gaze. "You can't go."

Susanna swallowed hard. She had to maintain a sunny disposition so as not to intensify Mother's storm. "Why not?" She'd managed to keep her voice just above a whisper.

"It's not prudent for a young woman—a single woman—to travel west without her family."

Her mother did enjoy rubbing in the fact that Susanna was yet unmarried. "I asked Father about making the trip, and he agreed."

"That man is clay in your hands, and you know it. You could plead a case for letting you ride a bucking horse in a sticker patch, and your father would relent." The vein in her mother's neck pulsed. "Just because you get your way doesn't make it a good decision."

"I'm not getting on a bucking horse. I'm boarding a train with a respectable family who will accompany me to Denver."

"And what will you—a single woman with no significant means—do in Denver?"

"Helen's brother lives there."

"And how do you expect that fact to be of help to you?"

"Mr. and Mrs. Granstadt will look after me, and I'll have Helen to keep me company." Susanna opened the trunk lid and met her mother's steely gaze. "I'm sure Denver's seams are bursting with confectionaries. I'll have no trouble finding a job as soon as my feet hit the depot platform."

"A respectable job?" Her mother ran her hand along the ruffle on the bedcover. "I've heard stories about the women out there."

"I'm not one of *those women.*"

"Perhaps not, but neither are you the most discreet of young women."

A shiver ran up Susanna's spine. "What happened with Trenton…Mr. Van Der Veer was a simple misunderstanding." One she could readily resolve, given the chance.

Her arms crossed, Mother raised an arched eyebrow.

"He got cold feet. It happens." And all Susanna needed to do was warm them up.

Mother dipped her chin. "So, did Mr. Van Der Veer run on cold feet to New York, or is he in Denver?" Her eyes narrowed. "Is that why you're so set on going there?"

"Why must you be so hurtful, Mother? You know I haven't heard from Mr. Van Der Veer, and I don't expect to." Susanna quivered her lip as though she might cry. "I'm set on going because my best friend is moving to Denver, and I could use a change of scenery."

And the prestigious photographer was working just behind Pikes Peak. A much shorter trip from Denver.

TEN

renton chased the broom through the house, still swept up in the memories of Friday's events. In record speed, he'd gone from reviewing applications for a portrait painter to being caught in a tongue-twisting misunderstanding. And the woman was now his employee.

He scooped a pile of dirt into a dustpan and carried it back outside where it belonged. Even if Jesse had been right about Trenton needing a change of scenery and a change of pace, things were happening too swiftly here for his comfort. The fast and furious way of the West wasn't his way. Driving his wagon of supplies across New York City from one opera house to another and one political campaign office to another would feel like a summer picnic right now.

A small studio, open four or five days a week. Being his own boss. That was all he'd wanted when he rented the shop on First Street. He hadn't considered employing anyone else.

He marched through the two-bedroom house, collecting the throw rugs as he went. He set the armful of rugs on the edge of the porch. He shook out a striped rag rug, laid it over the porch rail, and reached for another one.

He should send Mrs. Peterson a letter by courier this very day and tell her there had been a mistake. His mistake, thinking he was ready to expand the business after only two months in town. Why couldn't he be content with the progress he'd made and with business as it was? One or two sittings a day wasn't bad business, and it had been enough until he talked to the spitfire mine owner, Mollie Kathleen Gortner.

It wasn't his idea to draw attention to himself in political circles or in newspapers. If he'd still wanted that life, he would've gone to New York without Susanna. But it felt good to have his feet on the ground. A place to call home.

He was shaking out the last rug when a man rode up on a sorrel and leaned forward in the saddle. "Mister, you need yourself a woman."

Some folks would agree, say finding a wife was his next step. Trenton had a stable business and a home. But finding a wife wasn't a smart choice or a realistic conclusion for him. Not after his stretch in Kansas. Trying to be neighborly, he nodded anyway.

The wiry fellow dismounted. He wrapped the reins around the hitching rail and walked bowlegged into Trenton's yard. "You the new camera man, are you?"

"Yes, I opened the Photography S-Studio in town. Trenton Van Der Veer." He glanced at the rug hanging in front of him like a curtain.

"Joseph Weatherly." Joseph slapped his dusty cap on his leg, an apparent substitute for a handshake. "My place is up on the next road. Practically neighbors, you and me." He spit a stream of brown into Trenton's lawn. "Got me a sister in Manitou Springs. She done lost her husband in a lumber accident."

"I'm sorry." Trenton meant it. Sorry for Joseph's widowed sister, and sorry Joseph was trying to sell her to him like a swayback mare.

"Real good cook, Millie is." Joseph pressed his hat onto his head. "You can bet she would've had them rugs shook out and laid back down yesterday."

"About done. Thank you." Trenton waved, then pulled the rugs from the porch and went inside. There was a good chance Joseph wouldn't be the last neighbor to want to marry him off. Next time he'd shake out the rugs after sundown.

He laid the striped rag rug in the kitchen in front of the sink and carried the others to their respective places of service. When he set the last rug on the pine flooring in front of the bookcase, his writing box caught his eye.

He'd started over here in Cripple Creek but with little chance he'd forget what he'd left behind. Maybe it was time he wrote to her. He probably needed to reconcile his past if he had any hope of a future here. What if he'd simply imagined or misconstrued her words and acted on a misinformed impulse?

He carried the writing box to the kitchen. After spreading a piece of stationery on the table, he dipped the fountain pen into the ink.

Dear Susanna,

He set the pen down and leaned back in his chair. He should have considered what he'd say to her, if he had anything to say, before going to the trouble of starting a letter. He capped the ink and returned the box to the bookcase.

A walk to town seemed a more reasonable exercise.

Saturday morning Willow positioned a floppy hat on her head, pulled her reticule from the wardrobe, and strolled down the stairs. She didn't know what she would say to Ida, but Miss Hattie was right. Ida would want to know about her artistic opportunity at the Photography Studio, and she'd be excited for her. But was Ida ready to return to work, to let Willow go? Only Ida could answer those questions, and it was time Willow asked them.

Willow walked outside under a cloudy sky and pulled her shawl tight. Although it was only the middle of September, autumn seemed anxious to push summer out of the picture. Rain had pelted her bedroom window for the better part of the night. And from the look of the gray wall shrouding Pikes Peak and the Sangre de Cristos, the surrounding mountains were still getting pounded.

Dodging a mud puddle at the end of the walkway, Willow started up the hill toward the First Congregational Church, where her brother served as pastor. The steeple towered above rooftops, a beacon of faith and hope, and the white-trimmed parsonage, including a picket fence, stood behind the brick church building. The rosebushes lining the graveled walkway to the parsonage had recently been pruned.

Willow wiped the bottoms of her shoes on the rag rug. Before she could knock on the door, a lace curtain fluttered at the window, and Ida peered out at her. Soon Ida stood in the doorway, tears running down her face.

After closing the door behind them, Willow took Ida's hand and led her into the parlor. "Tucker isn't home?"

Ida wiped her tears. "He went to the hospital to visit one of our parishioners."

Help me, Lord. Give me the words You would speak to her.

Willow refused to ask her sister-in-law if she was all right. The answer was obvious. So obvious she couldn't fathom asking Ida to return to work on a regular basis. Swallowing her regret, Willow looked up at the first painting she'd done upon her arrival in Cripple Creek. A bank of fog obscured the top of Pikes Peak. The fog was beginning to clear for her, but not yet for Ida.

As soon as possible she'd send Mr. Van Der Veer a note by courier to let him know she couldn't accept the job as portrait painter. Her sister-in-law needed her still.

Ida wiped more tears from her face and seated herself on the sofa. "I don't know what's gotten into me."

"Grief has gotten into you." Willow sat in the rocker across from her. "You are the wife and the big sister trying to be strong for everyone else's sake."

"Vivian was here yesterday. She might be having her baby soon." Red rimmed Ida's blue eyes. "I should be feeling better by now."

"When Sam died, my grief took me down an unforeseeable path. For a long time."

"But I didn't lose my husband." Ida wiped her eyes. "I hadn't even felt my baby kick or roll as Kat has. I hadn't held my baby. I don't even know if it was a boy or a girl."

"But he or she was already a part of you. A life you and Tucker had created and anticipated."

Ida pressed her lips together and nodded. "It's hard to explain, but I already felt like a mother."

Willow squeezed Ida's hand. "You haven't talked to your sisters about this, have you?"

"I couldn't. Nell hasn't been able to conceive. Vivian is nearly ready to deliver her first baby, and Kat is carrying another child. They don't need to be thinking about my problems."

Willow nodded. She understood wanting to protect those around her. "You know how Sam died."

"Yes. Tucker told me Sam went into the river after him, and about how he blamed himself when Sam drowned."

Willow's heart raced after the memory, but she had to keep going. "Tucker wasn't to blame. No one was." Willow breathed another prayer for grace and guidance. "And because I was Tucker's big sister and loved him dearly, I tried to protect my brother from my grief. I felt I had to in order to assuage his grief, to comfort him, and to assure him Sam's death was an accident and he wasn't responsible."

"It's what big sisters do."

"Yes, but we need to be comforted too."

Ida nodded, her lips quivering.

"You've been worried about Tucker. And about me."

Another nod.

"You've been concerned about how your sisters feel because of their own pregnancies." Willow met Ida's gaze as she remembered Maria's wise counsel. "We have to look our own grief in the face before we can receive and accept the comfort we need."

A slight smile began to clear the clouds from Ida's blue eyes. "I'm so glad you stopped by." She straightened her back. "I know I haven't thanked you nearly enough for what you're doing for me at the icehouse."

Willow wanted to say she was glad she'd been available. She was, but—

"I needed time to work through what I was feeling. And Tucker, well, it's different with him."

Willow glanced at the mantel, her gaze settling on Tucker and Ida's wedding photograph. "Sam and I weren't married long, but he'd hung around our house for four or five years before that. Plus I've had a brother for much of my life. Men don't react to sorrow the way women do."

Ida nodded and looked at the rag rug beneath their feet. "He said he doesn't blame me."

Tears stung Willow's eyes. "Of course he doesn't. Losing the baby wasn't your fault." She softened her voice. "Only God knows why it happened." She wouldn't say there would be other children. She didn't know God's plan. "Tucker didn't know how to comfort you."

"So he cut the lawn and pruned the roses."

"Exactly. He felt the loss and was sad for you, but—"

"He hadn't had a baby growing inside him."

The image of her brother ripe with child prompted a laugh that erupted before Willow could stop it.

Ida's jaw dropped and her eyes widened, and then she began laughing too. "There's an image we won't soon forget. Speaking of Tucker, he told me about an advertisement he'd seen in the *Cripple Creek Times* and thought it might be of interest to you."

Willow sobered. Dare she think it was the advertisement Mr. Van Der Veer had printed for the studio job?

"We have a new photography shop in town, and the owner advertised for an artist who could paint portraits from his photographs."

"A Mr. Van Der Veer."

"You know him?"

"I applied for the job. *That* Saturday."

A familiar shadow crossed Ida's face.

Willow continued. "When I left the depot, I went to the library. I figured my mother had all but twisted your arm to give me a job, so I went to read the advertisements for employees."

Ida looked at her arm, a slow grin lighting her eyes. "She may have twisted some. You'd come to tell me?"

"And to check on you. I knew you had to be feeling badly not to see Mother off at the depot, but I never thought—"

"We were all surprised." Ida's voice trailed off to a short silence. "Did you ever hear from Mr. Van Der Veer?"

"That's why Hattie stopped by the showroom yesterday. The courier had returned my sample portrait with a letter from Mr. Van Der Veer."

"He offered you the job, didn't he?"

Willow nodded, keeping her smile to herself.

Ida leaned forward and grabbed Willow's hand. "That's wonderful!"

"You really think so?"

"You don't?" Ida straightened. "What, you're afraid you're going to miss selling iceboxes?"

Willow giggled.

"Wait a minute." A frown creased Ida's forehead. "I told Mr. Davenport you'd telephone him with the delivery date, as if you'd be working there forever. And you never said a word."

"You needed me."

"Well, now I need to go back to work."

"About that... I'm a little nervous about your return."

"Don't be." Ida folded her hands in her lap. "I'm feeling much better now. Besides, it'll be good for me to think about something else."

Willow cleared her throat. "That's not what I'm nervous about."

"Oh?"

"I'm not a businesswoman and definitely not a bookkeeper."

Ida laughed. "This is your way of telling me I may find a pile of loose numbers in my ledger Monday morning?"

"Yes. I did my best, but—"

"Don't worry about me. I'll manage just fine." Ida wagged her finger. "But you let me know if you need any help keeping track of the money Mr. Van Der Veer owes you."

Willow smiled. "Gladly."

Thirty minutes later, Willow had helped Ida pack the few baby things she'd already gathered and was on her way back to the boardinghouse. Miss Hattie had errands to run this morning. With her landlady gone, the boardinghouse would be a lonely place to celebrate. Willow's stomach fluttered with the prospect of working as a portrait painter. Now that Ida didn't need her help anymore, she could finally be excited about her new job.

Ice cream!

Her steps quickened as she walked down the hill toward town. At the bottom, she turned right on Bennett Avenue and stepped onto the boardwalk. Even on a Saturday morning, Cripple Creek buzzed. Carts wheeled up and down the muddy road. Horses whinnied and burros brayed. A gentleman doffed his bowler in a greeting, and she offered a quick nod in return.

Collins Pharmacy, one of the many new businesses in Cripple Creek, was situated in the middle of the block just west of Second Street. Willow carefully crossed at Third, dodging a boy cajoling a moody mule. Lace curtains framed the gilt lettering on the pharmacy door.

COLLINS

PHARMACY

ICE CREAM PARLOR

A matching lace curtain hung on the open eave above the door, fluttering in the breeze and waving her inside. Today was as good a time as any to investigate the pharmacy and taste the parlor's wares.

The heels of her high-top shoes tapped the black-and-white checkerboard linoleum. The left side of the store boasted row after row of drugs, medicinal liquors, balms, and various sundries. But the parlor area drew her to the soda fountain along the far wall. Willow stood behind the only open stool. On the wall behind the counter, rows of sparkling glass dishes and mugs lined the shelves in front of a large mirror. A big painted menu hung from the ceiling above the dipping cases and soda pulls.

The rotund man behind the counter offered her a toothy smile. "May I help you, Miss?"

Ignoring the label, Willow smiled. "Yes, please. I've come for some ice cream."

"You're in the right place." He stabbed at the countertop with his pudgy index finger. "Got us a special today. A large soda-water float with two scoops of vanilla ice cream for two bits."

"Mmm. I'll take one of those. Root beer soda, please." She pulled her coin purse from her reticule and laid a quarter on the counter.

He jerked the soda handle, partially filling the fluted glass, then reached into the cabinet, pulled out two perfectly round scoops of vanilla ice cream, and carefully dropped each one into the glass. He slipped in a tall teaspoon, added a spiral-striped paper straw, then slid her celebration treat to her with a flourish. "Here you go. One full-to-the-rim root beer soda with two scoops of vanilla ice cream."

"Thank you." Willow lifted the straw to her lips. Cold and sweet. Delicious.

An older man and woman sat on the stools to her left, a younger couple to her right. Round tables with red porcelain tops dotted the back corner of the pharmacy. Couples occupied four of the five tables. A lone man was seated at the far table, and he was looking straight at her.

Mr. Trenton Van Der Veer.

Willow gave him a polite nod, and he did the same.

Turning back around, she slid onto the empty stool and took a long drink of her creamy soda water, trying to ignore the fact that her boss was doing the same thing just a few feet away.

Two married people having ice cream alone and in a public place. Except she no longer had a husband.

Mr. Van Der Veer didn't need to know that.

Eleven

uesday, Hattie watched the action from her chair at the head of the dining room table. A long piece of white butcher paper stretched the full length of the table. The twentieth of September had arrived, and Mr. Sinclair was due in at the Midland Terminal depot at one thirty this afternoon.

All four of the Sinclair sisters had gathered at the boardinghouse to design a banner to ballyhoo his arrival. A wooden pencil box lay empty in front of Hattie. Each of the sisters had claimed a pencil, and the three youngest had lined up on one side of the table. Kat and Vivian, in the last weeks of their pregnancies, had chosen to sit while Ida officiated from the far end. She'd closed the icebox store today in preparation for the reunion with their father.

Ida tapped her narrow chin. "Do we want pictures on the sign or just a big, colorful *Welcome*?"

Vivian rested her hand on top of her rounded belly. Five days had passed since she'd been bothered by what Kat referred to as a *false start*. "You know Father. No frills."

Hattie swirled the ice shavings in her glass of lemonade. "He has four daughters, and he doesn't like frills?"

Vivian shook her head.

Nor did he favor talking on the telephone, at least not with the woman who had tended to his daughters in his absence. Nevertheless, Harlan Sinclair had fathered four delightful girls, and Hattie was eager to meet him. She leaned back in the cushioned chair and raised her glass to her mouth. She was more excited to greet his guest. She'd met Alma Shindlebower last year when Alma accompanied Vivian across the country, and the sisters' aunt had proven to be enchanting company. During this visit, Hattie would see that Alma spent more time with Boney. She sipped her lemonade, contemplating her reputation as a first-class matchmaker.

Nell bent over the banner and wrote a big swoopy *W.* "I vote for drawing embellishments on the letters. Then we can frame the word with our names."

A grunt and a groan in the opposite corner of the room drew everyone's attention. Thirteen-month-old William sat empty handed, staring at seventeen-month-old Hope, who stood over him waving a wooden block in each hand.

Kat rose from her chair with the speed of a desert tortoise. She looked in her daughter's direction and cocked her head. "Hope Joyce, are you sharing the blocks with your cousin?"

Nodding, the little girl widened her eyes and bobbed her curly locks. Hattie covered her mouth to stifle a laugh. The child had her mother's auburn hair and her father's blue eyes—a winning combination. Hattie should look away, but she couldn't bear to miss a minute with this family.

"Hope?" Kat dipped her sharp chin. "Did you take William's block?"

Hope copied the dipped chin and peered at her mother through dark lashes. Her lips pressed together, Hope handed one of the blocks to her younger cousin.

Kat leaned on the table. "Nanny Hattie has plenty of blocks for each of you. Don't you take his block again."

After a quick nod, Hope plopped on the floor beside William and reached into the cloth sack. She pulled out another of the blocks George had carved.

Hattie swallowed a bite of regret. She and George had expected to have a house full of children, and they would no doubt have had a baker's dozen of grandchildren by this time. But the good Lord had other plans for them. She diluted her residual regret with a generous swig of gratitude. The Lord had been so good to her. *Nanny Hattie.* What a gift it was to be a part of the Sinclair sisters' lives and their families. Hopefully that was a frill Mr. Sinclair could abide.

Hattie returned her attention to the banner. Vivian had pulled the paper to the edge of the table and with grand flourish wrote the *C* in *Welcome.*

Ida glanced toward the doorway. "I haven't seen Willow. Is she working today?"

Hattie moved the pencil box to the buffet. "She hasn't received any painting jobs yet, but she did come home yesterday with all sorts of art supplies. She has an old tintype of me and is upstairs practicing her portrait painting."

Kat covered her mouth. If she was trying to hide her yawn, she hadn't managed it. "Does anyone know the photographer she'll be working for?"

Ida shook her head. "Tucker and I haven't met Mr. Van Der Veer yet, but knowing my husband, I'm sure he'll be paying a visit soon." She started on the second *E* while Kat filled in the center of the *O* with a red pencil.

"I haven't yet met him either, but Mollie Kathleen spoke highly of his work at the last Women for the Betterment of Cripple Creek meeting." Hattie sipped her lemonade. "Said he's a childhood friend of Jesse's, at the livery."

Vivian dotted the *i*'s in her name and looked up at Ida. "Do you think Father will like Cripple Creek, after nearly two-and-a-half years of living in Paris, France?"

"I hope so." Ida looked at the sign. "It was, after all, his idea we all come here."

Upon the recommendation of his railroad buddies, Mr. Sinclair had sent his daughters out west to this mining town to find husbands. Hattie had heard the story, even lived a good portion of it with the girls, and she still had trouble understanding how a father could do such a thing.

She stood and retrieved the pencil box from the buffet. "I'm sure your father will love Cripple Creek because his girls are all here and you'll be a family again." Or at least that was how it should be.

Hattie glanced at the leaning tower of blocks Hope and William had built. Mr. Sinclair was a blessed man to have such delightful offspring, times four, and he'd soon meet his sons-in-law and two grandchildren for the first time.

Vivian laid her pencil on the table. "I was pretty upset with him for not taking me to Paris."

Nell focused on Vivian's rounded middle. "And now?"

"I got over it."

"As soon as she met Deputy Carter Alwyn." Ida winked.

Vivian turned a lovely shade of red. "I must admit, he is a distraction."

Ida stood back from the table. Tapping her sharp chin, she studied the sign.

"Good enough, big sis?" Kat tapped her chin too.

Ida swatted Kat on the shoulder. "I sure hope new baby Cutshaw isn't as ornery as you are."

"Well, if he takes after his sister, we know he will be."

"He?"

"My mother-in-law is sure it's a boy." Kat patted her abdomen. "She said when she carried Morgan her belly was the same shape—low and round."

"She could be wrong." Willow strolled into the dining room, wearing a plain brown frock. "Sam's sister said her baby like to have climbed into her throat, she carried him so high."

"A boy?"

Willow nodded.

"That's how I felt carrying Hope." Kat turned to Vivian. "Do you think you'll have a boy or a girl?"

Nell giggled. "As big as you are, you could deliver one of each."

"Twins?" Her eyes widening, Vivian pressed a hand to each side of her middle.

Kat shrugged, a little too playfully.

Vivian wagged her finger.

"We can't help ourselves," Ida said, between giggles. "Teasing you has always been so much fun."

"For you, maybe." A grin eased into Vivian's golden-brown eyes.

Hattie reveled in the patter between the girls. Did the no-nonsense man she'd talked to on the telephone know how blessed he was? If he did, would he have run off to Paris and left his daughters to fend for themselves?

She shook her head as if the action could chase away her poor thoughts of a man she hadn't yet met. It wasn't fair to judge Mr. Sinclair. His daughters were all spirited but gracious, God-fearing women. And their father was no doubt a very nice man.

The telephone jangled as if to scold her for thinking such uncomplimentary thoughts. William squealed, Hope clapped, and the tower of blocks tumbled to the floor. More squealing.

Hattie trudged to the kitchen. Shame on her for passing judgment. Mr. Sinclair had lost his wife—the mother of his children—then a few years later lost his job and his home. He had no choice but to roll with the changes.

She lifted the earpiece off its hook on the wall and spoke into the cone. "Happy Wednesday, Myrtle."

"Thank you. Doctor Morgan Cutshaw is on the line for his wife." The operator spoke in a rush.

"Is she there?" Morgan's voice sounded taut, like a violin string wound too tight.

"I'll get her." Hattie wanted to ask if everything was all right, but like Mr. Sinclair, the doctor sounded like a man on a mission. Instead, she let the earpiece hang from its wire and took quick steps to the doorway. "Kat, it's Morgan."

Kat stood, her eyebrows pinched. Hattie and Ida followed her into the kitchen. Kat picked up the earpiece. "Morgan?"

While Ida added wood to the stove, Hattie pulled a tin of peppermint tea from the shelf.

"A train wreck?"

Ida dropped a piece of firewood on the floor and rushed to her sister's side. "Father?"

Hattie met Kat's tense gaze. "Where?"

"Anaconda. In Phantom Canyon."

Hattie looked at one sister, then at the other. "That's the Florence Line."

Ida blew out a breath. "It's not Father's train."

Hattie patted Ida's arm. Mr. Sinclair had booked passage on the Midland train. But still, the midday train from Florence was always full of people and cargo. There would be injuries, if not worse.

She breathed a prayer and set the tin of tea on the counter. The railroad would be taking a load of folks out to help with the wreckage and to tend to the passengers, and she needed to be on it. Thankfully, she had readied her guests' rooms. Perhaps Willow would help prepare the family dinner tonight.

"I want to, Morgan, but I'm not sure I should." Kat ran her hand over her swollen belly. "I didn't sleep much last night, and I have Hope—"

Ida leaned toward the cone. "I'll go."

Hattie pulled off her apron. "Me too."

It seemed Mr. Sinclair would have only three of his four daughters at the depot to greet him. He'd be minus a landlady as well.

Willow watched from the front porch as Vivian, Kat, Nell, and their little ones strolled the walkway to Kat's carriage for a sweet reunion with their father.

Fighting a pang of grief, Willow walked back into the empty house and closed the door. The phonograph was silent, and so were the pots and pans in the kitchen. Miss Hattie had gone with Ida to offer aid at the site of the train wreck. No other boarders lived here until Mr. Sinclair and his sister-in-law's arrival later this afternoon.

She was alone.

Leaning against the door, Willow looked up at the colorful banner hanging from the second-floor landing—"Welcome!" While the Sinclair sisters were saying a long-awaited hello to their father, she was still struggling to say good-bye to her own.

She needed something to do. Something new to say hello to. And painting portraits was the best prescription for what ailed her. Her work with Mr. Van Der Veer would help occupy her time, as well as her mind, while adding roots to her new life here.

Her meeting with him late Friday afternoon seemed to go well. Recalling her sudden exit and innocent return to the studio made her smile. The way the man's jaw dropped, it was a wonder he didn't bruise his chin on the flooring. She'd seen the amusement in his eyes too. His wife was no doubt the compliant sort, and he wasn't accustomed to having a woman take charge. Normally she wouldn't be so brash, but they'd gotten off to a confusing start. And it worked out all right. After all, he did hire her.

But she hadn't heard from him since. A polite greeting on his way out of the ice-cream parlor didn't count.

She turned away from the banner and walked to the kitchen. That and the parlor were her favorite rooms in the house—cozy spots for keeping company. Homey and comfortable. Mr. Boney had recently repainted Hattie's kitchen a pale yellow with barn-red molding around the ceiling and the doors. It was a cheery room.

Willow set her reticule on the kitchen table and headed for the chromed stove. She'd never lived in a place with such a modern cook stove. She and Sam had taken their meals at the dining hall at seminary. The asylum may have had a nice stove, but she never saw it. And Aunt Rosemary's was functional enough, like the one at the parsonage, but certainly not pretty.

Willow lifted the handle from its hook on the end of the stove and opened a front lid. She could see a faint glow, so she gave it a gentle blow to wake up the fire. She lowered the lid and picked up the kettle, carrying it to the faucet above the sink.

The flowing water seemed a fitting metaphor for her thoughts. She wanted purpose in her life and she needed a livelihood, but what if she wasn't ready for a job? After all, she'd married Sam soon after finishing school and had never held a real job. She'd only sold a few of her portraits and landscapes to family and friends.

Willow pulled a floral mug from the shelf and tossed in a spoonful of tea leaves, continuing her deliberations. She'd buried her father, and her mother had returned to Colorado Springs, but she wasn't truly alone. She was indeed among friends. She had Miss Hattie and the Sinclair sisters. She was sure to form friendships in her church family. Who knew? She and her employer's wife might also become friends.

Speaking of her employer, if she didn't hear from him this afternoon, she'd return to the Photography Studio tomorrow and inquire about his contacts and his advertising. Perhaps she'd even create an advertisement of her own that they could post around town.

In the meantime, she'd enjoy a cup of tea and a slice of Miss Hattie's vanilla pound cake with berry sauce. Too bad she didn't have anyone to enjoy the refreshment with her, but she wouldn't feel sorry for herself and be a weeping Willow. Sam wouldn't want that for her. Neither would her father. She'd enjoy the spread she'd set out and pursue contentment.

She was savoring her last forkful of cake when the doorbell rang.

Archie, the same young man who had picked up her application package, stood on the porch with a large manila envelope. "Missus Peterson, another delivery from Mr. Van Der Veer, the photographer."

Her very first assignment, no doubt. "Yes, thank you. Come in." She hurried to the kitchen and returned with his tip.

When Archie had closed the door behind him, Willow grasped the string on the envelope and slid out a neatly written note atop two photographs.

20 September, 1898
Dear Mrs. Peterson,
Enclosed you will find your first assignments as the portrait painter for
The Photography Studio.
   Mrs. Gortner, owner of the Mollie Kathleen Mine, would like a
14 x 20-inch portrait on canvas. I have enclosed the printed photograph.
   Mr. Flinn, from the office of Eugene Flinn, Assayer, wants his
family photograph colorized.
   Please let me know if you have any questions.
Cordially,
Mr. Trenton Van Der Veer

The job was real. Mr. Van Der Veer had truly hired her, and she was now officially a commissioned portrait painter.

If only she were so confident.

TWELVE

I da stood between Hattie and Morgan. They were three of about thirty people, mostly men, who had crammed into the stock car, including two of the Sisters of Mercy, distinguishable in their black habits. A switch engine groaned as it tugged the car up out of the valley toward Phantom Canyon. Most of the men were miners, but a man with a box camera and a tripod tucked under his arm leaned against the slats in an opposite corner. Likely Willow's new boss, Trenton Van Der Veer.

Willow *would* see Father before Ida did. She sighed.

Hattie patted Ida's arm. "Your father will understand your not being at the depot, dear. He'll be proud of you serving others."

Father *would* understand. He'd do the same if the situation were reversed—forsake his own plans to help others. But disappointment still goaded her. She and her sisters had waited a long time for Father's visit, and she'd so been looking forward to meeting his train, to welcoming him and Aunt Alma upon their arrival. To telling him about the baby she carried.

She pressed her hand to her stomach. The baby she'd lost.

As the short train rounded the next curve, Ida caught sight of the wreck. Her gasp was one in a chorus of them. The engine, all the cars, and the caboose lay on their sides, wheels up, on the ballast below the rails. Fifty or so people dotted the embankment like worker ants. Many seemed to be assisting the injured while others milled about.

The stock car buzzed with chatter. Speechless, Ida breathed a prayer for the injured, then for wisdom and skill for all the helpers.

"Remain calm, and don't get in the way." Morgan's voice boomed above the buzz. "We'll assist passengers with the greatest need first, according to the severity of their condition."

As their transport drew closer to the wreckage below the bridge, Ida couldn't stop blinking. The disturbing image didn't go away. The locomotive lay in a heap, twisted, some of its pieces detached. Two passenger cars lay behind it, having slid several feet down the embankment. Three freight cars and the caboose lay in a zigzag, bringing up the rear of the calamity. Talk was that a rail on the downhill side had given way.

When their train came to a shuddering halt, one of the miners on board flipped the latch and slid open the door. Chaos erupted as people crowded the exit. So much for Morgan's directive to remain calm. They were all in the way, some risking injury by jumping to the ground. Others sat on the threshold to lower themselves to the gravel roadbed.

As Ida and Hattie allowed Morgan to lower them to the ground, the cries for help assaulted their ears. How would they know where to begin? With Hattie at her side, Ida picked her way down the embankment behind Morgan. Medical bag in hand, her brother-in-law took long strides toward the passenger cars.

"I'm a doctor," Morgan shouted.

"Over here!" The woman's cry came from under a rock overhang, several feet away from the far passenger car.

Hattie tapped Ida's arm and pointed to a young woman with antsy children. "I'm going to check on those families."

Ida nodded.

Morgan picked up his pace, and so did Ida. A wisp of a woman stood over a motionless man with no obvious injuries. He lay in the dry creek bed as if in blessed slumber.

"You have to help my husband." She blew at a strand of white hair that dangled from beneath her bonnet. "Harold was resting so peacefully until the train bumped off the tracks. He helped me out of the train and to the shade here, then said he needed to finish his nap." She wrung her feeble hands. "Now he won't wake up."

Ida met Morgan's stoic gaze, and her breath caught. The elderly man lay motionless. Placing her arm around the woman's back, Ida watched as her brother-in-law reached to the man's collar and placed two fingers on his neck.

Morgan stood. "I'm sorry, ma'am. Your husband is gone."

Narrowing her cloudy blue eyes, the new widow shook her head. "No, that's Harold, all right. Harold Sweeny. Look at his big nose."

Morgan looked at Ida. "I'd say his heart gave out. I need to help the injured."

"Go. I'll see to her."

"Doctor!" The call came from between the two passenger cars, where a groaning man sat on the ground, holding his leg.

Morgan answered the call, and Ida returned her attention to the confused woman at her side. "My name is Ida."

Smiling, the woman looked at her deceased husband. "Missus… I'm Harold's wife."

Her blank expression pierced Ida's heart. This poor woman was alone now. Ida fought the tears stinging her eyes and clasped Mrs. Sweeny's hand. "There is someone I'd like you to meet. Do you see that nun there by the bridge?"

Ten minutes later, Ida left Mrs. Sweeny with Sister Mary Claver Coleman. She looked for Morgan but spotted Hattie first, a gaggle of children gathered around her. It looked as if she'd chosen to distract them with her storytelling. It didn't look like help was needed there, so Ida started toward the group of folks milling about near the second passenger car.

"Cherise! Cherise!"

The distant plea came from behind her, the man's voice reminding her of the suppertime call from her childhood.

But it couldn't be him; he wasn't here.

She walked toward another of the nuns, thinking Morgan may be nearby.

"Ida! Ida, is that you?"

Her heart racing, Ida spun around and stared into the ashen face of her father. "Father! Why are you here? You're supposed to—" She stared at the knot on his forehead. Other than that, he didn't look injured, but she'd never seen him so agitated. "Are you all right?"

"I'm fine, but you have to help me, daughter."

Where was Aunt Alma? What were they doing on this train? By this time, her sisters had gone to meet them at the Midland Terminal depot.

"Is it Aunt Alma? Is she hurt?"

Father frowned as if her question confused him and shook his hatless head. "No. I can't find Cherise."

"Cherise? Who—"

"She came with me from Paris. I'd gone into the lavatory. I never should have left her side. We have to find her."

He'd brought a woman with him to Cripple Creek?

Ida followed her father back to the farthest passenger car. She'd never seen him move this fast. Nor had she seen him this uneasy. Not since the night her mother succumbed to pneumonia. This woman who had accompanied him from France couldn't be as important to him as their mother, could she?

Her father darted around a cluster of people, shouting the name *Cherise.* In pursuit, Ida picked up her skirts. Harlan Sinclair wasn't much for corresponding, but he *had* sent a handful of letters over the past two years. Not once had he mentioned having met a woman named Cherise.

But then during the past several months his only communication had been a brief telegram stating the date and time of his arrival on the Midland Terminal Railroad. Not on the Florence and Cripple Creek Railroad. Nor had he mentioned a guest. Hattie had been the one to tell her Father had telephoned the boardinghouse and asked for two rooms. That meant he and this Cherise weren't married, at least not yet. Since he hadn't said for whom he'd reserved the second room, Hattie had assumed the guest was Aunt Alma.

Prior to today, Ida would've chosen the word *logical* as an adjective befitting her father. Now he raced toward a fallen train car, pushing people aside like a madman.

"Father!"

He stopped just short of the tipped car and faced her. "I've searched everywhere else." He pressed his palm to the side of his head as if it pained him.

He wasn't all right. Morgan needed to look at him. Ida stared at her father while she listened for sounds in the car. She didn't hear any noises coming from inside. "I'm sure others have searched the car."

"I wasn't with her. She could've been hurt…buried by baggage and overlooked." He pressed his right foot to a frame rail and looked at her. He'd aged. The laugh lines that once framed his blue eyes had been replaced by worry lines. He clamped onto a brake line and started to pull himself up the exposed underside of the car.

"Your head hurts. You shouldn't be doing that." Sighing, Ida pushed up the sleeves of her linsey-woolsey dress. "I'll go in and look for her."

He stepped down, his shoulders sagging. "Thank you."

She decided to attack the end of the car, hoping the door could be opened. She checked the laces on her boots, then tucked the ruffled hem of her skirt into her stockings and started climbing. Using the pickets as ladder steps, she made her way up the railing, muttering to herself.

This Cherise must have been very important to Father, because there hadn't been so much as an embrace before he put her to work. He'd left Portland in April of '96. Ida hadn't seen him in two years and five months. A "glad-to-see-you" would've been nice.

The door was open. As gently as possible, Ida lowered herself into the car. Crouching on the lavatory door, she peered into the clutter. The bolted seats stood on end, looking like rows of vacant confessionals. Carpet bags, boxes, and other personal belongings lay strewn on the windows now facing the ground. Light streamed in through the windows that now served as a ceiling. Ida stepped carefully on the window frames, wending her way past the seats and through the mishmash.

A shuffling sound stopped her. Had she heard someone, or had she only imagined the sound in her desperation to find Cherise and appease her father?

"Is someone in here?"

Silence.

"Cherise?" Ida stepped over a broken lamp. "Cherise, I am Mr. Sinclair's daughter. Are you in here?"

Dark eyes peered at her from around a seat. As a tentative child emerged from her hiding place, Ida saw a curtain of long black hair. Red rimmed the young girl's eyes. Tears streaked her round face.

"You are Cherise?"

"*Oui*, Cherise. *Vous connaissez mon Monsieur Sinclair?*" The child sniffled. "Pardon. You know my Monsieur Sinclair?" Her accent was thick, but understandable.

Father had brought a little girl with him from France?

The man waiting outside wasn't the father she knew.

THIRTEEN

*T*renton set up his tripod on a hillock in the dry wash above the twisted train. He'd received news of the derailment by telephone from the president of the Florence and Cripple Creek Railroad, who had asked him to take pictures for their investigation. Before Trenton had gotten out of the studio door with his equipment, Bart Gardner, editor of the *Cripple Creek Times,* nearly ran him down. Bart had come to ask Trenton to capture a couple of crisp photographs for display in the newspaper office.

Folks from nearby farms had come to help. At least one doctor had come out to treat the injured. He'd heard of at least one death already, an elderly man whose wife was frail and confused. He'd seen two Catholic nuns comforting the frightened and handing out food to the hungry. He'd watched a matronly woman gather children about her. She'd soon had them laughing at her stories. He'd even witnessed a young woman climbing into one of the tipped passenger cars to rescue a panicked little girl.

Trenton positioned the cape on the camera and inserted the frosted glass. Perhaps his choice to photograph people rather than landscapes wasn't completely driven by his need to make a dollar. He'd all but forgotten there were benevolent people in the world. The photographs he planned to take of the participants here today would champion the human spirit—their tenacity and their compassion.

Some folks who knew his struggle would say he had spirit. Others would call him hopeless. Swallowing his mother's bitter indictment once again, he ducked under the cape and framed the scene before calling for all to be still.

"After that day, I didn't want to see another cow. Ever."

Hattie watched as the eight children gathered around her waited for another story. Their laughter was sweet music to her heart.

"Another one, Miss Hattie." The request came from Bucky, the oldest of three siblings. "Tell another one."

Hattie glanced up the tracks. The switch engine had started its descent toward them. "I'd love to, but it'll soon be my turn to go home."

"Me too!" A pigtailed girl clapped and ran to her mother. The children began to scatter, reuniting with their families.

Hattie's smile was bittersweet. She loved telling the tales of her younger self—Adeline Pemberton. Soon the Sinclair sisters' sons and daughters would be old enough to gather at her knee for a story.

She glanced around the wreckage for any sign of Ida, who was probably more than ready to head back to town and join her sisters in welcoming her father to Colorado. The last time Hattie had seen the oldest Sinclair sister, Ida was handing a little girl down from a train car.

Even if Mr. Sinclair didn't like frills or making a fuss over things, he should be proud of his daughters.

"Group Two." Mr. Updike stood on the bridge, shouting into a megaphone. "Group Two: line up here." Using the megaphone as a pointer, the banker directed the crowd already forming.

The stock car creaked as it was pulled around the corner, ready for its second run into town. The first load included the two Sisters of Mercy and Mrs. Sweeny—the poor dear who'd lost her husband today—and those passengers who'd been most severely injured. Bruises, scrapes, and frayed nerves accounted for most of the maladies, although one man had suffered a broken leg and an older woman had swooned and cut her head.

Hattie heard her name and turned around. Ida walked toward her beside the man Hattie had seen outside the passenger car. Ida's hand rested on his arm while the little girl Ida had rescued clung to his other arm.

Ida cleared her throat. "Miss Hattie, I'm pleased to introduce you to Mr. Harlan Sinclair. My father."

Hattie blinked and then blinked again. He didn't fit the image she had conjured of him. "Your father?"

"Yes, ma'am." He reached up as if to remove a hat he wasn't wearing. Hattie noticed the dark knot on his forehead. "We spoke on the telephone."

She nodded. Actually she'd done most of the speaking. "Hattie Adams." She seemed to have to force the words out. "Please. Call me Miss Hattie. It's a pleasure to meet you."

"This is Miss Cherise Renard." He rested a hand on the young girl's shoulder. "Cherise, this is Miss Hattie. We'll be boarding in her establishment for a while, remember?"

"*Oui.* Yes, Monsieur Sinclair." The little girl bowed for Hattie but never made eye contact.

Hattie looked to Ida for an explanation or at least a reaction to finding her father here—and with a child in his care. Ida's blue eyes seemed to hold only questions.

As the stock car clunked to a stop, they all joined the line to board. Fifteen minutes later, Hattie wiped beads of sweat from the back of her neck. The car was even more crowded on the return to Cripple Creek than on the trip down the canyon.

Ida stood nearby with her father and the young girl who had traveled halfway around the world with him. Hattie hadn't been able to learn much, but Ida did tell her that after she'd pulled Cherise from the train car, Morgan had checked the child and Mr. Sinclair for any injuries. Mr. Sinclair's knot was a goose egg of a bruise, enough to cause a whopping headache but nothing more serious. Morgan had stayed behind in order to return with the last group.

While the car inched up out of Phantom Canyon, Hattie braced herself against the side slats. Why hadn't Mr. Sinclair given his daughters enough information about his visit to help prepare them to meet his guest? Instead, he'd chosen to surprise them, which was not at all considerate. And to make matters worse, Hattie had made suppositions about his guest. His tight-lipped reservation had led her to expect Alma Shindlebower. Hattie blew out a breath of frustration. At nearly fifty years old, she should know better than to form assumptions. Thanks to her, the sisters had been expecting their aunt. But no. A French girl she guessed to be about eight years old now clung to Ida's father like a bee to a flower.

How did a man with grown children end up with a little girl from a foreign country? Where were her parents? Ida was sure to have at least as many questions about Cherise as Hattie did, but Mr. Sinclair's focused attention on the child didn't leave any room for inquiry or explanation. He should have told his daughters about the girl, warned them his affections would be divided.

As his landlady, Hattie wasn't in a position to pry into his personal affairs. But she was also a friend to his daughters, and Nanny Hattie so wanted to set the man straight in his priorities.

"Grievous words stir up anger." Hattie recalled the verse from the book of Proverbs and drew in a deep breath.

"Mrs. Adams."

Turning to face Mr. Sinclair, Hattie thought about correcting him again, suggesting he call her Miss Hattie. She chose not to. Perhaps it was best they remain on more formal terms. If she considered him an acquaintance rather than a friend, she wouldn't be quite so tempted to speak her mind.

At least that was what she told herself.

Fourteen

illow sat at the easel in her room. The photograph of Mrs. Gortner was propped against the canvas. A round table worked well
for displaying her drawing pencils and keeping her erasers handy. She'd already
sketched an outline of the dowdy woman sitting behind a library table. She
might even have the rough work finished before the Sinclair sisters returned
with their father and their aunt. But before she could start painting in any
colors or shading, she needed to meet Mrs. Gortner. Mr. Van Der Veer had
captured the mine owner's visage in his sepia photograph, but that didn't help
with skin tone or eye color.

Mr. Van Der Veer hadn't provided her with a completion date for either of
the two projects, an important detail as far as she was concerned. If not for all
the excitement, she would have gone to the studio to see him this afternoon.

A hubbub of horse hooves and wagon wheels drew her gaze to the window and the ground below. Kat stopped her carriage at the hitching rail. The
same number of people occupied the carriage as when she drove it away from
the house. The sisters had gone to meet Mr. Sinclair and Miss Shindlebower
at the depot. Where were they? Surely there hadn't been a problem with the
Midland train too.

Willow set her pencil on the table and hurried down the staircase. She
opened the front door just as Kat stepped onto the porch with Hope straddling
her hip. William slept in Nell's arms, and Vivian waddled up the steps behind
them.

"Where's your father?" Willow asked.

"That's what we'd like to know." Kat brushed past her, and Nell and Vivian followed their sister inside.

Her mind reeling with questions, Willow closed the door behind them. "The train?"

"It came in without him," Kat said, her brown eyes intense. "The agent here telephoned the depot in Colorado Springs for us." She lowered Hope to the floor.

The little girl flashed wide blue eyes. "Blocks?"

"Yes. You may bring the blocks in here." Kat wagged a finger. "Remember, you're not to touch Nanny Hattie's pretties."

Hope bobbed her acorn-brown curls and darted toward the dining room, where Miss Hattie kept the blocks and a few other toys in a bottom drawer of the buffet.

Kat returned her attention to Willow. "We found out that a Mr. Harlan Sinclair had purchased two tickets for today from Colorado Springs to Cripple Creek."

Nell looked at the snuffling bundle in her arms and walked toward the parlor. "But last night he canceled his passage." She laid William on one end of the sofa. Still asleep, the chunky tyke curled on his side and rooted into his blanket.

Willow sat on the sofa beside Nell. "Why would he do that?"

"That's what we'd like to know." Vivian lowered herself into the rocker near the hearth.

Kat seated herself in the Queen Anne chair. "That, and where they are."

"Perhaps they decided to stay in Colorado Springs another night?" Willow watched Hope stroll into the room dragging the cloth sack of blocks.

Nell stiffened. "What if one of them fell ill?"

Poor Nell always thought the worst. "Perhaps they simply needed more time on that end to… I don't know, shop or rest?" Willow said. "He didn't reschedule their passage?"

"He hadn't yet." Kat directed her daughter to play with the blocks on the opposite side of the room from where William napped.

"I'll bring you some tea." Willow stood. Although sipping tea was a dawdling activity, it somehow seemed to help pass time more quickly. "The kettle should still be hot."

Vivian nodded. "Thank you." She seemed short of breath. Not quite panting, but winded. Had she experienced another contraction?

At the window, Willow saw the courier step onto the walkway. Another portrait job so soon? "Archie's here. I'll see to him, then bring in the tea."

She met the postmaster's son at the door.

"This one's not for you, Missus Peterson." He waved a folded, single sheet of paper. "It's a telegram for Missus Raines. I heard she was here at Miss Hattie's."

Nell joined Willow at the door. "She has gone to assist with the train derailment. I'll sign for her."

"Sure thing, Missus Archer." He handed Nell the telegram.

"It's from Father." Her eyes wide, she spun toward the parlor.

Willow looked back at the young man. If he was waiting for a tip… "Her father missed his train today, and she is anxious to receive word."

"That's all right." He shrugged and gave his cap a tug. "I hope it's good news."

"Thank you." She closed the door.

"Oh no!" Nell's exclamation spilled out of the parlor. "They booked passage on the Florence and Cripple Creek!"

The train that wrecked. Willow hurried into the room. Kat and Vivian read over Nell's shoulder.

"You're sure?" Willow joined them near the silent phonograph.

Nell waved the telegram. "He sent this from Colorado Springs early this morning. Said he was too anxious to wait for the late morning train, that he'd be arriving two hours earlier, on the Florence and Cripple Creek Railroad."

Kat stood over her daughter, staring at the block house Hope was building, her brow creased. "What do we do?"

Willow's stomach knotted. How quickly life could change. If it were her father in question, the carriage out front would already be on the move. But it wasn't her father. Nor was it her place to tell her friends what they should do. They knew their father. She didn't. "I'm sure they're a little shaken, but fine." *Please let it be so, Lord.* "Ida's there," she said. "And so is Morgan."

"She's right." Nell returned to the sofa and sat beside her sleeping son. "If Father and Aunt Alma were involved, Ida and Morgan will take good care of them." She smoothed her son's mussed hair. "This is where Ida and Hattie will expect us to be. We should wait here. We could start supper for Hattie."

"She planned to fix a pork roast." Willow glanced toward the kitchen. "If we work fast, we could have it all ready for them when they arrive."

Twenty minutes later, Willow chopped a clove of garlic and stuffed the pieces into the roast. Kat cut several potatoes in half while Nell snapped peas. Vivian had auntie duty. She sat at the kitchen table, amused by her niece and nephew, who perched in wooden highchairs and nibbled on toasted bread heels.

Willow and Nell were setting the table when a commotion out front caused them both to stop midstep and look at each other.

"That has to be them." Nell set the rest of the silverware on the end of the table and rushed out of the room.

Willow followed Nell into the foyer just as Miss Hattie swung the front door open and rushed inside with Ida on her heels. The landlady wore a stern look Willow didn't understand until Ida's gaze directed her to the man and child that followed them. The young girl clinging to his side looked seven or eight years old. Definitely not Aunt Alma. Ida's father had apparently brought a child with him instead of the aunt they'd expected.

"Father!" Nell cried.

"Nellie Jean." Fatigue edged Mr. Sinclair's voice.

Nell fell against him, and Willow's heart wrenched. What she wouldn't give to have more time with her own father.

"I've missed you so." Tears clogging her throat, Nell stepped back from him. "When we learned you were on the train that wrecked—"

Kat and Vivian spilled out of the parlor, each with a child at her side.

"Father." Kat hugged her father's neck.

Vivian was next to hug and kiss her father. "I'm so glad you're here. Are you—"

She must have caught sight of the young girl. The child hid behind him, her chin tucked to her chest and her face eclipsed by his unbuttoned suit jacket.

Ida stepped forward. "This is Cherise Renard. She traveled with Father from France."

"She did?" Kat's brow furrowed.

Mr. Sinclair looked at Willow. He had a bump on his head, and dark circles rimmed his eyes. "I'm Harlan Sinclair. You must be Ida's sister-in-law. She said you were a resident here."

"Yes. Willow Peterson." She offered her hand. "It's a pleasure to meet you, sir."

Vivian looked down at the girl, then at the door. "Where is Aunt Alma?"

Mr. Sinclair glanced at Miss Hattie. "I never said I planned to bring your aunt."

"Neither did you say you were bringing a child." Miss Hattie's comment sounded like a schoolmarm's scolding.

Willow glanced up at the colorful banner still hanging from the second-story landing. So much for the warm welcome. She'd been around Miss Hattie enough to know she was in a bad humor. Hopefully it was because she'd had a long day, witnessed the wreckage, and was tired. Not because she had already made up her mind to dislike Mr. Sinclair.

Although Willow suspected it was the latter.

Their little hands clasped above them, William and Hope formed a bridge near the wall. The cousins seemed content to play, oblivious to their grandfather's presence. Nell picked a bit of lint from her calico sleeve, then glanced at the second-floor landing and the *Welcome* sign she and her sisters prepared for their grand reunion with Father. So much for expectations. Father should have arrived hours ago.

At the Midland Terminal Depot.

With Aunt Alma.

Instead he'd chosen to bring a stranger to the Sinclair family reunion. Nell contemplated the little French girl clinging to Father's side like a coat pocket. Straight, dark hair framed a round face. Her eyes remained hidden, buried in the fabric.

Cherise didn't belong here. She was a motherless child in a foreign land. A single man had no moral right to put her in this situation.

Sighing, Nell glanced at the gathering in the entryway. She should be more generous in her thoughts—to both of them. They had, after all, been involved in a train accident. Father had a knot on his forehead to show for it. Of course she was grateful they weren't harmed, but she could think of no logical reason he should make this journey with someone else's child.

He was nearly fifty years old, a man without a wife. A father who hadn't seen his daughters in nearly two-and-a-half years. Was Cherise the reason Father had seldom penned a note to them? Had she replaced Nell and her sisters in their father's affections? Her thoughts were selfish, perhaps even silly, but she felt caught in conflicting emotions.

Father sniffed the air like a hound on a hunt, then glanced at the child. "Cherise and I haven't eaten since Colorado Springs, and this house smells mighty good. Like my girls have been cooking." He smiled as if he'd neither said nor done anything out of the ordinary and everything was normal.

Nell pulled her head up straight and squared her shoulders. "Willow prepared the pork roast. Kat baked the potatoes, and I snapped the peas while Vivian entertained your grandchildren."

Father met her gaze, his eyes the same blue as hers. "Wonderful. And Ida has quite a story to tell about her activities. Cherise was missing, and I was—"

"Beside himself." Ida's matter-of-fact statement was testimony that she too had been blindsided by his actions.

His hand on Cherise's shoulder, Father bent and whispered something to her in French. Was he reassuring the child in her unfamiliar surroundings? Nell's insides knotted. She'd needed reassuring the day Father put her on the train west to marry a man she'd never met.

Hattie cleared her throat and glanced toward the dining room. "For certain, that is a delicious fragrance coming from the kitchen." Could her father's new landlady sense the storm brewing? Hattie draped her shawl on the coat rack. "Mr. Sinclair, I'll put the finishing touches on supper while you visit with your daughters. It'll only take a few moments."

"I'll help you." Nell caught Vivian's attention on her way to the door. "You'll keep watch on William?"

Vivian nodded, her brown eyes narrowed in a knowing look. Their father's surprise had to be especially hard for Vivian to swallow. She wasn't yet sixteen when he left her in Maine to take the job in France.

Nell followed Hattie and Willow into the dining room. She stopped at the end of the table where she'd abandoned the stack of silverware. Willow continued into the kitchen, but Hattie paused and enveloped Nell's hand. She looked into Hattie's blue-gray eyes. Hattie had been like a mother to her the past two years. "This shouldn't be so hard."

"But it is."

Nell nodded. "I should be happy he's here… I am, but it's nothing like what I thought it would be."

"You expected your aunt to accompany him, not a little girl commanding his attention."

"Yes." Blinking back tears, Nell leaned toward her dear friend and whispered, "He hasn't even held his grandchildren."

"He will." Hattie's voice held more promise than her weak smile did. "Most men aren't given to such demonstrations. And your father did just cross the country and survive a train wreck. Give him time."

When Hattie disappeared into the kitchen, Nell busied herself placing forks, knives, and spoons beside the plates. *Help me, Lord. I don't feel the least bit patient.*

The table ready, Nell went to the kitchen to help carry out the meal. Hattie held the meat platter. Willow balanced the dish of peas in one hand and a bread basket in the other. Nell followed with a tray of water glasses.

She'd just cleared the doorway when Father strolled into the dining room, holding her son's hand. Her breath caught. Cherise followed directly behind him, grasping his coat.

Perhaps Hattie was right. They needed to get reacquainted, and that would take time.

In the meantime, her questions probably wouldn't be addressed tonight, let alone answered.

Susanna peered out the train window as if she could see into the darkness speeding by her. She probably could if Helen weren't burning the gas lantern overhead. Her thoughts seemed to roll in rhythm with the clacking wheels as the West Coast Zephyr sped farther away from Kansas and toward her intended destiny. As they'd crossed the flat expanse of the Great Plains, all she could think about was Cripple Creek and what she'd say to win back Trenton Van Der Veer, photographer to the rich and famous. She wondered how long she'd be stuck in Colorado before he married her and whisked her away to New York.

Helen flipped a page of a fashion magazine. "I can't believe we're nearly to Colorado." She yawned, not bothering to cover her mouth the way the women in New York's high society would.

"Yes, tomorrow." Susanna glanced at their tight quarters. "And if our berth wasn't so small, I'd be dancing." By the time she woke in the morning, assuming her excitement allowed her any sleep, she'd be viewing the famous Rocky Mountains of Colorado. Soon after that, she'd step onto Denver soil, the gateway to her new life. She regarded her slouched friend. "Are you sure your brother won't mind another houseguest?"

Helen cocked her head and raised a reddish eyebrow. "He won't mind. It's not like you'll be staying very long."

Susanna shook her head. No longer than it took her to secure a suitable ride from Helen's brother's home to Cripple Creek.

"Girls, it's time you thought about retiring for the night." Mrs. Granstadt stood in the doorway. "We have a big day ahead of us tomorrow."

"Yes, Mother." Helen closed the magazine and tucked it into her bag.

Susanna pressed her lips together to avoid a confrontation. Her own mother was no doubt still pouting. She hadn't even come to the depot to see Susanna off on her adventure. Her mother led a sad life, and that wouldn't be Susanna in twenty years. No, if she had her way, she'd be in New York by springtime.

When Mrs. Granstadt left the doorway, Susanna leaned against her friend. "You're twenty, Helen. So am I. Neither of us is a girl."

She was a young woman who would soon strike out on her own.

In the meantime, a little beauty sleep would do her some good. She glanced up toward her hidden sleeping cot. Her father had given her enough money to ride in this well-appointed Pullman car with Helen and her parents. She and her friend didn't have a private bedchamber, but they would at least be able to stretch out for their rest.

Within moments a round-faced porter stood in front of them. "Young ladies, are you ready for me to make down the beds?" With a white-gloved hand, he gestured toward the folded berth.

"Yes, we'd appreciate that."

Helen stood and moved into the aisle. Susanna followed her, watching the porter release the latches. The bed swung down and latched into place with a reassuring clunk.

"Is this your first trip to gold country?" the porter asked as he reached across the bed and pulled the linens into place.

"Yes. Neither of us has been there," Susanna answered.

"But my brother lives in Denver," Helen said.

And Susanna's future husband lived in Cripple Creek. Now all she had to do was convince Trenton. This time she wouldn't mess it up.

Fifteen

*E*arly Thursday morning Trenton unlocked the studio door and headed straight to the darkroom. When he'd finally returned from Phantom Canyon last evening, he'd developed the negatives and made ten prints. The dried prints hung on a line. His job this morning was to choose the best images, a few for the railroad and a couple for display in the newspaper office. Once he'd delivered those, he'd make a few more prints to display in the studio and have available for sale.

He freed the photographs from their clips and carried the stack to his desk. Despite the commotion and his several moves for different angles, the photographs were good quality. Now it was a matter of who would want various shots. The railroad president should be happy he'd managed to capture the wreckage from all angles, including a wide shot from above the bridge. The newspaper would most likely be interested in that shot and a couple of the ones he'd taken of the passengers.

The printed images took him back to the dry wash and the acts of kindness and heroism he'd witnessed. He'd had other plans for his Wednesday afternoon and evening, but his involvement in the canyon yesterday would go a long way in helping him become established in Cripple Creek. The jobs photographing Denver's politicians had been noticed by a few of the local mine owners, and the article in the *Denver Post* had gained him recognition with the Women for the Betterment of Cripple Creek. But if the railroads liked his work—

The bell on the front door jingled, interrupting his thoughts. Probably an anxious newspaper man.

Still holding the stack of photographs, Trenton stepped into the main office. A man he didn't recognize stood at the counter.

"Mr. Van Der Veer?"

"...Yes. T-Trenton Van Der Veer." Trenton extended his hand over the counter and the man shook it.

"Tucker Raines." He had a warm smile. "So, you're the photographer."

"I am." Trenton set the stack of pictures on the counter.

"It's my pleasure to meet you." Mr. Raines glanced at the photograph atop the stack—the image of the two passenger cars lying tipped and twisted in the dry wash. "I'm the pastor at the First Congregational Church."

Raines. Reverend Raines. "Your wife runs the ice company."

"Yes." Tucker chuckled. "Her reputation seems to precede me."

Trenton felt his cheeks warm. Why had he mentioned the man's wife? "I've known J-Jesse at the l-livery since we were school boys in Maryland... He's mentioned you and your w-wife."

"Jesse is a good man and quite the smithy." The reverend set his flat-brimmed hat down beside the photographs. "This world is even smaller than that. My sister is a businesswoman too, and I hear she's working for you now."

Trenton shifted his weight. A much smaller world than he was used to. "Mrs. Peterson is your sister?"

"She is."

"S-small world indeed."

Perhaps too small. His new employee's brother was a pastor. Childhood memories assaulted him, and he couldn't help but wonder if Reverend Raines, too, would think his stuttering was of the devil. As a boy, he'd assumed all pastors were the same. An opinion not easily changed. But Mr. Raines was probably only here to make sure his sister would be safe working for Trenton. Her husband would most likely call on him next.

"I didn't come in to talk about the women in my life—my wife or my sister," Mr. Raines said with another friendly chuckle. "I wanted to welcome you to town and invite you and your wife to our services at the Congregational Church." He raised an eyebrow. "That is, if you're not already attending elsewhere."

"Thank you." Trenton swallowed hard. He'd rather talk about his marital status than his church attendance. Fatigue and tension seemed to make it all the more difficult to coax the words out. That, and the memories. "I'm n-not m-married."

And he was content to remain single. Well, he was working on being content.

The reverend looked back down at the photographs. "These are from the wreck in the canyon yesterday?"

Trenton nodded.

"Mind if I have a look?"

"No. Go right ahead."

The reverend examined each photograph, his eyes widening with shock and amazement.

All the while, Trenton kept watch on the door, wondering when Mrs. Peterson's husband would show up.

Thursday morning after breakfast, Father and all the sisters gathered in the parlor. From where Kat sat on the sofa, she had a clear view of the game table in the far corner. But this wasn't a carefree Sunday afternoon in Maine. Nor had they assembled for a family checkers tournament. This wasn't the spring of '96. This was autumn, 1898, and much had changed. Not the least of which was that Father now had a young protégée named Cherise. Thankfully, the young girl was in the kitchen with Miss Hattie, Hope, and William, so she and her sisters should be able to speak freely.

A teacup in her hand, Ida crossed her feet under the wing-back chair and smiled at Father. "It's wonderful to have you here." Her blue eyes seemed to hold the same concern drying Kat's throat and holding her questions captive. Who was Cherise? Why was she in his company? What did he plan to do with her? How long did he plan to stay in town?

"Father, why are you traveling with an eight-year-old girl?" Nell sat beside Kat on the sofa, her back straight and her gaze as direct as her question.

Dressed in a herringbone suit, Father sat across from Nell in the Queen Anne chair. He rubbed the now-purple knot on his head. "I worked with Cherise's father in Paris. Pierre Renard was one of the engineers on my staff." He reached for his mug on the side table. "Soon after I arrived in Paris, Pierre's wife succumbed to an illness that had beset her for years."

"And what of Mr. Renard?" Vivian perched in an armchair on the other side of Ida. "Shouldn't he bring up his own daughter?"

Father's shoulders sagged. "He planned to come with me to America, he and Cherise. Then nearly two months ago, a riveted seam on a boiler burst and scalded him." He glanced at the empty doorway. "Pierre died within the week. We had already booked our passage on the boat."

Vivian gasped. "I'm sorry, Father."

Tears clouded Nell's eyes. "That poor girl."

Kat shivered at a memory from her own childhood. She was close to Cherise's age when her mother died, and she couldn't fathom losing her father too. And all within two years. "It must have been so hard for her to leave the land of her birth, the only home she knew."

"She cried the first two days on the ship and wouldn't eat." Father stared at the braided rug beneath his feet. "While he was bedridden, her father begged me to take care of his daughter. He made me promise I'd bring her to America with me, that I'd make sure she had a family."

Ida set her cup on the side table. "No one expressed concern when you took Cherise out of her home country?"

Father looked at Ida first, then at each of them. Silver tinted the hair at his temples. "I gave Cherise the Sinclair surname and traveled with her as I would a daughter of my own."

But he hadn't traveled with any of his daughters. He'd sent each of them away to sink or swim on their own.

"Father, I'm sorry for her loss and yours, but some would consider the action you took outside propriety," Nell said.

Father set his cup on the table a little too abruptly. "And what of leaving an innocent little girl on the steps of an orphanage?"

"Of course, you couldn't do that." Nell's posture softened. "I have many questions. That's all."

"We all do." Kat felt the baby in her womb wiggle, and she rested against the sofa. "Why didn't you tell us about your friend, about Cherise? You rented two rooms. When we heard that, we assumed Aunt Alma was accompanying you."

He took a drink of coffee, then met Kat's gaze. "I know you girls are fond of Mrs. Adams, but I think she talks too much."

"And you hold everything to your vest." Vivian shifted on the sofa, her jaw tight. "You hardly told us anything about your new life in Paris."

Nell tucked a strand of blond hair behind her ear. "You could've sent us a telegraph from New York."

Ida tugged the hem on her shirtwaist. "We should be grateful Father's here, that he and Cherise weren't seriously injured in the train wreck. Or worse."

Father rubbed his clean-shaven chin. "It's all right, Ida. I am indeed a man of few words, and you and your sisters have a lot to be curious about."

"It's not just curiosity, Father." Vivian's sigh blew the curls on her forehead. "You left home and sent us here without you." She straightened as if doing so would bolster her courage to continue. "You're finally here. Of course, we're all grateful you and Cherise are unharmed. But nothing's the same, not with us and not with you. I'm sure you have questions about our new lives."

Kat wished she could reach Vivian's hand and squeeze it. She understood her baby sister's frustration. After a two-year absence from them, they'd all expected Father to be more attentive. Instead, he was distracted by a stranger.

"What is a…an older man to do with a child?" Nell asked.

His jaw tight, Father stood and walked to the hearth. "I expected my daughters to be charitable and do the right thing." He looked at Ida. "I'm hoping one of my daughters will take her in."

Kat heard what he wasn't saying. The frown on Ida's face said she too had heard his expectation. Did he really expect Ida to take Cherise? Was that the duty of the oldest? Or was it assumed because she was childless?

Hattie stifled a yawn as she poured orange juice into a small glass. She hadn't slept but a couple of hours last night. Cherise had fallen asleep on the sofa in the parlor, and Mr. Sinclair had carried the girl up to the room directly above Hattie's bedchamber. Cherise had cried out to him, and she'd heard him trying to reassure his charge.

Hattie's mind wouldn't let her rest, her thoughts teetering between the poor girl and the man who had, for whatever reason, assumed responsibility for her. She glanced at the child seated at her kitchen table. Long, straight hair framed the eight-year-old's round face. A face shadowed by sadness. The girl had reluctantly released Mr. Sinclair to let him go to the parlor without her this morning. Except for the short time Cherise had spent in her room before breakfast, she hadn't let the man out of her sight.

Hope's giggle drew Hattie's attention to the two wooden highchairs. William pulled his hair up like wings. Thankfully, those two were content for now, entertaining each other.

Hattie set the glass on the table in front of Cherise. The little girl hadn't eaten much at breakfast but did agree to a second glass of juice.

Cherise gazed up at her. *"Merci, Madame."*

*"Je vous en prie, ma chère...*you're welcome, dear." Camille would be amused to know Hattie was using the French she'd taught her on the trail. Hattie didn't know this child's story, except that she'd traveled across the world with a man who wasn't her father. And without her mother. "I'm Miss Hattie." She pointed to herself.

Cherise took a sip of juice, then looked up at her. "Miss Hattie?"

"Yes, dear."

"You have mother?"

"I did." Hattie glanced out the window. "But she died." Something she had in common with far too many folks.

Cherise gripped her glass with both hands as if it might escape her. "Mine too. And Papa." Her bottom lip quivered.

Her heart aching, Hattie patted the girl's head. "You poor dear." However did a man Mr. Sinclair's age expect to care for this child? He'd raised a family and had daughters, sons-in-law, and grandchildren to get to know.

More than a little curious about the conversation taking place in her parlor, Hattie glanced toward the kitchen door. Each of the Sinclair sisters had a story to tell her father, a new life to share with him. They needed their father.

And Cherise needed a mother.

The kettle rumbled. As Hattie walked to the stove, her thoughts rumbled too.

What if she'd found herself in the same situation as Mr. Sinclair? Would she be able to raise an orphaned child?

It made more sense than a single man trying to do it.

SIXTEEN

Willow breathed in the cool morning air as she walked down the hill on Fourth Street. She glanced at the two envelopes tucked against her side. Today she'd meet Mrs. Gortner, her first client. But not before she stopped at the post office and then at the Photography Studio for a word with Mr. Van Der Veer.

"Good day, Mrs. Peterson." One of Miss Hattie's neighbors waved from her wagon.

Smiling, Willow returned the wave. "And a pleasant day to you, Mrs. Eger."

Willow liked the way the small town familiarity merged with the economic benefits and social opportunities of a large city. Yes, Cripple Creek was starting to feel like home. She considered Miss Hattie a friend, and she liked living close enough to Tucker and Ida for more frequent visits.

To the east, a sunbeam defied the clouds overhead and cut across the hills above the Midland Terminal depot. Autumn would soon chase away any lingering days of summer.

At the corner, Willow stepped onto the boardwalk. Bennett Avenue teemed with life in all shapes and sizes. Two-legged and four-legged. Businessmen on foot. Cowboys on horses. Even a boy walking a bleating goat.

An older couple dressed to the nines and engaged in lively conversation strolled toward Willow. The woman looked up and stopped. She smiled. "Pardon me, Miss. Might you know where we could find the Raines icebox store?"

Willow smiled. The town may be growing by leaps and bounds, but the world was small. She directed the couple to the showroom and bid them a good day. With the post office in sight, Willow crossed the street, thankful Ida had returned to work and would be the one regaling the couple with the features and benefits of the various appliances.

After mailing a letter to her mother, Willow proceeded up Bennett Avenue to First Street. She'd just turned the corner when Tucker stepped out of the Photography Studio, his fancy felt hat in hand.

Why would her brother visit her place of employment? He would have no cause, except to seek her out. Had something happened to Ida? to Mother? Her heart began to race, and her steps quickened.

He met her gaze. Smiling, he didn't seem the least bit distressed. "Hello, sis."

"Tucker." She glanced at the studio door behind him. "Is everything all right? Why are you here?"

"Everything and everyone's fine, as far as I know." He set his hat on his head. "I was just paying your employer a friendly visit to welcome him to town and to invite him to church."

"Is that all?"

"I am a pastor, you know."

"Mr. Van Der Veer has been in town for at least two months, and you waited until after he'd hired me to pay him a *friendly visit*?"

"Yes, well, I did happen to mention my sister was a businesswoman and that I understood she now worked for him."

"I'm not helpless."

A shadow crossed Tucker's face. "Seemed like a nice enough fellow. Talented too. I saw the photographs he took at the train wreck yesterday."

"Mr. Van Der Veer is allowing me the opportunity to prove myself as a painter. I think it will be a good partnership, and the timing of his family's move to Cripple Creek couldn't have been any better."

A grin made her brother's brown eyes shine. "You don't know."

"Know what?"

"Your boss is a single man."

Her face warmed. "You didn't tell him, did you?"

He shook his head. "No, I didn't speak of your business."

"Except to let him know I have a brother who thinks he has to watch out for me."

Tucker looked back at the studio door. "Guess I best let you get to work. See you at supper tonight."

She sighed. "I'm not sure I should come. Ida's father, your father-in-law, is new to town and…it's a family dinner."

He arched his eyebrows. "I'm part of Ida's family, and you're part of mine. Big sister, that makes you family too."

"But with the train wreck and Cherise, things are complicated."

"All families are complicated."

His matter-of-fact tone made her giggle.

"Besides, Ida knew about the complications before she invited you to supper."

She had. Hopefully, by tonight Mr. Sinclair will have answered his daughters' questions about the little girl he'd brought to America and eased their concerns. "All right. I'll be there."

Her brother touched the brim of his hat and strolled away, leaving her alone to face the man she'd happily assumed was married. But this was the nineteenth century, not the dark ages. Single women had every right to intermingle in society.

Willow stepped into the main office, and bells jingled overhead. Mr. Van Der Veer stood up from a desk situated between two closed doors.

"M-Mrs. Peterson." He walked toward her, wearing a crisp white shirt and no jacket. "You received the first of your assignments?"

"Yes." She set the envelope on the counter between them and began unwinding the string on the clasp. Mr. Van Der Veer was obviously successful in business, to have his own shop and be adding employees. Miss Hattie had told her about seeing a write-up on him in the *Denver Post*. He was well-mannered and pleasant to look at. Why wouldn't he be married?

She pulled Mr. Van Der Veer's note from the envelope. Because of her brother's meddling, she was having trouble concentrating. Willow blew out a breath. If Tucker hadn't interfered in her business, she wouldn't be any wiser. No wonder she'd seen her boss alone at the ice-cream parlor.

But it was good she knew he was a single man. And as long as he believed she was married, they'd be able to avoid any awkwardness. Besides, they wouldn't be together that much. She'd do most of her work at the boardinghouse.

"Is s-something wrong?" Concern creased Mr. Van Der Veer's forehead.

She needed to focus her thoughts and regain her composure. "Your note didn't mention a date of completion for either of the projects."

Mr. Van Der Veer reached for the note just as she held it out to him. Their hands collided. "Oh!" He pulled his hand back as if he'd been stung. Yes, it was good he continue to think of her as married.

She extended the paper, and he carefully took it from her, his ears taking on the color of a persimmon.

He stared at the note. "An oversight." He looked up, but not directly at her. "The thirtieth of S-September for the p-portrait and the third of October for the photograph. Does that sound agreeable, Mrs. Peterson?"

Colorizing a photograph wouldn't take more than an hour or two. She nodded. "That gives me more than a week to complete them both. That should be sufficient." She slid the note back into the envelope. "You said Mrs. Gortner owns the Mollie Kathleen Mine?"

"She does."

"I need to see her skin tone and hair color before I begin painting." Willow didn't bother looping the string on the envelope before tucking it beneath her arm. "I'm on my way to see her now. I'll return the completed portrait to you straightaway." She turned to leave.

"Mrs. P-Peterson." He moved to her side of the counter. "I p-promised you a tour of the st-studio."

She glanced at the two closed doors behind him.

"It is office hours," he said.

She was curious about the workings of a photography studio, and he'd given her no reason to distrust him. Besides, he thought of her as a married woman. "Since we'll be working together, I suppose it would be beneficial for me to know more about your business."

He motioned for her to follow him and opened the door on the left first. "This is my studio. Wh-where I conduct the sittings. Occasionally I'll take my c-camera equipment to the client, but I p-prefer to shoot the photographs here."

Willow stepped inside the small room, feeling as if she'd stepped into another world. And she had—into Trenton Van Der Veer's world of photography. A wooden box camera atop a tripod. Lights on movable stands. A Greek column. A corner full of furniture, including a library table and a deacon's bench. Several printed canvas backgrounds hung from a rod on the back wall.

"I like varying p-possibilities for a pose."

Willow studied a peculiar side table in the corner. Made of cast iron, it had a long, skinny neck, like a music stand.

"That's a Brady st-stand. A model's armrest, adjustable for s-sitting or standing." He slid into its narrow seat. "Civil War photographer Mathew Brady used it. If I have s-someone who can't stop fidgeting, I can s-stand them beside it and steady their arm, which tends to still their whole body."

He carried the Brady stand to the deacon's bench and lowered the flat surface on top. Sitting on the bench, he began to wiggle. He then rested his forearm on the flat surface and stilled. His smile deepened the creases on either side of his blue eyes. "It doesn't always work, but it's one of the t-tools of the trade I p-picked up while w-working in New York."

"You had a studio in New York?"

"No. I was p-portable in my photographic van, but I had several clients in the c-city." He motioned toward the door. "Next is the darkroom where I develop my photographs."

Willow followed him into the adjacent room. He pulled the chain on a hanging bulb, shedding dim light on a tidy worktable and shelves lined with various bottles and flasks.

"Those are the chemicals I use for developing the photographs."

Photographs of leaves and fences hung from a line. It seemed there was much to learn about this man. His photography skill was not limited to portraits. "I didn't know you also worked in landscapes," Willow said.

"More of a hobby, I suppose." He looked away. "They should be dry by n-now."

She watched him unclip one print, then another. He carefully laid each one out on the worktable, creating a collage. Under the counter sat several shallow boxes, their contents neatly ordered.

"You've done a good job on the photographs and the studio," Willow said. "It's well organized."

"Thank you." Satisfaction flickered in his blue eyes.

Her mouth suddenly dry, Willow moistened her lips and looked down at the photographs on the table. They had more in common than she'd realized—including a penchant for capturing landscapes.

And they were both single.

Oh dear, she needed to do away with that thought.

"I couldn't do m-much organizing in the van."

"No, I suppose not." She smiled. "It couldn't have been easy, making the switch from traveling and working out of a wagon to setting up a stationary business."

"At f-first, the adjustment was difficult, but it's g-growing easier by the minute." He met her gaze. His face reddened, and he abruptly looked away and took quick steps toward the door.

Willow followed him into the main office, feeling a bit flushed herself.

Stopping at the counter, he cleared his throat. "I'm anxious to see wh-what you do with Mrs. Gortner's portrait. I think your w-work will create quite the demand for our new method of p-portrait paintings."

"I hope you're right." For her sake, and for his.

He smoothed his neatly trimmed mustache. "We could set the portrait in the wi-window for advertisement before I d-deliver it." He glanced at the window behind her. "I'm quite sure Mrs. Gortner would be am-amenable to that."

"That's a wonderful idea." Even better than hanging a flier in the post office. "In two or three days much of the town folk will have seen it."

"Have you thought about a name for your b-business?" he asked.

Her business?

He crossed his arms. "You are a b-businesswoman, correct?"

She hadn't thought of herself as such. Grieved woman. Fragile woman. Widowed woman. Those were the titles she'd assigned herself.

She nodded. "I am a businesswoman. Yes." She'd added the second affirmation for her own benefit. "I'll have a name for you when I return with Mrs. Gortner's portrait."

"Until then."

The bells jangled on her way out. Thoughts of a name for her business powered her steps down Bennett Avenue to the livery. She hadn't considered assigning a name to the service she offered Mr. Van Der Veer's photography patrons. She had expected to work in anonymity.

At the corner, while she waited for a delivery wagon to cross, she made a mental note of the various shops and stores up and down the main streets of town. King's Chinese Laundry. Glauber's Clothing. Butte Opera House. Carmen's Confectionary. Etta's Fashion Designs, where Vivian Sinclair Alwyn worked as a designer. If Willow followed Mr. Van Der Veer's example, naming her business would be as easy as calling it what it was: "Portraits." But not very interesting or modern. Something more progressive would better fit Cripple Creek's new image as Colorado's up-and-coming cultural center.

Her employer wasn't a man easily defined. What possessed him to consider her need for a name for her business? She'd expected her work to blend into the background of Mr. Van Der Veer's artistic endeavors.

A considerate man. Most businessmen, even in the West, weren't known for sharing the spotlight with anyone, much less a woman.

Considerate and surprising. And not married. Willow moistened her lips.

"Mrs. Peterson."

She startled and jerked to her right. The tall woman from the icebox showroom strolled toward her, a broad smile on her thin face.

"Good day, Mrs. Johnstone," Willow said.

"I'm pleased to see you. The mister and I are quite happy with the icebox you sold us."

Willow felt her shoulders lift a notch. "That's good news."

Mrs. Johnstone shifted an ornate, oversized handbag to her other arm. "I went to the showroom to thank you for your recommendation."

Willow smiled inside and out. Was it too much to hope folks would respond as well to her paintings? That Mr. Van Der Veer would be pleased with her work? Perhaps she should wait to name her business. At least until she'd proven herself worthy of it.

"Mrs. Raines said you found other work," Mrs. Johnstone said.

"Yes, my work at the icehouse was temporary." Thankfully. "I work for the Photography Studio now."

Mrs. Johnstone raised a thin eyebrow. "You're a lady photographer?"

Willow suppressed the laugh that accompanied the thought of her trying to manage a camera and all that entailed. "No ma'am. I'm a portrait painter. An artist."

"Is that a fact?"

"I paint portraits from Mr. Van Der Veer's photography prints."

"That's nice." Mrs. Johnstone pressed a carefully manicured fingernail to her angled chin. "I'll have to tell my mister."

"Yes, please do. The studio is on North First Street." Willow glanced down the street behind them. "By the end of next week I'll have a portrait on display in the window." Thanks to Mr. Van Der Veer's good business sense and his willingness to take a chance on her.

"This is wonderful. We could have a photograph taken and then a portrait made for our son." Mrs. Johnstone moved the handbag back to her other arm. "Our boy is impossible to shop for. He's an attorney in Denver and has everything money can buy."

The street cleared momentarily, and Willow said her good-byes and crossed to the boardwalk on the other side.

When a breeze brushed her neck, she realized she was holding her head high. Perhaps with her new job here, she was taking a step toward the other side of grief.

SEVENTEEN

*T*he livery and blacksmith shop sat on a corner, back from the main road. Willow stepped into the barn through the gaping doorway and blinked to adjust her vision.

The scent of horses carried memories of the Raines family home in Stockton. Her father's barn wasn't this big, but it always housed three or four Belgians. She wasn't even tall enough to reach the drawer in the kitchen cupboard when her father first put her up on Blue, one of his delivery horses. Remembering, she could feel the pounding in her chest and hear her own squeals as her daddy rested his hands on hers at the horse's mane and clucked his tongue. As the horse walked the circle in the center of the barn, she'd felt like a princess riding atop her hero's steed.

"Ma'am?"

A voice as deep as a canyon drew her attention to the back corner. A mountain of a man in soiled coveralls stood in front of a forge. A piece of steel glowed yellow at the end of his tongs. Laying the scrap on the anvil, he started shaping it with a hammer.

"Don't mean to be rude," he shouted between ringing beats, "but I gotta shape this S hook before it goes cold. Should only take a minute."

"I understand." She wanted to say she wasn't in a hurry, but she didn't want to lie. She glanced at the open door at the back of the barn. He must keep his rental rigs outside.

He put the project back into the flames and gave the bellows a few pumps. "What can I do for you, Miss?"

"I need to go to the Mollie Kathleen Mine, and I'd like to rent a buggy." If she could get on her way, the visit with Mrs. Gortner needn't take long, allowing her to return to the boardinghouse in time to spend a few hours working on the portrait before the evening's festivities at the parsonage.

Straightening, he studied her from shoe to bonnet. "You have business out at the mine?"

"I have business with Mrs. Gortner."

"Well, you won't find her at the mine."

"Mr. Van Der Veer at the Photography Studio told me Mrs. Gortner owns the Mollie Kathleen Mine."

A smile broadened the blacksmith's already full face. "You know Trenton Van Der Veer?"

"I work for him."

"Well, I'll be." He jabbed the tongs into the coals and gave the bellows a few more pumps. "You're the lady Trenton hired to paint the portraits."

"I am. Mrs. Peterson."

"I'm Jesse. It's a pleasure to meet you." He pulled off his right glove, looked at his soot-covered hand, and smiled. "A handshake seems out of the question. I hear your artwork is quite impressive." He replaced the glove and returned his attention to the furnace.

"You did?" Had the compliment come from her boss? Tucker and Miss Hattie had seen her portrait of Sam and were no doubt patrons here. Yes, it was probably one of them.

He lifted the tongs again, tapping them on the edge of the forge. "Trenton and I are friends. I knew him before he was strong enough to hold one of them box cameras."

"He said he was new to town."

"Oh, he is. And our boyhood days are long past." Jesse resumed the punishment of the small piece of steel, speaking between beats. "When he wrote about his recent troubles, I talked him into making the move here."

Her employer had troubles? *Recent troubles.* It made sense that she was curious. After all, she did work with the photographer. But the less they knew about each other's personal lives, the better.

"Trenton's right about Mrs. Gortner owning that mine, but he hasn't lived here long enough to know much about folks yet." Jesse chuckled. "She owns the mine all right, but she doesn't spend much time out there."

"Do you know where I might find her?"

"Sure." He twisted the end of his work around the spindle, making one end of the hook. "Missus Gortner don't live too far from here. It's a lot closer than up the mountain to the mine. Just up the hill on Carr Avenue."

That would save her time. And money.

"You can walk right up Fourth Street and turn left. Their house has a miniature headframe and a bitty ore car out front."

"Thank you."

Willow moved the envelope to her other arm and stepped back out into the bright midday sun. At Fourth Street, she turned and walked up the hill past Golden Avenue. Why bother to own a mine if you weren't going to have a say in how it was run? Perhaps, Mrs. Gortner was the owner in name only, her husband's way of appeasing her while he called all the shots.

Mrs. Gortner lived in the same block as Miss Hattie's Boardinghouse, but one street up. Just as the livery owner had said, a sculpted-metal miniature of a mine headframe stood on one side of a graveled walk, an ore cart on the other side. The mine owner's New England–style house was ocean blue with a snow-white trim. Scalloped slats adorned the eaves, and filigree outlined the second story windows.

Willow stepped onto the porch between two pots of geraniums and pressed the doorbell. The bell responded with a sort of growling ring, and a dog's bark exploded on the other side of the door. Not the yip or shriek of a typical house dog.

The door swept open. A woman with her hair brushed back into a neatly coiffed chignon stood in front of her, smiling. A large mound of gray fur sat poised and quiet beside her, a black nose protruding in Willow's direction.

Willow moistened her lips. "I apologize for coming by unexpectedly, but might Mrs. Gortner be in and willing to see me?"

The woman's crooked smile deepened the creases at her eyes. "I'm Mrs. Gortner." She extended her hand. A sprinkling of freckles dotted the bridge of her nose. "Mollie Kathleen." Her handshake was as warm as her smile.

"I'm pleased to meet you, ma'am. I'm Mrs. Peterson. Willow Peterson."

"Lovely name—Willow."

"Thank you." Willow pulled the photograph from the envelope. "Mr. Van Der Veer hired me to paint your portrait."

Mrs. Gortner's moss-green eyes sparkled. "He hired a woman. Good for him." Stepping backward, she motioned Willow inside. "Come in. Come in."

Willow regarded the motionless dog. Only his tail moved, sweeping the polished pine floor behind him.

"Duffy is a purebred Irish wolfhound." Mrs. Gortner patted the dog's huge gray head. "As long as I use my happy voice, Ol' Duff is harmless. But he can be fierce if he thinks I'm being threatened."

Willow had grown up with a dog as part of her family, but that seemed a lifetime ago. Refusing to take her gaze from the dog, she stepped inside and around him into a well-appointed foyer. A gilt-framed painting of a hunting scene hung over a polished tiger-wood table.

Mrs. Gortner signaled the dog to follow her and brushed the corner of the table as if to remove a speck of dust. "I knew I liked the photographer the moment I met him."

So did Willow. Even if she and Mr. Van Der Veer had trouble understanding each other. Hopefully that was in the past.

"I'm sorry to trouble you," Willow said, "but I only needed to see your hair color and skin tone before I began painting." Which she'd done standing outside the door.

"No apologies necessary. Your visit is the mark of a professional. I say we go to my office, shall we?" Mrs. Gortner spun toward a closed door.

The mine owner's office could have held a bucket of dust, but no one would know for all the clutter. The clawed feet on the tiger-wood desk and tables told Willow the furniture was exquisite, but papers, catalogs, files, and boxes topped every surface.

Mrs. Gortner removed an apple box full of papers from one of two spindle-back chairs in front of the desk. "Have a seat, Willow."

Willow seated herself. The framed mine claim featured in Mrs. Gortner's photograph hung behind the desk. A small balance scale sat on one corner, a fist-sized chunk of quartz on the other.

Duffy sprawled out on a rag rug near the door while Mrs. Gortner sat back in her tufted green-leather chair behind the desk. "A woman portrait painter here in Cripple Creek—I love it. I can hardly wait to commend Mr. Van Der Veer on his choice of artist. We women have to stick together, don't we?"

"Yes ma'am."

"I don't cotton to being called *ma'am*. Might you call me Mollie?"

"Yes. Mollie. Thank you."

Leaning forward, Mollie met Willow's gaze. "So, have you decided on the color of my hair and skin yet?"

Willow swallowed hard. She wasn't accustomed to sharing the specifics of her process, but neither had she encountered anyone outside family as enthusiastic about her art. "I have."

The older woman cocked her head and raised her left eyebrow. "Let's hear it."

"I'm thinking of an almond." Willow raised her chin a notch. "Your hair the reddish brown of the outside, and your skin the creamy white of the inside."

"An almond." Mollie chuckled. "I like it." She tapped her rounded chin. "And I like you."

Willow sighed. That was good news. "I'm thankful." She pulled the photograph from the envelope and laid it in front of her host. "I'm planning to complete your portrait no later than next Thursday. Do you want me to paint the image as it is in the print?"

"Yes, but without any blemishes."

Willow hadn't noticed any blemishes. She glanced at the photograph.

"No freckles." Mollie covered her nose.

"I can do that." Willow took the photograph and slid it into the envelope. "Mr. Van Der Veer plans to speak with you about displaying your portrait in the studio window for a couple of days."

"I think it's a wonderful idea. A smart business decision."

Now all Willow needed to do was come up with a business name.

"Did your boss tell you I'm the one who told him to hire a portrait painter?" Mollie asked.

Willow shook her head and closed the clasp on the envelope. "We haven't actually spoken much."

"Well, I did." Mollie stacked her hands on the desktop. "I told him painted portraits were all the talk now and he needed to hire someone who could paint from his photographs. I told him that if he did, his quiet little business would boom."

A very direct woman, indeed. So why didn't she have an office at her mine? Willow glanced at the various mining artifacts decorating the office. "Would you think me discourteous if I asked a personal question?"

"If I own the Mollie Kathleen Mine, why don't I have my office out there?"

"Yes. I couldn't help but wonder."

"It's a long story. Do you have the time?"

Willow hadn't expected to enjoy this woman's company this much. "Yes, I'd like to hear your story."

Mollie sat back in her chair and smiled. "My son Perry left our home in Colorado Springs to come to Cripple Creek as a surveyor to map the mining claims in the spring of '91. All I heard from him was talk of all the gold here. So one day I loaded our wagon with supplies and joined the other wagons headed here for a visit. I set up housekeeping in the log and canvas tent Perry had recently completed." She tapped a bell on her desk. Three distinct dings. "Where was I?"

"The canvas tent."

"Ah, yes. That September Perry was out surveying when he saw a huge herd of elk. He came home and told me about it. I decided to go out and see for myself."

"Miss Mollie." The voice drew their attention to the doorway, where a young Chinese woman wore a black serving dress and held a silver tray.

"Yes, do come in, Ling." Mollie looked at Willow. "I hope you have time to enjoy a cup of tea."

"Thank you."

Ling set the tray on a table and served each of them a cup of tea and a small plate with one scone on it. The slight domestic hadn't yet cleared the doorway when Mollie resumed her story.

"I never made it up high enough to see the elk. I stopped to rest. When I looked downward, I noticed an interesting rock formation. It winked at me."

"Gold?"

Mollie nodded, her smile reaching her eyes. "Pure gold laced in quartz."

Willow lifted her cup to her mouth. "What did you do?"

"I'd seen several prospectors in the area. Forcing myself to remain calm, I hid the ore sample in my clothing."

Willow sipped the fruity tea. She was excited to start painting, but this was fun too.

Mollie peered at her over the rim of her cup. "I became the first woman here to discover gold and strike a claim in her own name."

"The first—that's amazing!"

"Although I own the mine, Perry is the one with the office there. For a rather silly reason, really."

"Silly?"

"Well, I think it is. As soon as I set foot on the mine site, the miners scrambled up out of the tunnels. Seems they're a superstitious lot and refuse to be caught in a one-thousand-foot vertical shaft with a woman on the grounds."

"That does seem silly."

"A wise woman chooses her battles carefully." Mollie lifted the scone from her plate. "So I have my office at home, where I can have tea and scones anytime I wish." She giggled and bit into the pastry.

Willow cut a corner piece with her fork and eased it into her mouth, as if her mother were there to correct any ill manners. A sweet bite of peach purée teased Willow's tongue.

"We all have one, you know. An inspiring story, not a gold mine." Mollie dabbed her mouth with a gold-colored napkin. "When we meet again, you can tell me your story."

Willow blinked. "Perhaps." Here in town, only family, which included the Sinclair sisters and Miss Hattie, knew her story.

"How long have you been married?" Mollie asked.

Willow gulped. This woman had treated her like a longtime friend. It was only fair she share this much. "Sam died."

Mollie's mouth formed an *O,* but no sound came out.

"Four years ago." And two months.

"Oh my, and you're so young." Mollie pressed her lips together. "Yes, I definitely want to hear your story. From widow to portrait painter. Sounds mighty inspiring to me."

"Thank you." What else could Willow say? She'd already said too much.

And now she wondered if it would be crass to ask her new friend not to mention her being a widow to Mr. Van Der Veer.

EIGHTEEN

da pulled back the lace curtain and looked out the parlor window. Everyone had arrived at the parsonage but Willow. Where was her sister-in-law? She glanced at her husband, who sat at the game table engaged in a heated checkers game with Nell. "Tucker."

He looked her way, his hand still in midair. "Did Nell pay you to distract me?"

"I'm concerned about your sister. Willow was definitely planning to come?"

"She said she would." He moved a king piece.

"Well, it's after six o'clock and the sun will set soon. Everyone else is here. You're not worried about her?"

"I wasn't. Should I—"

A knock at the door silenced him. Ida rushed to the front door. She shouldn't worry about Willow, but she did.

Willow stood on the porch. "Sorry I'm late." Her breathing sounded ragged. "I have had the best day."

"That's good news." She gave Willow a quick hug.

"I saw Mrs. Johnstone in town, and she told me how much she and her husband are enjoying the icebox. She thanked me for the recommendation. In addition, I had an interesting conversation with my boss. Oh, yes, and I saw my brother. I met Jesse at the livery, and then I had a lovely time with the woman who owns the Mollie Kathleen Mine."

"Whew, you've had a very full day." Ida's heart warmed. In the nearly two years she'd known Willow, she'd never seen her sister-in-law this happy. And after watching Willow lay her father to rest last month, she hadn't expected she ever would.

"There's more. I just spent two hours reorganizing my supplies and paints. I got so engrossed that I lost track of the time. I practically ran here."

"An interesting conversation with your boss, huh?" Ida closed the door behind them. "The one who's single?"

Willow huffed. "It wasn't *that* interesting." She glanced at the parlor door. "Is my brother in there? I'd like to pop him on the head."

"You really didn't expect he'd be able to keep a tidbit like that from me, did you?"

"I suppose not."

"Come help me put supper on the table. We've lots to talk about."

Willow ducked into the parlor and greeted everyone, then followed Ida into the kitchen. She glanced at the doorway behind them to see if anyone had followed, but they were alone. "Did your father give you the answers you wanted?"

Ida sighed, remembering the sisters' meeting with him that morning. "He worked with Cherise's father." She told Willow all she knew about the deaths of the girl's parents and the arrangement for her care.

"Poor girl." Willow took a bowl of carrot and raisin salad and the bread basket from Ida. "How kind of your father to follow through and bring her with him."

"I'm not sure how kind it was." Ida lifted the kettle of chicken and dumplings from the stove and followed Willow into the dining room. "She's in a foreign land with strangers. And my father is too old and too single to raise someone else's daughter."

Willow set the bowl and the basket at one end of the table. "Did he say what his plans are?"

"Only that he expects me to take Cherise and raise her as my own."

Willow's eyebrows arched. "Really? He said as much?"

Ida placed the kettle in the center of the table and followed Willow back into the kitchen. "Not in so many words, but he looked at me when he said, 'I'm hoping one of my daughters will take her in.'"

"Are you going to?"

No. That was Ida's quick and private answer. "Right now the child won't even leave his side long enough to talk to anyone else."

"Do you speak French?"

Ida shook her head and picked up the saltcellar and the pepper mill from the cupboard. "No. But Miss Hattie does."

"Cherise speaks some English."

"Yes."

"They've been here only one day." Willow lifted a tray full of empty glasses off the round table. "I'm sure this will all settle, given time."

Ida nodded and grabbed the stack of cloth napkins on her way to the dining room. "Now, I want to hear about your interesting conversation with your employer."

Willow set the tray on the buffet. "He asked me if I'd thought of a name for my business."

"He did?"

"I know. I was surprised too. I hadn't even regarded myself as the owner of my own business. And to have a man do so is, well, surprising." Willow tucked a strand of hair behind her ear. "I hadn't given any thought to a business name before his question, and I still haven't come up with any names I care anything about."

"Such as?"

"Mrs. Peterson's Painted Portraits." Willow giggled. "Too many *p*'s."

"I see your point." Ida grinned.

"I didn't care for Willow's Simulacrums either. It sounds like a medical procedure."

Vivian waddled into the dining room. "What are we doing?"

Ida swallowed hard at the sight. How was it possible that her baby sister could be so close to giving birth? Where had the time gone? "We need to think of a name for Willow's new portrait business."

"That should be easy enough." Vivian tapped her lips, something she was prone to do when thinking. "You want something fashionable." She eased into a chair and resumed the tapping. "How about Portraits by Willow?"

Portraits by Willow.

Vivian's suggestion had pluck and personality. But what of Mr. Van Der Veer? He'd named his business Photography Studio, which wasn't very original. He might think Portraits by Willow too conceited.

Willow lifted the tray of glasses from the buffet and began setting one beside each plate. Why was she concerned with his opinion, anyway? It was her business they were talking about, which made the name her choice to make. Mollie Kathleen used her given name in titling the Mollie Kathleen Mine.

Vivian sat at the other end of the table and began folding napkins into fans, her pregnant middle bumped up against the table's edge. Ida was hosting the supper, but why wasn't Vivian with her father? Nell had done the same thing at yesterday's supper, disappearing into the kitchen like a Martha set on her task. Willow sighed. If it were her father here, nothing would pull her away from him, even if he had brought a stranger to the family reunion.

She glanced at Ida, who set the saltcellar and pepper mill on the table. "The table will be a bit crowded tonight."

"It does look like we'll be rubbing elbows a bit, but—"

"You don't have to include me in all of your family gatherings. I'm all right. I have a wonderful place to live and an intriguing job." It was best she didn't mention she found her boss intriguing too. "I haven't felt this good in several years." Four years and two months, to be exact. "You have your father here.

Your sisters. Cherise." And she was more than a little anxious to return to her room and paint.

Ida pursed her lips as in a pout. "I like having you here." She rested her hand on Willow's forearm and met her gaze, her eyes a lighter shade of blue than Mr. Van Der Veer's. "And like it or not, you're family too."

"I like it. I couldn't have picked a better sister-in-law."

"Or substitute sisters." Vivian smiled. "And you fit right in."

"Who fits right in?" Mr. Sinclair led the others into the dining room with Cherise at his side.

"Willow." Ida's reply sounded abrupt, almost sharp.

"That's the beauty of a big family," Mr. Sinclair said. "There's always room for one more."

Ida's face paled. Was she thinking about the baby she couldn't carry or the child her father hoped she'd take in?

"Mrs. Peterson," Mr. Sinclair said, greeting her.

"Please call me Willow."

"Willow, then. Ida mentioned you're working with a photographer here in town."

"Yes, but I'm just getting started. Mr. Van Der Veer is new here. From New York."

"New York?" Tucker held a chair for Ida and then one for Willow before taking his place at the head of the table. "He told me he was from Maryland."

"That may be. In the past seven years, you've lived in Stockton, San Francisco, and Cripple Creek. And probably places in between. All the same, at some point, Mr. Van Der Veer worked in New York." Why were they talking about the photographer? And why was she defending him?

Tucker stared at her, an eyebrow raised, no doubt wondering the same thing.

Ignoring the question on her brother's face, Willow pulled her napkin fan from her plate and spread it on her lap. If he mentioned Mr. Van Der Veer was single, she'd…she didn't know what she'd do, but he wouldn't think it pleasant.

Mr. Sinclair cleared his throat as if Willow and Tucker needed a referee. "Now that I have our family back together, I'd be interested in having a portrait done. You'd recommend this Mr. Van Der Veer?"

Willow straightened against the back of her chair in an attempt to assure everyone concerned that her interest in her boss was strictly business. "Yes. He does fine work."

"Very well. Once we're more settled"—Mr. Sinclair looked at Cherise, concern etching his brow—"I'll speak to him about scheduling a sitting for a family portrait."

Willow nodded. A Sinclair family sitting would provide her the perfect excuse to watch the photographer at work. She was, after all, practically family. She counted all those at the table, besides herself. A dozen. With that many subjects, Mr. Van Der Veer was bound to need an assistant.

NINETEEN

You don't think Mr. Sinclair is a good man?"

"I didn't say that."

Hattie dropped the dishrag into the sudsy water and angled her head toward Boney. The miner stood at her side with a dishtowel draped over his shoulder. Tonight he wore clean black trousers and a forest-green shirt. She couldn't remember ever seeing him wear anything besides coveralls since he'd moved here right after George's death.

Boney added a freshly dried soup bowl to the cupboard and looked at her, his brow furrowed. "But you did break your rule because of him."

Hattie straightened. "My rule?"

"If you can't say something kind about a person, say nothing at all." Boney's lopsided grin added a Sunday shine to his silver-blue eyes.

Cringing, Hattie fished the cloth from the sink. "That was my mother's rule." Her mother's rule or not, it was a creed she usually abided by. She had yet to say much, if anything, kind about the Sinclair sisters' father. She met her friend's expectant gaze. "Mr. Sinclair wears his herringbone suit well." She couldn't suppress her smile.

Boney's laughter exploded like a rifle shot.

"All right." She took to scrubbing the second bowl. "I suppose I haven't been too charitable where he's concerned."

"You suppose?" He chuckled. "You've been gnawin' on the man like a mama bear. Before you ever met him."

"And you blame me?" She dropped the bowl into the rinse tub, causing a splash. "Those poor girls came out here from Maine without their daddy so he could take a job in Paris. He sent Kat west to marry a ruffian."

"I doubt—"

"And poor Vivian." She plopped two spoons into the tub. "His baby girl. It's a miracle she survived her entanglement with those outlaws last year. And Mister Sinclair hasn't the slightest notion what his daughters have been through."

"Nor they, him." Boney lifted a dripping wet bowl from the sink and toweled it off.

She pulled the plug in the bottom of the sink. Dirty water swirled and gurgled down the drain. Her friend couldn't be any more matter-of-fact about this. His was the voice of reason, a trait she normally appreciated. Not tonight. She wanted to be mad at her new tenant. Blame him for the pain she'd watched his daughters suffer in their first months in Cripple Creek. Every one of them had needed her father's careful watch and guidance.

Boney hung the damp dishtowel on a peg and pulled two cups from the countertop. He was right, though. She hadn't given much thought to what Harlan Sinclair had suffered the past two years.

"Kat told me her father lost his job in Portland and, consequently, their house." Boney motioned to the table. "I don't imagine his decision was an easy one."

Was it a man's unspoken responsibility to defend another man?

While she pulled the sugar bowl off the buffet, Boney carried the fresh coffee to the table. "What would you have done differently in Mr. Sinclair's stead? Kat said her father had a job opportunity in Paris that would pay for his housing and allow him to make enough money to bring back to America with him."

"Along with a little girl. Another one he couldn't take care of."

Boney pulled out her chair and met her gaze. "That's what this is about?"

Hattie's bottom lip quivered. "If our daughter had lived, George never would've abandoned her." Tears pricked her eyes and spilled down her face. Before she could raise a hand to wipe them, Boney pulled her into a comforting embrace.

"No, he wouldn't have."

George wouldn't have abandoned her either. Not if he'd had a choice. Her shoulders shuddered under the weight of her tears.

"Shhh. Shhh." Boney held her and smoothed her hair just as he had that day down at the river, thirty years ago. "It's going to be all right, Adeline."

She believed him. She'd lived a full and blessed life despite her losses. So would the Sinclair sisters. So would little Cherise.

Why was she so set on blaming Mr. Sinclair? And for what? The sisters were thriving despite their ups and downs. The Lord had His hand on them. She needed to listen to Mr. Sinclair's side of the story. She shouldn't judge him. It wasn't her place. And God didn't need her help.

❧

The driver helped Willow from the carriage while Mr. Sinclair lifted Cherise to the ground. The only light glowed from the back of the boardinghouse. Apparently, Miss Hattie was still up and in the kitchen, which was where the three of them were headed. Cherise had been having trouble sleeping since she'd arrived in America, and Willow had offered to warm a cup of milk for the child. Mr. Sinclair had started yawning before Ida could serve the peach cobbler and coffee. If not for Cherise's restlessness on the carriage ride, he no doubt would have fallen asleep.

Mr. Sinclair opened the front door, and Willow entered. She set her reticule on the entry table and walked to the kitchen.

Just inside the doorway, she stopped so abruptly that Cherise bumped into her, nearly knocking her off balance. Without taking her gaze from Miss Hattie, Willow righted herself. She wasn't surprised to see her landlady in the company of Mr. Boney, but she hadn't expected to see the widow in the miner's arms.

Mr. Boney eased away from Miss Hattie and regarded them with a warm smile. "Miss Willow." He offered her a slight nod, then looked up at Mr. Sinclair, who stood about three inches taller than he did. "You must be Harlan Sinclair."

Mr. Sinclair didn't extend his hand, instead giving a tight-lipped nod.

Her face the color of a ripe strawberry, Miss Hattie smoothed her apron. "Yes, I'd like to introduce Mr. Harlan Sinclair." She turned to the taller man. "This is my friend, Boney Hughes."

Mr. Sinclair drew in a deep breath.

Willow felt her own cheeks warm in the awkward moment. "I was going to heat a cup of milk for Cherise."

"Oh, let me." Miss Hattie pulled a cast-iron pot from the cupboard. "It won't take me but a moment."

"Mrs. Adams." Mr. Sinclair sounded like a cross schoolteacher.

Miss Hattie stilled and gazed at him, her face still red. "Yes, Mr. Sinclair."

He cleared his throat. "If this is the sort of behavior we can expect from you, consider this our last night here."

The wrinkles on Miss Hattie's forehead deepened. "This sort of behavior?"

"Yes." Mr. Sinclair lifted his chin and lowered his voice. "Entertaining men."

Willow gasped.

The pan escaped Miss Hattie's hand and thudded onto the linoleum. Her landlady burst into a robust laughter that moistened her eyes. Boney joined in, and Willow caught herself midchuckle.

Mr. Sinclair, looking not the least bit amused, spun around and stomped out of the kitchen with Cherise in tow.

Miss Hattie stilled, her eyes wide and her jaw slack. Mr. Sinclair had been the only one to take himself seriously…until now.

Friday morning Hattie stirred the pan of scrambled eggs and looked up at the cupboard that housed the can of pepper. A teaspoon of the spice would be plenty to impact Mr. Sinclair and would be visually undetectable if she also added cheese to his *special* eggs. What did it matter if she gave in to her ornery streak? The man was moving out first thing after breakfast anyway.

The banner no longer hung below the second-story landing this morning. Mr. Sinclair had apparently taken it down in his snit. At least he knew he'd worn out his welcome.

Hattie huffed and gave the eggs a spirited stirring. The memory of last night's events still swirled about her. All three of her boarders had gone to supper at the parsonage. Boney had stopped by for soup, coffee, and conversation. And by the time she and Boney had finished chatting about her curt male boarder, she'd felt convicted of her unfair impression of the man. Even felt guilty about speaking of him when she hadn't found anything good to say. She'd actually begun to feel sorry for him. But within moments, he'd stood in her kitchen with nary a greeting and jumped to insulting conclusions.

It was such a ridiculous notion that all she could do was laugh. She hadn't been able to stop giggling until she saw Mr. Sinclair stomp from the room with poor little Cherise at his heels. Shaking her head, Hattie flipped the hashed potatoes. She'd thought herself a more reasonable choice to parent Cherise than a single man, but even if she had seriously considered broaching the possibility, there was little chance now Mr. Sinclair would consider such a proposal. Not if he thought her improper.

"Mrs. Adams."

Speak of the— Hattie scolded herself for thinking such a dreadful thought, and turned to face Mr. Sinclair. "I'll bring breakfast in shortly. It's nearly ready."

He stared at his polished shoes. Was he formulating a lecture on the proper behavior of a lady? Well, she would save herself the singe from his hot air.

She focused on the bump on his head, now a yellowish-green. "Sir, since you're uncomfortable boarding here, I'll refund your first week's rent." Tears stung her eyes, and she blinked before removing the skillet of eggs from the stove. She'd failed her precious Sinclair sisters. She'd managed to house each of them with great pleasure, but she'd alienated their father. He hadn't been here even forty-eight hours of his four weeks, and he was already moving out.

"I'm not." His baritone voice broke into her thoughts.

"You're not what?" She scooped the eggs into a serving bowl.

"Uncomfortable."

Well, she certainly was. "Last night you stood in this very kitchen—"

"And I made an absolute fool of myself."

Of course he did, but she'd never expected him to know it, let alone admit it. She stopped and looked at him.

"I jumped to conclusions that were unfair."

Not to mention unflattering.

He looked straight at her as if he'd read her thoughts, his eyes an indigo blue. "I walked in and saw..."

"A soft answer turneth away wrath." Hattie set the skillet and spatula in the sink. He'd seen her and a man he'd never met in an embrace. She may have done a little jumping herself.

"I shouldn't have assumed the worst."

"A rather abrupt change of heart, wouldn't you say?" She resisted the impulse to plant her hands on her hips. "How do you know now that your conclusions were unfair?"

"When Mrs. Peterson brought the milk upstairs for Cherise, she mentioned you and Mr. Hughes have been close friends for many years."

"And if Willow hadn't told you that?"

"I would have come to my senses." He smiled, his lips lifting under a neatly trimmed auburn mustache. "Eventually." His smile deepened. "I hope you'll accept my apology for my unwarranted behavior."

"I suppose it was a logical assumption." She flipped the potatoes again and moved the skillet to the bigger burner plate on the stove. "You don't know me." And he did have her influence on Cherise to think about.

"I should've trusted my daughters' reports of you. Each of them regards you highly." He glanced at the empty doorway. "Fact is, they adore you."

"And I, them."

He swallowed hard. "I haven't much liked you because of it."

She felt her mouth drop open. "Because your daughters adore me?"

"Yes ma'am." He brushed his hand through his silver-tinted auburn hair. "They seem to respond to you the way they would their mother."

If she were here. Why hadn't she realized what was going on? It made perfect sense. He was jealous of her relationship with his daughters, concerned she was trying to replace their mother. That was why he'd been aloof.

"I'm sorry," she said.

He tugged his suit coat straight and met her gaze. "I'm not proud of the fact, but I've been a little jealous. I didn't receive a single letter from any of them that didn't mention you. Most of their writings sung your praises. I felt terrible about having to leave them and missed them so much. You were here to care for them, and I wasn't."

They seemed to have more in common than she could have guessed. "Don't feel bad. I didn't like you either."

The slightest grin edged up one side of his mouth. "But you do now?"

"I believe so." She pressed a finger to her chin. "I was angry with you for shipping your daughters off to the West. Before you returned to the house last night, Boney helped me see that I was being unfair in my judgment of you. I'm sure it was a decision you gave much thought."

He nodded. "And then I had to come along and stick my foot in my mouth." His smile reached his eyes. "Please call me Harlan."

She nodded. "Hattie." The acrid scent of charring tickled her nose, and she rushed to the stove. "The potatoes!"

Harlan removed the skillet and set it on the trivet on the countertop. Hattie flipped the hashed potatoes. They weren't charred yet, but quite dark and crispy.

"Just the way I like them," Harlan said.

"You like your potatoes burned?"

He grinned. "This morning, they're exactly what I deserve."

Her ears warmed. Good thing she hadn't added the extra pepper to the eggs. Blackened potatoes would be punishment enough. She hadn't burned anything since she and George first wed. Clearly, Mr. Sinclair was a distraction.

"Miss Hattie." Willow stood in the doorway. "Cherise was alone at the table." She pointed toward the dining room. "Is everything all right?"

"If you like burned potatoes, it is." Hattie met Mr. Sinclair's gaze, and they both laughed. The wide-eyed wonder on Willow's face tickled her funny bone even further, and she fanned herself.

"We were about to serve breakfast when the potatoes grew impatient." A wide grin on his face, Harlan picked up the skillet and held it steady while she slid the brittle potato remains into a serving dish.

"Thank you."

"It's the least I could do." He carried the dish of potatoes out of the kitchen.

Hattie pulled the plate of sausage from the warmer and handed it to Willow. Without answering the question written all over the young woman's face, Hattie picked up the bowl of eggs and followed Mr. Sinclair to the dining room.

She'd been wrong about him. The way his emotions had been sitting on his shoulders he could have been Atlas holding the earth. And now that he'd found his sense of humor, he was rather charming.

TWENTY

*W*ednesday morning, a week after Mr. Sinclair's arrival, Willow
walked down Golden Avenue toward First Street with a bounce
in her step and a cloth sack swinging from her elbow. She held the double-
wrapped canvas in front of her. Today she'd deliver Mollie Kathleen Gortner's
portrait, two days ahead of Mr. Van Der Veer's deadline. She'd actually made
her last stroke with the brush on Monday afternoon but let it sit all day yesterday to make sure it was dry enough to wrap. This was her first commissioned
painting, and she couldn't wait to experience her boss's reaction. Hopefully,
he'd be pleased with her work.

A chilling wind caught Willow's wool shawl. Golden and crimson leaves
fluttered on the breeze like autumn streamers in a ticker-tape parade. Bennett
Avenue also proclaimed the change of season. Barrels of bright red apples and
mounds of pumpkins framed the grocer's door. As she passed, she caught a
whiff of apple cider and paused for a moment to enjoy the sweet scent. Rich
colors and sweet aromas. The best time of year to step into her new life as a
portrait artist.

Rounding the corner at First Street, Willow saw a crumpled man propped
against the front of the smoke shop. She slowed her steps and studied him. A
slouch hat teetered on his unkempt head. His ample chin rested on his chest,
and his legs stretched across the boardwalk like logs dressed in filthy trousers.
He didn't move, and his eyes were closed in a whiskered face. Had he fallen,
lost consciousness? Was he dead?

He was someone's father. She had to at least check on his condition, even if it meant putting herself in harm's way.

Grasping the canvas with both hands, Willow stared at the man's chest, looking and praying for signs of life. His chest rose. A groan escaped his fleshy lips, and his eyes popped open. He peered at her and brushed the brim of his hat.

"Hello, ma'am." The pungent scent of alcohol assaulted her senses.

"Good morning, sir."

He straightened his back against the wall and bent his knees. Squinting at her, he pulled the hat from his head. "My apologies, ma'am. I'm afraid I may have stayed up too early and plumb forgot my manners." His words were slow and sloppy.

"Sir, are you all right?"

Chuckling, he scratched his chin through the scraggly beard that covered it. "Not too many folks 'round here call me sir." He yanked the flannel shirt over his rounded belly, then inched his back up the wall and stood on wobbly legs. "Name's Baxter."

"Mrs. Peterson."

Tilting to one side, Mr. Baxter braced himself against a post. "Some say I have me a drinking problem."

She glanced at her bag, then at him. "Have you eaten anything today?"

He cradled his chin between his thumb and fingers. "What day is this?"

"Wednesday."

"Had me some jerky for breakfast Tuesday."

"That won't do." Willow propped the portrait against her leg and pulled the bag from her arm. When Miss Hattie heard about all she planned to do in town today, her landlady suggested she pack a lunch. Willow held the sack out to Mr. Baxter.

"What's that, ma'am?"

"A sandwich, an apple, and pecan sandies."

His eyes widened and he licked his lips, then he shook his head. "I couldn't take your lunch."

If he didn't eat something, the alcohol would eat his insides. She'd heard her daddy say that about the old doctor in Stockton. "Sir, might you know of the Flinn family?"

"They have a little girl."

"Yes, sounds like them."

"He works at the mine." He glanced at the hill behind them. "They live in a cabin up on Pikes Peak Avenue, off Florissant, fourth place on the left."

"That is of great help to me. Thank you so much." She pushed the sack against his hand, and he took her lunch.

"I'm glad I could help you. You're a nice lady." He tucked his hat under his arm, reached into the sack, and pulled out the cookies.

"Thank you." She lifted her package off the ground. "Good day to you, Mr. Baxter."

"And to you, ma'am."

Turning, Willow looked up the street toward the studio. Mr. Van Der Veer stood outside on the boardwalk, looking her way. How long had he been watching her?

❧

Trenton turned away from the sight of Mrs. Peterson and trudged into the office. As he closed the door, the bells above his head chimed, and he scowled at them. Was the woman born yesterday? Her letter of application stated she'd lived in Colorado Springs the past year and a half. Before that she'd lived in California. Had she been wearing blinders and not noticed the wild ways of the West?

What was she thinking, talking to the town drunk as if he were the mayor?

He lumbered past the desk and into the studio. Lifting the tripod from beside the settee, he carried it back to the piano bench.

The bell rang again. His only employee had arrived. He needed to keep his concerns to himself. Her naiveté wasn't his problem.

"Mr. Van Der Veer?"

"I-I'm in the st-studio, Mrs. Peterson."

She sauntered into the room, holding a flat package on her hands.

"You finished the portrait?" he asked.

"Indeed I did." She set the package on the library table. "I can't remember the last time I've had that much fun. Moll…Mrs. Gortner is a delight."

Trenton set the tripod on the floor with more force than necessary. "According to your ap-plication, you're not so new to the W-West that you should be ignorant of its w-ways."

He bristled at his own words. He should have sealed his mouth shut the minute he returned to the office. He'd just called Mrs. Peterson ignorant. *Unaware.* That was the word he should have used. Would have used, if he'd meant to say anything in the first place.

Her green eyes darkened. "I beg your pardon."

Her puckered brow told him he had no choice but to finish what he'd started. He held her gaze. "I am a m-mite surprised that you are *unaware* of the w-ways of the West, is all."

"Ways of the West?" Her elocution was slow, deliberate.

"Yes. I don't expect w-women alone should t-talk to complete strangers, especially derelicts like Baxter."

She bristled. "It's not normal for a man to be passed out on the boardwalk."

"It is if he's a bummer."

"Really, Mr. Van Der Veer?" Her brow crinkled. "I'd expected you to be more charitable."

He didn't bother to ask why. He knew. Because of his stammering, he should be more understanding of others with uncomely conditions.

"It's not a matter of charity, Mrs. Peterson. It's common sense. And a flea has…more." The words jerked out in fits.

Her lips thinned.

He didn't care if she was offended. Her safety was in question. "Does your husband know you're sociable with riffraff?"

She squared her shoulders and stuck out her chin. "I can talk with whomever I please, Mr. Van Der Veer." Her eyes glistened with tears. "My husband is not here to care. He's dead."

Trenton felt himself jerk as if he'd received a punch to his midsection.

Before he could offer her a proper response, she spun around and marched out of the room, mumbling, "So much for Portraits by Willow."

He nearly fell over the tripod in pursuit, but the blasted bell rang as she bolted through the front door. All he could do was watch the storm pass by the front window. Following her now would mean making a scene, sure to intensify the cyclone he'd created.

Instead, he carried the package to the counter and removed the string. As he carefully unwrapped the portrait, he couldn't believe his eyes. Mrs. Gortner could have been standing there, looking straight at him. Mrs. Peterson—the widow—had captured the crook in the mine owner's nose and the sparkle in her eyes. And all with flawless color and tone.

He hadn't even looked at the portrait before she left. Hadn't had a chance to tell her how pleased he was with her work, let alone pay her for it. He needed to make amends.

At the desk, Trenton unlocked the cashbox. He slid her payment into an envelope and put it into his coat pocket. Now for an apology gift. Flowers weren't appropriate. Neither was a box of candy.

Ah. He knew what to get her. He looked at the wall clock: nine thirty. He had half an hour before his next sitting was scheduled to arrive. Ample time for a trip to the mercantile.

TWENTY-ONE

Willow headed in the opposite direction of where the Flinn family lived on Pikes Peak Avenue. After that encounter with her boss, she wasn't of a mind to meet a new client.

She couldn't work for a man with such little regard for humanity. Mr. Van Der Veer couldn't have surprised her any more if he'd climbed onto the rooftop and belted out a saloon song. Instead, he'd scolded her for talking to someone in need. He'd barked his rebuke like a mad dog. He'd probably never even talked to Mr. Baxter, and yet he'd called the man a *derelict. Riffraff.* She shuddered, thinking what the photographer might call her if he knew of her residence in the asylum. He had talent for capturing a person's image, but his vision was distressingly shallow. He couldn't see past his nose.

And in her shock and ire, she'd blurted out the truth. She was a widow. Alone, with no one to care what she did or didn't do.

Turning onto Bennett Avenue, she stepped onto the boardwalk and looked across the street. The wooden sign for Carmen's Confectionary swung in the breeze. A sweet wouldn't improve the situation with her employer, but a piece of candy might minimize the bitter taste of anger souring her tongue.

Willow crossed the street behind an older woman and her five children. After dodging a wagon full of grimy miners, she made her way past an assay office and a barbershop. In front of the confectionary, she paused to admire two delectable trays of indulgences displayed in the window. One held an assortment of frosted pastries. The other, an array of delicious-looking choco-lates. She licked her lips and reached for the door handle.

"Welcome." The rounded chin of the woman clerk barely cleared the counter.

"Thank you." Willow breathed deeply, savoring the rich aroma. Her gaze settled on the glass display case. Cakes, pies, turnovers, and a colorful assort-ment of candies. Caramels, rock candy pops, taffy, lemon drops, root beer barrels, peppermint sticks, licorice bits, and more. Which one should she choose?

"You here about the sign, señorita?"

Willow had to concentrate to discern the question through the woman's Spanish accent. She scanned the wall behind the counter. Posters hawked the latest in factory-made candies and syrups from the East.

"The Help Wanted sign in the window," the clerk said.

Turning back toward the door, Willow saw the back of a chalk slate propped in the bottom corner of the window.

"I didn't see it."

"No matter." The woman's hand darted into the air above a tray of fudge. "I'm Carmen."

"Willow Peterson." She shook Carmen's leathered hand, admiring her brown almond-shaped eyes, barely peeping over her ample cheeks.

"I'm looking for a young woman such as yourself to work the counter. Are you looking for a job?"

Willow had a job. If she still wanted it. "I might be."

An hour later, after a stop at the library, Willow stepped onto Miss Hattie's porch. The swing at the far end looked especially inviting. She pulled the pink cardboard box from Carmen's Confectionary out of the fabric sack that had held her lunch before she gave it to Mr. Baxter. She'd enjoy a piece of fudge before going inside.

She'd taken her first bite when the front door creaked open and Hattie poked her head out.

"I thought I heard someone out here." Hattie stepped outside, her gaze settling on the piece of candy in Willow's hand. "Mind if I join you?"

"On the swing? Or eating candy?"

"Both?"

Willow pulled a second piece of fudge out of the bag, handed it to Hattie, then glanced at the empty space beside her.

After seating herself, Hattie slowly raised the candy to her mouth and nibbled it. "Mmm." Her blue-gray eyes widened. "Carmen's?"

Willow nodded and bit off another sliver of fudge, letting it dissolve on her tongue. "I can't say the candy is better than the root beer soda at Collins Pharmacy, but it's a very satisfying match."

Hattie rested her hand on the arm of the swing and looked at Willow. "With all you had planned for your day, I didn't expect you until late this afternoon." Brushing a gray curl back from her face, her landlady glanced at the bag on Willow's lap. "Did you already eat your lunch?"

Willow sighed, remembering her boss's bark. "I gave my lunch away."

Hattie's eyebrows arched.

"It's a long story."

"Mr. Sinclair and Cherise are making the rounds of the sisters' houses today, starting with Kat's. They'll have supper with Vivian and Carter. So I'm a woman with nothing but time." Hattie popped the last bite of fudge into her mouth.

Where to begin? Willow set the box of fudge on the side table and rested her back against the swing's wooden slats. "I was nearly to the studio when I came across an unconscious old man slouched against the smoke-shop wall."

"Baxter?"

Willow nodded.

"And you stopped." A slight smile edged up Hattie's face.

"I did." Willow straightened. "If he was sleeping on the boardwalk, he obviously needed help. I wasn't sure he was even breathing."

"Not too many people would bother."

"Including my employer."

"Mr. Van Der Veer isn't the charitable type?"

"Mr. Baxter was nice and respectful. He told me where I could find the Flinn family, and I gave him my lunch. When I walked into the office, Mr. Van Der Veer didn't even look at the portrait I gave him. He'd seen me with Mr. Baxter and was too busy expressing his reproach."

"Your employer scolded you?"

Willow couldn't push the image from her mind: his jaw was rigid and his ears a bright red. "Practically spat the words at me."

Hattie blew out a breath, lifting the wispy gray hairs at her forehead.

"I couldn't believe it. I was so angry when he asked if my husband knew I was sociable with riffraff that I admitted my husband wasn't here to care because he was dead."

"What did he say to that?"

She shrugged. "I didn't give him a chance to say any more. I said, 'So much for Portraits by Willow' and marched right out the front door."

Hattie tittered and covered her mouth with knotted fingers. "I'd like to have been there to see the look on his face."

Now that Willow thought about it, she would have liked to see his face too.

"You should've seen Mr. Sinclair's jaw drop this morning when I told him I didn't like him," Hattie said.

"You didn't."

Hattie's eyes sparkled. "I did." She sighed. "But it's all right. I found out he didn't like me either."

"So, that's why the potatoes burned. You two were busy telling each other of your dislike."

"Yes. We were finally talking about our misconceptions, and, well, I got distracted." Hattie's face suddenly pinked, and she moistened her lips. "So much for Portraits by Willow? Did you quit?"

"No. But I'm of a mind to. I'll add the coloring to the Flinn photograph, but how can I work for a man who won't trust my judgment?" Willow worried the strap on her sack. "He said a flea has more common sense."

Hattie laughed. "He didn't."

"He did, and all without even paying me for painting Mrs. Gortner's portrait."

"It sounds like a terrible misunderstanding. I've had my share of those." A grin bunched the wrinkles at Hattie's mouth. "Just this morning as a matter of fact."

"It was a misunderstanding, all right. Mr. Van Der Veer thought he could boss me around, and he was wrong." Willow hadn't expected to paint portraits for the photographer forever, but only one?

Hattie laid her hand on Willow's. "Any chance Mr. Van Der Veer's impassioned reaction could've been rooted in concern for your safety?"

But she wasn't his charge. He'd hired her to do a job, and she'd done it. "Meddling. Plain and simple."

"It's not customary for women to even walk on the same side of the street when a town drunk is present."

Looking up, Willow met her friend's tender gaze. "I suppose I may have been a tad foolhardy. But after what I've been through, I see people differently. I know looks can be deceiving."

Hattie nodded. "Yes, and misunderstandings can be misleading."

Archie strolled up the street and turned onto Hattie's walkway. The courier carried a package, one much thicker than the canvas she'd delivered to Mr. Van Der Veer. Willow stood. If it were an envelope, she could hope her barking boss had finally looked at her work and sent her payment. An apology was probably too much to expect.

"Hello, ladies." Archie doffed his cap. "I have another delivery for you, Missus Peterson."

Willow dug into her bag, pulled out a few coins, and exchanged them for the package. "Thank you, Archie."

"You're a popular lady. Leastwise you are with the photographer."

"I work for him." She didn't bother to correct the present tense in her statement. Right now she only wanted to see what Mr. Van Der Veer had to say for himself.

Archie strolled down the porch steps toward the road, and Willow slid the string from around the package. Inside the butcher paper sat an envelope on top of four blank canvases. She opened the envelope, flipped through a stack of dollar bills, and looked at Hattie. "Payment for Mrs. Gortner's portrait."

"It looks like a generous amount."

Sighing, Willow nodded and glanced at the empty envelope on her lap. "Yes, but no note of apology."

Hattie looked at the stack of canvases. "Those are new. Were you expecting them?"

Willow shook her head.

"My George liked to give me nonverbal apologies." Hattie giggled. "One time he gave me a brooch. My favorite was when he bought me a fine dress after his blasted dog tore mine from the clothesline." She paused. "Perhaps Mr. Van Der Veer prefers to act out an apology as well."

"It doesn't matter." Willow wrung her hands. "Carmen had a Help Wanted sign in the window at the candy shop, and I'm tempted to apply."

Miss Hattie straightened.

"Ida is back to work at the store full time, so selling iceboxes is no longer an option. Working with candy would be better than working for a sourpuss."

~⚬⌇⚬~

Vivian set three cups on the serving tray, then added a bowl of sugar and a pitcher of cream. The week since her father's arrival had been a swirl of family activity. Tonight was the first time she'd be able to visit with him without her sisters present. She drew in a deep breath before carrying the tray to the parlor. She couldn't wait any longer to tell Father about her recent past, but how was she to talk about such things with Cherise at his side? She felt bad for the child, but the girl's ever-present neediness was making it difficult for Vivian and her sisters to catch Father up on their new lives.

Her midsection suddenly tightened, and she gripped the edge of the counter. Since the first episode at Ida's nearly two weeks ago, she'd experienced the tightening on five occasions. This was the sixth. Another false start? Vivian made herself take a long, slow breath, counting off the seconds. How many more of these episodes would she experience before her baby was ready to make its appearance?

Was she ready to be a mother? The reality grew by bounds with each contraction.

Father walked into the kitchen without his dinner jacket. He stopped suddenly and stared at her as if she'd grown a second nose. "You're as white as your mother's cream sauce."

Vivian rolled her bottom lip between her teeth. She couldn't remember ever missing her mother as much as she did in this moment. If Mother were here... Tears sprang to her eyes. "I'm fine," she said, her voice quivering.

"Oh dear." Father wrung his hands. "You're in pain."

She was in pain, but the tightening of her abdomen wasn't to blame. Again, it had eased off rather quickly. She let go of the counter and took slow steps to the table.

"I should get your sisters." Father glanced toward the door. "Morgan. He's a doctor. I should telephone him."

"It's not the baby."

"But you had hold of the cupboard as if you'd crumple if you didn't." He pulled a chair out from the table and held it for her.

Accepting his helping hand, Vivian eased into the chair. "I've had a few practice contractions the past couple of weeks, and I just had another one."

His eyes widened. "Practice?"

"Yes. Kat said my body is practicing for the process of giving birth."

Her father paled, his cheeks puckered as if he were sucking on a lemon.

"The tightening didn't last long. I'm fine now." Tears rolled down Vivian's cheeks, betraying her.

"Then why are you crying?" He pulled a handkerchief from his coat pocket. "Something's bothering you. What is it?"

She breathed in the sweet scent of lavender soap as he blotted her tears. This was her chance to tell him. But how? She folded her hands and rested them on the table's edge, watching him sit in the chair beside hers. "You've been in Cripple Creek for a whole week."

His blue eyes narrowed, further creasing his wrinkled brow. "My arrival... my being here is cause for tears? I thought you'd be happy to have me here."

She reached for his hand. "I am. I missed you terribly. But—"

"I had no choice, Vivian."

She knew he'd lost his job in Portland. She knew he *needed* to take the job in Paris.

"I had to bring Cherise with me. I thought you girls would—"

"Would what? Understand?" She let go of him.

"I thought that when you heard her mother and father were gone, you'd see that Cherise needs me."

Her bottom lip quivering, Vivian met his sad gaze. He was disappointed in his daughters...in her. "I watched my mother be buried. I wasn't as young as Cherise is, and maybe I'm the most selfish girl in the world, but I needed my father too."

His eyes watering, he blew out a sigh. "This is different. You have Carter, and he seems like a real good man."

She pressed her fingers to the ring on her left hand. "He is a fine man. But Carter wasn't in Maine. Gregory was." Father's breath caught. She glanced at the empty doorway, then faced her father, her heart pounding. "I'm not the innocent girl you left with Aunt Alma."

His jaw hardened. "I never should have left you." The sadness in his eyes dried her mouth. "I'm sorry."

"For a time I did blame you and anyone else in my life, including God, but it's not your fault." She worried the handkerchief he'd given her. "There's more. I need you to know who I am, what I've done, and what Jesus has done for me."

Nodding, Father straightened in the chair and gave her his full attention.

A flutter in her womb drew her hands to her swollen abdomen. The new life inside her gave reassurance of the new life God had given her. After breathing a prayer of thanksgiving and asking God to comfort her father, Vivian related her story. Her fall with Gregory. Failing at every job she tried. Working for the madam, Pearl DeVere. Pearl's sudden death. Being held captive by an outlaw, and her confession and repentance. Then the bonus—God gracing her with Carter's love.

When she'd finished, Father wiped tears from his face. He captured her hands, his touch tender. "I wish you hadn't experienced all that pain. But I can see how God used your hardships to draw you deeper." He helped her out of the chair and enfolded her in a warm embrace.

God was so good. She looked into her father's loving eyes. "Thank you. I've kept you in here long enough." She pulled him toward the kitchen door. "I'm surprised Cherise hasn't come looking for you."

Father chuckled. "I am too. I haven't had much time to myself since Pierre died, especially after boarding the train to come west."

"I'm proud of you, Father."

He stopped. "Proud of me?"

"Yes. We were all taken aback by the surprise of Cherise's presence in your life, but you are doing right by her."

He shook his head. "I have no idea what the next step is."

"You will. God will show you." She wrapped her arm across his back and rested her head on his shoulder.

"You're right." He pressed her hand to his side. "I am a blessed man."

Cherise's laughter welcomed them into the parlor and drew their attention to the game table. Her husband sat across from the girl, his thumbs stuck in his ears with fingers splayed.

Carter met her gaze, his brown eyes brimming with love and mischief. "I'm teaching Cherise to play checkers."

"Trying the fine art of distraction on her, I see," Vivian said.

"So far, it's working." Carter glanced at Father, then back at Vivian.

"We talked." She smiled. "Thank you for distracting Cherise."

"My pleasure. This little one is quite the charmer."

"And so are you, Carter Alwyn." She patted his cheek.

TWENTY-TWO

*S*usanna raised her spoon from her plate and slid a bite of creamy mashed potatoes and gravy into her mouth. Helen's sister-in-law was a better cook than Mother. Less judgmental too. Susanna cut the slice of ham on her plate into bite-sized pieces and skewered one with her fork.

Helen's brother sat at one end of the table, regaling them with a story about the time he found a raccoon in their cellar. Whether truth or fabrication, his stories were always entertaining. And they never failed to spur Helen's father to at least try to top them. Later, they'd all sit out on the porch with coffee cups and neighbors, who would add their own stories to the banter.

Susanna set her fork on her plate and reached for her glass of cold apple cider. She liked Denver, and her friend's family was pleasant to live with. But this wasn't Cripple Creek. And she was no closer to her intended destination than she was when she first arrived in Colorado last week. She didn't have enough funds with her for dillydallying. If she didn't make her way to Cripple Creek soon, she'd have to look for a job here. She needed to find Trenton before winter and move quickly.

"Miss Woods."

She set her glass down and looked up at the beak-nosed fellow across the table from her. "Yes, Mr. Johnstone?"

Dressed like a suit model, Mr. Johnstone was an attorney in Denver. He was nice enough, and she should be impressed, but he didn't seem to have much of a sphere of influence if he represented the likes of Helen's family and had time to dine with them.

"Have you lived in Denver long?" he asked.

"No, I moved here with Miss Granstadt."

Helen's brother cleared his throat and slathered butter onto a thick slice of raisin bread. "Miss Woods lived in Kansas, the same town my family is from."

"Scandia, correct?" Mr. Johnstone asked.

"Yes." Susanna hated to admit having come from such an isolated place, but she had proven she had what it took to get out of there.

"And your family?"

"My parents and two younger brothers remain in Kansas." She reached for her water glass. "How about you, Mr. Johnstone? Do you have family in Colorado?"

He patted his mouth with his napkin. "Please, call me Walter. I don't have any family in Denver, but I do have a married sister who lives in Ouray with her family."

She hadn't heard of Ouray, but then, Colorado had never been the topic around her house. Until she'd read the article in the *Denver Post*.

"And my mother and father live in Cripple Creek," Mr. Johnstone continued.

Susanna could have sworn she heard music. She pressed her back against the chair spindles. "Cripple Creek, you said?"

"Yes. It is south of here, about a day's train ride."

"What a small world this is, Walter." She fixed her gaze on him. "I have a dear friend who lives in Cripple Creek. And you said your folks live there?"

Walter nodded like a mule pulling against his harness. "As a matter of fact, I plan to head that way on the seventh of October."

Was she dreaming? Not much more than a week away. Susanna leisurely raised her finger to her face. Twirling a soft curl at her temple, she offered Walter one of her most welcoming smiles.

Perhaps she was closer to reuniting with Trenton than she'd given herself credit for.

⚬⚭⚬

Hattie startled, her heart pounding, her skin damp. She'd been dreaming, a nightmare.

She felt the bed. There were no babies here.

But there was a little girl upstairs. Cherise.

The child's cries drifted from the room above Hattie, a sharp knife piercing her heart. Cherise was living a nightmare—motherless, fatherless, and alone in a foreign land.

Hattie sat up and folded her hands in her lap. She'd heard Cherise's cries most every night the girl had been here. After Cherise finally left Mr. Sinclair's side and went up to her room for the night, the whimpering would begin within an hour.

Tonight was different. Her room pitch black, Hattie stared toward the window. It was the middle of the night. No doors above her clicked open or shut. The poor child was alone.

Thankful for the electricity in her home, Hattie switched on the table lamp and pulled her dressing gown from the back of a chair. After lighting a candle lantern, she slid her feet into sheepskin slippers and climbed the stairs to the middle room, right off the second-story landing. The child's cries weren't as sharp now but still a steady sob.

Breathing a prayer, Hattie opened the door wide enough to hold the lantern in the crack. The little girl lay at the foot of the bed, curled in a ball, her bedcovers in a tangle. "Cherise, dear."

"Mama." She rolled over and peered at Hattie, her eyes red and her face wet. *"Je veux Maman."*

Hattie's heart wrenched. She closed the door behind her and hurried to the bed. Of course the child wanted her mama. "It's Miss Hattie."

"Je veux Maman."

"I know you do." Hattie blew out the candle and set the lantern on the bedside table. *"Je suis ici, ma chère. Vous n'êtes pas seul.* Shh. Shh. I'm here. You're not alone."

Letting her slippers fall to the floor, she reclined on the bed and held her arms out to the child. Soon Cherise clung to her, and their cries for mama and daughter blended, a prayer meant for the heart of God.

TWENTY-THREE

Willow pinned a golden-brown hat on her head and glanced at the corner table and the gift Mr. Van Der Veer sent yesterday. He hadn't said he was sorry for scolding her, but he'd included four new canvases with the payment for her first job.

She pushed the last hatpin through her curls, then walked to the corner and ran her finger across the white canvas. Its newness held such possibilities. Like a new life.

Had her new life as a portrait painter really ended before it had begun? If so, it was because of her pride. Mr. Van Der Veer wasn't the first person to misunderstand her actions and motives, and he no doubt wouldn't be the last.

She studied the Flinn photograph. A nice-looking family. The baby girl sat straight with a firm grip on a cloth bird. Willow's eyes welled and her throat constricted. She and Sam had wanted children. The day she'd burst through their apartment door with news that her art was expected to win a ribbon at the fair, he'd assumed she'd brought him *family news*. He'd flashed her the brightest smile she'd ever seen. Oh, how she wished now that Sam had been right. That she had his child to love and keep her company.

Pressing her hand to her heart, she prayed aloud. "I will trust You, Lord." Hearing herself echo her soul's promise somehow comforted her deep down.

Willow returned the photograph to the table. She'd meet the family to note the coloring of their eyes and hair, then she'd speak to Carmen at the confectionary. Standing at a candy counter wrapping packages of caramels or pastries and counting people's money didn't appeal to her in the least. She'd rather sell iceboxes. Her true preference was to capture the likenesses of the good people of Cripple Creek on canvas.

Hattie was probably right about Mr. Van Der Veer—he'd only meant to express his concern for her, even though it wasn't his place to do so. Some women might view his gruff reprimand as a gallant act. She just wasn't among them.

Misunderstandings can be misleading too.

But she hadn't misunderstood Mr. Van Der Veer. He'd made himself quite clear.

Did she want to work as a portrait artist badly enough that she could abide her boss's apathy toward folks like Mr. Baxter? Could she weather his moodiness?

Willow retrieved her reticule from the bed. Her answer was yes. She liked the work, and most of it could be done right here in her room.

At the bottom of the staircase, Willow poked her head into the parlor, where Hattie sat with her feet propped on an ottoman. A Bible lay open on her lap. "Miss Hattie?"

Her landlady's smile was warm.

"I'm on my way out now." Willow stepped inside the cozy parlor. "I'll see the Flinns, then go talk to Carmen. I intend to continue my work with Mr. Van Der Veer. I thoroughly enjoyed painting Mrs. Gortner's portrait."

Hattie smiled. "That's good news. You are too good at what you do to let a misunderstanding stand in your way. Are you sure you wouldn't rather drive my buggy up to the Flinns' place?"

"No, thank you. The walk will do me good. My father was fond of saying, 'Walking time is thinking time.'"

"Indeed, it is, and praying time." Hattie stroked her Bible. "Chapter twenty-one of Proverbs has me doing both. I've been guilty of giving Mr. Sinclair more than one haughty look."

Willow's heart winced. She remembered her own haughty response to Mr. Van Der Veer yesterday. She'd certainly been guilty of a prideful heart.

After a quick wave, Willow stepped out the front door, thankful for her time on the porch with Hattie yesterday. Fudge and confessions. Willow covered a giggle with her hand. She'd obviously mismatched Miss Hattie and Boney. Far more sparks flew between her landlady and Mr. Sinclair.

By the time Willow turned onto Pikes Peak Avenue, her breath puffed and her side ached. She paused at the corner and looked out over the valley. The Sangre de Cristo Mountains stood majestic in the distance. A breathtaking view. Smiling, she slowed her breathing and looked up the road. The fourth house on the left was a fairly new log cabin with a modest porch.

At the front door, Willow tapped the wooden knocker and glanced at the flour sack curtains in the window. No movement. Perhaps she should have sent the Flinns a message that she'd be calling on them.

Suddenly the door whooshed open and a man built tall and skinny like a telephone pole stood before her. Where were the wife and child? Had she misunderstood Mr. Baxter's directions? She should have given more credence to Mr. Van Der Veer's concerns. Had she put herself in harm's way coming up here alone?

Willow pressed her reticule to her side. "Mr. Flinn?"

His face void of emotion, the man nodded.

"I'm Mrs. Peterson, the owner of Portraits by Willow."

He furrowed his brow. "We don't want any." He shook his head and started to close the door.

"I'm the person Mr. Van Der Veer hired to colorize your family photograph."

The slight woman in the photograph appeared from behind the door. "A woman painter?"

"Yes ma'am." Willow had thought about having special calling cards made but hadn't been to see the printer yet. "I apologize for calling without invitation, but—"

Mrs. Flinn stepped forward. "Don't you worry none about that." Her smile didn't reach her pine-bark brown eyes. "I'm Myrna Flinn." She shook Willow's hand, then pulled her over the threshold. "Missus Peterson?"

"Yes. Please call me Willow."

The one-room cabin housed a ticking potbellied stove, a couple of worn armchairs, and a braided rug. The little girl from the photograph sat in a wooden highchair beside a rough-hewn table.

"This here's our girl, Ruby," Myrna said.

Ruby held a spoonful of what might have been oatmeal above a shallow tin bowl, and Willow guessed her to be less than two years old. She smiled at the child, noting the little girl's aqua blue eyes and creamy skin tone.

"Please, won't you sit for a spell?" Myrna pointed to one of the two chairs at the table.

"Thank you." Willow seated herself, but the woman of the house didn't sit. Instead her husband slid into the chair across from Willow.

Standing behind him, Myrna glanced at her sparse kitchen area and met Willow's gaze. "I'll fetch you a glass of water."

"No, thank you. I won't keep you long." Leaving her reticule on her lap, Willow folded her hands on the table and met Mr. Flinn's steely gaze. "As I said, Mr. Flinn, I'll be colorizing the photograph for you. I wanted to meet your family so I could do justice to the hair and eye colors for each of you."

He huffed. "It figures that dandy would hire a woman to do a man's job."

Willow reared her head as if she'd been struck, but she kept her tongue quiet. She'd let Mr. Flinn keep the job of slinging insults. Still standing behind her husband, Myrna worried her bottom lip.

He leaned forward, his elbows on the table. "Somethin' wrong with you too that you don't have a problem workin' for a man that can't even talk proper?" Mr. Flinn sneered. "Don't tell me you haven't noticed how the man spits and sputters his words like a simpleton or somebody that's afraid of his own shadow."

Willow had found Mr. Van Der Veer to be quite intelligent and his studio more organized than her armoire. *Barks. Spits.* Both were words she'd used to categorize Mr. Van Der Veer's speech, and both were products of his stammering, not anger.

"S-s-s-sit st-st-st-still." Mr. Flinn snickered. He sounded like a snake, and she'd had enough of his poison.

Willow stood, wishing she'd accepted a glass of water so she could throw it at him. "You would fault a man for stammering? I'd think long and hard on that, Mr. Flinn. Smug self-righteousness is an actual weakness, a very ugly one indeed." Choking the handle on her reticule, she regarded the trembling woman beside the highchair. "Good day, Myrna." She let herself out, her hand shaking as she clicked the door shut.

Willow looked over her shoulder at every turn to see if the insufferable Mr. Flinn had followed her. The walk down the hill, fueled by ire and fear, went much more quickly than her ascent. Whether her anger was righteous or not, she was furious. How could that sweet woman live with such a hateful man?

Turning right onto Bennett Avenue, she heard someone calling her name. She jumped, even though it was a woman's voice and a familiar voice. Her sister-in-law walked toward her.

"I'm on my way to the telegraph office. Saw you round the corner." Ida gave her a quick hug. "Are you coming from the boardinghouse?"

"I wish that were the case. I wouldn't mind starting this day anew. The whole week, in fact."

Ida raised a thin eyebrow. "I don't think I've ever seen a scowl on your face. Have you been tangling with a vermin?"

The image made Willow smile. She stepped closer to the building to let people pass on the boardwalk. "Yesterday I tangled with my boss. Today, a client. Most likely a former client now."

"Doesn't sound like you to tangle with anyone."

"Yes, well…" Willow sighed. "Mr. Van Der Veer stutters. He became annoyed yesterday, and I thought he was yelling at me." She blew out a long breath. "Now that I've had time to think about it, I know it was the stammering that made the words jerk out and sound like he was barking at me."

"Where are you headed now?"

"Carmen's Confectionary."

"Nothing like a bite of candy to soothe battle wounds. Think I'll join you." Ida hooked Willow's arm. "It's been too long since we've talked, and I'm in the mood for a story."

Willow took the first step. "I just wish I knew it was going to end well."

As they strolled up Bennett, she regaled Ida with tales of Mr. Baxter and her boss's scolding, then of Mr. Flinn's prejudice against businesswomen and men with stuttering issues. She was telling her about the Help Wanted sign in the window when they crossed the street in front of the candy shop.

"Well, if you start missing iceboxes, you know where to find me." Ida's grin warmed Willow's heart and felt like a well-timed gift from God.

Twenty-Four

Trenton pulled the brush through his stallion's mane and looked up at Jesse. "Why do I always make such a mess of things?"

Jesse tossed a pitchfork full of hay into the stall. "Because you insist on talking to women?"

Trenton chuckled. He could always count on two things from his friend: laughter and truth.

"If we men insist on talking to women, we're sure to be misunderstood." Jesse leaned on the pitchfork.

"The reason we're b-both still single."

"Speak for yourself, buddy." Jesse jabbed Trenton's shoulder. "I'm single by choice."

Trenton nodded. He'd made the choice to remain single, but that hadn't been his plan.

"Misunderstanding or not, it seems to me your employee overreacted to your concerns."

"Agreed." Trenton set the brush on the shelf. "J-just the same, her work is a cut above, and I chased her off."

"It couldn't have been that bad."

Trenton grimaced. "I told her fleas have more c-common sense than she does."

"No."

Trenton nodded. "I asked if her h-husband knew she was sociable with riffraff."

"What'd she say to that?"

Trenton refrained from squaring his shoulders and jutting out his chin in the retelling. "I can talk with whomever I pl-please, Mr. Van Der Veer. My husband is not here to c-care. He's d-dead."

Jesse let out a long, low whistle.

Trenton left the stall. "Life was easier living out of a van...that moved from t-town to town."

Jesse raked his hand through his hair. "I never said setting down roots would be easy. Only that it was time you did it."

"Well, it's not w-working out." Trenton sank onto a bale of hay. "Mrs. Peterson left the office before I'd p-paid her for the p-portrait."

"Did you send it to her?"

"Archie took it to her, along with f-four new canvases."

"A generous gesture. And you apologized for upsetting her?"

Trenton scrubbed his cheek. "Not in so many words."

"You thought the gift would say it for you."

"You know me too w-well." Trenton stared at Jesse's firing furnace at the back. "Haven't heard a w-word from her."

Jesse hooked a thumb in his coveralls. "You're gonna need the Lord's help to fix this."

Trenton's back tensed.

"You've been on your own for a long while, and you don't think you need anyone, but..." Jesse's sentence trailed off.

Maybe Trenton did need someone, but it wasn't God. "If G-God cared about me like you've said, things wou-would've been different."

"How do you know things aren't better than they would be if He didn't care?"

Good question. Had God stopped him from marrying the wrong woman?

Trenton stood and dusted off his backside. "I suppose it isn't fair to blame G-God for my insensitivity to Mrs. Peterson's b-benevolence." She'd obviously lived through a lot more than he'd given her credit for, and those experiences were probably what made her more compassionate than many of the other women he'd met. His trials should have done the same for him. Perhaps, if he had Jesse's faith, they would have. He slid his hands in his trouser pockets. "You think it's improper for me to go to the b-boardinghouse where Mrs. Peterson lives to apolo-gize?"

"It would be if you didn't take candy with you."

Trenton drew in a deep breath. "I'll stop at the c-confectionary first."

"Good thinkin'." A wide grin filled Jesse's face.

"Thanks."

Waving, Trenton walked outside and headed up Bennett Avenue. He wasn't sure showing up at the boardinghouse uninvited was his best idea, and taking candy with him seemed forward, but he had to do something to make things right. Even though he hadn't been wrong in recognizing the danger Mrs. Peterson could put herself in by talking to inebriated old men, he was mistaken to allow his fear to magnify his reaction. If the tears glistening in her green eyes weren't seared into his memory, he might be able to believe he hadn't compared her common sense to that of a flea and asked about her husband's knowledge of her behavior.

Two blocks down, Trenton stopped in front of the confectionary. Four youths walked out, and one held the door for him. After he thanked the young man, Trenton stepped inside and was met by a host of appetizing scents. Caramel. Taffy. Chocolate. He closed the door.

Two young women in fashionable bonnets stood at the counter with their backs to him. One was engaged in a conversation with an older woman behind the candy case. The other young woman studied the trays of delectable indulgences, which was what he wanted to do.

He took a few steps forward, and the woman glanced in his direction. She looked familiar. He would remember if she'd been in for a sitting. And she wasn't the librarian or a waitress from the café. Where else would he have seen her?

Ah, the train wreck. Yes, she was the woman who had climbed into the tipped car to rescue a little girl.

Smiling at him with a hint of recognition in her eyes, she tapped her companion's shoulder.

The woman in the stylish brown hat turned, and he wondered how he hadn't recognized her sooner. It was his employee—at least he hoped she still worked for him. The frown bunching her cheeks didn't bode well for him.

He removed his hat. "Mrs. Peterson. How are you f-faring?" Stupid question.

Her mouth softened. "If you're asking if I'm still angry with you, no." She glanced at her companion, then back at him. "Perhaps a little. But not for all the same reasons."

Was he supposed to understand that?

The woman from the train wreck cleared her throat.

Mrs. Peterson pulled herself upright. "Mr. Van Der Veer, permit me to present to you my sister-in-law, Mrs. Tucker Raines." Very properly, she addressed her companion. "Mr. Van Der Veer is a renowned photographer." She turned to him. "Mrs. Raines manages the Raines Ice Company."

"Ida Raines." The reverend's wife reached out and shook his hand. "I saw you taking photographs in Phantom Canyon, and I'm happy to meet you officially."

"Yes, and I, you. I saw you l-lifting a little girl out of one of the wr-wrecked cars."

"As it turned out, my father was on that train and traveling with the child."

"And they're both w-well?"

"Yes. Thank you."

He returned his attention to Mrs. Peterson. "I didn't get a chance to t-tell you I like your b-business name—Portraits by Willow."

Without any reaction to his compliment, she moistened her lips. "Could we step outside?"

He motioned for her to lead the way to the door, then held it for her.

"Excuse, Missus Peterson?"

Mrs. Peterson turned toward the petite woman behind the counter.

"You sure you don't want the job here?"

Mrs. Peterson looked at him, a puzzling gleam lighting her eyes. "I'm sure." Swinging her reticule, she stepped out onto the boardwalk and pointed to the empty bench in front of the post office. When he joined her on the far end of the bench, she shifted to face him. "I don't want to keep you from your business."

He glanced toward the confectionary. "I came to buy you candy."

Her cheeks turned bright pink, a shade complimentary to the pine-cone brown curl dangling at her ear.

"You came for a j-job?" he asked.

"No. There happened to be a Help Wanted sign in the window, and—"

"You have a job."

She raised her rounded chin. "After yesterday, I wasn't so sure I wanted it."

Another helping of her startling but refreshing directness. "I p-planned to bring the candy by the boardinghouse with a proper verbal apology for my p-poor behavior."

She drew in a deep breath. "You may prefer I buy you candy to accompany my own apology."

"Your apology?"

"I went to see the Flinn family this morning, and the man was nigh to impossible to—"

"W-worse than I am?"

She smiled, and he wished he'd had his camera set for it. "Worse. He's a bigoted troublemaker."

Her severe pronouncement knotted his stomach.

"I may have lost the job of colorizing their photograph. I'm usually not given to fits of rage, but I'm afraid his blathering set me mad."

Trenton fought the chuckle bubbling in his throat. "Worse than measuring your c-common sense against that of a f-flea?"

"Much worse, actually. Mr. Flinn doesn't approve of your decision to hire a woman for what he considers a man's job."

"Oh." Trenton met her gaze. "It makes no d-difference what he thinks. You're the artist I hired, and it's his p-privilege to have you working on his photograph." He paused, waiting for a couple to pass. "To avoid any f-further misunderstanding, I'm apologizing for the insensitive handling of my c-concern, not for the concern itself."

"Fair enough."

"One more thing." He worried the brim of his hat. "I'm f-finding it hard to believe a man's disapproval of a woman working in business, as outdated as it is, would be enough to make you that m-mad."

She blanched, then stood and met his gaze. "He knows nothing about God's intentions for women or God's view of difficulties, such as stuttering."

Standing, Trenton set his hat squarely on his head. Mr. Flinn had ridiculed his speech, and Willow Peterson had gotten mad enough to stand up to him in his own home. This was no ordinary woman. Concerned she may be able to read his thoughts, he looked away.

"We best return to the candy store before my sister-in-law comes looking for us," Mrs. Peterson said.

He nodded and motioned for her to take the lead.

Instead she kept her gaze on him steady. "Less common sense than a flea? Really?"

He felt his ears burn. "Are you ever going to f-forget that?"

"I could be persuaded." She glanced toward the candy shop. "I like the pecan fudge."

And he liked her.

He should have known she was a widow. Boardinghouses were for single women. And a married woman didn't take herself out for ice cream.

At least now he knew his attraction wasn't being directed toward a married woman.

TWENTY-FIVE

*A*n autumn rain tapped a steady rhythm on the fringed roof over Hattie's head. She'd taken Harlan Sinclair up on his offer to drive them to church this morning. Willow kept Cherise company in the backseat.

Hattie couldn't take her mind off the little girl whose story had captured her heart. She hadn't heard Cherise's cries the last couple of nights, but the child had to be unbearably lonely. At eight years old, she should be in school, spending time with children her age. And the poor girl had only brought two changes of day clothes with her. Today, she wore a blue pleated wool skirt and white button shirt with a band collar.

Hattie stole a quick glance at the man seated beside her. Silver streaked his neatly trimmed hair and auburn mustache. Since their talk in the kitchen Friday morning when she burned the potatoes, things had been different between them. The strain had disappeared, and they'd enjoyed several conversations during meals and laughed over tea or coffee in the parlor. He'd begun to share some of his experiences working in Paris and getting to know Pierre Renard. She told him stories from her ten years of running a boardinghouse.

Perhaps she'd earned the right to mention her concern about Cherise's education. But she'd wait until this evening after the child was tucked in for the night. In the meantime, she'd talk to Vivian about making something new for Cherise to wear. Hopefully to school, where she'd learn more English.

When the white steeple came into view, Harlan slowed the two horses to an even gait. Despite the rain, folks milled about outside under umbrellas. Hattie pulled two umbrellas off the seat. She'd found the small one for Cherise. One of the many things people tended to leave at the boardinghouse when they departed.

She glanced back at the round-faced Cherise. *"Êtes vous allée à l'église en France?"* Her French was a little rusty, but hopefully the girl understood she was asking about her church attendance in France.

"Oui. With Papa and Monsieur Sinclair."

"Our church services…umm…*réunions de l'église* are a little different here, no?"

"Oui. More fun."

Hattie smiled and nodded. Tucker was definitely less formal in the structure of the services. She'd heard Morgan refer to it as Holy Spirit–inspired spontaneity. As she turned back around, she met Harlan's gaze.

His smile revealed perfectly even teeth. "How is it that you know French?"

"Camille, my best friend on the trail, was French."

"The Oregon Trail?"

"Yes. My family traveled in a wagon from Missouri to California."

He looked at the road ahead, then back at her. "Another story you can tell me over coffee."

❧

Willow watched as Mr. Sinclair jumped down and rushed around the surrey. He held his hand out to Miss Hattie and helped her to the ground.

It seemed her landlady had at least two good prospects for a husband, even if she wasn't in the market for one. Hattie obviously enjoyed an ease and a history with Mr. Boney Hughes since their youth. But Mr. Sinclair had a flair for genteel manners and a definite family connection. A family Hattie already loved as her own.

"Thank you, kind sir." Smiling, Miss Hattie straightened her floral straw hat.

"You're most welcome, ma'am."

They may not realize it yet, but there was an undeniable attraction between her landlady and Ida's father.

Willow helped Cherise down from the surrey, but as soon as her feet touched the ground, it was the older woman's hand that Cherise snagged. A broad smile filled Mr. Sinclair's face as he captured the child's other hand.

Perhaps Ida wouldn't need to make a decision about taking in the child.

Willow followed them to the church steps. Mr. Sinclair steadied Miss Hattie's large umbrella over their heads while Miss Hattie held the small one until the two umbrellas collided. Their laughter stirred Willow's heart. She and her father liked to walk in the rain. He called the raindrops angel kisses.

Watching the older couple climb the stairs together with Cherise made her question her certainty that Sam had been her only chance for love. For the first time, she found herself hoping he wasn't.

At the door, Miss Hattie glanced over her shoulder. "Dear, you said Tucker invited Mr. Van Der Veer to church. Are you expecting he might attend this morning?"

"Tucker did say he extended an invitation, but Mr. Van Der Veer and I haven't talked about his church attendance."

What made Miss Hattie think of the photographer in this moment? Ah, the matchmaker in her must have decided Mr. Van Der Veer was a candidate.

Was that such a bad notion? He certainly had some noble attributes. Not the least of which was his commitment to hire an employee based upon his or *her* qualifications for the job. His appreciation for her work certainly counted. And for some reason the pecan fudge he'd bought for her tasted even better than that she'd purchased for herself the day before.

At the back of the sanctuary, she found herself inspecting the congregation for a man with broad shoulders and hair parted down the middle.

❦

Trenton leaned back in his porch chair, watching a steady rain spit into the pools of mud forming across the road. Before five o'clock that morning, big drops had pounded his roof and woken him.

Sundays were his toughest day of the week. His one consistent day off work, and he didn't know what to do with his time. He'd already scrubbed the kitchen counter and washed out the icebox, changed the sheets on his bed, unpacked a box of books, and written his mother a letter. And it wasn't even ten o'clock. He lifted his second mug of coffee to his mouth.

He'd thought about seeing if Jesse wanted to ride to Dome Rock with him. He'd heard talk about the landmark and wanted to photograph the monumental rock. But it was Sunday. His friend would be in church.

And so would Willow Peterson. Seeing how her brother was the pastor, church attendance was probably a family requirement. He took a long swig of hot coffee, then felt a smile spread across his face. What was he thinking? His employee wouldn't attend church just because a man told her to, even if the man happened to be her brother. No, she was a woman of faith in her own right. He couldn't say why he knew that, but something about her told him she'd relied on God when her husband died. And her ongoing confidence in God drew him to her.

Sitting beside her on the bench in front of the post office on Thursday had felt right. He thought better of himself when she was around. He didn't feel judged or condemned. When he thought he'd chased her off and lost her as an employee...well, he didn't want to think about it. She'd forgiven him for the flea imbroglio. Even if it was something neither of them was likely to forget.

"I could be persuaded. I like the pecan fudge." Her green-eyed smile had weakened his knees, like to have knocked him on his backside.

Straightening, Trenton set his coffee cup on the side table. After locking the front door, he pulled the collar up on his coat and took quick steps around the mud puddles toward the First Congregational Church.

The white steeple reminded him of the little cabin-church his family had attended in Maryland. His pulse quickened. He couldn't help but wonder how different his life would have been...would be, if he'd been able to put that experience behind him. If he hadn't lumped all pastors and believers together. If he hadn't blamed God.

Trenton noted the matching brick parsonage set behind the church, then made his way up the steps. Singing drew him through the outer doors. Wiping his shoes on an entry rug, he listened to the voices blending on the refrain: *"Blessed assurance, Jesus is mine!"* Assurance—a feeling he'd never experienced.

He wiped rainwater from his face and glanced at the closed door leading into the sanctuary. This was his first church service since that December day right before his tenth birthday. The pastor's condemning pronouncements and hellish cries still echoed in his memory.

The foyer here was close enough.

TWENTY-SIX

*I*da hadn't seated her father beside Hattie at the supper table, but that's where they belonged—together. Even though the two of them had talked through their foibles, they had yet to figure out they were a good match. Her father sat at the end of the table. Cherise sat between him and Hattie, who was quite attentive to the child's needs. As a mother might be.

Father hadn't said any more to Ida or her sisters about taking in Cherise as their own. He seemed more comfortable caring for her. Perhaps he—

"Miss Ida."

Ida looked across the table at Cherise. The little girl's dark hair, topped with a bright pink ribbon, cascaded over her shoulders. Probably Hattie's doing. "Yes?"

"I will...." She glanced up at Father.

Stilling his fork midair, Father smiled at her. "Attend?"

"Yes, attend." Cherise copied his pronunciation to the letter. "I will attend school." Excitement and apprehension etched her brow.

Ida's heart ached again for the fatherless child. How could she have been so petty to have entertained jealous thoughts toward Cherise? "Going to school will be wonderful."

"Yes, I liked school very much." Kat sipped her water.

"Monsieur Sinclair is a wise man." Miss Hattie leaned forward and gave Father a warm smile before returning her attention to Cherise. "School will be good for you, dear. You'll meet girls and boys your own age and learn more about America." She repeated it in French, stumbling over only a couple of words.

Ida met the little girl's timid gaze. "You'll do fine."

Cherise smiled, taking Ida back in time to her days as the *big sister* to little Vivian, now swollen with a child of her own.

Ida blinked back a tear for the baby she'd lost and scooped a spoonful of chilled pea salad. Cherise felt more like a little sister to her than a daughter.

An hour later, Ida carried a stack of dirty dishes to the kitchen. They'd finished their supper, and the men had retired to the parlor. Vivian remained in the dining room with Cherise, Hope, and William while Willow, Kat, and Nell helped Ida clean up. Hattie had taken a tray of coffee to the men.

Kat lifted her hands out of the dishwater and looked at Willow. "It may be wishful thinking, but it looks to me like your landlady may be smitten with my father."

"I've been thinking the same thing." Willow added a bowl she'd just dried to a stack on the countertop.

Ida slid a plate with two slices of leftover roast beef into the icebox. "You live with her. Has she said anything about him?"

"Only that they'd been talking and she thought much better of him." Willow cleared her throat. "But actions can speak louder than words."

"It doesn't hurt to hope." Kat dipped her hands back into the water.

Nell set the stack of bowls in the cupboard. "What about you, Willow?" She pinned Willow with the look of a desperate romantic.

Willow gave Nell a shy smile. "Your father is nice enough, but not my sort."

Nell didn't miss a beat. "And how about Mr. Van Der Veer? A man who buys pecan fudge for a woman seems like a good sort."

Willow shot Ida a look that could melt a block of ice.

"I might have mentioned something about it," Ida said. "I thought it was awfully sweet of him and didn't think you would mind my sharing it."

A loud gasp pulled Ida and the others back to the dining room. Vivian stood beside the table. Her face bright red, she stared at the floor. "I'm wet."

Liquid tinged a light pink had formed a puddle on the wooden floor.

"Your baby is ready." Kat stepped forward and wrapped her arm around Vivian's shoulders.

Vivian glanced at the children. "I can't have the baby here! I need to go home."

Carter rushed into the room and stared at the puddle. "Is it safe to move her?"

"Your floor. I'm so sorry." Vivian's forehead glistened with perspiration.

"I can mop it." Ida brushed Vivian's arm. "I'll do anything for my new niece or nephew."

Kat laid her hand on Vivian's swollen abdomen. "Are you having any pain?"

"Yes. My back aches, and I feel tight."

Her hand still on Vivian, Kat looked at Ida. "We'll use your bed."

Where she'd lost her baby just weeks ago. "Yes."

Morgan ducked into the room. "I'll go to the house and get the rubber sheet."

Ida's heart pounded. Women did this all the time without doctors, but this was her baby sister they were talking about. "You should stay. I'll go."

Morgan raised his hand, signalling a stop, and glanced at his wife. "Kat's done this before."

"With you." The coloring in Kat's face was a shade lighter. "You'll be back soon?"

He nodded and darted toward the kitchen door.

"Oh dear." Father came to an abrupt halt in the doorway, his eyebrows arched.

Hattie nearly collided with him from behind. She peeked around the blockage. "Are we having a baby?"

Father paled. "Not me. I'll be in the parlor. Better yet, telephone me at the boardinghouse as soon as my grandchild arrives."

Kat walked beside Vivian, their arms intertwined, as she and Carter guided her sister toward the bedroom. No more false starts. The contractions had come on fast and strong. When another one hit, Vivian stopped midstep and doubled over just outside Ida and Tucker's bedchamber. Kat glanced toward the front door, ready for her husband to return. Thankfully, they lived only a few blocks from the parsonage, and Morgan should be back any minute with the rubber sheet. If not, they may be delivering a baby on the bed without it.

Vivian latched onto the doorframe, her breath ragged and her brow damp.

Carter looked at Kat, concern etched in his brown eyes. "What do we do?"

"We're doing it—getting her to the bed." *The sooner, the better.*

Kat breathed a prayer for all of them. She'd helped Morgan deliver Iris's baby at the hospital two years ago and she gave birth to Hope last year, but those two experiences scarcely prepared her to be a midwife. She'd feel better if Morgan was here. But he wasn't, and there was no time to be concerned with how she felt. Her sister and Carter needed her to remain calm, at least in appearances.

Viv arched. "My back feels like it's on fire."

"It's not." Kat rubbed her sister's lower back. "I thought Hope would never come, but Viv, it seems you may be one of the lucky and deliver your baby fast."

"But Ida's bed." Viv's breath was ragged. "I can't—"

"Don't concern yourself with that, sis." Ida slipped past them and into the bedroom, carrying the rubber sheet, which meant Morgan had returned.

"Where's Morgan?" Kat asked.

"He said he'd be in the parlor with the husbands, that Vivian and the baby were in good hands with her sisters."

"My sisters." Vivian worked to draw in a deep breath and resume a snail's pace toward the bedroom. "Nell?"

"Nell went to the kitchen. She'll be along with water and towels soon." With each step Kat felt her own baby's kicks and wondered if she could deliver Vivian's baby from a sitting position.

They'd crossed the threshold and made it as far as the dressing table when Viv cupped her abdomen with both hands, pulling Kat's arm with her. "All that practice has made our baby impatient...and I feel like I need the chamber—" She grabbed the dressing table and grunted.

"You're pushing!" Kat hadn't meant to shout.

Vivian nodded, her breath shallow and her face tight.

In one swift move, Carter scooped Vivian into his arms and rushed to the bed. Ida had just tucked in the last corner of the sheet, a dressing gown draped over her shoulder. Carter laid Vivian on the bed.

Kat regarded her older sister. "There's no time to change her clothes."

"The baby's coming already?"

Nell rushed in, huffing and puffing. A curl of steam swirled above the pot she carried to the washstand.

"Now that you're settled... I'll do my waiting in the parlor." Carter leaned over and kissed Vivian's forehead before leaving the room. Vivian groaned again as Carter closed the door behind him.

"We need to get her ready," Kat said. With Ida and Nell's help, she raised Vivian's skirt, pulled off her pantaloons, and laid a cotton sheet over her lower extremities. "I need to see how close we are."

Vivian nodded, her belly tightening, the strain coloring her face. Nell set a short stack of towels on a bedside table, and Ida brushed Vivian's hair back from her face.

Kat settled into position at Vivian's knees and lifted the sheet. A tiny head slid toward her. "Woo-wee, this little guy is in a hurry!" Kat looked at Ida. "Throw me a towel." Her heart raced as she caught two dry towels and bent to catch the baby.

Vivian curled toward her, pushing and groaning.

Kat's eyes watered as a wiggling, slippery new life landed in her arms and screamed. "I have a niece."

A sweet smile replaced the pained scowl on Vivian's face. "I have a daughter?"

"You surely do. She's on the tiny side, and beautiful."

A sob escaped Vivian as she plopped back onto the pillow.

"Let me clean her up a little." Kat quickly patted the little one dry, then swaddled her and laid her on Vivian's chest. "Morgan will come cut the cord."

"That certainly went quickly." Nell leaned over the bed beside Ida for a peek at their new niece. "She is beautiful."

"I'll go get Carter and Morgan." Ida left the door open behind her.

Breathing a prayer of thanksgiving, Kat washed her hands at the washstand. She was watching the new mother nuzzle her newborn daughter when Vivian suddenly groaned and pulled her knees up.

Kat returned to the bed and lifted the sheet. "Oh my!"

Hattie pressed a puzzle piece into the lower right corner of the jigsaw. Harlan sat across from her at the parlor table. He'd driven her and Cherise back to the boardinghouse in an attempt to escape the certain drama of the impending birth.

Cherise was content playing on the sofa with a couple of dolls Hattie kept on hand, alternating English with French as she entertained her captive audience.

Harlan grunted, trying to push the same puzzle piece into the same spot for the third time. "I can't believe my baby girl is having a baby."

"I know." Hattie lifted her teacup from the saucer. "Feels like Vivian arrived in Cripple Creek just a few months ago." She drained her cup of the tepid tea. "But it also feels like time has been flying by. Soon Kat will have another child."

Hattie couldn't help but wonder how many grandbabies her baby might have given her by now if the Good Lord had chosen to leave her here on earth.

"Time didn't stand still then like it is now." Harlan ran his hand through his silver-tinted auburn hair. "It's been hours since we left the parsonage."

Hattie glanced at the mantel clock. "Two hours and twenty-five minutes to be exact."

"Feels like it all started yesterday." He looked at the puzzle, then up at her. "They promised to telephone us, didn't they?"

"Yes, Ida said she'd telephone with the news. I'm sure we'll hear from her soon."

At least she hoped so. If not for Harlan's sake, for hers. They were both as jumpy as crickets and needed something else to occupy their minds. The puzzle was no longer an adequate distraction.

"Have you gone to the school to register Cherise yet?" Hattie asked.

"I took her to meet the principal on Friday." Harlan looked across the room at Cherise. "It won't be an easy adjustment, but she needs to be around children. Cherise enjoys Hope and William, but it's not the same. She needs time with children her own age."

Had his eyes been that blue when they'd first met just weeks ago? How could she not have liked this man?

Harlan laid the troublesome puzzle piece on the table and met her gaze. "May I ask you something?"

She nodded, her mouth suddenly dry.

"If it's presumptuous of me, just say so."

Presumptuous? Whatever did he intend to ask her? She moistened her lips.

He glanced at the child. "Cherise needs new clothes. Will you go shopping with us?"

She stilled in surprise. "That was your bold question?"

"I don't wish to take advantage of the fact that you love my daughters or that Cherise and I are renting rooms in your home."

"Oh, fiddle-faddle. I count you as a friend, and shopping for a little girl? I'd love to." Harlan had four grown daughters, but he'd asked her to go with him and Cherise. Hattie's heart did a little dance. It felt so good to be included in this family.

Needing to get a grip on her emotions, she looked away and focused on the red flames flickering in the fireplace. She'd do well to remember that being included in a few of the Sinclair family goings-on didn't give her a permanent place in Harlan Sinclair's life, lest she start grasping at any crazy romantic notions. At her age?

"I expected one of my daughters to take Cherise in," Harlan said, his voice lowered.

"Expected? As in past tense?"

He glanced at Cherise, then returned his attention to Hattie and leaned toward her. "Truth is, I don't think I can give her up." She could barely hear his whisper over Cherise's chatter. "Even to one of my own daughters."

She shouldn't be surprised. His care of the little girl made it obvious that he adored her.

"I'm sure it sounds crazy for an old man like me to entertain the thought of raising an eight-year-old girl himself."

"I don't think it's a crazy thought." Hattie made herself look into those blue eyes. "But I do think the undertaking would be easier if you didn't try to do so on your own." Her breath caught. His creased brow told her he was wondering what she meant. So was she.

The telephone jangled, and they both jumped from their chairs, nearly colliding in the doorway. Laughing, Harlan stepped back and let Hattie go first. "It is your house, your telephone."

She rushed to the kitchen and pulled the cone from its hook. "Hello? Ida?"

"Yes, Miss Hattie." The operator had a thick Spanish accent. "I'll connect her."

"Thank you, Eva." Hattie handed the telephone cone to Harlan. He was, after all, the grandfather. He should hear the news first.

His eyes widened and his face paled.

"Ida? Is Vivian well?" Hattie asked.

He nodded, and a deep sigh escaped her.

"Two!" he said.

She moved closer to him. "Twins?"

Tears brimming his blue eyes, he nodded again. "Victoria and Veronica."

"Thank the Lord." Two more girls. Now poor William was outnumbered three to one. Hopefully, Kat would deliver a boy to even it out some.

Harlan said good-bye to Ida and faced Hattie, his gaze tender. "Mother and daughters are doing well." He drew in a deep breath. "I have four dear daughters. Four attentive sons-in-law. Four rambunctious grandchildren, with number five on the way. And a dear friend." He enfolded her hand in his. "I am a blessed man."

And she, a blessed woman. With weakening knees. As nonchalantly as possible, she rested her other hand on the countertop to steady herself. Perhaps age wasn't the issue she thought it was when it came to romance.

TWENTY-SEVEN

*M*onday morning Trenton paid for his breakfast and stepped out of the Third Street Café under a cloud-rimmed sky. The rain had finally let up sometime after midnight, but another storm was on its way. The thick air cradled dampness and the scent of rain as he walked to the studio.

Jesse usually joined him for breakfast on Monday mornings, but a big job had his friend working dawn to dusk this week.

It was just as well they didn't meet today. Trenton would have been tempted to tell Jesse he'd darkened the doors of a church yesterday. No sense raising his friend's hopes. Jesse might think his prayers had been answered and Trenton had finally given in to God, which he hadn't. He'd left on the last song, but not before getting a view into the sanctuary through the tiny window in the door and glimpsing the back of Willow Peterson's head. He didn't get away before he heard her brother preach a sermon from Romans, chapter 5. *"Justified by faith." "Peace with God." "Access by faith into this grace." "While we were yet sinners, Christ died for us."*

If what the reverend said about all that was true, Trenton had a lot more thinking to do. He may have heard that message as a little boy visiting his grandmother's church, before time and experience weighted his heart, but he couldn't remember. His grandmother had given him a Bible thirty-some years ago, and it was still tucked away in his trunk. Maybe it was time he dug it out.

Ready to cross the street, Trenton looked up and saw Mrs. Flinn walking toward him with little Ruby in tow. He waited for her on the boardwalk.

"Good day, Mr. Van Der Veer."

"Mrs. F-Flinn." He brushed the brim of his top hat.

"I'm glad to see you. I wanted to commend you for the artist you hired. Not too many men would trust a woman to do the job."

"M-men like your husband?"

She nodded, her cheeks turning pink. "He's behind the times."

Bigoted, according to Mrs. Peterson.

"I hope Mrs. Peterson will still colorize our photograph, although I wouldn't blame her if she chose against it. My husband can be quite thoughtless at times."

"Mrs. P-Peterson did m-mention your husband's, uh, issues with us, but she didn't indicate her p-plans." If he knew her at all, he guessed he'd see her in the studio today with the colorized print. "I suppose the greater question is whether or not Mr. Flinn still intends to p-pay for the work." Of a woman artist, hired by a man who stuttered. He kept the last comment to himself.

Mrs. Flinn raised her chin. "It doesn't matter what he'll do or not do. I sold a quilt. I have the money to pay for Mrs. Peterson's work."

"Very well." Today was the deadline he'd given her for the job. He'd soon know one way or the other. "Could you st-stop by later this week?"

"Yes. I'll be back in town on Thursday."

"Until then." Trenton continued to First Street and found himself looking for the man Mrs. Peterson called Mr. Baxter. He wasn't anywhere near the tobacco shop, but Mrs. Gortner stood at the window outside his studio. He picked up his pace. "Good day, Mrs. Gortner."

"Oh my." She stared at the portrait Willow Peterson had painted of her. "Mr. Van Der Veer, I expected that dear girl would do a fine job, but this is—"

"Extraordinary."

"Indeed, it is. Especially considering what she had to work with." Her laughter rocked the feather plumes on her green hat.

Bells jangled while he held the office door open for her. She paused in the doorway and met his gaze, leaving mere inches between their faces. "You have a gold mine in Mrs. Peterson."

"Yes ma'am."

"And the frame? Who made that?"

"I did. I have a s-small wood shop in my house."

"You run your own business and frame photographs and portraits with your hands? You're quite the Renaissance man, Mr. Van Der Veer." Mrs. Gortner smiled. "And you're single, correct?"

The summary of his abilities was complimentary, but why would his marital status be of any concern to her?

"Your silence tells me it is so." She continued into the office and turned to face him. "You do know that Willow Peterson is a widow, do you not?"

"I d-did know that. Yes." Thanks to his insensitivity to her benevolent ways. "But her m-marital status has no bearing—"

"On her employment with you. Of course not."

He closed the door and joined her at the window. "I could deliver your p-portrait this afternoon, if you like."

Mrs. Gortner held her head high like a royal. "A business partnership with Willow Peterson is one thing. A personal relationship is a whole different matter."

His neck warmed and his collar suddenly felt too tight.

"I know these things can take time to grow," Mrs. Gortner continued. "No time like the present to plant a seed."

He nodded, but he couldn't say why. There wasn't much chance Willow Peterson would care to nurture such a seed. She had gone to great lengths to ensure he believed her to be a married woman. She'd even submitted a portrait of her late husband, leaving out that he was deceased.

"I like to do my part in helping other women get their business off the ground," Mrs. Gortner said. "I say we give folks ample opportunity to see Willow's fine work. Why don't you bring the portrait by on Friday?"

"Yes. I'll do that. Thank you."

"Hopefully you'll soon have another of her portraits to display. I'll take my portrait to our Women for the Betterment of Cripple Creek meeting next week and see if I can stir up more business for your gold-mine girl." She winked, and embarrassment burned the tops of his ears. It was time he considered growing his hair a smidgen longer.

He looked away in time to see the portrait artist in question standing outside the window, looking at the portrait. She had an envelope tucked under her arm.

Mrs. Gortner noticed her too and smiled. "I'd say she's admiring your framing handiwork."

When Mrs. Peterson noticed them, she stepped inside, automatically ringing bells above the door.

"It's so good to see you, dear." Mrs. Gortner gave Willow Peterson's shoulders a quick embrace. "We were talking about you."

"You were?" Mrs. Peterson looked at him.

"Yes." He smiled past his fear that Mrs. Gortner would try to do a little more gardening in front of his employee. "We were talking about the wonderful j-job you did." *That you're a gold mine.* And that Mrs. Gortner had planted a troubling and intriguing seed in his mind. He'd be fine as long as it didn't take root. His heart couldn't bear another drought.

"I didn't do the framing or make the business sign." Mrs. Peterson met his gaze, her green eyes looking like polished emeralds. "The frame is perfect."

"He made it himself." Mrs. Gortner pointed at him.

"You did?"

He nodded.

"I didn't know you did woodwork."

"He's apparently a man of many undiscovered talents." The mine owner's smile was too wide.

"Are you happy with the portrait, Mollie?" Mrs. Peterson asked.

"I adore it." Mrs. Gortner glanced at the envelope in Mrs. Peterson's hand. "I'll take my leave and let you two tend to your business." She smiled at him. "And to the seeds."

Mrs. Peterson's brow creased. Time to change the subject.

"Thank you, again, for your b-business," Trenton said. "You can expect the p-portrait on Friday morning. Early, if that's all right."

"Early Friday is fine with me. I'll see you then, Mr. Van Der Veer." Mrs. Gortner turned to Mrs. Peterson. "And you, dear, need to come by for another cup of tea sometime soon."

"I'd like that."

"Perhaps next week."

They both watched Mrs. Gortner leave the studio, bells ringing behind her.

Willow Peterson faced him. "She's quite a woman, isn't she?"

He drew a deep breath. "Yes, and an apparent devotee of our work." His mind hung up on the word *our*. He and Mrs. Peterson did make a great team. Him taking the photographs, her painting the portraits, and him making the frames for them. A great professional team.

Mrs. Peterson set the envelope on the counter. "What seeds are we to be tending?"

His mouth went dry. He'd hoped Mrs. Peterson had forgotten the woman's odd comment. "Apparently, Mrs. Gortner is fond of gardening."

"Oh." Her mouth formed a perfectly shaped *O* and her face framed it in red.

"I saw Mrs. Flinn in town today," he said quickly. "She hoped you'd still add the coloring to their family photo despite her husband's offensiveness."

"I did, for her." She slid the photograph from the envelope. "And for you. You're a professional. I need to be one as well. And I'm sure Mr. Flinn won't be the last rude client we encounter."

"Likely not. But you do have the prerogative to deny such a person service."

"Thank you." She smiled, deepening the dimple on the left side of her face.

Clearing his throat, he studied the photograph. "Very nice work. Mrs. Flinn will be in on Thursday to pick it up." He wouldn't make Mrs. Peterson wait until then for her payment. He slid the photograph back into the envelope and carried it to his desk. When he had her payment, he pulled a job order from the box and returned to the counter. "I have your percentage for you. And a new job."

"Really?"

"Yes." He handed her the money, careful not to brush her hand.

She slid the payment into her reticule and looked up at him. "You're an answer to my prayer." Blushing again, she swept a curl from her forehead.

Him, an answer to prayer?

"My prayer for a new beginning." She moistened her lips. "You're giving me the chance to do what I love to do—paint. And I'm thankful."

"I know the need for a fresh start."

She opened her mouth as if to speak, but didn't. If she was about to ask about his fresh start, he was glad she didn't. He'd said too much. He needed to keep their relationship professional. For her sake.

"I have two women scheduled for sittings late this week," he said, "and they both said they'll want portraits painted. But one of the couples I photographed last week commissioned a portrait." He pulled the photograph from the envelope. "The woman said they know you, that you recommended my services."

She looked at the photograph. "Yes. Mr. and Mrs. Johnstone. I sold them an icebox."

"I appreciate the referral. Would M-Monday, the seventeenth, give you enough t-time?"

"Yes. That's two weeks. I can let it finish drying that Saturday and Sunday."

Sunday. Church. Was it wrong to attend church because of a woman and not out of a devotion to God?

⌐⌐∾⌐⌐

Willow slid the photograph of Mr. and Mrs. Johnstone back into the envelope, her mind in a swirl. Her boss was fast becoming an encouraging friend, and it felt good to have someone besides a family member recognize and appreciate her abilities as an artist.

Trenton flipped the Open sign over on the door. She thought about reminding him of Tucker's invitation to visit the church but decided that might be an infringement on Mr. Van Der Veer's personal life. She'd have to talk to God about that later. In the meantime, she had another painting job to do and couldn't wait to start on it.

"Looks like you might have company." Mr. Van Der Veer held the door open for a short, bulky man hidden behind a big bouquet of sunflowers.

Mr. Baxter lowered the bouquet and gave her a smile that revealed several gaps in his teeth. "Hello, Missus Peterson. These are for you." He handed her the flowers, his smile deepening.

"Mr. Baxter, you didn't have to bring me anything."

"And you didn't have to give me your lunch." He was clean and his brown eyes were clearer.

"I wanted to."

"That's what I'm saying… I wanted to give you flowers." He looked at Mr. Van Der Veer. "I hope you don't mind me bothering you at work."

"It's no b-bother." Her boss smiled at him. "Lovely flowers d-deserve a lovely lady."

Mr. Baxter nodded.

Willow pressed her hand to her warm chest and returned her attention to the bearer of gifts. "Thank you, Mr. Baxter." Holding the flowers to one side, she leaned forward and kissed his bristly cheek.

He chuckled. "You remind me of my daughter. Carolyn was sweet like you."

"Was?"

"Yes ma'am. She died of infection when she was nineteen."

"I'm sorry."

He ran his hand through a mass of wavy gray hair. "Carolyn would want me to stay away from the bottle." He met her gaze. "Wish I could. Your kindness, Missus Peterson, gave me enough courage for today."

Tears rimmed her lower lids and slid down her cheeks. Poor Mr. Baxter was in a battle she hoped he was strong enough to fight. To think God would use her to encourage him warmed her heart. God was good. He *had* been all along, but her eyes were finally open to it. Now she was seeing Him everywhere she looked. Even looking back on her time in the asylum, she saw His provision of people like Maria and the many there who'd helped her find her way back.

Had God placed her in Trenton Van Der Veer's path to help him in his new life in Cripple Creek? Or had He placed Trenton here for her benefit?

"There's not a thing wrong with this dress, Susanna." Helen held up a lovely taffeta gown with a wasp waist. "You would look exquisite in it."

"You know it isn't right for me."

Helen huffed. "Because it isn't purple?"

"Exactly. Purple is the color of royalty, and I need to feel like a princess when I see Trenton."

Helen dropped the hanger on the clothing rack. Her green eyes narrowed. "So, do I have this right? You're not going to Cripple Creek to see Trenton unless you can find a purple dress?"

"I will find a purple dress. I will see Trenton." Susanna continued her search at another rack. "If shopping is too much work for you, you can go back to your brother's and leave me to find the correct dress without distraction."

"Pardon me, ladies." A full-faced woman shuffled toward them. "I couldn't help but overhear you." She smiled at Susanna, revealing a thin scar at her eyebrow. "Did you say you're looking for a purple dress?"

"I am. Not too frilly but charming."

"I see. To charm a special young man?"

"Yes." Pay no mind that Trenton Van Der Veer was seventeen years her senior and hardly considered a young man.

The attendant's smile widened. "You're in luck, young lady. I received a shipment from Chicago just this morning. It's still in the back room, but I remember seeing a very handsome purple dress."

"I'd love to see it." Susanna crossed her fingers behind her back and watched the woman shuffle past a curtain.

Quickly returning with a satin treasure draped over her arms, the curvy woman stopped directly in front of Susanna and studied her from hat to shoe. "The dress may need a nip or tuck here or there, but no man will be able to resist you in this dress, dear."

"Perfect!" Soon Susanna would have Trenton nibbling humble pie from her hand. This time, she wouldn't do anything stupid to ruin her chances of wearing the new purple dress to charm the stage managers in New York.

That evening, Willow knelt on a rag rug with a wide paintbrush in her hand. The four fresh canvases Trenton had sent last Wednesday lay on old newspapers on the pine floor in her bedchamber. Before she could use them, she needed to undercoat them to avoid any cracks. She dipped the brush into pure white paint and coated the third canvas.

Everyone else in the house had no doubt drifted off to slumber hours ago. Even Cherise was quiet tonight. Willow's mind, however, refused to give way to such a frivolous activity. Not when the day—the past week, actually—had given her so much to think about.

A vase of cheery sunflowers sat on a round table beside the rocker. When Mr. Baxter brought them to her at the studio as a thank-you gift for her kindness, Trenton treated him as a valued guest, not unwanted riffraff. He'd even engaged in chitchat with Mr. Baxter, calling both the flowers and her lovely. Her face warmed in remembrance.

She'd thought of Trenton Van Der Veer only as her employer until they sat on the bench in front of the post office and talked about Mr. Flinn's prejudice against them. She'd even teased him some about his apology, and he'd bought her a box of pecan fudge. Not at all what she'd considered customary behavior for business associates.

Setting the brush on the palette, she glanced at the portrait she'd propped in the rocking chair—the likeness of a vibrant twenty-year-old man with a sturdy chin and warm sienna-brown eyes. In some ways, it seemed she'd painted Sam's image yesterday. But a lifetime had passed. Six years ago, she'd set up her sketch pad and easel at the shore of the San Joaquin River. After they'd enjoyed a picnic lunch, Sam posed for her. She'd presented the portrait to him as a wedding gift.

She still missed him terribly, and she couldn't think of anything she wouldn't give to spend one more day with him, to hear his voice again.

"Oh, Sam." Tears stung her eyes. "I never expected death to part us so soon. Why did you have to go and leave me alone?" She leaned away from the drying canvases.

When she'd finally emerged from the fog of melancholia and been released from the asylum, she was set on reconciling with her family and building a new life. Finding a job. Spending time with her brother and getting to know her new sister-in-law. She'd done all of those things and found pleasure in them. God had even provided her with work that fulfilled her dream of being a painter. She enjoyed Miss Hattie's company, and her room was comfortable, but a longing for something more niggled at her.

At one time, she'd wanted—expected—a home of her own. A family of her own.

"What am I to do?"

Talking to the painted image of a dead man wasn't normal. Was it?

Sam couldn't help her now. He wasn't hers to hold. Her new life without him and without her father was hers to live. She needed to decide what she wanted.

Right now it was easier to say what she didn't want. She didn't want to be alone.

Sam would always hold a special place in her heart, but she refused to let memories and unfulfilled dreams of their life together anchor her to the past.

Tasting salty tears on her lips, she lifted the portrait and kissed Sam's canvas mouth. She turned the canvas and set it back in the chair, facing away. "Good-bye, Sam."

Breathing a prayer for strength, she dipped the paintbrush in the white paint.

She was like these canvases. The Lord had applied a thick base coat to her, to prepare her according to His purpose. Only God knew what she'd say hello to, but she surrendered herself for that something more.

TWENTY-EIGHT

*H*attie stood in front of her wardrobe, looking through her clothing choices. None of which seemed suitable this morning. Her navy blue dress was too plain. Her red dress, too flashy. Her white shirtwaist with a skirt seemed too stuffy. She hadn't spent this much time selecting an outfit since the last time George had taken her out for supper at Maggie's Third Street Café, nearly eleven years ago.

Sighing, she closed her eyes and reached into the wardrobe. The first outfit she touched she pulled off its hook. Opening one eye, she peeked at her choice. Thankfully, she'd chosen her blue calico dress. Not too bold, but not too sedate either. She smiled, remembering that Vivian told her the print made the blue in her blue-gray eyes shine.

After Hattie had dressed and laced her brown boots, she pinned on a navy blue hat, then wrapped a matching wool shawl over her shoulders and took one last look at herself. The mirror had decided to be kind to her today. She glanced at the tin of red talcum on her dressing table. The rouge may have helped too.

Her chance to shop for clothes with an eight-year-old girl came only once in…forty-six years, so far. She smoothed the scalloped collar at her neck one more time.

"Miss Hattie?" Cherise's voice wafted to the second floor.

Oh, dear, she'd kept them waiting. "*Venez.* Coming." Hattie plucked her handbag from the round table and rushed to the door, stopping short to take inventory.

Boots, check.

Dress, check.

Hat, check.

Handbag, check.

It seemed like a silly exercise, but lately she hadn't been thinking clearly. And the distractions had taken hold the same day Harlan Sinclair arrived in town.

Hattie stepped onto the landing and looked toward the bottom of the staircase. Harlan stood beside Cherise, his arm draped on the little girl's shoulder, looking up at Hattie. He smiled, and her knees weakened. A coincidence? Or was it just another of the mysterious effects this man seemed to have on her?

She rested her hand on the polished pine railing and, as if she were sixteen and he'd come to escort her to a cotillion, she took measured steps toward him.

As she approached the last few steps, Harlan's eyes widened and a boyish grin reached his silver temples. He held his hand out to her. A dapper gentleman, Mr. Harlan Sinclair.

Shifting her weight to better support her weak knees, Hattie smiled and placed her hand in his as she took the last step. Strong but gentle hands. "Thank you, kind sir."

Harlan dipped his chin. "My pleasure, my lady."

"You are beauty, Miss Hattie," said Cherise.

Harlan looked into her eyes. "Truer words can't be spoken."

Heat rushed up her neck, and she stifled the nervous giggle in her throat. "Thank you."

Harlan looked at their connected hands and let go.

Feeling a sudden chill, Hattie turned her attention to Cherise and cupped the girl's soft cheek. "Thank you, dear. You are beauty too."

"I get a pretty dress?"

"We'll do our best," Harlan said. "Won't we, Miss Hattie?"

We. Hattie swallowed those same cotillion butterflies gathering in her throat and nodded.

"Your buggy awaits you." Harlan opened the front door. While she'd dithered over which dress to wear, Harlan had gone to the livery and brought her horse and buggy to the house. She could get used to this.

Cherise slipped her hand into Hattie's, and Hattie practically floated down the porch steps. In the front seat beside Mr. Sinclair, Hattie couldn't help but think Harlan and George would've gotten along well.

Harlan gave the reins a gentle snap. The mare lunged forward, and they were on their way to town for a day of shopping fun.

Hattie glanced back at Cherise. The child's smile melted her heart. She could get used to this too. But she wasn't a schoolgirl, and Harlan Sinclair clearly had enough women in his life—four daughters, Cherise, and now *three* granddaughters. Nell had been right about Vivian having twins. Thankfully, Vivian and both her tiny new daughters were faring well.

Hattie looked up at their grandfather. "Harlan, do twins run in your family?"

"My mother was a twin, but unlike Veronica and Victoria, her twin was a brother." He looked at her. "You and your husband never had children?"

A sweet little face came to her in a memory. "George and I had a daughter, Katie Louise." Hattie moistened her lips. "She died at eight months old."

His laugh lines deepened into a frown. "I'm sorry."

"Thank you. I awoke one night and the room was too quiet. I rushed to her cradle, but I was too late. She was already in God's arms."

"No wonder you are so dear to my daughters." His blue eyes shimmered. Were the tears for her? "You're an amazing woman, Hattie Adams." He was still speaking when he returned his attention to the road.

A rather intimate conversation to have in an open buggy bumping down Fourth Avenue, stopping and starting at each crowded intersection. But Harlan was easy to talk to.

"Can we see the babies today?" Cherise asked.

He glanced back at Cherise. "After our lunch, if Miss Hattie has the time."

Hattie smiled. "I'd like that."

All the time in the world didn't feel like it would be enough.

Thirty minutes later, Hattie was happily squeezed into a fitting room with Cherise. The little girl squirmed as Hattie fastened the buttons on the first of five dresses they'd found for her to try on.

"Miss Hattie?" Cherise looked up, her dark eyes shining. *"Je t'aime."*

Hattie's fingers stilled and tears clogged her throat. "I love you too, dear."

"And Monsieur Sinclair?"

"He loves you too." His actions toward the child clearly told her so.

"You love him?"

Hattie gulped air and coughed. "He is a very nice man."

"You laugh with him."

"I do." Hearing those two words come from her mouth warmed her face.

"You do love him?"

"I'm very fond of Mr. Sinclair. Yes." Why wouldn't she love him? After all, they were practically family.

Because of his daughters.

Trenton pulled another print out of the tray and hung it on the line. His Wednesday had started earlier than usual. And far more abruptly. He'd been deep into a delightful dream when his neighbor's dog began barking relentlessly. He'd later discovered the dog had good reason but not good sense. The canine had lost a predawn stare-down with a short-tempered polecat, and the unfortunate mutt was outside being forced into a tub of suds.

When Trenton's attempt to return to sleep failed, he'd decided a brisk walk to Mount Pisgah and back might provide much-needed time for contemplation. He'd returned to town and opened the office at eight o'clock.

Now, as he slid the last print out of the fixer, he recalled the dream. Again. Willow Peterson walked toward him wearing a frilly pink dress and beaming a smile that rivaled the brightest ray of sunshine. Mollie Kathleen Gortner walked beside her, carrying a garden spade. Tucker Raines stood with Trenton, holding an open Bible.

Trenton returned the fixer to its jug and stowed it under the printing table. Pausing, he shook his head. It was only a dream. A crazy dream inspired by a delusional mine owner who liked to talk about marital status and seeds that need tending. He wiped the table and tidied the shelf of chemicals above it. He and Willow may have planted seeds of friendship, but he couldn't expect anything more. He wasn't marriage material—a blithering fool and a heathen to boot. He picked the trimmings from the day's prints from the floor.

The bell sounded on the outside door.

"W-welcome. Be r-right—"

"Morning, Trenton. It's only me." It was the voice of the man who had stood beside him in the dream with an open Bible.

Had Tucker seen him through the window in the sanctuary door? Maybe the little old man who'd seen Trenton sitting in the foyer told him. Or was he here for a different reason? Mrs. Peterson?

"Be r-right there, R-Reverend." He pulled the chain on the light in the darkroom and stepped out into the office.

Reverend Raines stood at the counter. "Tucker. Please call me Tucker."

"Is your sister all right?"

"She's fine, as far as I know. I haven't seen her since Sunday, but she seemed fine at church. She even won a game of checkers at our Sunday lunch." Tucker removed his felt preacher's hat. "Never mind that it was an eight-year-old girl she beat." Chuckling, he met Trenton's gaze as he feigned seriousness. "You can't tell her I said that."

Trenton raised his hand as if to take a vow. "I wouldn't dream of it." Ironic word choice. And here he was talking to the brother of the subject of his recent dreams. "We men have to stick together." He glanced at the wood stove in the corner. "You want a c-cup of coffee?"

"Sounds good. Feels like an early snow is on its way."

"C-coffee's boiled." Trenton pointed to the extra chair in front of the desk. "I didn't have electricity on the road in the photographic v-van."

Tucker seated himself and set his hat on the desk. "Sounds like we've both drunk a lot of campfire coffee. I was an itinerant preacher before coming to Cripple Creek."

This preacher wasn't anything like the fraudulent Reverend Olum. For one thing, Tucker hadn't looked down on Trenton or accused him of living a sinful life that caused his *affliction*. He was down to earth. He'd even told a funny story about himself in his sermon last Sunday. Trenton pulled two mugs from the bottom drawer and filled them with hot coffee.

"Thanks." Tucker took a full mug from him. "Have you always had a stammer?"

"S-since I was a boy, sch-school age, I guess."

Tucker blew across the top of his coffee. "And photography, how long you been interested in that?"

"Almost as long. My mother was d-dragging me to see another sp-speech therapist when we had to w-wait for a photographic van to roll by." Trenton paused. "I s-stared at the poster on the side until she pulled me away. The next day I saw the m-man taking photographs in front of the courthouse. I talked to him while my mother was in the dry-goods store." He took another deep breath. It felt good to get the whole story out. "What about you? Born with a Bible in your hand, were you?"

Tucker chuckled and gulped coffee. "Nope. Mine wasn't a churchgoing family. Until my father's last couple years of life, he figured he was good enough to get to heaven, if there was one. He wouldn't admit to needing any help. Probably assumed he could talk his way in when the time came."

Sounded familiar. Trenton resisted the impulse to loosen his collar.

"My brothers-in-law and I gather on Wednesday mornings for Bible study and prayer," Tucker said. "We meet at Morgan Cutshaw's house on Carr Avenue. I just came from there. You're welcome to join us next week, if you like."

Trenton slid his finger along the inside of his collar. It was so much easier to avoid such discussions and expectations when he was on the road, moving from town to town. "I'll think about it."

Tucker nodded, and his lazy smile said he knew a dismissal when he heard one. He pushed himself up in the chair and set his coffee mug on the desk. "I almost forgot what I came here for. We're having a church picnic a week from Sunday, on the sixteenth. I thought it'd be nice to have a group photo taken."

"Folks m-might object to me w-working on Sunday."

Nodding, Tucker plucked his hat from the desk. "Then I guess you'll have to come take photographs for the sheer fun of it." He stood. "We'd pay you a sitting fee. And folks who want to pay for prints can stop by the studio during the week."

Trenton sighed. "Fair enough."

"But you'll want to make sure you allow plenty of time to sample my wife's potato salad and Miss Hattie's fried chicken. Not to mention my sister's apple pie."

Willow Peterson. The perfect reason for him to attend.

"I'll be there, and I can have prints ready by Monday afternoon."

"I'm happy to hear it." Tucker brushed the brim of his hat. "Good day then." He was almost to the door when he turned. "It was good to see you in church this past Sunday." A grin crept across his face. "Maybe this Sunday you'll venture all the way into the sanctuary?"

Trenton smiled. "I'll think about that too."

Yep. He liked Reverend Raines. It was his feelings for the man's sister that troubled him.

TWENTY-NINE

*N*ell wrapped another diaper around Victoria. The fifth since she'd arrived at the cabin this morning. Thankfully only one of the twins was having issues with Vivian's milk today. Content to sleep away the hours, Veronica made sweet sleep noises in the cradle while Vivian gathered their dinner dishes. Her sister had already washed a load of diapers and hung them on the line.

Now, her hands full of soup bowls, Vivian turned toward the sink and tripped on the base of the cradle.

"Ouch!"

Nell instinctively bent over the cradle to protect Victoria, but somehow Vivian managed to keep hold of the dishes and steady herself. She straightened.

"How ever did you manage not to drop those?" Nell asked.

"Practice. Good to know I learned something of value during my days as a hostess." The sarcasm added a shimmer to Vivian's brown eyes. When she finished pinning the diaper, Nell pulled Victoria's dress down and lifted her from the bed. The crunch of wagon wheels on the rocky road out front drew Nell and Vivian to the open window. Father sat tall beside Miss Hattie, at the reins in her surrey. Cherise sat behind them, next to a mound of packages. Today was the grand shopping day for school clothes.

Without looking away from the window, Vivian stroked the top of

Victoria's hairless head. "They're all smiling. I'd say the shopping excursion was a success."

"Perhaps in more ways than one?"

Vivian dipped her chin and nodded, a grin framing her thin lips.

The three of them looked every bit a family, despite the extreme age spread between Cherise and the adults. Now that Nell had observed her father with the child and gotten to know her better, it wasn't surprising that he wanted to provide a home and a family for her.

"They do make a rather sweet family, don't they?" Vivian arched a thin eyebrow.

"I was thinking the same thing." Nell walked to the door. "I doubt he'd be able to turn Cherise over to any of us now."

"I think it's Father's turn for a second chance, and I'm praying he'll see the light and take a wife."

"Miss Hattie? Do you think—"

Vivian opened the door and stepped out onto the small stoop. "You watch the two of them together for a few minutes," she whispered, "then tell me what you think."

Hattie cradled baby Victoria in the crook of her arm and breathed in her sweetness—a blend of talc and mother's milk. This day bubbled with bliss. Shopping with Cherise and Harlan, then lunch at the Third Street Café. Harlan had told them about the report he'd submitted to the railroad after the train wreck and about the letter they'd sent, offering him a job in the Cripple Creek District. He planned to remain.

Yes, a blissful day.

Nell was at Vivian and Carter's house helping Vivian with the twins. She showed Cherise how to hold three-day-old Veronica, the other twin.

Vivian came in from outside carrying a basket of diapers. She shivered. "Sun's still shining, but it feels like it could snow tonight." She sat on one end of the sofa and set the basket on the floor in front of her. "I don't normally fold clothes in the parlor, or when I have guests, but..."

"We're all family here." Harlan seated himself in a wing-back chair across from Hattie.

Vivian looked up from the diaper and met Hattie's gaze. "So... Father said you three have been clothes shopping."

"We have indeed."

"That must have been fun." Hattie recognized the lilt in Nell's voice. The third-born Sinclair sister was an incurable romantic.

"It was an enjoyable time." Hattie shouldn't have looked at Harlan, but she did, and his tender smile stirred her own romantic notions.

"Hattie really has an eye for sensible fashion." He still hadn't looked away. "Thank you."

"And she's so good with Cherise." He smiled at the child. "You'll look like a princess in school next week."

"I show my clothes?" Cherise's enthusiasm startled Veronica and the baby whimpered.

"We've kept Miss Hattie out long enough." Harlan glanced from Cherise to each of his daughters. "But there is something I'd like to discuss with her before we take her home. Would you girls mind entertaining Cherise for a few minutes?"

Vivian looked up from the diaper she was folding, amusement shining in her brown eyes. "We don't mind."

Harlan bent toward Hattie and reached for baby Victoria. "Do you mind a private conversation?"

Hattie shook her head, unable to form words around the questions clogging her throat. She handed him the snuffling bundle. What could he possibly need to speak to her about that required privacy?

He kissed his granddaughter's forehead and carried her to Vivian. A moment later he returned to the sofa and extended his arm to Hattie. She stood and laid her hand on his arm, feeling his warmth through the jacket. He led her into the entryway and glanced back toward the room where two of his daughters remained. Apparently their whispers had reached his ears too.

"I'd hoped we could speak privately, but it may be too cold outside for lingering," he said.

"My mantle will keep me warm enough."

"Very well." Harlan pulled her wool cape from a coat tree and laid it over her shoulders. She looked into his azure blue eyes and nodded, not at all sure what she was agreeing to. He held the door open. "I thought we could sit on the porch for a spell."

Hattie stepped past him, breathing in the scent of shaving soap and hair tonic.

When the door clicked shut behind them, Hattie noted the chairs normally cluttering the porch were missing. She moistened her lips and seated herself on the porch swing. She pressed her hand to her stomach to still the soaring butterflies and glanced at the empty space beside her. Harlan sat down. His elbow brushed hers, sending a shiver up her spine.

"I think Cherise is happy with the clothes we found her," she said.

He nodded, his clean-shaven chin not more than a foot away from her own. "You are so good with her. So kind." Pausing, he drew in a deep breath. "You should be a mother."

Hattie swallowed hard. She agreed, but she trusted the Good—

Harlan captured her hand, jolting her thoughts and drawing her gaze. His blue eyes blazed with intensity. "Hattie, will you do me the honor of becoming my wife and mother to Cherise?"

Hattie leaned against the wooden slats on the swing. Yawning to clear her ears would be rude, but she couldn't have heard him right. She pressed her teeth together in a discreet yawn.

"Please marry me, Hattie Adams."

She hadn't imagined it—he was actually proposing marriage. Whatever had gotten into him? He'd been in town only two weeks, and they hadn't really spoken to one another for the first three days. Now he wanted to marry her?

She was very fond of Harlan Sinclair, and she admired him for wanting to raise Cherise as his own daughter. She worried the seam at her bodice. What he was really saying was that she should be *Cherise's mother,* not necessarily his wife.

He cleared his throat and squeezed her hand.

"I'm sorry to keep you waiting, but this is all quite sudden, and I'll need to think on it."

Drawing in a deep breath, Harlan smoothed his neatly trimmed mustache. "Thank you. I should be grateful you're at least willing to consider it."

She wouldn't have agreed to that much if she hadn't already come to love him.

꩜

Willow stepped back to assess the images on the canvas. Holding up the photograph Trenton had taken of Mr. and Mrs. Johnstone, she compared the lines and tones to what she'd already painted. She was happy with the slope of Mrs. Johnstone's forehead and the angle of her hazel eyes, but Mr. Johnstone's bulbous nose was another story. Perhaps it was time she shifted her attention to sketching the deacon's bench in the photograph. The change in focus might provide a fresh perspective.

Thinking about the bench, she remembered sitting in the church pew Sunday morning, hoping Trenton might appear. But she never saw him. His church attendance shouldn't be her concern, but because of their affiliation as employer and employee, God might consider him her neighbor. It made perfect sense that she'd take an interest in his spiritual state. Why, she didn't even know if he was a man of faith.

Tucker had spoken with him, invited him to church. But she couldn't very well ask her brother about Trenton's faith life. He might misunderstand her interest. She dipped a clean brush into the burnt sienna and painted feather strokes on the bench she'd sketched.

She didn't need a pastor to make the inquiry for her. Tucker had recently exhorted the congregation to be bold in sharing their Christian beliefs. Given the right opportunity, she was perfectly capable of speaking to Trenton about such things. And if he didn't appreciate such a personal discussion, what could he do about it?

He could fire her.

Willow's spine stiffened, and the brush strayed into Mrs. Johnstone's rust-colored skirt. Her employer might lecture her on keeping personal concerns personal, but surely he wouldn't fire her. Would he? After all, her inquiry was for his eternal well-being. She couldn't possibly imagine her life without her trust in God, her faith in Jesus Christ. She couldn't bear to even consider the dire consequences of life without His help.

She set aside her brush and palette and walked to her bedside table. Her prayer journal lay beneath her Bible. Until the right opportunity presented itself, she could at least pray for Trenton, and there was no time better than the present.

❧

Ida had walked to the icehouse with the list of the icebox deliveries for tomorrow. The trip had given her the opportunity to visit with Otis and catch up on each other's family happenings. Now, as she returned to the showroom, she pulled her cape tight against the chilled air and glanced at the gray sky. All day she'd looked forward to seeing her new twin nieces on her way home from work. If she didn't close the store soon, the impending snowfall would blanket her cape before she arrived at Vivian's. All she had left to do was count the income for the day and ready it for deposit.

As she reached the showroom door, her father rounded the corner of the building alone. Cherise hadn't started school yet. How had he managed to separate himself from her? "Father, it's good to see you."

He embraced her and opened the door. "Do you have time for your father?"

"Of course." She shed her cape and hung it on the peg. "Is Cherise all right?"

"Yes. She's at home with Hattie." He fidgeted with his hat. "Baking, I believe."

Something was obviously bothering him. "The three of you were going clothes shopping today."

"We did."

He obviously hadn't come to discuss Cherise's new school wardrobe. Was he here to ask her to take Cherise?

"Can we be seated?" he asked.

She nodded and walked to her desk. Father waited for her to sit, then seated himself across from her.

"You know about the job offer I received," he said, "and that I plan to make my home here."

She smiled. "Yes, and I'm very pleased. We all are."

"Starting next week, after Cherise is in school, I'll be a railroad inspector for the Cripple Creek District."

"They'll be fortunate to have you."

He rubbed a scratch on the desktop. "Your Miss Hattie is a natural with children. And she's obviously very fond of our family."

Ida folded her hands on the desk and found his pensive gaze. "Father, does this visit concern Miss Hattie?"

"I asked her to marry me."

Ida startled.

"You girls know Hattie and love her," he said. "And so does Cherise."

"What did she say?"

"She needs to think on it."

"She's only known you a short time."

"But I feel like I met her two years ago in Nell's letters."

"You two didn't even like each other the first few days."

He smiled. "True. But that was a misunderstanding."

Ida intercepted the grin tugging at her cheeks. Willow had told her about finding Hattie and Boney in the kitchen one evening and Hattie and Father in the kitchen the next morning, laughing over burned potatoes.

"We're quite compatible," Father said. "We both love my four daughters. And she's very good with Cherise."

"She is." Miss Hattie had been able to put the child at ease in this new country and make her feel at home. That was why he wanted to marry her? "You want to keep Cherise and raise her yourself."

He nodded. "I know I'm not a young man anymore, but is that so bad a desire?"

"No. Cherise obviously trusts you and loves you. And Miss Hattie." Ida braced her chin, resting her elbows on the desk. "Did you propose to Hattie merely so she could be a mother to Cherise?"

He stood and brushed his graying hair back from his temples. "A mother for Cherise is part of the reason and why I don't want to wait any longer than necessary to complete our family."

"What about your feelings for Miss Hattie?" Ida laid her hand on her father's arm. "She won't marry for any reason but love."

"Well then, I'm thankful she loves Cherise." Father stood and turned toward the door. "I'll just have to hope her affection for Cherise will be enough."

THIRTY

riday morning Susanna pushed a pin into the stylish straw hat on her head. Wool was a more suitable choice for October, but straw was more durable for travel, and the wider brim offered additional protection should she find herself exposed to the sun during their occasional stops.

Occasional stops.

Her hands stilled. She looked at Helen, who sat on the bed, lacing her boots. "The West is a wilderness."

"Uh-huh." Helen peered at her, skepticism arching her eyebrows. "After that arduous train ride from the Mississippi, you're just now figuring out why it's called the Wild West?"

"The train had a necessary."

Helen straightened into a sitting position, the cynicism disappearing from her face. "Oh. Dear." A grin tugged at her lips.

Sitting at the dinner table with Walter Johnstone nine days ago, discussing his trip to Cripple Creek, Susanna had tossed social proprieties aside and given no thought to necessities when traveling alone with a man with whom she'd shared only one meal.

"Knowing you, you'll manage just fine." Helen squared her shoulders and swiveled them.

Susanna refused to acknowledge her friend's mockery. "You're right. I managed to get out of Kansas and make my way all the way to Colorado."

Breathing past her concerns, Susanna resumed her task. She was no delicate flower afraid of a little wind. She could do this. Her plan was foolproof. By this time, Trenton had to be as lonely as a rooster in a rabbit hutch and no doubt plagued with second thoughts about leaving her.

"I'm going to miss you." Helen pulled her boot laces tight. "After fifteen years of being around you, I've grown used to having you around."

"I'll miss you too." Susanna meant it. Helen had been a good friend to her, but she needed more. She needed a bigger life. "Denver isn't all that far from Cripple Creek. And you can look forward to coming to New York to visit me and Trenton."

Helen tittered. "Possessing even a fraction of your confidence would be enough for me." Susanna, satisfied her hat was secure, tucked the pin box into her satchel.

Helen tied the bootlace into a bow. "Trenton did leave you behind. What if, after all you've been through to get there, he's not pleased to see you?"

"Don't be silly. The photographer is the least of my worries." Susanna added her journal to the bag, then glanced around the room to make sure she hadn't forgotten anything. "I am, however, a bit nervous about spending the next few days cooped up in a carriage with the lawyer."

Helen stood and smoothed her skirt. "Are you afraid he'll bore you to death?"

"You were at the supper table. The man is anything but a riveting conversationalist."

Helen faked a big yawn, patting her mouth. They both giggled.

The slap of horse hooves and wagon wheels on the rocky road in front of the house quieted them and set Susanna's heart to racing.

Helen looked at the timepiece on her bedside table. "Mr. Johnstone may be sleep-inducing, but he is punctual—a minute past sunrise."

Smiling, Susanna grabbed her satchel and followed her friend to the door. She'd surely miss Helen's dry sense of humor, even her sarcasm.

Standing on the porch, Susanna blinked feverishly. She couldn't say for sure what she'd expected Walter's wagon to look like, but the one parked in front of Helen's family's house certainly wasn't it. Two draft horses were harnessed to a long buckboard with a canvas stretched over hidden figures as uneven as elephants and field mice sandwiched together. Helen's father and brother were already loading her trunk behind the rickety driver's seat. Did Mr. Johnstone really expect her to travel on that?

"Good morning, Miss Woods," the lawyer said, smiling at her from the driver's seat.

She drew in a fortifying breath. "Mr. Johnstone."

"I decided to make my trip do double duty and drive the wagon with some furniture for my folks. Triple, if I count transporting you too."

Some women might like the way his dark hair swept back, plastered to his head. Susanna wasn't one of them. And why hadn't he shipped the furniture to his parents by rail or hired a freight wagon to haul it? She had a lot to say but thought better of speaking her mind. The road ahead of them would be long enough without any dissention. She needed him on her side.

He reached for her satchel. "I like a woman who doesn't keep a man waiting."

She handed over her bag, mustering the sweetest smile she could manage. "I'm ready."

At least it was partly true. She was ready to be in Cripple Creek but in no particular hurry to make the trip in this contraption.

"This is all quite sudden, and I'll need to think on it."

Sunday morning Hattie walked from the surrey to the church steps beside Willow and behind Harlan and Cherise. Tomorrow the sweet child would start her classes. With the new wardrobe Hattie had helped pick out. She sighed.

Cherise twisted and faced her. "Are you well, Miss Hattie?" The child had heard her sigh. Concern laced her brown eyes.

"*Je vais très bien.* I'm fine, dear." Hattie smiled. "And I'm happy to be at the Lord's House." That much was true.

Harlan met her gaze, the question of marriage still evident in his handsome features. She looked away, and he resumed his walk to the steps.

Absent-mindedly, Hattie greeted her fellow parishioners. Four days and four sleepless nights had passed since Harlan had proposed. She'd spent the nights mulling over the same possibilities. She loved him and the child he intended to raise. The entire Sinclair clan, for that matter. But if she'd ever thought about a second marriage, she would have wanted it to be like the first—two people marrying because they loved one another and couldn't imagine life without the other. Would her and Harlan's love of Cherise be enough for a marriage of convenience? Was she being selfish? Should she settle for such a union for the sake of the child?

After greeting the Sinclair sisters and kissing their babies' soft cheeks, she joined her friend Etta Ondersma. They sat on the same side of the building as the Sinclair family, but several rows behind them. Hattie's heart ached. She could be sitting up there with them, part of the family.

Hattie opened her Bible to the third chapter of Proverbs and read the fifth verse in an attempt to capture her confusing thoughts.

"*Trust in the* LORD *with all thine heart; and lean not unto thine own understanding.*"

Nell's husband, Judson Archer, was the singer in the family. He stood at the podium with a hymnal open in his hands. "Join me in singing to the God of our past, present, and future. Hymn number 177. ''Tis So Sweet to Trust in Jesus.'"

God knew what she needed, and she knew what she wanted. Hattie flipped through the pages of the hymnal and then settled into her alto part, surrendering her heart anew.

Lord, what do You will for me?

Trenton opened the flap window in his woodworking room. The first snowfall of the season Wednesday night had burdened the trees, but it had melted by Friday afternoon. The morning air was crisp and dry. He leaned toward the opening and breathed in the refreshment.

Sunday.

He tightened the miter clamp on a strip of pine. The day of the week never mattered much to him on the road. He was usually in the photographic van, headed to the next town, content to wander. Until Jesse suggested he put down roots in Cripple Creek. Maybe his current restlessness had nothing to do with wandering or roots and everything to do with what he'd left behind in Kansas—his dream of taking a wife and raising a family. He loosened the clamp and repositioned the board to cut the other end.

Tucker Raines wasn't judgmental or pushy. The reverend had seen him through the small window to the foyer, but he hadn't pointed him out and made a spectacle of inviting him inside.

He was a restrained *and* clever man of God. By inviting him to the men's Bible study first, he'd made attending the church picnic seem harmless. He'd presented it as a job. But Trenton never should have agreed to participate, even if it afforded him the opportunity to see Willow in a social setting and taste her apple pie.

"Maybe this Sunday you'll venture all the way into the sanctuary?"

He wasn't ready for that, but he *was* curious.

Trenton laid the backsaw on the worktable and went to the trunk in his bedroom. Kneeling, he dug through the worn winter clothes to where his Bible lay. The best way to figure out what the reverend was talking about last Sunday was to read that fifth chapter of Romans for himself.

THIRTY-ONE

Monday morning Hattie set her teacup in its saucer and looked across the small kitchen table at Harlan, an activity that had grown comfortable. The unanswered question between them, however, was most uncomfortable. She'd never been an indecisive person and hated that she'd kept Harlan waiting on her answer since Wednesday.

He'd sent Cherise for her schoolbag, and Willow hadn't come down for breakfast yet, affording her an opportunity to give her answer. She smiled, praying for the right words and the courage to speak them.

Harlan set his coffee cup on the table, wrapping his hands around it. His eyes were a deeper blue this morning. "This afternoon I'll find another place for me and Cherise to live."

She pressed her lips together, willing herself not to object to his plans. It made sense that they not be under the same roof, given the personal nature of their relationship.

"Your silence is your answer," he continued. "I shouldn't have expected you to marry me out of your fondness for Cherise."

Hattie set her cup in the saucer, its rattle stretching the silence. She should tell Harlan why she couldn't marry him. That she loved him but refused to settle for a marriage of convenience, even though she loved Cherise and wanted to help him raise her.

A tear rolled down her cheek, and she brushed it away. "I'm sorry. I wish—"

Cherise dashed in, wearing her new green dress. "My bag is by *porte*."

"Door." Hattie offered her the English word. She'd miss these opportunities to help the child learn the language.

Harlan shifted his attention to his charge. "Very good." He stood. "We'll have our breakfast, little one, then see you off to school."

Cherise gave Hattie's neck a squeeze. "I like new dress."

"And you look lovely in it, sweet girl."

Harlan and Cherise left the room hand in hand.

At the stove, Hattie contemplated if being loved by a man was overrated. Women throughout history had settled for being cared for, and most had done quite well. Cherise loved her. Couldn't that be enough to make them a family?

Midafternoon, Hattie pulled the tray of apple tarts from her oven and set it on a trivet. Cinnamon and apple scented the kitchen, and she breathed in its tantalizing fragrance.

Autumn had come to Colorado, her favorite time of year. She glanced out the window at the sycamore tree. Its swaying branches waved crimson, golden, and burnt-orange flags. The cooling winds signaled relief from summer's heat. Hattie sighed. She knew better than to entertain schoolgirl notions at her age, but she'd let herself think Harlan Sinclair could be her autumn, that he'd swept into Cripple Creek, bringing a change of seasons with him.

Taking part in four weddings in less than two years had obviously softened her heart toward the prospect of a second marriage. But George had done too good a job of cherishing her. She wasn't ready to be the wife of a man who didn't love her, no matter how much she loved Harlan, Cherise, and the entire Sinclair family. She couldn't settle for anything less than love.

A knock on the kitchen door alerted her that Boney had arrived for coffee and chatter. A well-timed visit, if her friend was ready for the insurmountable task of cheering her up.

"Come in." She filled his coffee mug and met him at the door.

Boney stepped inside, wearing trousers and a coat with a new felt hat. He sniffed the air like a hound on a hunt. "You must have known I was coming." She loved her whiskered friend's boyish grin. "You've been baking again." He lifted the tray off the countertop and took it and his cup to the table.

Baking usually helped her think, but she'd been doing far too much of both lately. She carried two plates and forks to the table, along with her cup of tea. "You're all shined up for the second time in less than a month. If I didn't know better, I'd think you were trying to woo me." She smiled and seated herself.

Boney's bushy eyebrows knit together. "I gave up on that a long time ago."

Hattie nodded. And for good reason. She didn't love him in that way.

He tugged on his neatly trimmed beard and sat down. "I have been seeing someone though."

"It's about time. You aren't getting any younger."

Boney opened his mouth as if to speak, but didn't.

"Harlan asked me to marry him." Hattie hadn't meant to blurt it out.

Boney blew out a long whistle. "You win. Your news is bigger than mine." He pointed a crooked finger at her. "You go first."

"Wednesday was a heavenly day. Harlan took Cherise clothes shopping and invited me along. We had such a grand time picking out skirts, frocks, and shirtwaists, even a couple of bonnets." She sipped her tea. "He bought my lunch at the café and took me and Cherise to the cabin to see Vivian's twins."

"It sounds like a cozy family time to me."

"It was." Dreaminess laced her voice, but she didn't care. "Then he said he wanted to talk to me privately." She stirred a little more sugar into her cup. "We went out on the porch swing. That's where he proposed."

Boney let out a low whistle. "And?"

"I said no."

Boney hung his head and peered at her. "You still have that bad habit, do you?"

She swatted at him as if he were a buzzing fly. "This is different."

"I would've thought so. You love him, don't you?"

"I might."

Boney slid an apple tart onto each of their plates and added forks. He looked at her, the lines at his eyes softening. "Remember, I've seen love on you before."

"I remember." Boney was there when she fell for George.

Boney sat back in his chair. "You love the little girl. And if you love Harlan Sinclair, why did you turn him down?"

"He needs a mother for Cherise. That's why he asked me."

He sighed and shook his head. "That's not enough for you."

"You know me well." Hattie reached for her teacup. "Now it's your turn. You said you're seeing someone. Anyone I know?"

"Etta Ondersma."

"Etta? I sat beside her at church yesterday, and she didn't mention anything to me about a fuzzy old miner courting her."

"Etta knows you and I are close friends. And I wanted to tell you myself. I knew I'd be coming over today."

"That's good." At least one widow in the district would…

"Are you jealous?" he asked.

"Don't be silly. We're not children, and this isn't the school yard." No matter how they acted at times. She reached across the table and patted his hand. "Companions are important, and I'm happy to hear you and Etta are together."

Boney raised his hand, his eyes wide. "Whoa. Back up the wagon. I haven't proposed or any such thing. I saw her at the post office, and we got to talking. Mostly about you. We went to the ice-cream parlor and visited. She invited me to the church picnic Sunday."

Hattie knew Boney. He wasn't superficial. He had been living in dusty coveralls for more than a dozen years and didn't slick up on a whim. He'd known Etta and her late husband for several years. He and Etta were already friends, which could form a solid foundation for a marriage.

Hattie wagged her finger in front of him. "One bite of Etta's sourdough bread rolls at the picnic, and you'll be in love."

"Then you ought to make sure Harlan gets a big dose of your fried chicken." He laughed, and she joined him.

A silly thought. But as soon as he left, she'd head to the grocer and buy three of his biggest chickens.

Thirty-Two

*S*usanna spritzed her neck with a rose-scented toilet water. She set the bottle on the tiny dressing table in her room and pressed her wrists into the spray. While camped in stage stops between Denver and Cripple Creek, she'd feared this day would never come.

She'd underestimated how long and dirty a six-day wagon ride between the two cities would be. Not to mention Mr. Johnstone's dreariness. He could bore a laughing hyena. And it was just her luck the attorney decided to leave his carriage at home so he could deliver a wagon full of furniture to his parents.

Despite her fear that she'd die in a scratchy bedroll out in the middle of nowhere, he did finally deliver her to a boardinghouse in Cripple Creek. That was late yesterday morning, nearly thirty hours ago. After two hot baths, she was finally feeling clean and rested enough to make her debut in town.

Susanna pulled the calendar and fountain pen off her bedside table, noted her arrival, and circled today's date. Friday, the fourteenth of October—the day she would reunite with Trenton Van Der Veer. She tucked a fresh handkerchief and a floral fan into her reticule, then lifted the purple hat off the bed. She used the pearl hatpins her father had given her last Christmas and pinned the hat in place, allowing for a flirtatious tilt. Adding a touch of rouge to her lips, she took one last glance at herself in the mirror. The purple dress she'd found in Denver was fitted perfectly and offered just the right balance between respectable lady and vixen. She pulled a golden curl down to frame her eyes, then nodded. Her reunion with the prestigious photographer would be fully developed by sundown.

Descending the staircase at the Downtowner Inn, she practiced what she hoped would be a tantalizing gait. She'd telephoned a boardinghouse called Miss Hattie's before leaving Denver, but the woman had no rooms available. This dive would have to suffice until she was able to move into a nicer place with Trenton.

The afternoon air was crisp, but the sun warmed her as she made her way to Bennett Avenue. The proprietor of the inn told her where she could find the Photography Studio, her first stop in town. Unlike Scandia, Cripple Creek's main street boasted new brick and sandstone buildings with brightly painted factory storefronts. Among other shops, including a confectionary, she'd seen a millinery, a fashion designer's shop, and at least two opera houses. The quaint little city would do until she was able to convince Trenton to pursue their dream of a studio in New York.

On First Street, she blew out a long breath and looked up at the wooden sign hanging over the boardwalk ahead of her: Photography Studio. She'd have to talk to Trenton about her ideas for a more creative business name. Something so trite would never do in a fashionable city like New York. But first things first.

Approaching the window in front of his shop, she fluffed the flouncing at her neckline and moistened her lips. Before she reached the door, a large framed sign propped in the window captured her attention: Portraits by Willow.

Susanna stared at it. Trenton had no doubt made the frame, but since when had he started offering painted portraits? And who was Willow?

She'd save the questions for later, after she'd melted his cold heart. She practiced an enticing smile in the reflective glass, then sauntered to the door. Locked. Then she noticed the slate board propped on an easel behind it.

I'll return at 4:00 p.m. Trenton's handwriting—neat and tidy.

Susanna knocked anyway, just in case he was there, behind one of the two closed doors on the back wall. No response. Just her luck that she'd gotten all gussied up for him, and he wasn't even here. She sighed, then lifted her chin. She'd just have to return after four o'clock.

In the meantime, she'd find out who this woman was who apparently worked for Trenton. All she needed was a busybody. She'd seen the post office on Bennett Avenue. Perhaps someone there could point her in the right direction.

Returning to the main street, Susanna chided herself for not considering the possibility that she might have competition for Trenton's affections. She hadn't given the likelihood a single thought. Why would she? The newspapers back home prided themselves on reporting the desperate need for women in the West. Why, she'd even read advertisements asking women to travel to California or Colorado as mail-order brides. A dreadful thought.

If Denver was an indicator, the reports of an overpopulation of men were accurate. The city where Helen's brother lived boasted a much higher percentage of men than women, and if the case here in Cripple Creek was any different, she had yet to see evidence of it. At least nine of the ten people she passed on the boardwalk or saw milling about were males.

Susanna glanced across the street at the post office. She'd cross at the next corner. She just knew she had nothing to worry about. Willow of Portraits by Willow was probably an ugly, old spinster with heaps of time on her hands for painting. Although her business name didn't sound particularly spinsterish. If not a spinster, then Willow was most likely a hag who had come west to snag a husband. Either way, Susanna needn't worry. Trenton was a man of culture and principles. He wouldn't become romantically entangled with a defective or married woman.

Susanna was across the street and approaching the post office when a boy not much past puberty stepped out the door, carrying an armload of packages.

"Excuse me, sir," she called.

He glanced behind him, then back at her, a shock of dark hair spilling over one eye.

"I was speaking to you, young man."

Nervous laughter shook his gangly shoulders. "You're new in town."

"I am, but I have friends here."

"My father's the only *sir* in our family. I'm Archie."

"Looks to me like you're doing the work of a *sir,* Archie."

He glanced at the packages. "Yes, well, among other things around here, I'm a courier."

"A very important job." She pressed a fingertip to her chin, tilting her head slightly. "Speaking of which, Archie, I understand you do a fine job delivering packages for my friend Trenton Van Der Veer, the photographer over on First Street."

"Yes ma'am. Gotten real busy since Mr. Van Der Veer hired Missus Peterson and they started sending packages back and forth."

Mrs. Unless he'd hired someone else as well. "Willow Peterson?"

"Yes. Portraits by Willow—has a nice ring to it, don't it?"

"It does." Just as she'd suspected, his portrait painter was married. "They must keep you awfully busy running back and forth to her place."

"Nah. Miss Hattie's isn't all that far." He glanced up the hill behind her.

Miss Hattie's Boardinghouse. The very one she'd called first for a room.

Why would a married woman take up residence at a boardinghouse?

Trenton signed the note and slid it into the package with the four photographs. Three people had commissioned portraits and one more wanted color added to the print. Hopefully, this person would be more agreeable with Willow than Mr. Flinn had been. If not, he'd cancel the job himself. The money was of far lesser value than her smile.

How anyone could be so rude to such a kindhearted woman was beyond his understanding. The image of Willow sitting at the counter in the ice-cream parlor sprang to mind. She'd looked so innocent and childlike sipping her creamy root beer. He'd like nothing more than to sit at one of those red tables with her.

Another foolish dream. He hadn't given himself to daydreaming until Willow balked at his scolding and blurted out her marital status. Her ability to enjoy life in the wake of adversity drew him to her. That and her intelligence. And the dimples.

He'd hoped Willow would have finished the Johnstones' portrait early and brought it in this afternoon. He'd rather hand the new photographs to her personally than send them by courier. She may have come by when he was out for his late lunch. He wound the string around the clasp on the envelope and looked at the wall clock: half past four. Probably too late to expect Willow to come by, but she'd no doubt appreciate knowing she had more work for next week. He'd take the package to her at Miss Hattie's Boardinghouse.

Trenton cleaned off his desktop and gulped the last of his lukewarm coffee. When the bell jingled on the door, he nearly choked on the sharp liquid.

Staring in disbelief, he stood. "Su-Susanna?"

She walked toward him, waggling from head to foot like a worm in rich soil.

"Why are y-you here?" he asked.

She took slow steps toward the end of the counter. "We had unfinished business when you had to rush off."

Talk about a skewed perspective. "How d-did you f-find me?"

"Were you trying to hide?"

He walked to the potbellied stove at the far wall and lifted the lid. Good. The fire was out. "I wa-wasn't trying to hide from anyone. C-Colorado wasn't one of the s-states on your list."

"Nor was it on yours." She rounded the end of the counter and rested her long, slender fingers on its edge. "You're a man of many surprises, Trenton."

"Y-you don't b-belong here." And neither did he belong here alone with her.

She draped her long blond hair over her shoulder. "I belong with you."

He leaned back, trying to regain some lost space, and glanced toward the door.

"Are you expecting Mrs. Peterson?"

How did she know about Willow?

Smiling, she looked at the sign in the window. Of course, the advertisement—Portraits by Willow. But her married name? It didn't matter. Susanna needed to leave.

He let the lid slam shut on the stove. "Y-you and I…are no longer b-betrothed."

"You never said that."

"I guess I assumed you'd f-figure it out when I c-caught you k-kissing the cabinetmaker. Or, at the v-very least, when I d-drove off in my wagon and ne-never returned."

"That was a peck on the cheek. We went to school together. I was just saying good-bye to him before you and I wed."

"I heard w-what you said to him."

"That only proves you can't believe everything you hear."

"Or that I c-can't believe anything you s-say." He grabbed his keys off the desk. "You have to l-leave."

"Why? Because you are involved with a married woman?"

Feeling slapped in the face, Trenton scrubbed his cheek and drew in a deep breath. Susanna didn't know him at all. How could he ever have entertained the thought of marrying her?

"N-not that it is any of your b-business," he said, "b-but Willow is a w-widow."

He hoped to at least see a hint of remorse, but it was amusement that brightened Susanna's eyes as she took a step toward him.

❧

Willow shut the door on her bedchamber and carried the package down the stairs. She'd finished the portrait yesterday afternoon, and it had finally dried after a full twenty-four hours. That meant she was cutting it close for catching Trenton before he left the studio for the day.

Stopping in front of the mirror in the entryway, she leaned the paper-wrapped canvas against a table leg. She adjusted a hatpin and brushed her cheeks. Satisfied that she looked more rested than she felt, she retrieved the package and stepped outside. When the cold air hit her, she reconsidered her decision to deliver the portrait. If her visit to the studio only concerned handing in the completed job, she'd rather perch by the fireplace in the parlor with a good book.

Sunday was coming, and for five days she'd been thinking of little else but her urgency for Trenton's soul and the invitation she'd prayed about.

Willow held the package against her as a barrier to the cold breeze and quickened her steps. So far she'd only painted two portraits from Trenton's photographs and colorized one. Mollie Kathleen's portrait was in the studio window for nearly a week with her business sign. By this time, Willow had expected to have more work than she could handle. Hopefully, Trenton would have a package of photographs for her.

Praying for the right words, she strolled up the boardwalk toward the Photography Studio. The closer she came to it, the faster her mind shuffled the memories of her recent time in Cripple Creek. Trenton Van Der Veer seemed to have the biggest stack of memories. From their first meeting and seeing him alone in the ice-cream parlor, to sitting on the bench with him in front of the post office and then accepting the fudge he bought her at Carmen's Confectionary. She blew out an unladylike breath. Entertaining such thoughts did her no good. He hadn't given her any indication he needed or even wanted a romantic relationship or a family. And most importantly, his spiritual convictions were still in question.

The plain wooden shingle still hung over the boardwalk. If she had enough time, she'd mention her ideas for a more fashionable name for his business and a more colorful sign. She stopped at the window to admire the advertisement one more time.

Portraits by Willow
Inquire Within

A fresh start far better than she'd imagined. Yes, she'd be forever grateful to Trenton for believing in her abilities when others would have turned her down simply because she was a woman.

She was reaching for the door handle when she caught a glimpse of Trenton behind the counter.

With a woman.

In close proximity.

Her insides twisting, Willow pulled her arm back and stepped away from the door as if it were hot. Trenton apparently wasn't as innocent as she'd imagined him. She leaned the canvas against the metal storefront, trying to steady her racing pulse. Feeling like a spy in a dime novel, she hid behind the column framing the doorway and peeked in the window.

The blond woman in a playful purple dress caressed Trenton's face. Willow's own face burned, witnessing such brash familiarity. Even if it was inside his own place of business.

How could he do this?

Her left hand knotted. But what she was feeling couldn't be jealousy. She had no cause to be jealous of this woman. She was merely Mr. Van Der Veer's employee, and he was free to conduct his personal life according to his own…

The young woman was so elegant looking. And she touched him.

Willow shuddered. She might have admitted to a twinge of jealousy if she weren't so disappointed. She grabbed the portrait and whirled around. She'd let Archie deliver her work.

This was her fault. Trenton hadn't made a personal commitment to her. She'd allowed her longing for love and family to set him on a faulty pedestal.

And if that woman hadn't just knocked him off it, she'd gladly bean him with the canvas and do so herself.

Susanna's fingers trailed Trenton's cheek. His skin tingled under her touch. It felt good.

But it didn't feel right. He couldn't trust himself to touch her hand to remove it, so he backed away. What was wrong with him? He couldn't let Susanna ensnare him again. He'd been expecting Willow to walk through the door. That was who he'd hoped to see...wanted to see.

Susanna stood frozen in place, hurt narrowing her blue eyes.

Trenton clasped his hands behind his back and drew in a deep breath. "You have to st-stop touching me."

"I'm sorry. I—" Her bottom lip quivered. A big tear rolled down her face. "I was just so glad to see you." In slow motion, she raised her hand to her face and swept away the tear. "I'd hoped you'd missed me too."

He had. The woman he'd once believed her to be, at least. He'd missed the idea of settling down with a wife and building a family.

"You can't stay."

"But I've come all this way."

"That was your doing, not mine."

"The way I feel about you, Trenton... I had to see you. We'd made plans for a wonderful life together." She pressed her lips together and sighed. "We were to be married."

"*Were.* That's past tense, Susanna."

She stretched the curl dangling beside her eye. "You can't tell me you were happy with the way things ended between us."

How could he be? She'd hurt him, and he'd turned tail and run, hoping to cause her the same kind of humiliation and pain. The guilt had ridden in the wagon with him, following him into his new life here. And now she'd done the same.

"Are you happy, Trenton?"

"I wasn't expecting you...this." He buttoned his jacket. "I need some time."

"Of course." She pressed her reticule to her midsection and gave him a silky smile. "I'm lodging at the Downtowner Inn."

"I'll telephone you there. Tomorrow."

She met his gaze and nodded. "Thank you." She turned and sauntered out the door with the same theatrical finesse with which she'd entered.

He sank into his chair. She'd left him alone to think. An impossible task, because right now his thoughts were as untrustworthy as his senses.

THIRTY-THREE

$\mathcal{S}$aturday morning Trenton stopped short of Golden Avenue and glanced at the envelope under his arm. Archie had brought the Johnstones' portrait by the studio early. What had gotten into him that he hadn't let the courier deliver the photographs to Willow?

If Willow had wanted to see him, she would have delivered the canvas herself. Thankfully, she'd chosen not to. The thought of her walking in while Susanna was trying to rekindle their relationship made him cringe.

"Mister?" A huge, sweaty man sat atop a mule-drawn wagon hauling a load of firewood. "You gonna go, Mister?"

"Yes. Thank you." Trenton waved at the driver and finished crossing the street.

He needed to see Susanna and pay for her return fare to Scandia, but he wanted to take care of this business first. He'd simply hand the package to the boardinghouse proprietor and be on his way. That was it. Although he'd be working during the picnic, he'd at least see Willow tomorrow. He found himself looking forward to the entire day. He knew a few of the folks, including some he counted as friends—Tucker Raines and his wife. And, of course, Willow.

The two-story boardinghouse stood at the end of a graveled walkway, looking bright and cheery in yellow with white trim. A few hardy sunflowers lingered in clay pots on the porch.

He'd stepped up to the door when it swung open. A woman with silver hair stared out at him, her mouth open and her blue-gray eyes wide. "Oh my lands. I hadn't a clue there was anyone out here."

"S-sorry, ma'am. Didn't mean to frighten you." He almost reached up to remove his hat, but remembered he hadn't worn one today. "Trenton Van Der Veer."

"You startled me some is all." She looked him up and down. "You're Willow's employer."

"Yes ma'am."

"Hattie Adams. I own this place." She extended her hand, and he obliged her handshake. "A good, strong handshake. Says a lot about a man, you know."

Trenton nodded, without a clue why he'd agreed with her. Or why he'd given her such a firm handshake. Given yesterday's circumstances, he felt more like a worm.

"It doesn't take much to put the color of beets into your face, does it?" she asked.

He laughed. "No m-ma'am, it doesn't. I inherited my f-father's fair skin."

She stepped back from the door. "Most folks call me Miss Hattie. Do come on in."

His feet leaden, Trenton held up the envelope. "Thank you, Miss Hattie. But if I could ask you to deliver this to Willow, uh…Mrs. Peterson, I'll be on my way."

"Don't be silly. What if she has questions for you?"

"The note I included is qu-quite thorough."

"I'm sure she'll want to see you." Miss Hattie motioned for him to join her inside. "She was in the kitchen last I heard."

He was in no hurry to see Susanna again, despite his warring emotions. Willow, however, he wasn't seeing nearly often enough to suit him. He closed the door behind him and followed the matronly woman through a well-appointed entryway.

⤴

Willow laid a crust over the apple pie filling and pinched the top and bottom
layers together into a scalloped edge. She wiped the flour on her hands onto her
apron. Despite her lack of sleep, she'd already scrubbed her paint palette clean,
washed and hung her clothing, and prepared two pies.

Since no one else was around, as Mr. Sinclair and Cherise had moved in
with Kat and Morgan for the time being, and Miss Hattie didn't mind how
Willow looked, she wore her plain checkered frock. She hadn't even bothered
to tame her hair in an upsweep. After what she'd witnessed from outside the
Photography Studio yesterday afternoon, her overactive mind had kept her
awake into the wee hours. She'd spent most of those hours writing letters to
Mother, Aunt Rosemary, and Maria.

She carried both pies to the stove and slid them into the oven. While the
pies baked, she'd clean the kitchen and finish reading one of the books she'd
borrowed from the library. Later, she'd take a short nap. A lazy afternoon
would suit her fine.

Trenton would have received the portrait last night and, hopefully, would
have more work for her on Monday. If he wasn't too busy with the woman who
couldn't keep her hands off him.

As Willow gathered the dirtied bowls and utensils, she heard the front
door close and remembered Miss Hattie was on her way to the Blue Front
Grocery for another chicken for tomorrow's picnic.

"Willow, dear?" Miss Hattie called.

"Did you forget something?" Willow lifted the stack of dishes off the table
to carry them to the sink.

"I met up with a visitor at the door. Someone who came to see you."

"To see me?" Willow turned. "Who is—"

Her employer stood in the doorway, looking quite rested with his hair
parted in the middle and slicked back with hair tonic. He wore brown trousers
and a grass-green shirt, not his usual business attire.

"Trenton." Why had he come to the boardinghouse?

"I should've waited for you in the p-parlor, but I'm glad I didn't. I wouldn't have wanted to m-miss this sight." He smiled, making her wonder if flour caked her face.

She removed the apron. She doubted the blonde in his studio would ever be caught with her hands in flour.

He sniffed and glanced at the oven. "Apple pie?"

"Two, for the picnic tomorrow."

"Your brother inv-vited me…to take photographs."

She wanted to ask if he planned to bring his lady friend with him but refrained. It was best they keep their private lives just that—private.

Trenton looked at the envelope he held, then at her gooey hands. "I have more jobs for you and p-payment for the Johnstones' portrait. Archie delivered it this morning. I was going to l-leave this with Miss Hattie, but she insisted I hand it to you myself."

Willow looked past Trenton at Miss Hattie. Amusement danced in her landlady's blue-gray eyes. "Yes, Miss Hattie is like that."

Miss Hattie tittered. "I'll clean the kitchen and watch the pies, dear. Why don't you and Mr. Van Der Veer conduct your business in the parlor?"

"Thank you." Willow faced Trenton. "I best wash my hands first."

Trenton nodded. The sight of his warm smile warred with the memory of what she'd seen through the window. She soaped her hands and scrubbed them under running water until they were clean.

"Here you go." He pulled the hand towel off the counter and handed it to her. "You did an excellent job on Mr. Johnstone's nose."

She giggled and dried her hands.

"On b-both of them."

"Both of his noses?"

Trenton's musical laugh followed her out of the kitchen and into the parlor. She sat in a wing-back chair, and he sat in the armchair, with only a side table between them.

She liked this man. Or at least she had until she'd seen him with another woman. She'd experienced jealousy, but it was more than that. He'd seemed a man of integrity, unlikely to be leading a double life. Until yesterday afternoon, she hadn't seen or heard any evidence he was involved with anyone. His attentions toward her, including his visit this morning, would lead her to believe his interest in her may run deeper than mere employment. And yet she'd clearly witnessed an intimacy between him and that woman.

Trenton cleared his throat. "I knew you'd finish the p-painting early, and I thought you m-might bring it in yesterday afternoon."

Willow rested her hands on the chair arms and looked at him. "I did."

His brow creased.

"I was there. Outside the window."

He swallowed hard. "You should've come in."

"To interrupt you and look like a fool?" Her voice, louder than she'd intended, cracked on the last word.

"To rescue me."

"You didn't look like you needed rescuing."

"Looks can b-be deceiving." His gaze collided with hers. "So can f-first impressions. Remember?"

She recalled their first meeting, and her heart melted.

Trenton stood and paced the room. "Do you care to hear my story?"

"You don't have to tell me, if you'd rather not."

"B-but I do." He met her gaze. "I want you to kn-know me."

She wanted to know him better, especially if he hadn't been guilty of what she'd imagined. "Yes. I'd like to hear it."

"I came to Cripple Creek from K-Kansas. That's where S-Susanna is from."

"The woman in the studio?"

"Yes. She and I were betrothed, and we planned our wedding for last month."

He was going to marry that young woman? She wanted to know why it had fallen apart, but it wasn't her business to ask. Instead, she picked a piece of lint from the arm of the wing-back chair. After an uncomfortable pause, she looked at him.

"I learned S-Susanna wasn't at all the w-woman I thought her to be," he said, "and I b-broke the engagement."

"And left Kansas."

"Yes. R-rather abruptly."

"She followed you here?"

He nodded. "I didn't know until yesterday, when she showed up at the s-studio." He looked at her, the anguish in his eyes confirming that he spoke the truth. "I sent her away."

"I didn't see that part."

"Except to p-put her on a train b-back to Kansas this afternoon, I want nothing to do with…with Susanna." The last phrase rushed out as one word. "You have to b-believe me."

"Why does it matter what I believe?"

"I care that you kn-know the truth."

She stood. "I have something I need to show you. Will you come with me?"

"Yes." Bewilderment creased his brow.

She held up a finger and hurried to the kitchen to let Hattie know of her plans, then went up to her room. She swept her hair up and changed into a walk-about-town dress.

When she returned to the parlor, Trenton smiled and followed her down the porch steps. They walked the few blocks to the church in silence but for the street sounds.

As the steeple came into view, Trenton turned to her. "I was here Sunday before last."

"I didn't see you."

"You looked for me?"

Her face warmed. "I did."

"I sat on the bench in the foyer."

Her first impulse was to giggle but she didn't. "We don't bite, you know."

"I hadn't been in a church for...since I was a boy." He stuck his hands into his trouser pockets. "My p-parents were ashamed of m-me...my stuttering. My m-mother took me to one speech therapist and th-then another. They had me p-practice saying the alph-phabet and read with marbles in my mouth. They even tried to s-scare it out of me. When those t-tactics didn't work, my f-father talked to the p-pastor of the only church in town."

"What did they expect him to do?"

He raked his hand through his hair, then met her gaze. "Rid me of demons."

A sadness settled on her heart. "Your parents believed the stuttering was of the—"

"It was the worst day of my life."

"It must have been awful!" Willow didn't need to tell him Tucker was different. He knew it, or he wouldn't have visited the First Congregational Church at all. "I would've hesitated to attend church too."

She continued up the pathway toward the parsonage and knocked on the door. Nothing. She pulled a key out of her reticule and unlocked the door.

"Perhaps we should return another time," Trenton said.

"They won't mind we're here. My brother likes you."

"I'd like to keep it that way." His easy grin chased away the sadness.

"You have nothing to worry about." She opened the door and stepped inside. "Ida? Tucker?"

No answer. The chill in the house told her they'd been gone awhile.

"What I want to show you is in the parlor."

When they reached the parlor, she added wood to the stove in the corner. The settee offered the most comfortable and direct view, but they were alone in the room, and it wouldn't be proper to sit together. Willow walked to the settee anyway. Standing behind it, she looked up at the first painting she'd done in Colorado—a landscape of Pikes Peak rising out of a bank of gray fog, tipped in pure white.

"Magnificent!" Trenton stood beside her.

"I painted my life story there."

"You painted that?"

Willow nodded, praying for the right words. Even if he hadn't darkened the sanctuary, he'd come to the church. Trenton Van Der Veer was seeking God, and she believed God was running toward him.

"I knew you were a gifted p-portrait painter," he said, "but this is—"

"When my husband Sam died and the grief hit me, I felt as if I had slipped into a thick fog bank."

His hand rested on the back of the sofa, his tender gaze fixed on her.

She drew in a deep breath. "I became so despondent that my father didn't know what else to do but to have me committed."

His eyebrows arched. "Y-you were institutionalized?"

"Yes." If he thought less of her, she didn't see it in his blue eyes.

"You don't owe me an explanation."

Willow held his gaze. "But I also want you to know *me* better." She never thought she'd be eager to tell her story.

His smile gave her all the encouragement she needed, and she explained what she'd learned about melancholia, told him about Tucker visiting her every week even though she couldn't remember or respond until she started receiving his letters from Cripple Creek.

"I never would've guessed you'd been through all that. You must've been so lonely."

"Somehow I knew God was there, with me, through it all."

"How did you know?"

"Even when I felt alone, I believed God's promise to never leave me or forsake me. I trusted that He would always meet my needs, and He has, even when I didn't recognize His hand." She glanced at the painting, then back at him. "The Lord's presence and His grace transcend all circumstances. God was in the fog with me and helped me break through it. Nothing can separate us from the sacrificial love of Jesus the Christ. Not the death of a husband, a father, melancholia—"

"Stutters and stammers?"

She shook her head.

"B-broken engagements?"

"No. Not a sorely misguided preacher either." She breathed another prayer for him. "God will use all our brokenness for good, if we'll allow it. And for those who believe in Jesus and accept His love, there is no condemnation."

"That's what Tucker was saying about the p-passage in Romans that Sunday."

She nodded, unable to press words past the tears clogging her throat.

He reached for her hand and squeezed it lightly, his touch warming her heart. "Thank you."

"You're welcome." She glanced at their joined hands, then into his glistening blue eyes.

Tucker and Ida appeared in the parlor doorway, their mouths gaping open. Trenton released her hand and stepped away, allowing for the proper space between them. But right now, it wasn't her reputation camped on Willow's mind. It was what she'd seen in Trenton's eyes and felt in his touch.

"When the front door was unlocked, we figured it was you in here, Willow. Robbers wouldn't use a key or leave the door open." Curiosity laced her brother's brown eyes.

Trenton shook Tucker's hand. "Willow...we came to look at her painting."

"It's good to see you again, Mr. Van Der Veer." A wide smile accented Ida's high cheekbones. Her sister-in-law was clearly amused by the surprise of finding the two of them together.

"Thank you. P-please, call me Trenton."

Willow glanced at the landscape. "I wanted to tell Trenton my story, and I knew it would be easier looking at the painting."

"Ah." Tucker stoked the stove and glanced at her. "Was I one of the good guys?"

"Always." She winked at her brother.

Ida removed her cape. "If you two haven't had lunch yet, I hope you'll join us."

Trenton met Willow's gaze. "I'd like to stay, but I have some business to attend to."

Susanna.

Willow nodded. The sooner he saw her on the train back to Kansas, the better.

"Another time then," Tucker said.

"Yes, I'd like that," Trenton said. "Thank you."

Willow would like that too. This was her best Saturday in four years. Trenton was indeed the man of integrity she believed him to be. He knew her story, and he hadn't cowered.

Run to him, Lord.

Thirty-Four

*M*eals with strangers, isolation, and a cold shoulder.

Susanna must have lost her mind to chase after a man who'd rejected her. She'd been just as desperate the day Helen walked in with the *Denver Post* as the day Trenton left her in Scandia with no prospects for a better future.

Trenton Van Der Veer was a bit eccentric with all his flasks and plates and saws, but still charming. A bit embarrassing at times with all the stammering, but a true gentleman with a talent that could take him—and her—into the homes of the upper tens in New York City. His connections with high society could gain her a spot onstage in one of the most prestigious opera houses in the country.

She hadn't expected Trenton to welcome her with open arms, but neither had she thought he'd resist her persistent attentions. That he'd leave her... alone.

Susanna walked to the window. Sighing, she pulled the tattered curtain back and looked outside. Men, women, and children packed the streets, all of them going somewhere with someone or something. Sunlight touched everyone but her. She let the curtain drop.

He said he'd do some thinking and they'd talk today. He'd had all night to ponder. It was nearly ten o'clock, so where was he? She'd already telephoned his studio but received no answer.

Trenton had changed.

No doubt the fault of the widow Willow Peterson, his portrait painter. Trenton had flinched and backed away from Susanna when she touched his cheek, but not before she'd made sure the woman outside the window had gotten an eyeful.

Would a mere employee or casual observer have scampered off like that? Not likely.

Still, Susanna was no better off than before she arrived in town. She couldn't just sit around waiting for the photographer and feeling sorry for herself. If Trenton preferred the more independent businesswoman-artist type, then she knew just how to put herself in the running.

Cripple Creek had at least one opera house. Her charms may not have worked on Trenton yesterday, but most opera house managers were men, and it wouldn't hurt to try her luck on one.

She glanced from the potbellied stove to the tiny table, from the too-soft chair to the single bed. If she stayed here a minute longer, she'd need the undertaker.

Thirty minutes later, Susanna stepped onto the boardwalk and strolled toward the Butte Opera House. She'd donned her mint-green taffeta dress and obtained a little information from the dowdy Mrs. Michaels, proprietor of the Downtowner Inn. According to her, a Mr. Myron Wilcox managed the Butte Opera House, and Susanna was on her way to meet him.

Clouds hung over the mountains that rimmed the pretty valley. Mrs. Michaels had told Susanna all about the fires of '96, and the new brick and sandstone buildings had given the city a fresh face. This was, after all, now "the center of commerce in the new state of Colorado."

She passed Glauber's Clothing, a millinery, even a fashion design store. She could live here and sing at the Butte until Trenton, or some other influential man, was ready to take her to the stages of New York.

Susanna continued to the opera house. These days, and especially in the West, plenty of women were making their own way. And she would be one of them. Was that what Willow Peterson was doing, or was she banking on Trenton's help and affections too?

The Butte Opera House wasn't as big as she'd hoped. It was little more than a storefront wedged in the middle of the block, but it was at least elegant, with gilded filigree and lettering on the glass door and side window. Susanna stepped into a small vestibule. Posters of past performances lined the walls. A rounded woman with a broom looked up from a side hallway.

"Can you tell me where I can find Mr. Myron Wilcox?" Susanna asked.

"He's in his office." The cleaning woman pointed to a closed door behind her.

"Thank you." Susanna tugged her skirt straight and took slow strides to the door. She moistened her lips before knocking.

"Come in." It seemed ironic that the manager of an opera house would sound like he'd been chewing on gravel.

A man with a hook nose sat behind a desk cluttered with papers and a stained porcelain coffee cup. He peered at her over wire-rimmed spectacles.

"Mr. Wilcox?"

"That's me." He studied her from the laced high-top shoes on her feet to the feather on her hat.

"I'm a singer, Mr. Wilcox."

His laugh stung her ears. "They all are, honey."

Squaring her shoulders, Susanna ran her finger along her jaw. "I'd like to audition for you."

He stood. His belly hung over his belt. "That's not how this works, missy."

"Susanna. Miss Susanna Woods." Her indignation was fast becoming fury.

"We bring in top-billed singers. I don't pull 'em in off the street." Another coarse laugh. "Where you from?"

"Kansas, but—"

"But nothing. You don't belong here." He stepped around the desk and looked her over again. "Leastwise, not as a singer. You might try the other opera house if you're okay with showin' your knickers in a vaudeville act."

Trenton reluctantly walked away from the parsonage. If he hadn't promised Susanna he'd think about what had happened between them in Kansas and what she'd said yesterday in the studio, a crowbar couldn't have pried him away from Willow Peterson and her family today. But he'd given Susanna his word, and it was already nearly noon. If he had any hope of seeing her onto a train today, he needed to get to it.

Pulling his coat tight, he turned left onto Bennett Avenue. He'd go to the depot first to see about the schedule. Saturdays seemed to draw even more people into town. Men, women, and children riding in wagons, pulling carts, and walking dogs. But the streets were no more crowded than his mind was with thoughts and images.

The image of Pikes Peak shrouded in clouds mingled with the image of Willow standing with him behind the sofa, her hand in his. The compassion he'd seen in her eyes. He hadn't told anyone about that pastor's attempt at exorcism. Not Susanna. Not even Jesse.

The Midland Terminal Railroad depot buzzed with activity. After he'd managed to obtain the train schedule for the day, Trenton walked to the Downtowner Inn, asking God for guidance.

Him…praying. That was definitely something new. And the thanks was due to Reverend Tucker Raines and his sister. Trenton had been right about Willow. She was a woman of confounding faith. *"God was in the fog with me and helped me break through it."* Her statements still echoed in his mind, challenging his heart. *"Nothing can separate us from the sacrificial love of Jesus the Christ."*

In sharp contrast to Miss Hattie's Boardinghouse, the Downtowner Inn sat in the middle of a busy city block. No front porch. No flowers. No lace curtains in the windows. If this was all Susanna could afford, perhaps she'd be anxious to accept his offer.

Trenton opened the door, jangling a bell overhead. When he stepped into a cramped entryway, a stick-thin woman appeared from a side doorway and wiped her hands on a soiled apron.

She looked him over and grinned, revealing gaps in her teeth. "You lookin' for a nice room and got yourself lost, did you?"

"No m-ma'am. I'm Trenton Van Der Veer. I'm here to see—"

"That's the new photographer's name." Her eyes narrowed. "You're him?"

"Yes ma'am."

"You here to see Susanna Woods, are you?"

"I am."

"She left this morning after breakfast."

Until he heard his deep sigh, Trenton hadn't realized he'd been holding his breath. Dare he entertain the relief easing the tension in his shoulders? Had Susanna really given up and left town on her own?

"No doubt she'll be back before dinner," the woman continued.

His shoulders tightened. "Miss Woods didn't l-leave town?"

The proprietor shook her head in short wobbles. "Didn't take her bags with her, if she did. Besides, she's paid up for another week."

If Susanna was still in town, he obviously hadn't gotten through to her. "Did Miss Woods mention where she was going?"

"Not a word about it."

Well, there was nothing he could do for Susanna if he couldn't find her. And he refused to hunt her down. He didn't want to take any chance at encouraging her childish notion that the two of them could become a couple again. He'd much rather purchase a box of pecan fudge for a certain portrait painter.

✺

Hattie pulled another of her shirtwaists from the line and dropped the clothes-pins in her apron pocket. She added the shirtwaist to the basket on the ground, also adding to the list of reasons she missed having Mr. Sinclair and Cherise around the boardinghouse. She liked having men's shirts and little girls' dresses hanging on her line. She added more pins to the apron and a dressing gown to the basket.

Having Harlan and Cherise in the house had stirred something inside her. They'd felt like family. Now Kat was preparing Harlan and Cherise's meals and laundering their clothes, and she already had more than her share to do. A doctor's wife. A mother with a little one and another baby on the way. A monthly column to write for *Harper's Bazar*. And now she was an experienced midwife. Kat didn't have any time to spare.

Hattie pinched the last pin and released her navy-blue walking skirt. She was considering paying Kat a visit this afternoon to offer her help when a styl-ish young woman stepped around the corner of the house. Hattie added the folded skirt to the stack of clothes in the basket and smiled at her guest. "Good day."

"Mrs. Peterson?" As the young woman drew closer, her brow crinkled and a slow smile lit her blue eyes. A beaded reticule hung from one arm. "You're Willow Peterson?"

"No, dear." Hattie felt a peculiar satisfaction in upsetting the young wom-an's expectations. "Willow is much younger than I am."

"Oh." The young woman's mouth lingered in the shape of an *O*.

"Willow is one of my boarders. I'm Hattie Adams, the owner." Hattie untied her apron and dropped it into the basket, then picked up the bundle and, balancing it on a hip, walked toward her guest. "You are?"

"Yes, of course, pardon my poor manners, ma'am." Her guest straightened and tugged at the scalloped hem of her paisley jacket. "I'm Miss Susanna Woods."

"Miss Woods." The niggle in Hattie's stomach kept her from saying it was a pleasure to meet her. It may have just been the two extra pieces of sausage she'd eaten at the breakfast table, but something didn't feel quite right.

Miss Woods's eyes narrowed, and she cocked her head. "Mrs. Peterson didn't mention me?"

"No." Hattie shifted the basket to her other hip. "But we've both been busy chasing our tails to get where we're going."

Miss Woods quirked a thin eyebrow. "Might you know when you expect her?"

"Well, it's hard to say. Fact is I've lost track of time."

"Last I checked, it was half past eleven."

"My, oh my, but time is flying." Hattie tucked a pesky strand of hair into the bun at the back of her head. "I would've thought they'd have returned by now."

Miss Woods moistened her lips. "They?"

"Yes. Willow and her employer left here well over an hour ago."

Her visitor's shoulders drooped. Did this have more to do with Mr. Van Der Veer than Willow?

"Would you like to come in and have a cup of tea while you wait?" Hattie asked.

Miss Woods pressed her reticule to her midsection. "No. Thank you."

That settled it. A young woman who refused tea with her was clearly up to no good. "May I give Willow a message? Does she know where to find you?"

"No thank you." Miss Woods drew in a deep breath. "I'd rather surprise her. Good day, Mrs. Adams."

Hattie nodded. "Miss Woods."

She didn't like to make a habit of judging strangers, but if she was pressed to offer her opinion, she'd pronounce that one a tower of trouble.

THIRTY-FIVE

*W*e've both been chasing our tails to get where we're going."

What kind of gibberish was that?

Susanna marched down the hill toward Bennett Avenue. Trenton—*her* Trenton—was with Willow Peterson. And that woman at the clothesline likely knew where he'd taken her, but wouldn't say. Susanna wouldn't have lasted a full day living in that house, no matter how comfortable the amenities or delectable the food. Hattie Adams was a mother hen, and Willow was obviously in her brood. Was Hattie Adams that way with all her boarders, or just the ones trying to steal another woman's man?

Susanna had hoped to at least meet Willow. How else was she to determine the best approach to the situation?

At the corner, she glanced both ways on Bennett. It wasn't a bad looking town, with shiny new brick buildings lining its main street and plenty of people coming and going for commerce and culture. But Cripple Creek wasn't New York, and she hated roadblocks and detours. Willow Peterson, Myron Wilcox, and Hattie Adams among them. She'd experienced more than her fair share of diversions and frustrations since her arrival in town, and she'd had enough.

She slid her hand into the empty seam pocket on her skirt. Her father had given her enough money for the train to Denver and to tide her over until she'd found a job, but it was more costly to lodge here than she had anticipated. It was time she came up with a new plan. She seated herself on the empty bench in front of the post office and tucked her reticule, with the small amount of cash that remained to her, under her skirt.

Whatever was she to do now?

The mere thought of appearing in a vaudeville act liked to have brought on the vapors. Was she to give up on Trenton after traveling all this way? Perhaps she should return to Denver and find a man there? The image of Mr. Johnstone seated beside her on a rickety wagon for days on end made her yawn and want for a washstand. No thank you. Being a city lawyer might make him a good provider, but it didn't make him a good partner. But she couldn't return to Kansas, not like this.

She squared her shoulders. Susanna Woods was not a quitter, and she wouldn't leave town without her man. All she needed was a plan to get her back on track. If Trenton Van Der Veer did have romantic notions toward Willow Peterson, he'd forget them. And Myron Wilcox would rue the day he refused her an audition. Even Hattie Adams would take notice. Yes, all she needed was a fresh approach. She gathered her reticule, lifted her chin, and stood.

A Help Wanted sign in a shop window on the next block had caught her attention. The job would certainly qualify as another dreary detour, but considering where she and Trenton first met, perhaps this particular deviation could work to her advantage.

"Miss Woods, do you have any questions?"

Susanna looked up from the price listing she'd been studying. Her new employer slid a tray of caramels into the display case under the counter. A crowd from the midday show at the opera house had just left the shop with boxes of sweet treats.

"Except for the absence of buttermints, the list looks pretty much the same as my father's offerings," Susanna said.

Miss Carmen tugged her smudged white apron down at her waist.

"Westerners seem to prefer horehounds, licorice, caramels, taffy, and fudge." The apron would stop at the knees on anyone of average height, but the candy maker's draped her calves, becoming a fringe on her simple cotton frock. "Opera goers seem to favor caramels and chocolates, about cleaned me out. I'll be in the back if you need me."

When Miss Carmen disappeared through the swinging doors, Susanna pulled a damp cloth from a bucket of warm water and wiped down the inside of the display case. She should be entertaining those opera goers instead of serving them. If she hadn't just started her job when they'd come in, she would've broken into an aria. Let them tell Mr. Wilcox he was a fool not to hire her. Instead she was cleaning sticky residue off glass shelves. Not much had changed for her. Rejected in Kansas. Rejected in Colorado.

When the bell above the door jingled, she returned the rag to the basket and greeted her customer, midturn. "Welcome to—"

Her former fiancé came to an abrupt halt halfway to the counter. His eyes bugged, Trenton looked as if he might turn right back around, but he didn't. Clearing his throat, he took deliberate strides toward her.

Breathe, Susanna. Breathe.

Trenton was a more complicated man than she'd given him credit for. Willow Peterson was probably more genteel and composed.

She could do genteel and composed.

"Susanna?" Trenton glanced toward the swinging doors, no doubt looking for Carmen. "I didn't expect to s-see you here. B-behind the counter."

"You were right to take some time to think, Trenton. It gave me time to do a little more thinking myself."

"It did?"

"Yes. A lot of time and miles have passed between us. I know I've changed considerably, and I'm sure you have too."

His brow creased, he stared at the display case, no doubt contemplating the changes.

"I didn't mean to rush you, Trenton." She relaxed her tone for emphasis. "It was wrong."

"Yes, well, thank you." He met her gaze. "I knew Miss Carmen was looking for help, but…" He glanced at the window where she'd seen the Help Wanted slate. "You work here?"

"Yes, as of this afternoon." She pressed her ring-deprived left hand to her collarbone. "When I didn't hear from you…"

"I…didn't expect to be busy this morning, but—"

"I understand." She swallowed the truth—she knew he'd been busy entertaining Willow—and offered what she hoped was a demure smile. "Time can slip away when you're working."

He nodded. "I went by the Downtowner Inn, but you'd already left."

"Cripple Creek is a booming city. I can see why you like it."

Trenton shifted his weight. "It's c-certainly not New York, b-but I'm adjusting to it."

"I thought about it and decided the best way for me to meet people is to work in town, and since I know this business…"

"But—"

"I wondered if you still have your sweet tooth. Did you come for chocolate-dipped strawberries? We still have some, even though strawberries will soon be completely out of season."

The back doors swung open and Miss Carmen spilled out, carrying a tray of chocolates. "Mr. Van Der Veer. Nice to see you again, and so soon."

A sudden blush tinged his ears pink. "And you, Miss Carmen."

"Miss Woods, would you bring the tray of pecan fudge from the kitchen?"

Was her employer trying to get rid of her? Was Carmen another of Willow Peterson's mother hens?

Breathe, Susanna. Breathe.

"Of course." Susanna did a slow spin toward the swinging doors.

"He'll need a pretty pink box too, won't you, Mr. Van Der Veer?" Miss Carmen said.

"Yes ma'am."

Her hands curled into fists, Susanna stomped into the back room. Willow Peterson apparently favored pecan fudge, and Trenton favored her.

For now.

He was wound tighter than a cheap pocket watch, not ready to go home or even to the studio.

Trenton walked up Bennett Avenue without a destination in mind. His insides churned with each step. Susanna should never have come looking for him in the first place. He had picked up the train schedule for her with the intention of offering to pay her fare back to Kansas, but he hadn't had the chance to make the offer. Instead of leaving town as she should, Susanna secured a job at the candy store, the very spot his and Willow's relationship began.

He needed a man to talk to. Jesse was in Victor today. Trenton had met a lot of the businessmen in town, but it was Tucker Raines who came to mind. Trenton smiled and turned up the hill toward the First Congregational Church. If anyone had told him he would one day think of a reverend as his friend, well, he would have thought it absurd.

Susanna *was* right about one thing—Trenton had changed. His lifestyle, his thinking, and what he'd believed for so many years. Not all preachers were the same. Tucker had come by the studio and befriended him, not judged him. Even when he'd found Trenton in his house with Willow this morning, he'd welcomed him to stay for lunch.

The white steeple came into view and another thought crossed Trenton's mind. He wanted to talk with Tucker, but what if Willow was still visiting?

He'd take that chance. Seeing her always did him good. Besides, he needed to tell Willow that Susanna was still in town, to reassure her that it wasn't his preference.

He'd just walked past the church building and was on the path to the parsonage when he heard Tucker call his name. Trenton turned toward the voice coming from the foyer.

Tucker walked down the front steps of the church toward him. "If you changed your mind about lunch, you're a little late."

Trenton chuckled. "No. Do you have a f-few minutes?"

"Sure. How about a cup of coffee?"

"Sounds good."

"Ida's gone to work at the icebox showroom for a couple of hours. I was looking over my sermon notes for tomorrow when I saw you walk by." Tucker led the way up the steps and through the familiar church foyer to the open door of a small office. He tapped the top of an armchair, then walked to a potbellied stove in the corner. "Have a seat."

Trenton seated himself and studied his surroundings. The space was small but comfortable. A Bible, an oil lamp, and a pair of reading glasses sat atop a modest desk. Trenton was especially thankful for the two chairs and table off to the side. Sitting across the desk from Tucker would've felt too formal. Although nothing about this preacher seemed stuffy or starched.

Tucker handed him a cup of steaming coffee, then poured one for himself and sat in the second armchair.

Trenton drew in a deep breath. "I would imagine Willow st-stayed for lunch."

"She did, and I know she wished you could've stayed too."

"I would have preferred to stay." Trenton gulped down some coffee. "Did she s-say anything about seeing a w-woman in my office yesterday?"

Tucker's eyebrows formed an arch, and he shook his head.

"She came fr-from Kansas."

"Someone from your past?"

"Yes. We were to be m-married, but she proved to be s-someone I could not be married to."

Tucker set his coffee mug on the side table between them and leaned back in the chair.

"She showed up in the studio yesterday afternoon and was...uh, making advances—"

"When Willow came by?"

Trenton nodded, sighing.

Tucker blew out a low whistle.

He took another gulp of coffee. Why was he talking to Tucker about his woman trouble? Especially when the trouble was that he cared about Tucker's sister and what she thought of him. Given the recent changes he'd been thinking about, the answer shouldn't have been that puzzling. He'd spent a lot of years running from who he was and who others believed him to be, and now he wanted to be known by those he cared about. And he counted Tucker among them.

"I sent Susanna away. And until this m-morning, I didn't know Willow had witnessed our discussion."

Tucker peered at him from over the top of his cup. "You care for my sister."

"I do." Trenton's choice of words caused a warm blush to rush up his neck. "Very much, I'm afraid." It shouldn't matter that Susanna had remained in town, except he considered her a loose cannon, unsure of her next move. She'd been too gracious in the confectionary.

"Susanna is the reason you didn't stay for lunch?"

Trenton nodded. "I took the afternoon t-train schedule to the inn, but she w-wasn't there. I thought I'd get some candy for Willow, so I went to the confectionary."

Tucker smiled. "She'll like that."

"Susanna was behind the counter."

"She plans to stay?"

Trenton shrugged. "She won't find what she's looking for. There's not much chance she'll be here long."

"She didn't come here to find you?"

"Yes and no. She fancies herself a singer."

Tucker lifted his cup from the table and met his gaze. "And you have connections in New York."

"It took me awhile to figure out, but yes, that is what she's hanging her hopes on."

"You were smart to walk away from that one."

Trenton drew in a deep breath. "All th-that said, I would like very m-much to court your sister. If you have no objections."

Tucker raised a thick eyebrow. "If you haven't noticed, Willow has a mind of her own."

Trenton had noticed, the very first time they'd met. He chuckled and nodded. "In our discussion about the j-job as portrait p-painter, I offered her a seventy percent commission. Wi-Without batting an eyelash, she said, 'Seventy-five percent seems more equitable.'"

Tucker chuckled. "That sounds like my sister, all right."

"There's more."

"Oh?"

"I told Willow why I'd determined to never s-set foot in a church again, w-why I'd decided I didn't need God in my life."

"And now?"

"I was listening in the foyer that Sunday. What you said started me thinking, and set me to reading the Bible my grandmother gave me. This morning, Willow talked about the sacrificial love of Jesus the Christ. She said that for those who believe in Jesus and accept His love, there is no condemnation." Trenton leaned forward, his elbows on his knees. "I need that. I need Him."

"That's great news." Tucker's smile was genuine. "And for what it's worth, I approve."

"Of me needing God?"

"Of you courting my sister."

Trenton liked the sound of that.

Tucker walked to his desk and brought a worn leather Bible back to the chair. "Let's talk about your decision."

THIRTY-SIX

*S*unday morning Willow lifted her two apple pies off the backseat of the surrey. Thankfully, Mr. Sinclair and Cherise had also arrived at the church early. Without hesitation, Mr. Sinclair reached for Miss Hattie's generous pan of fried chicken, while Cherise grabbed two loaves of honey-wheat bread. Miss Hattie carried a stack of tablecloths.

Mr. Sinclair lifted the corner of the lid on the fried chicken and licked his lips.

"Not a single bite until the picnic," Miss Hattie groused with a grin teasing her face.

He pretended to reach into the pan. Miss Hattie shifted the tablecloths and swatted at his hand. Mr. Sinclair and Cherise laughed. Cherise peeked into the bread sack, sniffed, and pretended to take a bite.

Miss Hattie wagged her finger at the child, then looked at Mr. Sinclair. "What a fine influence you are." Her smile defied the mock sternness in her voice.

"She can't catch both of us, Cherise," Mr. Sinclair said.

"But I'll catch you, Harlan Sinclair." Miss Hattie's face flushed. "I know precisely how many pieces of chicken I cooked, and every last one of them better be there when the picnic begins."

The three of them were already more of a family than some families, and they belonged together. There was no doubt in Willow's mind Mr. Sinclair loved Hattie. Did he not know it?

The church kitchen door was propped open. Ida looked at Willow from the stove. "I'm glad you're here. I'm short two workers."

Willow set her pies on the table next to a cake and smiled at her sister-in-law. "I do like to be needed. I understand why Vivian's not here yet, with the twins to care for, but where are Kat and Nell?"

Ida looked at her father. "Morgan telephoned after you left the house. Kat's baby is on its way. Nell went to be with her."

"More babies to bounce on your knee." Miss Hattie sounded farther away than the stool in the corner. "That's wonderful."

"It is wonderful," Mr. Sinclair said, "but my girls are making a nervous wreck of me."

"Two babies again?" Cherise's eyes shone like black diamonds.

Miss Hattie squeezed the child's shoulders like a mama would. "We do like babies, don't we?"

Cherise nodded. "I like holding them."

Mr. Sinclair smiled at Hattie. "If you ladies will excuse me, I'll leave you to guard my chicken while I go find a couple of my sons-in-law."

Willow's heart told her Trenton would be in the sanctuary this morning. She'd rather go find him, but it looked like she'd be helping her sister-in-law until the service started.

❧

Trenton drove his buckboard to the First Congregational Church Sunday morning. After their talk yesterday, Tucker said he was welcome to store his photography equipment in the reverend's office until the picnic.

As the familiar steeple came into view, an unfamiliar anticipation stirred inside Trenton. For the first time in his life, he felt drawn to attend church and truly ready for something more in his life.

Willow seemed ready too. She'd cared enough about him to show him her painting and share her story.

At the hitching rail, he pulled his tripod off the floor of the wagon.

"Trenton Van Der Veer?" An unfamiliar man's voice drew closer.

Trenton turned toward a warm smile. "Yes. Trenton." He shifted the tripod and shook the man's hand.

"Judson Archer." Clean-shaven, he wore trousers and a dress shirt. "I'm one of Tucker Raines's brothers-in-law."

"Yes, one of the men in the Wednesday morning Bible study."

"That's right, and if you're thinkin' about marryin' Willow, you're welcome to join us."

Trenton's mouth went dry. Tucker hadn't mentioned any prerequisites.

Judson's laugh was as easy as his smile. "I was teasing. Tucker said you were coming today, that you could probably use a little help." He took the tripod from Trenton and glanced at the wagon. "Anything else?"

Trenton pulled the camera and the box of glass plates off the wagon floor. "I'll grab these. Thanks." He followed Judson up the steps and through the foyer, searching for Willow in the gathering crowd.

"Tucker says you're new in town," Judson said.

"About three months now."

As Judson turned down a hallway, he spoke over his shoulder. "Good to have you here—in town and at the church." The man with the permanent smile tapped on a closed door. "It's Judson and Trenton, the photographer."

"Trenton." Tucker's voice was welcoming. "Come in."

Tucker and a dark-haired man in a black leather vest rose from armchairs. Trenton recognized the second man as Cripple Creek's chief at the police department.

"I didn't m-mean to interrupt."

"You didn't." Tucker shook Trenton's hand. "We meet for prayer every Sunday morning, and we just finished. Glad you came." He glanced toward the table. "You can set your things back there. I'll lock my office, and we can come get 'em before the picnic."

"Sounds good."

Tucker turned to the dark-haired man. "Carter, I'd like you to meet my friend Trenton Van Der Veer, Cripple Creek's new photographer."

Trenton shook Carter's hand. "You're the police chief."

Tucker slapped Carter's back. "And father to a fresh set of twin girls."

"Congratulations." Carter Alwyn had the *something more* Trenton was feeling ready for—a family. With Willow.

"Thanks." Carter lifted a steaming cup off the desk. "I've seen your shop on First Street."

"Stop in next time," Trenton said. "I keep hot coffee on the stove too."

Carter tugged the points on his vest. "Good to know. Thanks."

Tucker looked from Carter to Judson. "These two are part of Willow's extended family—they both married Sinclair sisters. My third brother-in-law, Dr. Morgan Cutshaw, is home pacing the floor while his wife delivers their second baby." Tucker lifted his Bible from the desk and looked at Trenton. "Guess we better get in there before our women come looking for us."

Trenton liked the sound of that.

After the church service, Willow carried her two pies to the tables the men had arranged for the picnic. Walking beside her, Ida held Hattie's pan of fried chicken.

"Do you want the desserts anywhere in particular?" Willow asked.

Ida breathed what Willow recognized as a thinking breath. "On that far end, perhaps?" She pointed to the table closest to the sycamore tree.

Willow nodded and carried the pies to the last table. She, Ida, Vivian, Cherise, Hattie, and Etta Ondersma, among other women, were setting out the lunch. They'd already carried out the table settings. Tucker had announced that they would first satisfy their bellies, then gather for the camera.

Etta was right behind them with a big basket of her sourdough rolls. She studied Willow's pies. "Apple?"

"Yes. My specialty." According to Sam, anyway. She was anxious to find out if Trenton agreed.

Etta's gaze swept the three food tables and the growing bounty. "Everything looks delicious."

Willow nodded, making room for the pineapple upside-down cake Vivian carried toward them, but her mind wasn't focused on lunch. She watched as Trenton started up the hillock with his tripod and camera bag. He'd not only come to the church this morning but joined the congregation in the sanctuary. She was already seated beside Ida and her family when Trenton walked in with Tucker, Carter, and Judson, looking relaxed and happy to be there, and sat on the aisle next to Judson.

She was anxious to talk to him about what had happened yesterday with Susanna and with Tucker, but he was here to do a job and needed to set up for the church photograph. This wasn't the time or place. If he'd shared anything about Susanna with Tucker, her brother hadn't said. But before Tucker went to his office this morning for prayer, he did mention Trenton's visit to the church yesterday afternoon and that her employer had placed his faith in Christ. Her own heart was still soaring and praising God for answered prayer.

"He's a good man."

Willow turned toward Vivian. "He is."

"And it looks to me…" Vivian paused as she studied Willow's face. "I'd say you've changed your mind."

"Changed my mind?"

"The day of my wedding last year, you said you'd had your turn at love."

She remembered. "Yes, the memory of Sam was still too fresh."

"And now?"

"I may have changed my mind." She held Vivian's brown-eyed gaze. "Any word from Nell on the baby?"

"Not yet, ye lady of diversion."

Willow offered her honorary sister a coy grin and curtsied before starting back to the church kitchen for another load of food. She knew who she'd choose for a second chance at love, but it wasn't up to her. After Trenton's troubles with Susanna Woods, she wouldn't blame him for shying away from opening his heart again.

THIRTY-SEVEN

*H*attie spread the remaining pieces of chicken on the platter. Harlan had taken two thighs when he first filled his plate and come back for seconds. She smiled, remembering her conversation with Boney on Monday. She'd told Boney that after one bite of Etta's sourdough bread rolls at the picnic, he'd be in love. He'd laughed and told her she ought to make sure Harlan got a big dose of her fried chicken.

She'd done her part. Cooked up five fryers. The rest was up to Harlan.

A little boy returned for another slice of her honey-wheat bread, and she patted his head. After she cleaned up a couple spills on her tablecloth, she stole another look at Harlan. The dapper father of the Sinclair sisters sat cross-legged on a blanket under a sycamore tree, surrounded by his family. Hope wiggled on his lap, her giggles traveling on the slight breeze. Vivian sat beside him, holding one of the twins. Ida held the other twin, while Cherise rolled a ball with William.

Etta Ondersma approached and fussed with a couple of salad bowls. Concern fanned the lines that framed her hazel eyes. "You and Boney have been friends for a lot of years. Are you sure you don't mind that he and I are seeing each other? I would've told you, but Boney wanted to tell you himself."

Hattie removed an empty salad dish from the serving table. "I think it's wonderful. Unless you plan to tell me I can't see my friend."

Etta smiled. "I have no intention of breaking up any friendships." She stirred a potato salad and straightened a bread basket. "As a matter of fact..."

She glanced at the Sinclair family. "I'm hoping the four of us can go out to supper sometime."

Hattie sighed. "You, my friend, are suffering from a bad case of wishful thinking."

"I wouldn't be so sure about that. He can't seem to get enough of your fried chicken. He'd probably come back for more if you weren't watching him so closely."

"I'm not."

Etta creased her brow.

"All right. I am," Hattie said.

"And you're not alone. Whenever you're not looking at him, he's stealing a glance at you."

"He isn't."

"You know he is."

Hattie resisted the impulse to look at Harlan. "We're a couple of old widows behaving like schoolgirls."

"Fun, isn't it?"

It'd be more fun if Harlan Sinclair loved her.

"Hattie, you were so right about Vivian. She's a wonderful designer. Business has more than doubled since she opened the shop here." Etta brushed a graying tuft of blond hair from her cheek. "I wouldn't be surprised if it doubles again when she starts taking those adorable babies to the shop."

"You know I'll be there," Hattie said. Vivian's mother would have been so proud of her. Hattie certainly was. "All four of the Sinclair sisters are hard working."

"And talented. Just this week I read Kat's most recent article in *Harper's Bazar*. A mesmerizing story about our very own Doc Susie."

"Yes, I read it too. Wonderful writing."

Harlan walked toward the table alone, his steps purposeful. Where was he putting all that chicken?

"Hattie, can you spare the time for a stroll?" he asked. Her whipped butter wasn't as smooth as his voice.

Etta took the empty salad dish from her. "Boney and I will watch the tables."

Harlan offered Hattie his arm, and she laid her hand on his shirt sleeve, sending a shiver up her spine. They walked toward the parsonage in silence.

The butterflies were back in her stomach. He wanted to talk to her alone. Was it to plead his case that she'd be the perfect substitute mother for Cherise?

When they reached the parsonage gate, she looked at him. "Any word from Nell? Has Kat delivered the baby?"

"We're still waiting to hear." He guided her to the white cast-iron bench among the stand of golden aspen trees.

Hattie sat down, but he remained standing and cleared his throat. Knots replaced the butterflies in her stomach. Had something happened to Kat and the baby? Was that why he'd taken her away from the crowd?

"Are you sure everything is all right?" she asked.

He removed his bowler. "She's fine." He cleared his throat again. "At Vivian's, the day you went shopping with Cherise and I..."

"Yes."

"I'm afraid I may have misrepresented myself on the porch."

"Oh?" He hadn't meant to propose marriage?

"I asked you to marry me, to be my wife and a mother to Cherise."

"Yes. I remember."

He knelt on one knee in front of her.

The butterflies returned with reinforcements.

He clasped her hand in his and looked her in the eye. "Hattie Adams, it is a treasured gift to have a friend who has so generously poured herself into the lives of my four grown daughters these past two years."

Tears stung her eyes.

"And the way you've come alongside Cherise," he continued, "you've helped her in ways I never could."

"It has been my pleasure." Her voice cracked with emotion. Where was he going with all this?

"But, Hattie, it is especially wonderful when the woman you love can make the world's best fried chicken."

Tears spilled onto her cheeks. "The woman you love?"

He nodded. "I think I knew it the minute I saw the burned potatoes."

She blotted her wet face.

He squeezed her hand. "Hattie, would you do me the honor of marrying me?"

"I love you too, Harlan. Yes, let's be married."

She bent to kiss him on the forehead, and he surprised her, lifting his face and touching his lips to hers.

All her wishful thinking had found a home, and so had her heart.

Willow shifted her gaze from beneath the tree, where Trenton was setting up his camera and tripod, to the parsonage. She and Ida had both watched Mr. Sinclair take Miss Hattie away from her duties at the food tables.

"Did your father tell you his plan?" Willow asked.

Ida reached for her cup of apple cider. "Not in so many words, but I hope he's telling her the truth. His feelings for her aren't limited to her maternal qualities."

"I hope you're right. Anyone can see the two of them belong together."

"Sometimes what is crystal clear to others isn't as obvious to the people involved." Ida's eyebrow angled to match her grin.

And sometimes it was apparent to one of the people involved long before it dawned on the other. Did Trenton have any idea of her feelings for him?

"I suspect we'll have another wedding around here." Ida peered over the cup at her. "A double wedding, perhaps." There went that eyebrow again.

Willow's face warmed despite the cooling temperature. Her sister-in-law had posed it as a statement rather than a question. "Trenton and I are still getting acquainted with each other."

A demure smile lit Ida's face. "So are Tucker and I."

Willow remembered yesterday and her time with Trenton. *I want you to know me,* Trenton had said after she told him she didn't need the details of his past with Susanna. What Tucker said rang true for her—the more she knew Trenton, the more she loved him.

There, she'd admitted it. At least to herself.

"Nell!" Ida pointed to the road, and they both stood.

Nell scurried toward them.

Vivian walked up. "A niece or a nephew?"

"A nephew." Winded, Nell patted her chest. "Ezra Harlan Cutshaw."

"After Father," Ida said.

"And Morgan's grandfather." Nell drew in a deep breath.

Willow joined the sisterly hugs. "And they're well?"

"Yes. Kat and Ezra are doing fine. Napping." Nell studied the nearby blankets. "Where's Father?"

Vivian glanced toward the parsonage. "Father took Miss Hattie for a stroll."

"I see." Romantic notions colored Nell's voice. "We'll tell them about the baby later."

Ida nodded. "I suspect he and Hattie may have big news of their own by then."

When the sisters started comparing notes on their father's relationship with Miss Hattie, Willow decided to go for a stroll by herself. Announcing her departure would only draw unwanted attention and speculation, which would probably have been too accurate for her comfort, so she slipped away during a hardy laugh.

She visited for a moment with Boney, then headed to the food tables. Etta Ondersma was busy talking with a couple of other women at the far end. Willow searched out her pie plate: empty. She bent to the crate under the table and pulled out the second pie.

"Saved one for the photographer, did you?" Etta stood beside her.

"Not the whole pie."

Etta laughed. "If I'd-a let him, Boney would've eaten the whole basket of my sourdough rolls."

Hopefully, Trenton would go for her apple pie like Mr. Sinclair had gone for Miss Hattie's fried chicken and Boney for Etta's rolls.

"Don't you worry, dear." Etta patted Willow's hand. "This'll be our little secret. Vivian mentioned you were working for Mr. Van Der Veer and that it was going...well." She pursed her lips, and Willow found it difficult to believe anyone around here—the city of hopeless romantics—could keep a secret.

If only Trenton could be counted among them.

"You go ahead, Willow." Etta shooed her toward the hillock where Trenton stood behind his tripod.

Willow had just walked away from the tables when a woman in a red hat stepped in front of her.

"Willow, as in Portraits by Willow?"

"Yes." Willow lowered the pie and looked into the smug face of the woman she'd seen in Trenton's studio. Hattie had told her the woman had shown up at the boardinghouse yesterday looking for her. The woman she assumed had already left town. "Willow Peterson. And you are?"

"Susanna Woods." A smirk added sparkle to her blue eyes. "The woman you saw with Trenton."

Heat rushed into Willow's face. Miss Woods had seen her watching from the boardwalk. No wonder she'd touched Trenton the way she had.

"I'm his fiancée," Miss Woods said.

"Former fiancée is closer to Trenton's understanding."

"Well, well. It seems Trenton has found himself quite the gullible fan."

"A soft answer turneth away wrath." But if her Heavenly Father didn't give her a soft answer soon—

"Did Trenton tell you we were together yesterday at the confectionary?" Miss Woods asked.

After he'd gone to the parsonage with her, and they'd shared their stories with one another? She glanced toward the men at the tripod. Trenton and her brother were engaged in a conversation that seemed to leave them both oblivious to her situation.

Miss Woods clucked her tongue. "Shame, shame on Trenton."

Willow moistened her lips. She knew Trenton Van Der Veer. If he was at the confectionary with Miss Woods, he had a noble explanation. After a deep breath, she met the other woman's haughty gaze. "Here's what is a shame, Miss Woods. It's that a handsome woman like yourself, still blessed with youth, would think so little of herself as to pursue a man without affection for her. For what? A career?"

Miss Woods huffed, the sparkle gone from her eyes.

"Don't you want more? The love of the right man, for instance?" Willow sighed. That was what she'd known with Sam, and she was finally ready to experience love with the right man again.

"You don't know me. Or what I want." Her lips pressed together, Miss Woods spun and sauntered toward the hillock. Toward Trenton.

"Are you all right, sis?" Tucker stepped up from behind and braced her elbow. Willow turned and looked up into his tender face.

"I am. Thank you." She drew in a deep breath. "That was Susanna Woods from—"

"Trenton's past. He told me about her. Some of us don't give up very easily."

"But… I feel sorry for her. She's come all this way, and Trenton doesn't want her here."

"Is that what you said to her?"

"I told her it was a shame for a handsome young woman like her to pursue a man who had no affections for her."

"True to who you are, you spoke the truth." Tucker glanced toward the hillock. "Now you need to trust him. He'll know what to say to her."

If only she were so sure.

THIRTY-EIGHT

*W*hile the others cleaned up the picnic area, Trenton folded the tripod and slid it into its sack. He'd taken three photographs of the First Congregational Church family, as Tucker referred to them. And, surprisingly, today he felt like part of the family. He considered it amazing that he'd been so comfortable sitting in the sanctuary this morning. In front of the preacher, no less.

Now if only he felt half as good about his predicament with Susanna. She'd made the decision to come to Cripple Creek, and it was her choice whether to leave or not. But she was imprudent and alone here, and he couldn't help but feel bad for her.

"What you did was amazing." Willow walked up the hill toward him with a pie plate in her hands, a vision of remarkable grace and beauty. "How many photographers would attempt to assemble and organize sixty squirming men, women, and children?"

Not many that he knew.

"I brought you a reward." She glanced at the dish.

"You saved half of a p-pie for me? However did you manage?"

Pink tinged her cheeks, the perfect complement to her burgundy plaid shirtwaist. "Believe it or not, I hid it in a crate under the table."

"For me?"

She nodded, a smile teasing her tantalizing lips.

He accepted the dish, his mouth watering for more than just the pie. "Thank you."

She dipped her chin. "You may want to reserve your thanks until after you've tasted it."

He scooped a forkful of apples and savored the sweetness. "Mmm. Thank you." Her apple pie was sweet, but her lips were the true distraction. If they weren't in public, with her brother less than thirty feet away, he'd likely try to steal a kiss from her.

"I don't want to spoil your dessert," Willow said, "but Susanna looked quite upset when she left."

"I t-told her I shouldn't have just run away. I should've t-told her the truth."

"The *truth*?"

"The real reason I couldn't m-marry her."

Willow quietly took his hand. "What was it…the real reason?"

"I didn't l-love her. I thought I did. B-but I didn't know what love was. I told her I was sorry for the embarrassment I'd c-caused her. She'd hurt me, and I childishly wanted to do the s-same to her."

"What did she say?"

"If she was to accept my apology and my decision, wh-what was she to do?"

"You told her you'd purchase her train ticket?"

"I did."

Willow's eyes glistened. "You, Trenton, are indeed a man of integrity and a very generous man."

"She asked me if it was you."

"Me?"

"Who had taught me what love was."

Her breath caught. "What did you tell her?"

"That she could th-thank God for the lesson, and that credit was due you f-for the introduction."

A tear rolled down Willow's cheek, and Trenton desperately wanted to reach up and touch her face. She brushed it away before he could give in to the temptation. She was so genuine. At the confectionary, Susanna had attempted sincerity and failed miserably.

The candy! He cleared his throat. "You distracted me so much with the p-pie that I almost forgot I have s-something for you." He handed her the pie plate and bent over his box of camera supplies. He pulled out the pink box of fudge and handed it to her.

"That's why you were at the confectionary," Willow said, smiling.

"Susanna told you?"

"She gave me her version." Willow set her hands over his and met his gaze. "I like your version better."

"I'm sure I do too."

While he savored a few more bites of pie, Willow ate a piece of the pecan fudge, giving him knee-weakening smiles. When he could wait no longer, he set the dish on top of the box and looked into her warm eyes, drinking in the assurance that her interest in him exceeded their professional relationship.

"I don't want to rush you," he said.

She stilled.

"M-might you be ready for courtship?"

A slight grin deepened her dimples, and his heart did a flip. "I suppose it depends on who the caller is."

"Me. I want to court you." *Kiss you. Marry you.* But first things, first.

"Yes."

"The ice-cream parlor this Tuesday at four o'clock?"

"Yes."

Her smile was far more valuable than anything to be found in a gold mine.

※

Ida held two corners of the quilt, and Tucker folded the other two corners. "Your sister is going to be all right."

He nodded, his brown eyes glistening with tears. "Trenton's a good man. He came by the church yesterday for a talk and surrendered his life to Christ."

"That's wonderful." Joy and relief caused Ida's voice to quiver. She retrieved the picnic basket from the grass littered with golden leaves. "She loves Trenton."

"Even I can tell."

They were laughing when Father and Miss Hattie returned from the parsonage and diverted their attention. Hattie's hand rested on his arm, and the smile on her face tickled Ida clear to her toes. Her father had obviously admitted to himself and to Hattie that he loved her.

Father stacked his other hand on Hattie's and regarded the family gathered around them. "We have some news."

So did they, but Kat's baby news could wait a couple of minutes.

Father looked at Ida, Nell, and Vivian. "Your Miss Hattie has agreed to be my wife."

Cherise squealed and rushed to Father. He and Miss Hattie wrapped the child in a tearful embrace.

Tears streamed down Ida's face. God was handing out second chances to Father and Hattie, Cherise, and Willow. Ida joined in the celebratory hugging and looked at her husband. She so wanted to tell Tucker that God was giving them another chance at parenthood, but she needed to be sure.

THIRTY-NINE

Willow stepped out of the mercantile behind Hattie and breathed in the crispness of autumn. Each of them clutched a package. Willow had purchased more paints and brushes while Miss Hattie collected eyelet ribbon in preparation for her wedding next month. How was it possible that it could be Saturday already, that a whole week had passed since the church picnic?

Now that Willow thought about it, it was Trenton's fault. Last Sunday she'd agreed to courtship. Consequently, she was living the busiest week of her life. Monday, Trenton had photographed her in the studio, then the two of them had gone to the parsonage for supper with Tucker and Ida. Tuesday, they'd sat at one of the red tables in the ice-cream parlor and talked about anything and everything over root beer sodas. Wednesday, a midday stroll to Mount Pisgah. Thursday, lunch at the Third Street Café. Last night, Trenton had come to supper at the boardinghouse, and they'd bundled up to sit on the porch swing. They gazed at the night sky until she couldn't stop yawning and the stars blurred.

And that was only a list of her time with Trenton. It seemed every mine owner in town wanted a photograph taken and a portrait done.

Hattie stopped in the middle of the block, her eyebrows arched. "Where are we going next?" She glanced at their packages. "Do we have time to take these home before the sitting?"

"We started early. It can't be later than ten o'clock. We should have plenty of time. Unless you get to primping." Willow grinned. Since the morning Hattie burned the potatoes with Mr. Sinclair in the kitchen, her landlady was spending a lot more time at her dressing table.

Hattie feigned shock and tapped Willow's shoulder. "I would like to change into my blue calico dress. I didn't want to wear it shopping and take the chance—"

"That it wouldn't be perfect for the Sinclair family photograph?"

Hattie nodded, her blue-gray eyes glistening, "I never would've imagined that I'd marry again, and into the Sinclair family, no less." She turned toward the Fourth Street corner. "God is so good."

"Indeed He is."

They crossed the street and walked up the hill to the boardinghouse on Golden Avenue.

Hattie stepped onto the front porch first and peered down at the stationery peeking out from under the door. "That wasn't there when we left."

"Maybe Trenton came by."

"Or Harlan." Hattie stepped to the side as she inserted the key into the door, allowing Willow access to the letter.

Willow shifted her package to one arm and bent to retrieve it. "It has my full name on it, but it isn't Trenton's penmanship."

Hattie unlocked the door and pushed it open. "A client, perhaps?"

Willow set her package and reticule on the entry table next to the vase of sunflowers, then carried the envelope into the parlor. Standing in front of the warm stove, she slid the stationery out of the envelope and started to unfold it. "It's from Miss Woods."

Hattie walked into the room. Her eyes widened, deepening the creases that framed them. "That could be interesting."

Or distressing. Neither Willow nor Trenton had heard a word from Susanna, nor seen hide nor hair of her, since her appearance at the church picnic last Sunday. They had both avoided the confectionary, and, thankfully, Susanna had stayed away from them.

Until now.

Given the young woman's spite on Sunday, Willow wasn't sure she wanted to read the note. She finished unfolding the rough piece of parchment paper anyway and read aloud.

Greetings to you, Willow Peterson,
What you said Sunday set me to thinking. I thought I knew what I
wanted...until I met you. It doesn't feel good to admit it, but you were
right. I do consider myself to be a handsome woman, with much to offer
the right man.

Hattie tittered. "You said all of that to her?"

Willow shrugged. "I do remember saying she was a handsome woman and something about it being a shame that she would waste time pursuing a man who didn't have affections for her."

"You must have had the power of the Holy Ghost behind your words."

Willow was thankful but wondered where Susanna was headed with the declaration. She returned her attention to the letter.

I do want someone who will love me for who I am. Trenton deserves
the same. Please tell him he's free of me. This morning, I will board
the train for Denver. Miss Carmen misses you both at the
confectionary.
With warm regard,
Susanna Woods

"She's leaving."

"That's good news."

It was, but mixed feelings plagued Willow. She tucked the letter into the envelope.

"You're going to the depot, aren't you," Hattie said.

"I can't say why, but yes." Willow pulled her reticule off of the entry table and reached for the door handle.

"I'll meet you at the studio," Hattie said, rushing the words.

Willow nodded as the door closed behind her. She proceeded to the street and down the hill at an unladylike pace. She hadn't heard the train whistle blow to signal departure yet, but she knew the time was short. It made no sense that Willow wanted to see the young woman again, but she did.

At Bennett, she crossed the street and turned left. She'd just passed Jesse's livery when the train whistle blew. She hitched her skirt at the side seams and picked up her pace again. The depot was busier than a beehive and no doubt just as noisy. She maneuvered between horses, wagons, and carts and dashed to the platform.

Susanna wasn't there. Willow glanced toward the stream of people pouring out of the depot, then up at the train. Walking past the second passenger car, she spotted Susanna. Her blue eyes wide and her jaw lax, the young woman looked as surprised to see her there as Willow was surprised to be there.

Smiling, Willow held up the envelope, then pressed it to her breast.

Susanna returned her smile and nodded. She'd been a bit foolhardy and shameful in her nefarious pursuit of Trenton, but Willow wanted to believe that Denver held more promise for the young woman.

The locomotive belched a noxious cloud of sulfur-scented steam as it strained to take up the slack in each coupling, the metallic clunks deafening.

Susanna waved.

As Willow watched the train chug up the mountain toward Ute Pass, waves of relief and concern washed over her, along with gratitude for the right words and God's use of them to help Susanna move on.

You're guiding Trenton, Lord. Guide her too.

☙❧

Trenton studied the studio, from column to Brady stand, from settee to tripod. After photographing the entire church congregation, the Sinclair family should be easy enough for him to frame, even with fifteen members. He draped a Greek column backdrop over the rod on the back wall, then positioned the settee in front of it, leaving a few feet between them for creating layers.

On his way to the darkroom for prepared plates, he caught himself humming again. Something he'd been doing all week—since Sunday evening when he'd returned home from the picnic. He was especially given to humming after returning from spending time with Willow. At every hint of a sound or shadow, he glanced toward the office and the main door. The Sinclair sitting was still half an hour off, but he expected Willow to arrive early, which probably explained the humming. Today, it was "Bedouin Love Song." Yesterday, a tune from some silly romantic play. He seemed to alternate between the two, even though as recently as last month, he wouldn't have recalled either.

"Hello?" The bell above his door accompanied the voice as if on cue. But it was Miss Hattie's voice, not Willow's.

"I'm b-back here, Miss Hattie."

Willow's landlady peeked into the darkroom. "There you are."

"Yes. I'm j-just gathering supplies for the s-sitting." He stopped. "You look especially n-nice today."

"Why, thank you." She relaxed the shawl about her, revealing the crocheted lace accents at her neckline.

He drew in a deep breath for dramatic effect. "I can see where we could have a p-problem."

"Oh?"

"Mr. Sinclair m-may have trouble taking his eyes off you long enough to l-look at the camera."

She tittered, waving a gloved hand. Her wide-brimmed hat may be a distraction too, or at least a positioning challenge. No matter. He'd made a sport of guessing what kind of hat Miss Hattie would wear next. He had his answer for today, and he'd make it work.

"I'll show you where you all will gather." As he stepped between the dark-room and the studio doors, he glanced toward the street out of habit.

"Willow said she'd meet me here. I'm sure she'll be along in a few minutes," Miss Hattie said.

He nodded and carried the glass plates to the table next to the tripod. "Thank you, again, for the supper last night."

"It was my pleasure. My love of cooking is one of the reasons I wanted to open a boardinghouse."

"I k-know Willow enjoys l-living there."

"And it's been thrilling to watch her flourish in the new life God has given her here." Miss Hattie sighed. "You have overcome much as well. What an incredible journey you've had as a child with a stammer and as an apprentice on the move."

"I'm th-thankful I'm not that child or that a-apprentice anymore."

She nodded, bouncing the hat brim like an Oriental palm fan. "We're all thankful you chose to settle here."

"Thank you, m-ma'am. I am too."

"Life is ever changing, even when settled in one place."

He could certainly attest to that. Meeting Willow, working with her, and courting her this past week had changed everything. His business life, his spiritual life, and his personal life.

Miss Hattie cleared her throat. "Did Willow tell you Mr. Sinclair and I have set a date to be married? Thanksgiving Day. Don't you think it's a perfect day for a wedding?"

He met her gaze and offered her a slight grin. "I do, actually."

When the realization of what he wasn't saying dawned on her, she tipped her head and a generous smile lit her eyes.

The outside door opened, and he leaned toward her and whispered, "For now, it's our secret."

Miss Hattie pressed a gloved finger to her mouth and nodded.

"Willow?" He stepped into the main office just as Willow reached the end of the counter. "I was beginning to think you'd changed your mind about being my assistant today."

"No. I've been looking forward to it."

He gazed into her eyes, his soul drinking in the love he saw there.

She pulled an envelope from her reticule. "Susanna is gone. She left on the morning train."

"I don't understand. She didn't ask me for the ticket I'd offered her. How did you—"

"Miss Hattie and I returned from the mercantile this morning and found this note from her." Willow pulled a piece of stationery from the envelope and handed it to him.

He went from reading it with a smile on his face to trying to read through tears.

"I just came from the depot," Willow said. "I felt compelled to see her off. Her being alone and all."

Compassion ran through Willow's veins. Yes, the reasons he loved her were filling his heart to the brim.

Miss Hattie was still in the studio, but he didn't care if she stepped out and was a witness. He'd waited long enough.

Trenton laid the letter on the counter. "You, Willow Peterson, are an invaluable treasure." He rested his hand on her cheek, trailed his finger down her face, then lifted her chin. Quivering, she leaned toward him. Their lips met, and her kiss was every bit as sweet as he'd imagined.

It wasn't going to be Mr. Sinclair's distraction that caused a problem during the sitting, but Trenton's own distraction. Susanna's chapter in his life story had come to a close. And Willow Peterson was proving to be an undeniable leading lady.

FORTY

*W*illow sat in her bedchamber, hooking her calfskin boots. Trenton had been courting her for two feverish weeks. Root beer sodas at the ice-cream parlor. Sitting together in church. Sunday lunch with the Sinclair family. Buggy rides. Walks to the library. Dinner with Tucker and Ida at the Third Street Café. But today felt different.

Trenton said he planned to take her somewhere special. Despite her persistent questioning, he refused to divulge the destination. She'd even told him she needed to know so she could dress appropriately. His answer still made her smile. *"You, my dear Willow, could dress in tatters and look lovely."*

The only hint she'd been able to tease out of him was that their destination involved a full day of travel. At breakfast this morning, Miss Hattie offered a few guesses, but they couldn't be sure.

Willow captured the last button on her boot. Since he'd used the word *special,* she'd chosen to wear her burgundy walking skirt, her frilly cream-colored shirtwaist, and a bolero jacket for a dash of panache. She took the jacket from her wardrobe. Next, she pinned a black felt riding hat into place and slipped a pair of black crochet gloves into her reticule.

She glanced in the mirror and fussed with a sassy curl at her ear. Satisfied with her appearance, she smiled at the new woman looking back at her. She'd come a long way from being a girl paralyzed by grief and then a frightened Colorado newcomer. She was a businesswoman in love with an enchanting man. She laid her hand on the ribbon-trimmed ruffle at the bodice.

Sam would approve of her moving past her loss. He'd like Trenton Van Der Veer, and he'd want her to have a family of her own.

Here in Cripple Creek, God was giving her the chance to do just that.

Looping his black string tie, Trenton stood mesmerized by the photograph hanging on the wall in his bedroom. It wasn't the printed image that truly enthralled him but the actual woman who had agreed to courtship. These past two weeks had afforded him the best days of his life, thus far.

He donned his sack coat and went to the kitchen for the picnic basket. Then he tucked a quilt under his arm and lifted his bowler off a peg on his way out the front door.

Jesse waved from the driver's seat on a shiny black carriage. His friend had agreed to drive Trenton and Willow to their destination in style.

The rest was up to him.

And to Willow Peterson, the woman of his favorite dreams.

After subjecting himself to Jesse's teasing, Trenton climbed into the carriage, leaned against the cushioned seat, and breathed a prayer for God's guidance.

When Jesse stopped the carriage in front of the yellow boardinghouse, Trenton stepped onto the walkway that led to the front door. It seemed someone had stretched the walk since yesterday afternoon when he'd brought Willow home from the ice-cream parlor. Removing his hat, he stepped up onto the porch and rang the bell.

Footsteps in the foyer quickened Trenton's pulse, but it was Miss Hattie who opened the door.

"Good day, Miss Hattie."

The proprietor looked him over and smiled. "Why, Mr. Van Der Veer, if you aren't a sight for sleepy eyes."

"Thank you, ma'am. Given the r-right incentive, I can c-clean up pretty good."

She waved him inside. "You always look polished, but today, well, there seems to be a little something extra."

He winked. Determined not to divulge his plans, he swallowed his anticipation and looked toward the staircase. Willow stood on the landing looking like an angel.

"Trenton." Her welcoming smile transported him to heavenly realms. "I'm ready."

"Me too."

Miss Hattie tittered. "You two are goners."

"Yes ma'am." He knew he, at least, qualified. He didn't shift his attention from the adorable woman who took slow but sure steps toward him. The woman who had told him he was an answer to her prayers.

They had so much in common. When he didn't even know what he needed or how to pray, God had answered him.

Ten minutes later, he and Willow were in the carriage, headed out of Cripple Creek, with Jesse at the reins.

"I asked J-Jesse to come along to d-drive so I could s-sit here with you. I hope you don't mind."

"Do I look like I mind?" Willow placed her hand into his.

"Me neither, but J-Jesse may if a storm rolls in."

Willow looked out the window at the blue sky overhead. "Just how long do you expect us to be gone?"

"All day."

She brushed the quilt on the seat beside her.

"I put that there s-so you'd have to sit closer," Trenton said.

"I figured as much." She grinned and glanced at the picnic basket at her feet. "It might be a little brisk outside for a picnic." She tugged at the lapel of her jacket. "But I suppose it depends upon where you're taking me."

"Exactly."

Her mouth tipped into a demure smile. "So, am I dressed appropriately for our destination?"

"Perfectly." He swallowed his amusement. "Would you like a clue?"

She pursed her lips.

"All right then." He paused for dramatic effect. "David the psalmist asked God to l-lead him to it."

"To what?"

"To something that is higher than him."

Her green eyes flashed. "To the rock that is higher." Her shoulders sagged. "You're taking me to a rock?"

"Not to just any r-rock. We're going to a rock that is higher. Dome Rock."

Her dimples deepened, and his breathing became shallow.

They sat in comfortable silence as the carriage wound its way through grasslands, across a rushing stream, and into a ponderosa pine forest. As they approached massive outcroppings of Pikes Peak granite, Willow pointed to three bighorn sheep.

Jesse stopped the carriage in front of the most spectacular pillar. It stood hundreds of feet above the canyon floor. Trenton's boyhood friend climbed down and peeked in the door at them. "All right, you lovebirds, this is Dome Rock. I'll be takin' my lunch sack over there." He pointed toward a stand of bare aspen trees.

"Thanks, b-buddy."

"Don't mention it." Jesse hooked a thumb in his coveralls. "I'll bring the favor up later. When it best suits me."

Trenton laughed, and Willow giggled.

Jesse waved and walked off, leaving them alone.

Trenton helped Willow to the ground. Turning toward the rock, he felt his jaw drop.

Willow faced the landmark. "It's magnificent!"

They stood side by side, admiring the amazing sight. Emotion clogged his throat. *Help me get the words out, Lord.*

Trenton turned toward Willow and brushed the silken curl above her ear. "I like the psalmists. It's like they speak for me when I can't s-speak for myself."

A tear spilled onto her cheek, and he wiped it away.

"God is the Rock that is h-higher than my past, my mistakes, my frustrations…and you led me to Him."

Her lips quivered. "The Rock that is higher than losing a husband, or yourself."

"Yes, and God is the Rock I want to b-build our life upon."

"Our life?"

He pulled the ring from his waistcoat pocket. Holding it up between them, he looked into the emerald green eyes that seemed to peer into his heart. "Willow, I never expected to f-feel this way about anyone. But you have p-proven to be a most pleasant surprise." He drew in a deep breath. "I love you."

"I love you too." Her whisper echoed off the rock and landed deep in his heart.

"I want to spend the rest of my life with you."

"Me too. Will you marry me?"

He chuckled. "That was my line."

"Well then, yes!"

He lifted her chin and leaned into a kiss that felt like the promise of forever.

FORTY-ONE

*W*ednesday morning Willow sat at the game table, her fountain
pen poised above a piece of stationery. In her last letter to Mother,
she'd described her job with Mr. Trenton Van Der Veer, but she'd left any
personal feelings out of the correspondence. She hadn't even mentioned her
boss being single. Perhaps, on the outside of the envelope, she should warn
Mother to seat herself before reading the news.

Not sure where to begin her story, Willow set the pen to paper.

Dearest Mother,
I think of you often, and hope you are well. That Aunt Rosemary is well.
I am—

"Be sure and tell your mother hello for me." Miss Hattie sat on the sofa,
waving the latest copy of *Harper's Bazar*. "And tell her I'm looking forward to
seeing her and your aunt." Her blue-gray eyes sparkled. "Soon."

"I will." Willow stared at the fireplace, watching the yellow flames dance
across a burning log. "It seems I have a whole lot to tell her."

"That you do." Miss Hattie flipped a page of the magazine. "I can't believe
Trenton took you all the way to Dome Rock for a carriage picnic. How
romantic!"

"It was. The whole day." Trenton had draped the quilt over the facing seat in the carriage and spread their lunch on it. They ate together, enjoying the cozy interior of the carriage and the clear view of the Dome.

Willow held up her left hand and glanced at the promise ring he'd slid on her finger. "We're getting married!" She tapped the tip of the pen on the table. "How will we ever be ready in only three weeks?"

Miss Hattie closed the magazine and smiled. "Dear, have you forgotten who we have helping us?" A grin deepened the lines at the corners of her mouth. "The Sinclair sisters—all five of them. I've watched the four oldest ones put together each other's weddings. Whirlwinds spinning on a dime, and with breathtaking results. The youngest, well, Cherise has already told me which dress I'm wearing and suggested I buy a new pair of shoes for the occasion."

Her dear friend and fellow bride-to-be was right. They were meeting Ida, Kat, and Nell at Vivian's shop this morning. And if Vivian was making her dress, Willow had nothing to worry about.

"After school, Cherise will come here for a tea party and a fashion show." Miss Hattie looked at the mantel clock. "I suppose I should let you finish your letter. It's nearly time for us to leave."

"I would like to drop it at the post office when we go out." Willow dipped the pen and returned her attention to the stationery.

The photographer I told you about, well, he is single. But only for another three weeks.

An hour later, Hattie watched Vivian drape Willow with one fabric and then another. Taffeta. Chiffon. Velvet. And then a sateen, a new arrival at the design shop. Ida and Nell picked out fabrics, and Kat looked through an assortment of ribbons and lace for trimming Willow's gown. Hope twirled a purple ribbon on her head, while William played with a wooden horse in the corner. Hattie didn't know how it was possible with all the cackling going on, but Vivian's twins slept in the cradle. Her heart full to overflowing, Hattie bounced the carriage that held Kat's newborn son, Ezra.

"What do you think of this, Nanny Hattie?" Smiling, Willow wrapped a yard of sateen over her shoulders and spun around like a music-box angel.

"It's stunning, dear." Hattie pressed her free hand to her chest. "But I agree with Trenton; you'd look lovely in tatters."

Willow's cheeks pinked.

Ida held a swatch of pink chiffon. "Yes. Tucker would say Trenton Van Der Veer is a man in love over his head."

"He should know." Willow winked at her sister-in-law.

Vivian took the material from Willow. "Looks to me like you've settled on the fabric."

"Are you sure you're going to have time to make my dress?"

Vivian carefully folded the chosen fabric. "I've made the dresses for all of my sisters, and they've never been late. I don't intend to break my streak with you, my honorary sister." She added a strip of lace to the makings for Willow's dress.

"Thank you. But they gave you more time." Willow glanced at the cradle. "And that was before you were the mother of twins."

Nell brandished a pair of pinking shears. "I'll help with the cutting."

"Sounds like my dress is in good hands." Willow met Hattie's gaze. "And now it's your turn. Cherise is right—you need a new pair of shoes for your walk toward your future as Mrs. Harlan Sinclair." She looped Hattie's arm.

"If she's wearing her blue calico dress," Ida said, "I assure you Father will not be looking at her feet."

Hattie tittered, and the others joined in, their laughter music to her ears.

Ida cleared her throat. "I have news." She pulled two swatches of fabric from a basket. One was blue, the other pink. Her eyes rimmed with tears, Ida pressed her hand to her midsection. "I told Tucker this morning that I don't know if I'll have a boy or a girl come June."

Her sisters squealed, and Hattie breathed a prayer of thanksgiving.

The family was ever growing. And soon her family ties would be official.

FORTY-TWO

28 November, 1898

Thanksgiving Day. Willow pulled the new striped curtain back from the window in Miss Hattie's bedchamber. Snow drifted to the ground. Ida stood at the dressing table, brushing Miss Hattie's silver-gray hair into a soft bun. Cherise stood nearby, twirling a parasol and humming a happy tune.

"I have so much to be thankful for." Miss Hattie met Willow's gaze in the mirror. "The perfect day for a wedding, don't you think?"

Willow swished the bell-shaped skirt on her gown. "Make that two weddings."

"I hear the wheels. He's here!" Cherise grabbed Hattie's hand. "I ready!"

Hattie pressed the child's hand to her lips. "Me too, sweet girl of mine. I'm ready too."

With Ida at her side, Willow followed Cherise and Hattie to the foyer, wondering if she might trip over the child's broad smile.

Jesse stood at the end of the walkway dressed in dark trousers and a white shirt. The pair of palominos that had pulled her and Trenton to Dome Rock stood harnessed to a white carriage in a winter wonderland. Yes, the perfect day for a wedding and for beginning a lifetime as Mrs. Trenton Van Der Veer.

Vivian, Kat, and Nell met them in the foyer of the First Congregational Church. After hugs, the three sisters left to join the other guests in the sanctuary. Boney and Tucker stepped out of the hallway.

Boney smiled at Willow, then kissed Hattie's cheek. "Lucky fellows, those two."

Tucker faced Willow and took her hands in his. "Sis." His brown eyes glistened with tears, causing her eyes to fill.

She squeezed his hands. "I know." She was thankful for God's gift to her—family and a second chance at love.

The rising piano music sent shivers up Willow's spine.

Boney held his arm out to Hattie. "Are you ready?"

"Nearly overcooked."

Chuckling, Boney propped the sanctuary door open and escorted Hattie down the aisle.

Willow peeked inside at those gathered for their celebration of love and marriage. Mother. Aunt Rosemary. All five of the Sinclair sisters, Hope, William, baby Ezra, and the twins. Otis and Naomi Bernard and their four sons. Mollie Kathleen. Mr. Baxter, Carmen, Mr. and Mrs. Johnstone. Boney and Etta. Jesse. She was home.

Harlan Sinclair reached for Hattie's hand at the front of the aisle, and they both turned to watch Willow enter.

Drawing in a deep breath, Willow met her brother's tender gaze. "Yes," she said in response to his unspoken question. Ready and impatient. She rested her hand on his arm and might have sprinted up the aisle if Tucker hadn't held her back with his deliberate pace.

Trenton waited for her at the first row of pews, his eyes widening as she drew close. He wore a full tuxedo and held a familiar pink candy box in his hand.

A husband *and* a box of fudge. What a day! "Thank You, Jesus."

Smiling, Trenton looked up. "To the Rock that is higher."

READERS GUIDE

1. Willow Peterson, Ida Sinclair's sister-in-law, is back in Cripple Creek as the main character. When Willow's beloved Sam drowned, she had an emotional breakdown and spent time in a mental asylum. Standing at her father's graveside, Willow and those who love her fear she may succumb to sorrow once again. What do you do to protect your mental health when you face grief? What Bible verses do you turn to for a faith that overcomes?

2. Trenton Van Der Veer, Cripple Creek's new photographer, stammers and grew up belittled because of it. He even found himself humiliated in front of a congregation of churchgoers. What would you have said to Trenton to help him separate that experience from his perception of the heart of God?

3. Often it takes a crisis, hitting rock bottom, before a person recognizes his or her need for God, acceptance, repentance, and surrender. What was Trenton's low point...his point of need? How did Willow minister to Trenton? What steps did she take in preparing her heart to minister to him?

4. Miss Hattie, the proprietor of Miss Hattie's Boardinghouse, is an influencer. Who, in this story, did Miss Hattie influence and how did her influence affect them? What qualities do you look for in an influencer?

5. Willow Peterson and Hattie Adams, both widows, find a second chance at love in a second romance. Have you had such an experience?

6. Willow and Trenton were both misunderstood and ridiculed because of their differences—her because she was a woman and him because of his speech impediment. What would you say to them about who they are in God's eyes?

7. Harlan Sinclair, the single parent of four grown daughters, finds himself the guardian of eight-year-old Cherise, which creates conflict. What are some emotions or situations that often cause friction between adult children and their parents? What strategies did the Sinclair sisters and their father use for reconciliation?

8. Cherise buried both of her parents at a young age, became the charge of a guardian, and moved to a new country. But God provided her with the compassionate Mr. Sinclair and Miss Hattie to love her and care for her as their own. Has God ever brought someone into your life who surprised you with an outpouring of love and grace?

9. Mollie Kathleen Gortner is a historical figure who lived in Cripple Creek at the time this story takes place. Ignoring her fictionalized personality and behavior, what do you think of Mollie's accomplishments as a business woman in an 1890s mining town? What qualities do you imagine Mollie Kathleen must have possessed that made it possible for her to become the first woman to stake a mine claim in her name in the Cripple Creek Mining District?

10. This story is full of wounded servants. Hattie had buried her husband and baby girl. Willow had suffered struggles in her family relationships and was in a mental asylum. Ida had miscarried, losing her baby. Despite her deep desire to birth her own baby, Nell still can't conceive. And, yet, these hurting people didn't allow themselves to remain self-focused. In what ways did the wounded serve others? What verse or verses from Scripture do you think support this theology?

Mona is available for book club conference calls, where she joins your book club for a prescheduled, twenty-to-thirty-minute conversation via speakerphone or Skype. **When possible, Mona is happy to add an "in person" visit to a Book Club in a city she's visiting.** For more information, please contact Mona through her website: www.monahodgson.com.

Author's Note

*T*hank you for joining me on my adventures with the Sinclair sisters and their Colorado community.

In each of The Sinclair Sisters of Cripple Creek novels, you meet at least one real-life woman from Cripple Creek history. I introduced Mary Claver Coleman, the Reverend Mother of the Sisters of Mercy, in *Two Brides Too Many*. In *Too Rich for a Bride,* business entrepreneur Mollie O'Bryan helped add layers to Ida Sinclair's journey. Doctor Susan Anderson, known as Doc Susie, came alongside our cast of fictional characters in *The Bride Wore Blue*. Mollie Kathleen Gortner is the primary real-life woman in *Twice a Bride*. Like the women in the previous stories, Mollie Kathleen's portrayal in the story is a fictionalization.

In keeping with my commitment as a storyteller of historical fiction, I'm required to play with facts and actual locations to best meet the needs of my stories.

Harper's Bazar, the magazine I feature in the series, offers a spelling twist. If you're like me, you wanted to add another *a* after the *z,* but until the November 1929 issue, the magazine was spelled with only two *a*'s.

The Glockner Sanitorium, which was one of many tuberculosis or consumption treatment centers in Colorado during the 1800s, is where Willow's father spent the last year and a half of his life. You might be tempted to fix the spelling of *Sanitorium* to the more common and modern spelling— *Sanitarium*—but my research shows the historical spelling featured more *o*'s than *a*'s.

While the Butte Opera House was most likely still called the Butte Concert and Beer Hall at the time this story takes place, I opted to adopt its current title. Also, the manager I characterized was a fabrication to move Susanna along in her Cripple Creek experience.

I've enjoyed our time together in this four-book series. Excitement mingled with sadness as I neared the end of this last story. But I have big news! WaterBrook Press and I are partnering for a second set of stories, beginning with three novellas that form a prequel. More big news—at least two of our beloved Cripple Creek characters will join us in the new series. I can't wait!

My prayer is that in whatever state you find yourself as you read, my stories will lead you to the Rock that is higher than you and I. Higher than any heartbreak or success. Higher than any circumstance.

Please plan now to join me in my next series. Until then, may you experience freedom in God's grace, walk in His joy, and bask in His peace.

Your Friend,
Mona

ACKNOWLEDGMENTS

On some levels, writing is a solitary undertaking. But it is also a process requiring a team of supporters. Many people rallied around me in the various stages of this book and The Sinclair Sisters of Cripple Creek series.

- My hubby, Bob—my first reader, technical support, home manager....
- My agent, Janet Kobobel Grant of Books & Such Literary Agency.
- My critique partner and writing bud, DiAnn.
- My editors, Shannon Hill Marchese and Jessica Barnes.
- The entire WaterBrook Multnomah—Random House team.
- My brainstorming and writing-retreat buds, Lauraine and Eileen.
- My sisters, Cindy, Tammy, and Linda.
- My prayer partners. Thank you, Mom, and all.

A big thank-you to all of these listed, and to all who aren't, who made it possible for me to accomplish my dream of writing novels for you.

Now unto the King eternal, immortal, invisible, the
only wise God,
be honour and glory for ever and ever. Amen.
—1 Timothy 1:17

ABOUT THE AUTHOR

*M*ona Hodgson is the author of The Sinclair Sisters of Cripple Creek series and nearly thirty children's books. Her writing credits also include hundreds of articles, poems, and short stories in more than fifty different periodicals, including *Focus on the Family, Decision, Clubhouse Jr., Highlights for Children, The Upper Room, The Quiet Hour,* and the *Christian Communicator.* Mona speaks at women's retreats, schools, and conferences for librarians, educators, and writers, and is a regular columnist on the *Bustles and Spurs Blog.*

Mona and Bob, her husband of forty years, have two adult daughters, two sons-in-law, and a gaggle of grandchildren.

Learn more about Mona, find readers' guides for your book club, and view her photo album of current-day Cripple Creek, at Mona's website: www.monahodgson.com. You can also find Mona at www.twitter.com /monahodgson and on Facebook at www.facebook.com/Author.Mona.

OTHER BOOKS BY MONA HODGSON

HISTORICAL FICTION
Two Brides Too Many
Too Rich for a Bride
The Bride Wore Blue

CHILDREN'S BOOKS
Real Girls of the Bible: A 31-Day Devotional (Zonderkidz)
The Princess Twins and the Kitty (Zonderkidz I Can Read)
The Princess Twins Play in the Garden (Zonderkidz I Can Read)
The Princess Twins and the Tea Party (Zonderkidz I Can Read)
The Princess Twins and the Birthday Party (Zonderkidz I Can Read)
The Best Breakfast (Zonderkidz I Can Read)
Thank You, God, for Rain (Zonderkidz I Can Read)
Bedtime in the Southwest (Northland Publishing)

For a complete and current listing of Mona's books, including any out-of-print titles she may still have available, please visit her website at www.monahodgson .com.

Coming February 2013

An Original E-Book
Novella

Dandelions
on the Wind

ONE

*S*hoo. Shoo." Maren Jensen spoke the words as much to her own thoughts as she did to the chickens pecking at her bootlaces. She reached into her apron and tossed handfuls of potato peels and corn in a wide arc. The cackling chickens scattered to be first to the bounty. This was not the home she had pictured while traveling on the boat from Denmark nearly two years ago. But then she still had more of her sight. At least for now, the widow and her granddaughter and the quilting circle were her family.

Inside the stifling hot coop, Maren dodged the roost and reached into the first of the five nests along the back wall. With all of the eggs gathered, she felt for the pole and ducked under it, taking the most direct route out of the smelly henhouse. She pressed her bonnet against her ear to stop the onslaught of hot August air and stepped into the chicken yard, through the gate and into the ruts leading to the barn. The parching wind stung her eyes and whipped her apron.

She folded one of the double-hinged barn doors and clamped it open, then stepped inside, squinting against the near darkness. The strong, sweet smell of damp hay filled her nostrils. The cow scent was strong and not so sweet. Both reminded her of the farm her family had lost in Copenhagen. And the farm Orvie Christensen had promised her in his letters.

After Maren hung the basket of eggs by the door, she climbed the wooden steps to the hayloft. Cows bawled and horses whinnied below while she tugged hay from a stack and tossed it over the edge and into the swinging mangers at the stalls. She repeated the task on the other side, flinging hay into Duden and Boone's stall. She dropped a couple forkfuls of hay onto the center of the barn floor before climbing down to attend the cows. Her stomach growling, she realized too many hours had passed since her bowl of oatmeal porridge. Hours filled with domestic work, music, and a spirited four-year-old.

Maren stopped at the top of the ladder and brushed her hands together to dislodge any remaining hay stems from her woolen gloves. She would feed the hogs and mules, milk the cows, and then go inside for her dinner. She had planted her boots on the first two rungs of the ladder when a raspy baritone voice split the still air.

"Good day, ma'am."

Maren jerked and her boot slipped, causing her chin to strike a step. Wincing, she released her grip and fell backward. Fear caught a scream in her throat. The hay she had thrown down broke her fall, but still she landed flat on her back. She fought to recover her breath and gather her wits. A staccato heartbeat pounded in her ears. The deep voice did not belong to George Williams who ran the farm for Mrs. Brantenberg, or to anyone in the Williams family.

Blinking, she willed her eyes to focus in her limited circle of vision. Brown curls swerved every which way on the head of a man she did not recognize. Scrambling to right herself, she edged toward the wall near the cow stall.

"Ma'am." An American accent. Not one of Mrs. Brantenberg's German neighbors. "Are you well?"

"Yes." She felt along the wall for a makeshift weapon. When she found the shovel, she lifted it off its nail and held it up.

"I mean you no harm."

Holding the shovel steady, Maren widened her shoulders and raised her smarting chin.

"I apologize. I didn't—"

"Didn't what, sir?" This man may be harmless, but he was no less a nuisance. "You did not mean to burst into my barn and cause me to take a topple?"

"You are not Mrs. Brantenberg." Confidence supported his statement.

Did he know Mrs. Brantenberg, or had someone in town told him to expect an older woman?

"I am Maren Jensen." When soldiers had chosen to camp on the farm last year, Mrs. Brantenberg taught her the less said the better. She could not make out his facial features in the shadows, but she did see one arm in a sling. "And you are?" Silence ticked off the seconds.

"People call me Woolly."

He moved closer, and while repositioning her heavy weapon, she blinked to focus her vision.

"With a name like Jensen, and that accent, I'm guessing you're from Denmark."

"Yes."

He removed his cap. "I do apologize for the disturbance, ma'am, or is it miss?"

Of course, it was Miss. No one would have her. Not as she was.

"*Ja,* Miss Jensen." Her employer had never mentioned anyone named Woolly. He had to be a drifter looking for work. And with work to finish she had no time to waste. "You'll find Mrs. Brantenberg at the house."

"Thank you, Miss Jensen." His voice held a pleasant tone, although it sounded a bit gravelly, like he'd been out in the weather for a long spell. She should be nicer to the gentleman, but she couldn't afford to be. Chores were obligatory and niceties with strangers were not.

He turned to leave the barn and quickly faded into darkness. Maren lowered the shovel and listened as the door closed behind him. If she ever did have a home of her own, it wouldn't sit beside a well-traveled road. Especially not during or immediately following a war.

She's ashamed *of* her past *and* has no faith *in* her future. *Or* grace.

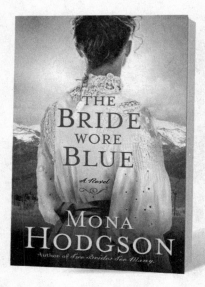

Vivian has made one bad decision too many and now she's looking for a fresh start. But between the lies about her past and the lies about the present, there's no room to accept help—or love—from her sisters or anyone else. Not even from that interesting sheriff's deputy who has his eye on her.

Read an excerpt from this book and more on
WaterBrookMultnomah.com!

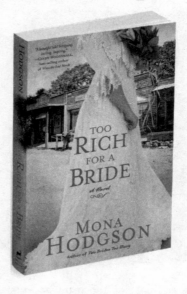

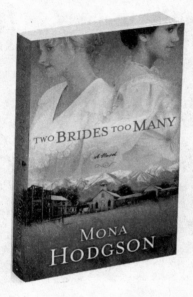

Coming Soon:
Three eNovellas for Historical Fiction and Romance Fans!

Available early 2013 wherever eBooks are sold.

When three women form a quilting group in St. Charles, Missouri, just after the end of the Civil War, their growing friendships carry them through the burdens of life and the joys of love.

Also look for the first novel in the Hearts Seeking Home series, coming Summer 2013!